LORD OF THE
CHANGING WINDS

The griffin struck at Bertaud's face with a beak like a blade, but somehow Bertaud's sword was in the way. He had no notion how it had come into his hand—his left hand, for the white griffin had his right pinned in its grip.

He cut at its head, so close to his own, and it flung him away. He fell hard, to sand that flickered with little ripples of fire; he rolled fast to get up, beating at a charred patch of cloth over his thigh, but made it only so far as his knees. The griffin, above him on the rock, wings spread wide, seemed as immense as the sky. It stared at him with fierce eyes of a hard fiery blue, and sprang like a cat.

"No," he cried at it without breath, without sound. He found himself more furious than terrified. He tried to fling himself to his feet, but his right leg would not hold, and he was falling already as the white griffin came down upon him. Darkness rose up like heat, or he fell into it, and it filled his eyes and his mind.

LORD OF THE
CHANGING WINDS

THE GRIFFIN MAGE TRILOGY: BOOK ONE

RACHEL NEUMEIER

www.orbitbooks.net

ORBIT

First published in Great Britain in 2010 by Orbit

A CIP catalogue record for this book
is available from the British Library.

ISBN 978-1-84149-873-7

Typeset in Times by Palimpsest Book Production Limited,
Grangemouth, Stirlingshire
Printed and bound in Great Britain by
CPI Mackays, Chatham, ME5 8TD

Papers used by Orbit are natural, renewable and recyclable
products sourced from well-managed forests and certified
in accordance with the rules of the Forest Stewardship Council.

 Mixed Sources
Product group from well-managed
forests and other controlled sources
www.fsc.org Cert no. SGS-COC-004081
© 1996 Forest Stewardship Council
FSC

Orbit
An imprint of
Little, Brown Book Group
100 Victoria Embankment
London EC4Y 0DY

An Hachette UK Company
www.hachette.co.uk

www.orbitbooks.net

This one's for my brother Brett—without whose advice,
instructions, and long-distance consultation,
my Web sites would either not exist or
would crash on a regular basis!

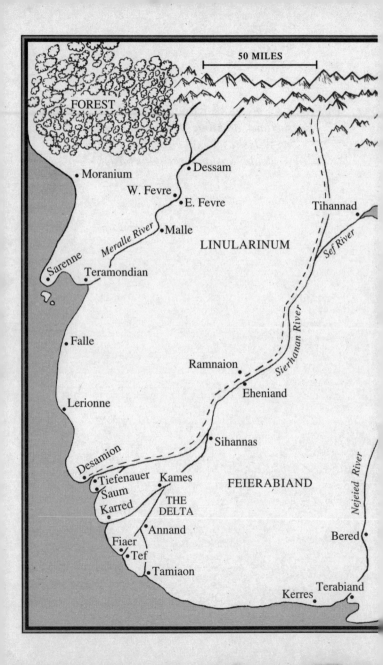

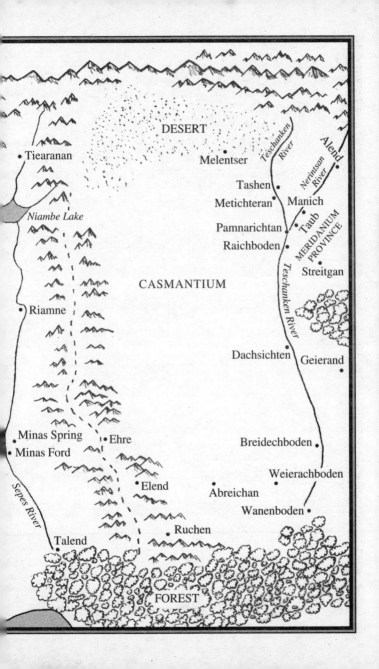

CHAPTER 1

The griffins came to Feierabiand with the early summer warmth, riding the wind out of the heights down to the tender green pastures of the foothills. The wind they brought with them was a hard, hot wind, with nothing of the gentle Feierabiand summer about it. It tasted of red dust and hot brass.

Kes, gathering herbs in the high pastures above the village of Minas Ford, saw them come: great bronze wings shining in the sun, tawny pelts like molten gold, sunlight striking harshly off beaks and talons. One was a hard shining white, one red as the coals at the heart of a fire. The griffins rode their wind like soaring eagles, wings outstretched and still. The sky took on a fierce metallic tone as they passed. They turned around the shoulder of the mountain and disappeared, one and then another and another, until they had all passed out of sight. Behind them, the sky softened slowly to its accustomed gentle blue.

Kes stood in hills above the high pastures, barefoot,

her hair tangled, her hands full of fresh-picked angelica, and watched until the last of the griffins slid out of view. They were the most beautiful creatures she had ever seen. She almost followed them, running around the curve of the mountain's shoulder, leaving her angelica and elecampane and goldenseal to wilt in the sun; she even took a step after them before she thought better of the idea.

But Tesme hated it when Kes did not come home by dusk; she hated it worse when her sister did not come home before dawn. So Kes hesitated one moment and then another, knowing that if she followed the griffins she would forget time and her sister's expectations. There would be noise and fuss, and then it would be days before Tesme once again gave reluctant leave for Kes to go up into the hills. So she stayed where she was on the mountainside, only shading her eyes with her hand as she tried to follow the griffins with her eyes and imagination around the curve of the mountain.

Griffins, she thought. *Griffins*. . . . She walked slowly down from the hills, crossed the stream to the highest of the pastures, and went on downhill, her eyes filled with blazing wings and sunlight. She climbed stone walls without really noticing them, one after another: high pasture to hill pasture, hill pasture down to the midlands pasture. And then the low pasture, nearest the barns and the house: the fence here was rail instead of stone. This meant Kes had no convenient flat-topped wall on which to put her basket while climbing over. She balanced it awkwardly against her hip and clambered over the fence with one hand.

Her sister, Tesme, spotted Kes as she walked past the nearest barn and hurried to meet her. The griffins, it was plain, had not come down so far as the house; Tesme's eyes held nothing of fire and splendor. They were filled instead with thoughts of heavy mares and staggering foals. And with worry. Kes saw that. It pulled her back toward the ordinary concerns of home and horse breeding.

"Kes!" said her sister. "Where have you been?" She glanced at the basket of herbs and went on quickly, "At least, I see where you've been, all right, fine, did you happen to get milk thistle while you were in the hills?"

Kes, blinking away images of shining wings, shook her head and made a questioning gesture toward the foaling stable.

"It's River," Tesme said tensely. "I think she's going to have a difficult time. I should never have bred her to that Delta stud. He was too big for her, I knew he was, but oh, I want this foal!"

Kes nodded, taking a step toward the house.

"I got your things out for you—they're in the barn— along with your shoes," Tesme added, her gaze dropping to Kes's bare feet. But her tone was more worried than tart, the foaling mare distracting her from her sister's lack of civilized manners. "You just want your ordinary kit, don't you? Don't worry about those herbs—somebody can take them to the house for you." Tesme took Kes by the shoulder and hurried her toward the barn.

In the foaling barn, Kes absently handed her basket to one of the boys and waved him off toward the house. Tesme hovered anxiously. Kes saw that she could not tell Tesme about the griffins; not now. She tried to make herself focus on the mare. Indeed, once she saw her, it became less of an effort to forget sunlit magnificence and concentrate instead on normal life. River, a stocky bay

mare with bulging sides, was clearly uncomfortable. And
certainly very large. She looked to have doubled her width
since Kes had last looked at her, and that had only been a
handful of days ago.

"Do you think she could be carrying twins?" Tesme
asked apprehensively. She was actually wringing her hands.

"From the look of her, she could be carrying triplets,"
Meris commented, swinging through the wide barn doors.
"I've been waiting for her to explode for the past month,
and now look at her. Kes, glad to see you. Tesme, just how
big was that stud?"

"Huge," Tesme said unhappily. "But I wanted size. River's not *that* small. I thought it would be a safe cross."

Kes shrugged. Usually crossing horses of different
sizes worked all right, but sometimes it didn't. No one
knew why. She looked at her kit, then back at the mare.

"Mugwort," she suggested. "Partridge berry."

"Good idea," said Meris. "Partridge berry to calm
her down and help her labor at the beginning—mugwort
later, I suppose, in case we need to help the strength of
her contractions. I have water boiling. Want me to make
the decoctions?"

Kes nodded.

Meris was a quick-moving little sparrow of a woman,
plain and sensible and good-humored, equally at home
with a foaling mare or a birthing woman. Kes was far
more comfortable with her than with most other people;
Meris never tried to draw Kes out or make her talk; when
Kes did talk, Meris never seemed surprised at what she
said. Meris was willing, as so few people seemed to be,
to simply let a person or an animal be what it was. No
wonder Tesme had sent for Meris. Even if River had no

difficulty with her foal, just having Meris around would calm everyone's nerves. That would be good. Kes gave the older woman the packets of herbs and slipped into the stall to touch River's neck. The mare bent her neck around and snuffled down Kes's shirt. She was sweating, pawing at the stall floor nervously. Kes patted her again.

"What do you think?" Tesme asked, seeming almost as distressed as the mare. "Is she going to be all right, do you think?"

Kes shrugged. "Jos?" If they had to pull this foal, she wanted someone with the muscle to do it. Jos had been a drifter. Tesme had hired him for the season six years past, and he had just never seemed inclined to drift away again. He was very strong. And the horses liked him. Kes liked him too. He didn't *talk* at you all the time, or expect you to talk back.

"I'll get him," Tesme agreed, and hurried out.

Kes frowned at the mare, patting her in absent reassurance. River twitched her ears back and walked in a circle, dropping her head and shifting her weight. She was thinking of lying down but was too uncomfortable to do so; Tesme, with her affinity for horses, could have made the mare lie down. Kes neither held an affinity for any animal nor possessed any other special gift—if one did not count an unusual desire to abandon shoes and sister and walk up alone into the quiet of the hills. She did not usually envy Tesme her gift, but she would have liked to be able to make River lie down. She could only coax the mare down with a touch and a murmur.

Fortunately, that was enough. Kes stepped hastily out of the way when the mare folded up her legs and collapsed awkwardly onto the straw.

"How is she?" Tesme wanted to know, finally returning with Jos. Kes gave her sister a shrug and Jos a nod. He nodded back wordlessly and came to lean on the stall gate next to her.

Foals came fast, usually. There was normally no fuss about them. If there was trouble, it was likely to be serious trouble. But it would not help, in either case, to flutter around like so many broken-winged birds and disturb the mare further. Kes watched River, timing the contractions that rippled down the mare's sides, and thought there was not yet any need to do anything but wait.

Waiting, Kes found her mind drifting toward a hard pale sky, toward the memory of harsh light striking off fierce curved beaks and golden feathers. Tesme did not notice her bemusement. But Jos said, "Kes?"

Kes blinked at him, startled. The cool dimness of the foaling barn seemed strange to her, as though the fierce sun the griffins had brought with them had somehow become more real to her than the gentle summer of Minas Ford.

"Are you well?" Jos was frowning at her, curious. Even concerned. Did she seem so distracted? Kes nodded to him and made a dismissive "it's nothing" kind of gesture. He did not seem fully convinced.

Then Tesme called Kes's name sharply, and, pulling her attention back to the mare, Kes went back to lay a hand on River's flank and judge how she was progressing.

The foal *was* very big. But Kes found that, after all, once the birth began, there was not much trouble about the foaling. It had its front feet in the birth canal and its nose positioned properly forward. She nodded reassuringly at her sister and at Jos.

Tesme gave back a little relieved nod of her own, but it was Jos who was the happiest. The last time a foaling had gone badly, the foal had been turned the wrong way round, both front legs hung up on the mare's pelvis. Jos had not been able to push the foal back in enough to straighten the legs; he had had to break them to get the foal out. It had been born dead, which was as well. That had been a grim job that none of them had any desire to repeat, and the memory of it was probably what had wound Tesme up in nervous worry.

This time, Kes waited until the mare was well into labor. Then she simply tied a cord around each of the foal's front hooves, and while Tesme stood at the mare's head and soothed her, she and Jos added a smooth pull to the mare's next contraction. The foal slid right out, wet and dark with birthing liquids.

"A filly!" said Meris, bending to check.

"Wonderful," Tesme said fervently. "Wonderful. Good *girl*, River!"

The mare tipped her ears forward at Tesme, heaved herself to her feet, turned around in the straw, and nosed the baby, which thrashed itself to its feet and tottered. Jos steadied it when it would have fallen. It was sucking strongly only minutes later.

After that, it was only natural to go to the village inn to celebrate. Tesme changed into a clean skirt and braided her hair and gave Kes a string of polished wooden beads to braid into hers. Tesme was happy. She had her foal from the Delta stud—a filly—and all was right with the world. Jos stayed at the farm, keeping an eye on the baby foal; he rarely went to the village during the day, though he visited the inn nearly every evening to listen to the news that travelers brought and to have a mug of ale and a game of pian stones with the other men.

Kes was not so happy. She would as soon have stayed at the farm with Jos and had bread and cheese quietly. But Tesme would have been unhappy if she had refused to go. She was never happy when Kes seemed too solitary. She said Kes was more like a silent, wild creature of the hills than a girl, and when she said such things, she worried. Sometimes she worried for days, and that was hard on them both. So Kes made no objection to the beads or the shoes or the visit to the inn.

They walked. The road was dry and firm at the verge, and Tesme—oddly, for a woman who raised horses—liked to walk. Kes put one properly shod foot in front of another and thought about griffins. Bronze feathers caught by the sun, tawny flanks like gold. Beaks that gleamed like metal. Her steps slowed.

"Come on," Tesme said, and impatiently, "There's nothing to be afraid of, Kes!"

Kes blinked, recalled back to the ordinary road and the empty sky. She didn't say that she was not afraid, exactly. It had been a long time since she'd tried to explain to Tesme her feelings about people, about crowds, about the hard press of their expectations. From the time she had been little, everyone else had seemed to see the world from a different slant than Kes. To understand, without even trying, unspoken codes and rules that only baffled her. Talking to people, trying to shape herself into what they expected, was not exactly frightening. But it was exhausting and confusing and, in a way, the confusion itself was frightening. But Tesme did not seem able to understand any of this. Kes had long since given up trying to explain herself to her sister.

Nor did Kes mention griffins. There seemed no place for them in Tesme's eyes. Kes tried to forget the vision of heat and beauty, to see only the ordinary countryside that surrounded them. To please her sister, she walked a little faster.

But Tesme, who had been walking quickly and impatiently with her hands shoved into the pockets of her skirt, slowed in her turn. She said, "Kes—"

Kes looked at her inquiringly. The light of the sun slid across Tesme's face, revealing the small lines that had come into her face and set themselves permanently between her eyes and at the corners of her generous mouth. Her wheaten hair, braided with a strand of polished wooden beads and tucked up in a coil, held the first strands of gray.

She looked, Kes thought, startled, like the few faint memories she had of their mother. Left at nineteen to hold their father's farm and raise her much younger sister, married twice and twice quickly widowed, Tesme had never yet showed much sign of care or worry or even the passage of time. But she showed it now. Kes looked down again, ashamed to have worried her.

"Are you all right?" Tesme asked gently. She usually seemed a little distracted when she spoke to her sister, when she spoke to anyone; she was always thinking about a dozen different things—mostly practical things, things having to do with raising horses and running the farm.

But Kes thought she was paying attention now. That was uncomfortable: Kes preferred to slip gently around the edges of everyone else's awareness—even Tesme's. Close attention made her feel exposed. Worse than exposed: at risk. As though she stood in the shadows at the edge of brilliant, dangerous light, light that would burn her to ash if it fell on her. Kes always found it difficult to speak; she never knew what anyone expected her to say. But when pinned by the glare of close attention, the uncertainty she felt was much worse. She managed, in a voice that even to her own ears sounded faltering and unpersuasive. "I—I'm all right. I'm fine."

"You seem preoccupied, somehow."

Since Tesme frequently noted aloud that her sister seemed preoccupied, even when she was paying quite close attention, Kes did not know how to answer this.

"There's something . . . *Is* there something wrong?"

Kes could find no words to describe the magnificence of bronze wings in the sun. She would have tried, for Tesme. But the mere thought of trying to explain the griffins, the hard heat they had brought with them, the strange look of the sky when they crossed it in their brilliant flight . . . She shook her head, mute.

Tesme frowned at her. "No one has been, well, bothering you, have they?"

For a long moment, Kes didn't understand what her sister meant. Then, taken aback, she blushed fiercely and shook her head again.

Tesme had come to a full halt. She reached out as though to touch Kes on the arm, but then her hand fell. "Some of the boys can be, well, boys. And you're so quiet. Sometimes that can encourage them. And besides the boys . . ." She hesitated. Then she said, "I like Jos, and he's a wonderful help around the farm, but Kes, if he bothers you, you surely know I'll send him away immediately."

Kes said, startled, "Jos?"

"I know you wouldn't encourage him, Kes, but lately I've thought sometimes that he might be, well, watching you."

"*Jos* doesn't bother me," Kes said, and was startled by the vehemence of her tone. She moderated it. "I like Jos. He wouldn't . . . he isn't . . . and he's too old, anyway!"

"Oh, well, Kes! He's not *that* old, and he's not blind, and you're growing up and getting pretty, and if he notices you too much, there are other places he could get work." But Tesme looked somewhat reassured. She started walking again, if not as quickly.

Kes hurried the few steps necessary to catch up. "I like Jos," she said again. She did, she realized. His quiet, his calm, the competent way he handled the horses. The way he never pressed her to speak, or seemed to expect her to fit into some unexplained pattern of behavior she couldn't even recognize. He was comfortable to be around, as so few people were. He had been at the farm for . . . nearly half her life, Kes thought. She could not imagine it without him. "He doesn't bother me, Tesme. Really, he doesn't. Don't send him away."

"All right . . ." Tesme said doubtfully, and began to walk a little more quickly. "But let me know if you change your mind."

It was easier to nod than protest again.

They walked a little farther. But then Tesme gave Kes a sideways look and added, "Now, if there's a boy you *do* like, you'd let me know, Kes, wouldn't you? I remember what I was like at your age, and shy as you are, you *are* getting to be pretty. You know you don't need to slip off silently to meet somebody, don't you? If you want to walk out with Kanne or Sef or somebody, that's different, but you would tell me, wouldn't you? There's a world of trouble for a girl who's too secretive, believe me."

Kes felt her face heat. "I don't like anyone!" she protested.

"That changes," Tesme said, her tone wry. "If it changes for you, Kes . . ."

"I'll tell you. I'll tell you," Kes said hastily, hoping to sound so firmly reassuring that Tesme would let the subject die. It was true anyway. Kanne? She suppressed an urge to roll her eyes, not wanting her sister to reopen the subject—but *Kanne*? Kanne was a baby, and too interested in himself to even notice a girl. Sef was almost as bad, all but welded to the smithy where he was apprenticed. Kes couldn't imagine either of them, or any other of the village boys, ever choosing to simply walk out across the hills and listen to the wind and the silence.

"All right . . ." Tesme said. She did sound somewhat reassured. "It's true you're not much like I was. On the whole, that's probably just as well." She glanced at Kes, half smiling and half worried.

Kes had no idea what to say to this, and so said nothing.

"You're yourself, that's all," Tesme concluded at last, smiling. She patted Kes on the shoulder and lengthened her stride once more.

The inn, set by the road near the river, right at the edge of the village, was all white stone and dark wooden beams. It had a dozen pretty little tables in its wide, walled courtyard, across from its stables, which were screened from the inn by small trees and beds of flowers. Jerreid and his wife, Edlin, and their daughters ran the inn, which was widely acknowledged to be the best of all the little country inns along the western river road that ran from Niambe Lake all the way down to Terabiand. The inn was not overlarge, but it was pleasant and very clean, and every window looked out onto one flower garden or another. And the food was good.

Many ordinary folk and even nobles broke their journey in Minas Ford as they traveled from the little jewel-pretty cities of the high north to the sprawling coastal town of Terabiand in the south—the Ford of the town's name had long ago been replaced by the best bridge anywhere along the river—and, as the saying went, everyone and everything passed along the coast at some time. And so a good proportion of everyone and everything traveled up from Terabiand and through Minas Ford eventually, and since Minas Ford was conveniently a long day's journey from Bered to the south and an easy day's journey from Riamne to the north, many travelers looked forward to a stay at Jerreid's pretty little inn.

Every upstairs room had a window, shutters open in this fine weather; every table, outdoors or in, was graced by a slender vase of flowers. Edlin made the vases of fine white clay, glazing them with translucent glazes in blue and pink and white. She made them to keep cut flowers, and she had the gift of making in her hands: It was common knowledge that flowers stayed fresh in one of Edlin's vases twice as long as they lasted in an old cracked mug.

Edlin also made tableware that was both pretty and very hard to break. She sold bowls and plates and platters from a shop behind the inn, leaving the running of the inn almost entirely to her husband and their three daughters. Edlin grew the flowers herself, though, and picked them fresh every week to arrange in the vases. That was, famously, as close to the work of the inn as she would come.

Jerreid, fortunately, seemed perfectly happy to leave his wife to her dishes and glazes and gardens.

"Tesme!" Jerreid said, as they came into the yard. He was a big, bluff, genial man with a talent for making his inn feel homey and all his visitors feel welcome. He'd been leaning against one of the outdoor tables, chatting with what looked like half the folk of the village—a big crowd for the middle of the day. There were no travelers present at the moment, although some would probably stop later in the day. But Chiad and his wife had torn themselves away from their farm to visit the inn, along with a dozen children and cousins and nephews. And Heste had abandoned her bakery for the moment—well, the morning bread was long out of the ovens, and perhaps she had a little time before she would start the pies and honey cakes for the evening. But Nehoen was also present, which was less usual. His big house with its sprawling lands lay well outside the village, and he did not usually come to the inn except on market day. And Caris had for some reason left her weaving to visit the inn, as well as Kanes and his apprentice Sef the smithy.

Kes looked at them all uneasily, wondering nervously whether she might guess what had drawn them all away from their ordinary business. She hoped she did not blush when she glanced at Kanne or Sef. How could Tesme possibly think—? Was Kanne even fourteen yet? And Sef! She looked hastily away from the smith's apprentice, aware that she probably *was* blushing, now.

"You seem happy," Jerreid was saying to Tesme. His smile, at least, seemed ordinarily cheerful. "How is your mare? River, wasn't it? She must have done well by you, yes?"

"Yes, yes, yes!" Tesme came across the yard, leaving Kes to follow more slowly. She took Jerreid's hands in hers and smiled at him. "A filly, healthy and big, and River's fine. We're celebrating. Have you any blackberry wine left, or did you drink it all yourself?"

"We've plenty—"

"But you might want to hold off on the celebrations," said Chiad. Dark as the earth he worked, serious by nature and not given to celebrations at even the best of times, he looked at the moment even more somber than usual. He slapped the table with one broad hand for emphasis as he spoke.

"Give the woman a chance to catch her breath!" exclaimed Jerreid, shaking his head in mild disapproval.

Chiad gave him a blink of incomprehension and instantly transferred his attention back to Tesme. "You've got your young foals down by the house, haven't you, Tesme? Do you know what Kanne saw this morning?" Kanne was Chiad's son, and he now sat up straight in his chair and looked important.

Kes knew. She heard it in Chiad's voice. She saw it in Kanne's eyes.

Tesme arched her eyebrows, still smiling, if a little less certainly. "If it wasn't someone underselling me with Delta-bred stock for cheap, I don't think I'll mind, whatever it was."

"You will," said Chiad, heavily, with a somber shake of his head. "Tell her, boy."

Kanne laid his hands down flat on the table and sat up even straighter, looking proud and important. "Griffins!" he said.

This had not been what Tesme expected, and she looked blank.

"Griffins!" Chiad said. He slapped the table, shaking his head again in heavy disapproval. "Of all things! Half lion, half eagle, and all killer! My barley is likely safe enough, but you'd best look after your stock, Tesme!"

Tesme still looked blank. She said after a moment, "Kanne, are you sure they weren't just eagles?"

"Now, that's what I said," Jerreid agreed, nodding.

"Sure, I'm sure," Kanne said importantly. "I *am* sure! I know what eagles look like, Jerreid! These weren't eagles or vultures or any bird!"

"Griffins never leave their desert," said Heste, frowning. Her attitude suggested that she had said this before, repeatedly.

"They do," said Nehoen, so patiently it was clear he'd said this before as well. "Griffins in the spring mean a hard summer." Nehoen was not sitting at the table. He had gotten to his feet when Tesme and Kes had entered the courtyard. Now he moved restlessly, leaning his hip against one of the tables and crossing his arms over his chest. He was old, nearly fifty, but he was one of the few gentlemen of the village and thus showed his age far less than a farmer or smith.

"What?" said Tesme, blinking at him.

Nehoen smiled at her. He owned all the land out on the west side of the village near the river, and he could not only read, but owned far more books than all the rest of Minas Ford put together. His grandmother had been an educated woman of the Delta, and had put great store by books and written learning. He explained now, "Griffins in the fall mean an easy winter, griffins in the spring a hard summer. They say that in Casmantium. There wouldn't be a saying about it if the griffins never left their country of fire to come into the country of earth."

"But why would they?" Tesme asked. "And why come so *far*? Not just so far south, either, but all the way across the mountains into Feierabiand?"

"Well, that I don't know. The mages of Casmantium keep them out of Casmantian lands—that's what their cold mages are for, isn't it?—so maybe if the griffins wanted to move, they had to cross the mountains. But why they left their own desert in the first place?" Nehoen shrugged. "Who can guess why such creatures do anything?"

"Griffins are bad for fire," said Kanes. The smith's deep voice rumbled, and everyone hushed to listen to him. "That's what I know. They're made of fire, and fire falls from the wind their wings stirs up. That's what smiths say. They're bad creatures to have about."

Smiths knew fire. Everyone was silent for a moment, thinking about that.

"Griffins," said Jerreid at last, shaking his head.

"Griffins," agreed Nehoen. He began a rough sketch on a sheet of paper somebody had given him.

Chiad's wife said, practically, as she was always practical, "Saying Kanne is right, as I think he is, then what? Fire and hard summers, maybe—and then maybe not. But it stands to reason a creature with eagle talons and lion claws will hunt."

"Surely—" Tesme began, and stopped, looking worried. "You don't think they would eat our horses, really?"

"Nellis stops wolves from eating livestock," said Chiad, laying a broad hand on his wife's hand.

She nodded to him and went on herself, "Jenned stops mountain cats. Perren stops hawks from coming after chicks." Perren was a falconer as well as a farmer, and gentled hawks and falcons for the hunt. Chiad's wife added, "I can keep foxes off the hens, and my little Seb stops weasels and stoats. But I don't know who's going to stop griffins eating your foals or my sheep, if that's what they want. What we need is a cold mage. I wonder why our mages in Feierabiand never thought to train up a youngster or two in cold magic?"

"We've never needed cold magecraft before," Chiad answered his wife, but not as though he found this argument persuasive.

His wife lifted her shoulders in a scornful shrug. "Well, and we don't need ice cellars until the summer heat, or a second lot of seed grain until a wet spring rots the first sowing; that's why we plan ahead, isn't it? They should have thought ahead, up there in Tihannad—"

"Now, now." Jerreid shook his head at Chiad's wife in mild reproof. "Summer we have every year, and wet springs often enough, but if griffins have ever come across the mountains before, it was so long ago none of our fathers or grandfathers remember it. Be fair, Nellis."

"Whoever thought or didn't think, it's my horses that are going to be eaten by griffins," said Tesme, sitting down rather abruptly at the table in the chair Nehoen had abandoned.

"They wouldn't eat them," Nehoen said, patting her shoulder. "Griffins don't eat. They may look part eagle and part lion, but they're wholly creatures of fire. They hunt to kill, but they don't eat what they bring down."

"That's even worse!" Tesme exclaimed, and rubbed her forehead.

Kes watched her sister work through the idea of griffins coming down on her horses. It clearly took her a moment. She wasn't used to thinking of the danger a big predator might pose if no one in the village could speak to it or control it.

In every country there were folk with each of the three common gifts. But just as Casmantian folk were famously dark and big-boned and stocky, Casmantian makers and builders were famously the best. There were makers everywhere, but more and better makers in Casmantium; to find makers with the strongest gifts and the deepest dedication to their craft, to find builders who could construct the strongest walls and best roads and tallest palaces, one went to Casmantium.

In the same way, one could recognize Linularinan people because they commonly had hair the color of light ale and narrow, secretive eyes, but also because they were clever and loved poetry. Everyone in Linularinum could write, they said, so probably it wasn't surprising that Linularinum had the cleverest legists. There were legists in Feierabiand, at least in the cities, but if you wanted a really unbreakable contract that would do exactly what you wanted, you hired a Linularinan legist to write it for you.

But everyone knew that if you needed someone with a really *strong* affinity for a particular sort of animal, you came to Feierabiand. As Tesme held an affinity to horses, others held affinities to crows or mice or deer or dogs. In Feierabiand, every town and village and tiny hamlet had one or two people who could call wolves and mountain cats—and more important, send them away. But griffins were creatures of fire, not earth. No matter how dangerous or destructive they might prove, no one, even in

Feierabiand, would be able to send the griffins back across the mountains.

Tesme was looking more and more unhappy. "Maybe you and Edlin would let us borrow the use of your lower pasture for a while?" she said to Jerreid. "Mine isn't big enough for all the horses. Will I have to move all the horses, do you think? How big are griffins? How many did you see, Kanne?"

"Dozens," the boy said. He sounded pleased about it. "Big."

Nehoen silently held out a sketch he'd drawn. It showed an animal with a savage look: a creature half feathered and half furred, with the cruel hooked beak and talons of an eagle and the haunches of a cat. Everyone crowded forward to look. Kes, peering over Kanes's shoulder, winced a little. The monster in the drawing was a crude misshapen thing, neither bird nor beast; it looked clumsy and vicious.

"Yes," said Kanne triumphantly. "Griffins!"

Kanes nodded heavily. "We need king's soldiers. That's what we need. Clean the creatures out before they settle in to stay."

Kes continued to study the drawing for a moment longer, not listening as everyone else spoke at once. It was all wrong. And what she found, though she didn't understand why it mattered to her, was that she couldn't bear to have everyone believe Nehoen's drawing showed the truth. So she silently took the paper from Nehoen's hand and picked up the piece of charcoal he had used for his drawing. Nehoen looked startled, but he let her have the charcoal. Nellis stood up, giving Kes her place at the table, and waved for Kanne to move, too.

Kes turned the paper over to the blank side and sat down. She had already forgotten her audience. She was thinking of griffins. Her eyes filled with fire and beauty. She turned the charcoal over in her fingers and set it to the paper. The creature she drew was not like the one Nehoen had sketched. She had a surer hand with the charcoal than Nehoen, but that was not the difference. The difference was that she knew what she was drawing.

The griffin flowed out of the charcoal, out of Kes's eyes. It was eagle and lion, but not mismade, not wrong, as Nehoen's griffin had been wrong. She gave this griffin the beauty she had seen. She had seen griffins flying, but the one she drew was sitting, posed neatly like a cat. It was curled around a little, its head tilted at an inquisitive angle. It was fierce, but not vicious. The feathers around its eyes gave it a keen, hard look. Its sharp-edged beak was a smooth curve, exactly right for its eagle head. The feathers flowed down its forequarters and melted smoothly into a powerfully muscled lion rear. Its wings, half opened, poured through the sketch with the clean purity of flame.

Tesme, looking over Kes's shoulder, took a slow breath and let it out.

Nehoen took the finished drawing out of Kes' hands and looked at it silently. Kes looked steadily down at the table.

"When did you see them?" Nehoen asked gently.

Kes glanced up at him and looked down again. She moved her hand restlessly across the rough surface of the table. "This morning."

Tesme was staring at her. "You didn't say anything."

Kes traced the grain of the wood under her hand, running the tip of her finger around and around a small knot in the wood. "I didn't know how. To talk about them. They . . . are nothing I know words to describe."

"You—" Chiad said incredulously.

"Hush," said Nellis, laying a hand on her husband's arm. "Kes, love—"

At the gate of the inn yard, someone moved, and everyone jumped and stared. Then they stared some more.

The man at the gate was a stranger. But more than a stranger, he was himself strange. He wore fine clothing, but unusual in both cut and color. Red silk, red linen, red leather—all red, a dark color like drying blood, except for low black boots and a black cloak. He did not wear a sword, though even in Feierabiand nearly all men of good birth carried one. But this man did not carry even a knife at his belt. He held no horse, and that was surely strangest of all, for how had a gentleman come to Minas Ford if not by horse or carriage?

The man's hair was black and very thick, without a trace of gray—although it was somehow immediately clear that he was not a young man. The lines of his face were harsh and strong. His eyes were black, his gaze powerful. He had a proud look to him, as though he thought he owned all the land on which his gaze fell. His shadow, Kes saw, with a strange lack of astonishment, was not the shadow of a man. It was too large for a man's shadow, and the wrong shape, and feathered with fire. Kes glanced quickly into her sister's face, and then looked at Nehoen and Jerreid and Kanes, and realized that although everyone was startled by the stranger, no one else saw that his shadow was the shadow of a griffin.

The black-eyed stranger with the griffin's shadow did

not speak. No one spoke, not even Jerreid, who liked everyone and was hard to put off. Everyone stared at the stranger, but he had attention only for Kes. And rather than speaking, he walked forward, straight to the table where she sat. He clearly assumed everyone would get out of his way, and everyone did, although Nehoen, getting abruptly to his feet, put a hand on Kes's shoulder as though he thought she might need protection.

Ignoring Nehoen, still without speaking, the man picked up the drawing Kes had made and looked at it. Then he looked at her.

Kes met his eyes, seeing without surprise that they were filled with fire. She took a breath of air that seemed stiff with heat and desert magic. She could not look away, and wondered what the man saw in her eyes.

"What is your name?" the man asked her. His voice was austere as barren stone, powerful as the sun.

After a moment, Nehoen cleared his throat and answered on her behalf. "Kes, lord," he said. "Kes. She doesn't talk much. And what is *your* name?"

The man transferred his gaze to Nehoen's face, and Nehoen stood very still. Then the man smiled suddenly, a taut hard smile that did not reach his eyes. "I am sometimes called Kairaithin. Anasakuse Sipiike Kairaithin. You may call me so, if that pleases you. And yours, man?"

Nehoen swallowed. He met the black stare of the stranger as though he was meeting a physical blow. He said slowly, reluctantly, "Nehoen. Nehoen, son of Rasas, lord."

"Nehoen, son of Rasas," said the stranger. "I am not your enemy." He did not say, I do not care about you at all, but Kes saw the merciless indifference in his eyes. When he turned his attention back to her, she looked down at the table. She said nothing. She did not dare speak, but beyond that, she simply had no idea what to say. The stranger seemed to see her exactly as she was, but she had no idea who, or what, he saw. In a way, she found this hard-edged perception more difficult to endure than the ordinary expectations of the townsfolk.

"Kes," said the man. He put down the drawing she had made. "My . . . people . . . have encountered difficulty. There are injured. We have need of a healer. You are a healer, are you not? My people are not far removed from this placc. Will you come?" He asked this as though Kes had a choice.

Kanes rose to his considerable height, crossed his powerful smith's arms across his chest, and rumbled, "Who asked you to bring your . . . *difficulties* . . . here, stranger?"

The man did not even glance at the smith. But Kes flinched. She could not understand how Kanes, strong as he was, could possibly think he could challenge the stranger. She could not understand how the smith could miss his contained power.

But Kanes, it seemed, was not alone in that inclination. Nehoen shifted half a step forward and said in a tone edged with hostility, "She's needed at her home." He looked at Tesme.

Tesme blinked. She had been staring at the stranger, wordless. Now she said in a breathless voice, "Kes. Come home," and held out her hand to her sister.

Kes did not move. She looked into the face of the

stranger and whispered, "You are a mage. As well as—" she stopped.

A swift, fierce smile glinted in the black eyes.

"Are you—" Kes began, and stopped again.

"I am not your enemy," the man said, harsh and amused. "Do this for me, and perhaps I will be your friend." Fire flared in his eyes. He said patiently, holding out his hand, "I have no power to heal. I think you do. Will you come?"

"Kes—" said Tesme.

"Look, Kes—" said Nehoen.

"I—you should understand, lord," Kes whispered, "I only use herbs."

The man continued to hold out his hand expectantly. "You drew that. Yes?"

Kes, lowering her gaze, looked at the drawing that lay on the table between her hands. It seemed strange to her now, how smoothly that image had emerged from her eyes, from her memory. Her hands closed slowly into fists. "Yes."

"Then I hardly think you will need herbs. It was not a herb woman I sought. Searching, it was you I found. Will you come?"

Kes found she wanted to go with him. She knew he was not truly a man; she knew he was not any creature of the ordinary earth. But she longed, suddenly and intensely, to go with him and see what strangeness he might show her. Kes got to her feet, not looking at anyone but especially not at her sister, and laid her hand in his. His long fingers closed firmly around hers. The stranger's skin was dry, fever hot to the touch. He tilted his head to the side, meeting her eyes with his power-

ful black gaze. There was nothing remotely human in
his eyes.

The world moved under their feet, rearranging itself.
They stood high up on the slopes of the mountain. Kes
caught her breath, blinking, and found the world had gone
as strange and beautiful as she could ever have wished.

The sun poured down with ruthless clarity upon the
rocks, which were red, all in twisted and broken shapes,
nothing like the everyday rounded gray stone of the
mountain. Griffins lounged all around them, inscrutable
as cats, brazen as summer. They turned their heads to
look at Kes out of fierce, inhuman eyes. Their feathers,
ruffled by the wind that came down the mountain, looked
like they had been poured out of light, their lion haunches
like they had been fashioned out of gold. A white griffin,
close at hand, looked like it had been made of alabaster
and white marble and then lit from within by white fire.
Its eyes were the pitiless blue white of the desert sky.

And, Kes realized, the griffins were not actually lounging. They were not relaxed. They lay on the sand or atop
the twisted red stone ledges, tense and tight-coiled, looking at Kes with fierce and angry stares.

The man at her side moved a step, drawing her glance.
The merciless sun threw his shadow out behind him, and
here in the desert that shadow was clearly made of fire. It
was more brilliant than even the molten sunlight. Flames
tossed around the shadow's fierce eagle head like feathers
moved by the wind. Its eyes were black.

The man said with harsh approval, "You knew, of
course."

Kes nodded hesitantly.

"Of course. You see very clearly. You are such a gift as

I had hardly hoped to find, woman, though it was for one such as you I searched. You are exactly what we need." He drew her forward, between gold and bronze griffins, into the shade cast by the shoulder of the mountain. His shadow paled in that relative dimness, like the edges of a clear flame, more sensed than seen.

A griffin lay there in the shade. It was, indeed, injured. A deep and bloody wound scored its golden lion flank, and blood speckled the bronze and black feathers of its chest. It lay with its mouth open, panting rapidly. Its tongue was narrow and barbed. Its eyes were open but blind, glazed with pain.

Kes stared at the wounded griffin in horror, as much at the ruin of its beautiful strength as at its pain. The stranger had said he needed a healer, but she had not imagined such desperate wounds and suffering. She had none of her things, not the sinews for sewing injuries nor the powders to keep infection from starting. And even if she had had those things, the griffin's wounds looked too serious for her skill anyway.

Another griffin crouched near the injured one like a friend or a brother: Something in this griffin's manner made Kes think of how Tesme would have hovered by her side if *she* had been hurt. She longed, suddenly and intensely, for Tesme; yet at the same time, she was fervently glad that her sister was not here. There was nothing in this place Tesme would have understood, and Kes felt, strongly if incoherently, that her sister's presence would only have offended the griffins and weakened Kes herself.

The guardian griffin had feathers of brilliant gold overlaid with a copper tracery. He sat up as they approached, tail wrapped neatly as a cat's around his feet, and fixed Kes with a brilliant copper-gold stare. She faltered, but Kairaithin drew her forward.

"There are others injured," Kairaithin said. He sounded . . . not concerned, precisely. Not like a man might sound, whose friend was injured. Kes did not understand what she heard in his voice, but it was nothing human. He went on, "But this is the worst. This is our . . . king. He must live. Far better for your people, as well as mine, if he should live."

Kes could not tell if he meant this as a threat, or merely as a statement. She moved forward hesitantly, kneeling by the wounded griffin. She put her hand to its chest, parting the feathers delicately. The injured griffin did not move; the other one shifted a foot, talons scraping across stone. Kes flinched back, but he did not move again. And Kairaithin was waiting.

The wound she found was a puncture, deep . . . she could not tell how deep . . . wide as well as deep. It was bleeding only a little, a slow welling of crimson droplets that ran, each in turn, along the lie of the feathers to fall, glittering and solid, to the sand. Tiny gemstones, rubies and garnets, sparkled in the sand under her knees. Kes blinked at them, fully understanding for the first time that these were truly not creatures of earth. That they were wholly foreign to this land and to her own nature. And she was expected to heal them? She cast Kairaithin a frightened glance.

"An arrow made of ice and ill intent," said the griffin mage, watching her face. "I drew the arrow and slowed the blood. But I have no power to heal. That is for you."

Kes laid her hand over the wound. She had no herbs, no needles, no clean water, nothing a healer would use at her craft . . . She touched the griffin's face, traced the delicate shadings of gold and bronze under the blind eye, moved her hand to rest on the rapid pulse beating under the fine feathers of the throat. She said, trying to sound helpless rather than defiant, "But . . . truly, lord, I know nothing but herbs."

"You know what you see. You know what we are. Are you not aware of your own power, poised to wake? Did you not know me at once?"

Kes did not know what the man meant by "your own power." True healers were mages, not mere herb women. She was not a mage. She knew very well she was not a mage. Mages were not simply gifted, as Tesme was gifted with her affinity for horses, as makers or legists might be variously gifted. There was always magic in making, in made things; everyone had that to at least a small degree. There was magic in spoken and, especially, written words—especially in Linularinum, where everybody learned to write. But the affinity to an animal, the ability to make or build, the legist's gift of setting truth down with quill and ink . . . all of those things were part of inborn, natural earth magic. Anybody could be gifted.

But mages were not merely gifted. They *were* gifted, but the gift wasn't enough to make a mage. Or so Kes had always believed. Mages studied for years and years, learning . . . Kes could not imagine what. And there were never many of them: the necessary combination of power and dedication were vanishingly rare.

It had never occurred to Kes to wonder how an old mage chose an apprentice, or how a young person, perhaps, found within herself the desire or capacity or . . . whatever it might be that might lead her to want to be chosen. Kes had never wanted anything like that. Kes had only wanted to be left alone, to walk in the hills and look at the sky and the pools and the growing things. Hadn't she? If the idea of being a mage had ever occurred to her . . . *would* she have wanted that? Did she want it now?

Now that the notion had occurred to her, Kes thought, uneasily, that she might almost want it. It would set her apart . . . but in a way that people could understand, or at least that they could be comfortable with not under-standing. And she had always been set apart anyway, or set herself apart, somehow. Mage-skill would have made her . . . made her . . . she did not know what. Something different than she was now. Wouldn't it? And yet, this griffin-mage thought *she* might be a mage? Even trying now to look inside herself, she could find nothing whatso-ever that seemed to her like *power*.

Kairaithin's power, on the other hand, beat against her skin like the heat of a bonfire. Kes closed her eyes and saw a black-and-red griffin move in the darkness be-hind the lids. *I have no power to heal,* he had said. What power *did* a griffin have, when he was also a mage? When she thought of the griffin, fire roared through the dark-ness. A voice like the hot wind of the desert said in her mind, *Anasakuse Sipiike Kairaithin.* She did not doubt Kairaithin's power. Was it possible the griffin mage had made a mistake about her?

"Searching, I found you, and so brought my people to this place," Kairaithin said to her, as though in answer to her unspoken question. With her eyes closed, it seemed to Kes that he spoke from a place very far away. "And so we are here; and so is Kiibaile Esterire Airaikeliu, Lord of Fire and Air. See him whole, woman, with insistent sight; pour through your heart and into him the fire that sustains him, and he will be whole."

Kes opened her eyes again and looked up at the griffin mage, baffled. *Insistent sight?* She laid her hand on the wounded griffin's chest and stared down at him, hoping for inspiration. His breath came rapidly. His blood, liquid as it left his body, was hot against her fingers. The gold-and-copper griffin stared furiously at her. She did not ask what the griffins would do if she could not heal their king. She thought instead of the griffin mage saying in his austere voice, *I hardly think you will need herbs.*

Could he be right? What, then, would she need? *See him whole, and he will be whole.* She stared down at the bloody feathers under her hands, and found she did indeed want to heal that terrible wound and restore the griffin to health and wholeness. She wanted that. But even so, she did not know what to do. She drew her hands back and looked helplessly at Kairaithin, afraid he would be angry, but simply at a loss.

The griffin mage did not appear to be angry, although perhaps impatient. He took one of Kes's hands in both of his and held it firmly. Heat struck up her arm, racing from her hand up to her shoulder and then spreading down toward her heart. Kes gasped. It did not actually hurt. But it was a strange feeling, as though her own blood had been turned into a foreign substance within her veins.

"Creature of earth," said Kairaithin, letting her go but holding her eyes with his. "You may yet learn to understand fire. Reach for fire and it will follow the pathway your will lays down for it, as a fire follows tinder across stone."

"Reach for it?" Kes said, faltering.

"Make it a part of your nature. I will give you fire. Let

the fire strike into your heart." The griffin mage bent forward, staring at her, willing her to understand.

Kes stared back at him. *Let the fire strike into your heart.* She pictured an arrow slanting down out of the sun at her, guided by Kairaithin's will: a burning arrow, a golden arrow trailing flames. She flinched from the image.

Beside her, the injured griffin shifted. His breath rattled in his throat. His eyes were blind, Kes thought, because they were filled with shadows.

She blinked, and blinked again, and then shut her eyes and turned her face up to the sky. Lord of Fire and Air. King of the griffins. His pulse beat under the tips of her fingers. His name beat in her own pulse. She said, not understanding her own certainty, "Why is he in the shade? He needs light."

The mage moved his hand and the rock above them shattered and fell away, raining far down the mountain in little pieces. The sun poured down. Kes thought about the fiery arrow coming down at her, and this time she didn't flinch. Instead, she did something that felt like calling out to it.

"Yes," said Kairaithin, his tone fierce and triumphant.

Mere image though it might be, the arrow seemed to blaze down and snap into Kes's body with an almost physical shock: The image in her mind of the arrow striking home was so vivid she gasped. She thought she could feel its sharp entry into her heart. There was a sharp-edged moment of agony, but then at once a sense of fierce satisfaction and a strange kind of wholeness, as though she had been waiting all her life for that arrow of light and heat to enter her. She felt filled with fire. It did not feel like power. It felt like completion.

Kes shut her eyes and held up her hands to the sunlight. She cupped the light in her hands, hot and heavy as gold, and then opened her hands to pour it out like liquid. She listened to the griffin's name in the beating of her blood. Kiibaile Esterire Airaikeliu. Creature of fire and blood. She stared into the sun, and then lowered her eyes to stare into his. She saw him whole, and blinked, and blinked again, her eyes filled with heat and light.

Beneath her hands, the pulse that had been so rapid steadied and slowed.

The king of the griffins moved his head and looked at her with eyes that were no longer blind, but clear and savage. The wounds were gone. When he rolled to crouch and then sit, his movements were fluid, effortless. When he struck at Kes with his savage eagle's beak, he moved fast as light pouring across stone.

Kes could never have ducked in time. But in fact she did not try to dodge the griffin's beak at all. She knelt in the sun and stared into fierce golden eyes, stunned as a rabbit by the gaze of an eagle, as much by what she had done as by the unexpected violence, watching light glance savagely off that curved beak as it slashed toward her face.

The gold-and-copper griffin interposed his own beak, blindingly quick, with a sound like bone striking bone. The king of the griffins turned his shoulder to the copper-traced one and stretched, muscles shifting powerfully under the tawny pelt of his haunches; he spread his great wings, shaking the feathers into place. They spread behind him, a tapestry of gold and bronze and black. He cried out, a hard high cry filled with something that seemed to

Kes akin to joy, but not a human joy. Something stranger and harsher than any human emotion.

Kairaithin had not moved, but he was smiling. The copper-traced griffin swept his head back and cried out, the same cry as the king, but pitched half a tone higher. The king swept his wings forward and then down, catching the hot breeze, and leapt suddenly into the air. The hot wind from his wings blew Kes's hair around her face and drove up from the ground a whirling red dust that smelled of hot stone and fire. Flickering wisps of fire were stirred to life in the wind of those wings; the fiery sparks turned to gold as they scattered across the sand.

The other griffin lingered a moment longer. *I am Eskainiane Escaile Sehaikiu*, he said to Kes, his voice flashing brilliantly around the edges of her mind. *When you would set a name to burn against the dark, think of me, human woman.* Then he said to Kairaithin, *I acknowledge your claim; you were right to bring us to the country of men and right to seek a young human with her magecraft on the very edge of waking.*

Kairaithin inclined his head in acknowledgment and satisfaction.

The coppery griffin spread wings like a blazing stroke of fire and swept into the sky, following the king. Kairaithin put his hand down to Kes. "There are other injured. I will show them to you."

Kes asked him shakily, "Will they all try to kill me?" She felt very strange, and not only because of the griffin king's unexpected savagery. She felt light and warm, but it was not, somehow, a comforting kind of warmth. It seemed to her that if she stood up she might fall into the hot desert wind and blow away across the red sand; she felt as though she had become, in some essential manner, detached from the very earth. But she took Kairaithin's hand and let him lift her to her feet.

"Perhaps some." The mage released her hand and tilted his head to look at her sidelong, a gesture curiously like that of a bird. He said after a slight pause, "Do not be offended, woman. These are not your own kind. Esterire Sehaikiu gave you his name, and he is not the least among us. Will you not then allow the king his pride? I will protect you if there is need. Will you come?" He offered her his hand again.

Kes got slowly to her feet, though this time she did not take the mage's offered hand. She looked at him wordlessly, meeting his eyes. She took a breath of hot desert air, tasting light like hot brass on her tongue. She thought of a red griffin with black eyes. Red wings heavily barred with black shifted across her sight. *Kairaithin*, she thought. *Anasakuse Sipiike Kairaithin*. His name beat in her blood like her own pulse.

"No," said the mage briefly, and moved his hand. A darkness fell across Kes's sight like the shadow of a great wing, and the rhythm in her blood faded with the light. His shadow looked at her; its black eyes laughed. "You could be powerful," Kairaithin said, that same harsh amusement in his voice. "But you are young. You would not be wise to challenge me, woman. Remember that I am not your enemy."

Kes looked at him. The black eyes met hers with absolute assurance. There was no trace of offense in his eyes, in his austere manner. She asked, her voice not quite steady, "Will you be my friend?"

He smiled slowly, a hard expression that was not like a human smile.

"Kairaithin," she said, tasting the word.

He shifted and glanced away, expression closing, and turned to show her the way he wanted her to go. "Come, woman. See the other injured."

Kes followed obediently. She wondered who in the world had had the temerity to attack griffins. With arrows of ice and ill intent. Had she not heard that, in Casmantium, some of the earth mages used a magecraft of cold and ice? And used it specifically against griffins, to keep them out of the lands of men? Such mages might, she supposed, make arrows of ice.

But griffins had always dwelled in the desert north of Casmantium; why would Casmantian mages now attack the griffins? Had the griffins first come south and threatened the cities of men? She wanted to ask Kairaithin. But she did not ask. She only threaded her way between stark stones, following the griffin mage. The sun rode its punishing track above. The griffins ignored their mage, but they turned their heads to watch Kes pass. Their eyes were the fierce hot eyes of desert eagles, unreadable. The griffins were beautiful, but Kes did not have the nerve to meet their stares.

The injured griffin Kairaithin brought Kes to was a slim dark creature, with feathers of rich dark brown only lightly barred with gold. The lion belly was cut across by a long terrible gash that had come near to disemboweling the griffin. Garnets lay strewn across the sand near it, some of them disturbingly large. The griffin lay half in the sun, half in the shade of a towering red rock shelf. Its beak was open as it panted; its eyes, dazed with pain and endurance, were half-lidded. It turned its head as Kairaithin stopped beside it, though, and looked at the mage, and then at Kes. Golden-brown eyes met hers. But this griffin did not seem savage. It seemed, more than anything, simply patient.

"Opailikiita Sehanaka Kiistaike," said Kairaithin.

There was something in his tone, something strong, but nothing Kes recognized. When she moved cautiously past the mage to put a hand on the leonine side of the griffin, it only turned its head away. She did not know if it was acquiescent to her touch, or simply refused to acknowledge her. Or whether it felt something else that she recognized even less. She was not absolutely certain she could heal it. She did not understand what she had done to heal the first griffin. But she wanted to heal it. The thought of the savage wound across its belly was like the thought of broken legs on a foal.

It was surprisingly hard to remember that the griffin was dangerous. That it would perhaps try to kill her. That she did not understand it. *Her*, she thought. She had not been paying particular attention, but she knew that this griffin was female. And young. Yes. The slimness of the haunches said this was a young griffin. She wondered if its composure was feminine in a griffin? Or was it part of just this griffin, an individual characteristic, like Jerreid's friendliness and Nellis's practicality and Tesme's slightly flurried kindness? She did not let herself think of Tesme for longer than an instant. Opailikiita. Opailikiita Sehanaka Kiistaike. Dark and slim and quick and graceful. Opailikiita. Yes.

Kes closed her eyes, then opened them, looking into the sunlight. The griffin's name beat through Kes's awareness. Through her blood. Kes stared into the dark, patient eyes, her own eyes blind with the fierce light of the sun, and groped for the memory of what she had done to heal the griffins' king. She seemed, in just those few steps it had taken to come to this griffin, to have lost the trick of it. She felt much like a child learning to walk, who could not keep his balance and fell every few steps. Of course, a child could cling to the hand of his father. What could Kes cling to?

She thought of fire and fiery arrows and put her hand out, blindly, to Kairaithin. His long angular fingers closed around hers, and again the half-familiar, not-quite-painful heat rushed up her arm. Her heart bloomed with fire.

It demanded no effort to see the griffin the way she should be, rather than the way she was. Opailikiita Sehanaka Kiistaike. Slim and young and beautiful, undamaged by malice or injury. It was more difficult to gather light and heat in her hands, as though half her mind had realized by this time that what she was doing was impossible and this realization interfered with her heart.

Kes blinked through the dazzle of heat, then closed her eyes and lifted a double handful of sand and gemstones. The sand was hot; the garnets rich even to the touch. Kes closed her hands around the grit, then opened her hands again, and looked down. Light pooled in her hands, molten and liquid, and she reached then to touch the injured griffin. And found, with no sense of surprise at all, that the griffin under her hands became whole.

This griffin stretched slowly and rose, and stretched again, fastidious as a cat. She did not strike at Kes, however. She angled her head to the side and regarded Kes from an eye that was unreadable, but not violent. Kes smiled, finding that her face felt stiff, as though it had been a long time since she had last smiled. The griffin leaped up to the top of the red rock that had sheltered her, stretched out in the sun, and began to ruffle her feathers into proper order with her beak, for all the world like a common garden songbird.

Kes looked at Kairaithin. He, too, was smiling. It was not a gentle expression on his harsh face, but he was clearly pleased. "Come," he said, and moved a hand to show her the way.

"She didn't try to kill me," Kes said tentatively.

"She would not," the griffin mage agreed without explanation. "This next one will try, I think. His name is Raihaisike Saipakale. He is quick in temper and embarrassed to have suffered injury. I will, however, protect you."

Kes believed he would. She followed the mage around broken rock and struggling parched grasses, thinking about wounds made with arrow and spear. Made with ice and steel. And ill intent . . . "Who makes such weapons?"

The mage gave her a severe look from his black eyes. "Mages."

This was singularly uninformative. Kes asked tentatively, "Cold mages? Casmantian mages?"

"Yes," said Kairaithin, but he said nothing else.

Kes wanted to ask him why the cold mages of Casmantium had done this, but she looked into Kairaithin's hard, spare face, into his black eyes that held fire and power, into the fiery dark-eyed shadow that shifted restless wings at his back, and did not quite dare.

Raihaisike Saipakale was lying in a patch of withered grass that had once been spring fed; Kes recognized the

site, but the spring was dry. The mostly buried gray rock
from which the water had seeped was cracked and broken, half-hidden by drifting sand. It was strange and disturbing to see a familiar place so altered; for a moment,
Kes found herself wondering whether, if she went home
now, she would find her home, too, half buried in desert
sand, the bones of the horses wind-scoured, Tesmé gone.
This was a terrible image. Kes paused, horrified, unable
to decide whether she thought it might be true.

"You may attend to the injured. The places of men remain untouched by the desert," Kairaithin said, watching
her face. His black eyes held nothing she could recognize
as sympathy, but neither did they hold deceit.

Kes took a shaky breath of hot desert air and turned
back to the wounded griffin.

This griffin had dreadful injuries across his face and
throat and chest; his blood had scattered garnets and carnelians generously through the dead grasses. Kes was
surprised he was still alive. But she was confident, this
time, that she could make him whole. She called light
into her eyes and her blood; she poured light through her
hands into the griffin and felt it shape itself into sinew
and bone, into bronze feather and tawny pelt. His name
ran through her mind, and an understanding of his fierce,
quick temperament. She made him whole, unsurprised by
the ferocious blaze of temper that accompanied his return
to health.

There were many injured griffins. The mage brought
her to one and then another, and another. He gave her
their names, and she made them whole. The names of
the griffins melted across her tongue, tasting of ash and
copper, and settled uneasily to the back of her mind.

She thought she would be able to recognize every griffin she had healed for the rest of her life, to recall each one's name like a line of poetry. Dazed with sun and the powerful names of griffins, she was startled to find at last that there were no others awaiting her touch and the healing light. She stood in the shadow of a red rock where Kairaithin had brought her and looked at him in mute bewilderment. The only griffin there was Opailikiita Sehanaka Kiistaike, and Kes knew the small brown griffin did not need further healing.

"Rest, *kereskiita*," Kairaithin suggested. Not gently, nor kindly. With something else in his tone. Not exactly sympathy, but perhaps . . . a strange kind of heedfulness.

It seemed, at the moment, enough like kindness. Opailikiita shifted, half-opening a wing in a gesture that looked like welcome, or something similar. *Come*, she said, a smooth touch against the borders of Kes's mind. The tone of her voice, too, suggested welcome.

Kes had not known how desperately weary she had grown until the opportunity to rest was offered. She did not answer the slim brown griffin. She did not think she was capable of putting words together with any lucidity. But she went forward and sank down in the shade where the heat was marginally less oppressive, leaned her head against Opailikiita's feathered foreleg when the griffin turned to offer her that pillow, and was instantly lost in fire-ridden darkness.

CHAPTER 2

On one particularly fine morning in late spring, Bertaud son of Boudan, Lord of the Delta, found himself standing in the courtyard of the king's winter house in Tihannad, watching the king of Feierabiand tease apart the delicate roots of young lilies so that they might be most aesthetically arranged in their waiting box. The morning was very fair, and Bertaud would rather, perhaps, have been hunting or hawking or even shooting at targets in the courtyard with the queen and her ladies to look on and applaud. But Iaor Safiad, in perhaps an excess of affection for his young wife, wished instead to wander through the gardens of his winter house, bury his hands in warm dark earth, and play with flowers. Bertaud shifted his weight, trying not to sigh.

The king finished with the lilies and washed his hands in a basin. Ignoring the towel Bertaud proffered, he shook his hands dry in the air and finally looked at Bertaud with a glint in his eyes. The king was not quite as tall as Bertaud and not quite as dark; though both men spent much time out of doors, the king's skin went golden in the sun rather than brown, and his dark hair, untouched as yet by any gray, picked up sun-bleached streaks and became almost tawny. In looks, Iaor resembled his mother far more than his great black bull of a father. But when he gave Bertaud a sidelong glance and observed, "You're bored," the mocking edge to his tone was very like the old king's.

Bertaud lifted his eyebrows. "Bored? How could I be?"

Iaor laughed—his own laugh. He was far less guarded in manner than his father had been, but with a wickedly sardonic edge to his humor, utterly unlike his mother.

The king's laugh pulled at uncomfortably deep places in Bertaud's heart. He couldn't help it; couldn't help that he admired and honored—and, yes, loved—Iaor Safiad above any other man in Feierabiand. Bertaud would never have insulted Iaor by claiming to feel toward him as toward his father. But as toward an older brother . . . the best and most admirable of older brothers . . . He might have admitted to that.

Bertaud could still remember how splendid and kind Iaor had seemed to him when he had first come to court from his own father's huge cluttered house in the Delta, which had been always crowded and yet never companionable. He had been only ten; Iaor more than twice that. But Iaor had seen something in the awkward, silent boy Bertaud had been, and had made him his own page, holding him at court long past the time he had been due to return to his father's house. Bertaud had tried to conceal his desperate fear of returning home, but Iaor had known it, of course. So he had kept Bertaud at his side for eight years, until Bertaud's father had suddenly died in a frenzy of rage and drink and Bertaud himself, though barely grown, inherited title to the broad, fertile lands of the Delta.

But when, only a few years later, Iaor's father too had suffered a stroke and died, it had been Bertaud whom Iaor Safiad had summoned to his side. And Bertaud had gladly left one of his many uncles to keep his own lands in order and returned to Iaor's court. Lord of the Delta, Bertaud hated the Delta; he had a hundred cousins but cared for none of them; all that he valued lay in this court, and most of all, the friendship and trust of the king. But Iaor despised sycophancy, and Bertaud would never risk giving any such impression. Now he waited a moment, until he was certain his voice would show nothing he didn't want it to show. Then he said, matching Iaor's drily mocking tone, "How could I possibly desire anything other than what you desire, my king?"

Iaor laughed again. "Of course!" he said. "And what I desire is to enjoy the last of the spring and think, for a moment, of nothing more complicated than lilies." Straightening his back, the king stretched extravagantly and then turned and stood for a long moment, looking around at the gardens and his house in palpable satisfaction.

The winter house of the king of Feierabiand nestled into the land at a place where three hills came together, where the little wavelets of Niambe Lake ran before the wind away from the rocky shore. A low, sprawling building built of the native stone, set against the winter gray of the lake, the king's house seemed a part of the land. Like the hills, it might have simply grown there long ago. The Casmantian kings might build magnificent palaces to impress both their own people and travelers with their grandeur and their skill as builders; the Linularinan kings might raise delicate towers and airy balconies to the sky; but Iaor Safiad was a true king of Feierabiand, and the kings of Feierabiand wanted a warm and comfortable house, one with small rooms that could each be heated by a single fireplace, with thick walls and soft hangings to keep in the warmth during the long winters.

The town of Tihannad had grown up around the king's winter house, or perhaps the king's house had been built by the lake because of the town; no one in these latter years remembered. But the town was like the king's house: low and plain and comfortable. Its homes were snugly built of stone, and its streets paved with more stone, with gutters to carry the spring's melting snow to the river that curved along one wall of the town. The wall went all around the town, a tall, thick barricade, though no one living remembered a time the wall had held back any enemy. The gates in the wall stood open day and night, and the wall itself, forgetful of the purpose it had originally been made to serve, did not present opposition to travelers.

In winter, the people of Tihannad dressed in warm coats of poppy red or gentian blue, put bells and ribbons on the harnesses of their horses, and went skating on Niambe Lake. They lit bonfires in the town square around which young men and women gathered to dance in the long evenings. They carved blocks of thick ice from the lake to store in deep cellars for summer, and then carved more blocks into flowers and swans and other fanciful shapes.

But though the people of Tihannad enjoyed winter, they loved spring. As soon as the west wind warmed and the snow melted, every house in Tihannad put out boxes and pots and half-barrels of flowers—blue and white pansies, pink kimee with huge fringed petals and delicate blue-green foliage, white trumpet-flowered moonglow, soft saffron-and-pink spring lilies. All the girls wore flowers in their hair, and children braided flowers into the manes of their families' horses on the slightest excuse.

The king's house was no exception to this joy in spring, for the king, too, took pleasure in the warming days and the bright flowers. The King of Feierabiand was a Safiad; his full name was Iaor Daveien Behanad Safiad. Safiads had ruled Feierabiand for three hundred years, and had generally ruled it well. Iaor Safiad had inherited his father's strong will along with his mother's self-possession, and this combination made some of his opponents uneasy. Nevertheless, Feierabiand was accustomed to Safiad rule, and even Iaor's most outspoken critics in his court did not truly expect to trouble his rule overmuch.

Iaor needed both assurance and determination, for no matter the season, he ordinarily had a good deal more to think about than lilies. As his father and grandfather had before him, Iaor Safiad kept a wary peace with Feierabiand's neighboring countries. To the west lay Linularinum—sophisticated, imperious, haughty Linularinum, always ready to believe that Feierabiand peasants would one day learn to accept the natural superiority of their western neighbor.

Linularinum was not exactly warlike. But a mere hundred years ago, King Lherriadd Kohorrian, high-handed and overbearing, had offended the Lord of the Delta and lost the allegiance of the Delta, which at that time had been one of Linularinum's more valuable coastal assets.

And everyone also knew that if Linularinum's current king, Mariddeier Kohorrian, ever saw a way to force the issue, he would not necessarily care whether the Delta wished to switch allegiance once more. No, if the old Fox of Linularinum glimpsed a chance to bring the Delta into his grasp, he would consider it a matter of pride to reach out and take it.

But in some ways Casmantium, across the mountains in the dry country of the east, presented a greater threat. Barely eighty years ago, it had conquered the small country of Meridanium to its northeast. Now Meridanium had a Casmantian governor and its people paid taxes to the Casmantian king in Breidechboden. Worse—from Feierabiand's point of view—Meridanium had been more than conquered; it had been absorbed. As Meridanium no longer seemed restive under Casmantian rule, the kings of Casmantium were free to consider other projects. Everyone knew Brechen Glansent Arobern was ambitious to add another province to his possessions; everyone knew he did not necessarily consider the current border his country shared with Feierabiand to be the last word on the subject.

So Iaor Safiad kept the Feierabiand armies blatantly visible on both borders. And he encouraged trade and business, since prosperous merchants always preferred peace and were seldom much concerned with who claimed what chunk of territory as long as the trade moved briskly. The old Fox of Linularinum would press only subtly at the river border so long as all his wealthiest subjects preferred to use the bridges for peaceful—and lucrative—trade. Similarly, as long as roads and harbors yielded trade and wealth, even the restless young king of

Casmantium seemed content to confine arguments over
road tolls and harbor dues to strong words rather than
flashing swords and spears.

Still, it was not astonishing that this spring Iaor Safiad
would find a moment or two for flowers. He had married
during the winter, his second marriage, and hardly before time, according to his court and kingdom. Iaor's first
wife had died without issue three years past and, by most
accounts, the king had not been half forward enough in
seeking another. Everyone hoped for heirs from his new
young queen.

The new queen, Niethe, was a beautiful young woman
from a good Tiearanan family, graceful as a fawn and
playful as a kitten, delighted with Iaor and her new life
and still charmingly amazed by her good fortune. And
the king was captivated by her. Once spring had arrived,
Iaor spent more time arranging flowers to please his new
bride than he did attending to the business of the kingdom, a propensity greeted with tolerant amusement by the
town, and with displeasure only by those of his court who
suspected that his preoccupation was merely a ruse and
that they might be targets of it.

Niethe was in her early twenties, little more than
half the king's age—her youth accounted fortuitous for
the production of heirs. But, despite any calculation
that had been involved in the match, Niethe seemed
as pleased by Iaor himself as much as by her new roy-
alty. Certainly she loved proof of his love for her. She
loved flowers, and loved best of all the ones her lord
brought to her with his own hands: She loved to be
courted and made much of. And the king made much
of her . . . a little overmuch for some of his court, who

found themselves, this spring, somewhat displaced from his attention.

Bertaud tried hard not to feel jealous of the new queen; he knew it was neither just nor sensible to resent Niethe. But sometimes he found Iaor's focus on his new wife a little trying. He supposed he would view the matter more favorably if he found a wife of his own—but the Lord of the Delta would need to marry a woman of the Delta, and as Bertaud had no desire at all to return to his own lands, he was not eager to pursue the question. He said now, mildly, "I suppose we must enjoy the spring while it lasts; soon enough we will have the full heat of summer closing down upon us."

"And then we will need to contend with the bother of moving to the summer house," Iaor agreed, but still smiling. "Well, we shall ride out when we can and, as you wisely suggest, enjoy the spring while it remains to us! But I fear, much as I might desire otherwise, we'll have no time for either hunting or hawking this morning. One of my judges has appealed a case to me. No doubt it will be some strange, convoluted matter, or why else appeal to me?" He made a face, though to Bertaud it was clear he was actually looking forward to finding out what the problem involved.

Iaor went on, "However, I have hope this judgment will not take long. Perhaps this afternoon there will be time to take the hawks out. You know the Linularinan ambassador just gave my lady one of those miniature falcons they are so proud of. A pretty little thing, though I have a certain doubt as to its ability to take anything so large as a rabbit."

Of course Iaor's first thought was of Niethe. Bertaud

would have died before allowing Iaor to glimpse any hint of jealousy, though sometimes he could not help but remember a time before the young queen had intruded into the closeness he had once shared with the king. He said smoothly, "I think they mostly hunt mice. Do you suppose the queen would like mice?"

"She might, if it was her falcon caught them. She thinks the bird is charming—well, so it is. We shall have to try it on young rabbits and see how it does. Or persuade the cooks to try what they might do with mice, hah? See if the judge is here, will you? I gave him the third hour."

They had arrived at the king's personal reception room, a small, cheerful chamber with broad windows, shutters thrown back this morning to let in the light and air. The king himself had a chair, set up on a low dais; there were no other furnishings.

The judge was, of course, already present in the antechamber—it would not do to risk keeping the king waiting, so the judge had come early, bringing with him the principal from his case. That proved to be a young man, about Bertaud's age, with bound wrists and—reasonably enough—a sober expression. The prisoner had a narrow face, brown hair, and long hands. From his dress, which was plain but good, he was likely the son of a tradesman or minor merchant. A guardsman was also present, standing behind the young man.

The judge was Ferris son of Tohanis, a man Bertaud knew a little. He inclined his head to the judge and said, "Esteemed sir." He did not glance at the other men, other than one swift look to be sure the guardsman looked professional and alert. The guardsman returned a small nod. The captain of the royal guards answered to Bertaud.

That responsibility did not normally accrue to the Lord of the Delta, but so Iaor had granted it, despite Bertaud's youth. Bertaud was fiercely proud of the honor and strove to be worthy of Iaor's trust—though with the royal guard, his duty largely consisted of leaving Eles, their captain, a free hand.

"My lord," the judge answered formally. "If I may ask—"

Bertaud smiled. "He is curious what you may have for him. He is, I believe, rather in the mood for tangled thoughts, and looks forward to finding out what you have brought him."

The judge nodded and sighed, not returning Bertaud's smile. "I hope his majesty's mood is still inclined that way after he hears me. This matter is not so much complicated as provoking—or so I have found it. Well . . . well, thank you, my lord, and is his majesty ready to see me, then?"

"If you are ready to present your case, esteemed sir, his majesty is prepared to hear it."

The judge was, of course, ready. Bertaud let him lead the way down the hall and to the small reception room.

The king nodded as they entered. The young man, guided by the guardsman, came forward to the foot of the dais and, pressed down by firm hands on his shoulders, went awkwardly to his knees. The guardsman stood behind him. The judge clasped his hands together before his chest and bowed.

"Esteemed Ferris," said the king. "What does your diligence bring me?"

The judge bowed a second time and straightened. He said, his manner somewhat pedantic, "Your majesty, this man is Enned son of Lakas. He was brought before me on charges of mayhem and murder. He has not denied guilt—indeed, his guilt is not in question. The circumstances are these: A Linularinan merchant—a dealer in salt, linen, and metals, who has traded in Tihannad every spring for the past seven years, a respected and wealthy man—offended against the father of this young man, Lakas son of Timiad. This Lakas is a tradesman of Tihannad. He makes goods out of linen, buying the linen from Linularinum, of course."

"Of course," agreed the king. "An equitable arrangement, I expect. And?"

The judge tilted his head to one side. "In fact, the Linularinan merchant, one Mihenian son of Mihenian, had for several years been going to some effort to ensure that the arrangement was *not* equitable. Indeed, due to certain contracts drawn up by a Linularinan legist, Mihenian's fortunes had risen substantially, whereas Lakas son of Timiad was very close to being ruined."

"Ah."

"On this fact being discovered—having exhaustively investigated the matter, your majesty, I am satisfied that it is a fact—Lakas went to the merchant Mihenian and attempted to gain satisfaction. However, confident that Lakas would not be able to collect monies owed him legally, due to an interesting principle of Linularinan law, which—well, your majesty, to be brief, Mihenian refused to regularize his dealings with Lakas son of Timiad. He was, in fact, directly insulting. He went so far as to strike Lakas in the face."

Iaor nodded, interested but also a little impatient.

"It being clear that the monies would be impossible to collect, and severely offended at Mihenian's callous disregard of his father's ruin, this young man then laid an ambush for the merchant and killed him. Due to an exceptionally alert guardsman, whose name, my king, I have given to the captain of your guard for commendation, he did not succeed in doing so secretly. When this young man was approached by the guard, he surrendered without resistance and cast himself on the mercy of the court; that is to say, my mercy."

"Yes?" said the king.

Ferris inclined his head. "Well, your majesty, I would be inclined to grant it, except of course I have no way to do so, legally. The Linularinan merchant behaved in a most offensive manner. It's true, of course, that Lakas son of Timiad might have brought charges against Mihenian for assault, only the witnesses to the act were all employees of Mihenian. And, legally, Lakas had no recourse for the business dealings that Mihenian had employed against him. Evidently, he was prepared to accept his losses and the blow to his pride, but his son was not."

"Nevertheless, despite the lack of disinterested witnesses, you are satisfied as to what occurred."

"Yes, your majesty."

"Then I, too, am satisfied."

Ferris inclined his head, gratified, and continued. "In the strictest legal sense, Mihenian son of Mihenian was not at fault. The contract was, to even the closest reading, legally unassailable. However, from the standpoint of disinterested justice, Mihenian clearly acted without regard for just and proper dealing. On the other hand, he was a citizen of Linularinum, which broadens the scope of this matter in a most unfortunate way."

"Yes," agreed the king, with distaste. Linularinan opinion was often too inflexible for his taste, but impossible to take lightly. As the people of Feierabiand frequently held an affinity to one animal or another, as the people of Casmantium were famous for their making and building, so the people of Linularinum were well known for the magic many of them could weave with quill and ink. "When you sign a Linularinan contract," the saying went, "count your fingers afterward—and remember as the years pass to count the fingers of your children and grandchildren."

When a Linularinan legist set the magic of the binding word into his work, a contract might unroll its meaning in unexpected directions—and be very difficult to rewrite. Iaor would not want to give the old Fox of Linularinum any opening to claim that legal impropriety had been done. Dismissing a justified charge of murder done upon a Linularinan merchant, for example, might very well provide such an opening.

"So I appeal to your majesty," said Ferris, opening his hands. He inclined his head.

"Yes," said the king again. He surveyed the young man. Enned son of Lakas looked back steadily. He was rather pale. But he had too much pride to flinch from the king's searching gaze. Looking at him, Bertaud was not surprised that this young man had been willing to risk his own life to retrieve his father's pride and punish the man who had ruined him. And what would the father think of that? Surely any normal father would be appalled? If not at the murder, than at this aftermath?

"Have you anything to add?" the king asked him. "Do you concur with what the esteemed Ferris has recounted?"

Enned bowed his head over his bound hands. "No, your majesty. That is, yes. Everything he said is true."

"You understand that the penalty for murder is death?"

"Yes, your majesty," the young man answered. He was afraid, Bertaud saw, but not defiant; he looked back at the king frankly and honestly. His voice was not, however, quite as calm as his face.

"Do you think your father would regard the trade of your life for the death of his business rival as a fair and good trade?"

The young man shook his head, stiffly. "His grief will be hard. I didn't mean to get caught. I'm sorry I was. And I'm sorry if you think I was wrong. But I can't be sorry I killed the Linularinan. My family was not wealthy, your majesty, but we were not poor, and my father worked hard to build our business. And he is a good man, and no one to cast aside like a beggar!"

"As you cast aside my law?"

Enned looked startled. Color rose in his face. "I . . . confess I didn't think of it that way, your majesty."

The king tapped his fingers thoughtfully against the arm of his chair. "My law exists for a reason. My courts exist to give legal recourse to wronged men. *I* am here to hear appeals, where the courts cannot give satisfaction. And yet you did murder on your own account, on account of your own pride."

The young man could not, evidently, think of anything to say.

The king leaned forward. "I conclude you are a fool." He looked, and sounded, more and more severe. "If every man whose business associates bested or offended him drew a knife, if the law were disregarded every time a rash young man felt his pride touched, how would we all live? And in what disorder? Enned son of Lakas, the esteemed Ferris brought you to me because he felt you deserved mercy he could not give you. I don't know that I feel so. If the Linularinan merchant offended your father's pride and your family's well-being, how much more have you offended my pride, and the well-being of my kingdom?"

The young man swallowed, bowing his head.

Straightening, the king looked thoughtfully at the judge.

Ferris shrugged, opening his hands. "If every man who did business was upright in his dealings with his business associates, then their business associates would not suffer through their actions and young men would not be offended, however proud they might be. Though I grant you, this one is proud. He is also the only son of his father. His father came to me and begged for the life of his son, which I, of course, have no authority to grant."

"But you would have *me* grant it."

"The law is stern, your majesty, but I serve it gladly. Except when it is flouted by men who use sly cunning to slip its proper bounds. Then I am unable to be glad in its service. Still, at such moments, as I am not the final authority, I have recourse. Your majesty, of course, does not. Forgive me if I was wrong to appeal to your majesty."

The king leaned back in his chair and stared for a long moment at the young man, who flinched under that stare at last, his gaze dropping to the floor.

The king's eyebrows lifted. He said severely, "My brother king Mariddeier Kohorrian will be offended, and rightly, if he finds his merchants cannot travel to Feierabiand without being knifed in dark alleys by proud young fools."

Enned son of Lakas said in a faint voice, "Yes, your majesty."

"Bertaud," said the king.

Bertaud straightened attentively. "My king?"

"Though he is without doubt a proud young fool, I am inclined to spare this young man's life. But do you see a way I may do so that would satisfy Linularinum?"

It was a reasonable question to throw to Bertaud. The Delta had belonged to Linularinum as often, in the convoluted history of the two countries, as it had belonged to Feierabiand. But a hundred or so years ago, when the King of Linularinum had become a little too overbearing in his attempts to force the Delta to comply with a handful of Linularinan laws that it did not favor, its allegiance had swung decisively toward Feierabiand. Even the cleverest threats devised by the most subtle Linularinan legists had done nothing but make Keroen son of Betraunes order a Linularinan banner made so he could throw it down under the hooves of his horse, trample it into the mud, and invite Daraod Safiad to make him an offer.

But more than any other region, the Delta still mingled the peoples and customs of both Feierabiand and Linularinum. Bertaud considered the king's likely intentions and desires against his own estimation of Linularinan attitudes. He said after a moment, "The Linularinan people respect, ah, creative interpretations of the law. This is not Casmantium: We have neither the custom of the murderer's *geas* nor the cold mages who might inflict it, for which I suppose Enned son of Lakas may well be grateful. But what if we borrowed the general idea rather than the actual practice? Perhaps you might require this man's life, rather than his death. You might give the young man

over to the army, my king, and thus take his life while not
requiring his death. Military service is hardly as severe
as the Casmantian *geas*, but perhaps it could be seen to
satisfy the requirements of the moment."

The king rested his elbow on the arm of his chair and
leaned his chin on his hand. "A worthy suggestion. And
you think Jasand or Adries will take him among his soldiers? A hot-hearted fool like this?"

After a moment, Bertaud realized where Iaor was
heading with this question. He didn't know whether to
laugh or groan and in the end made a sound midway between the two. Iaor smiled.

"Oh, earth and iron," Bertaud said resignedly. "All
right, then. Give him to your guard, if you must, and I
will take him. I'm sure Eles will be delighted by the gift
I'll bring him."

Enned looked from the king to Bertaud cautiously, bewildered, but beginning to hope that he might, in fact, not
die this day.

"Will you take him, then?"

"If it please you, my king."

"Then he is yours," the king said briskly, and waved a
hand to show the decision was made.

Bertaud gestured to the guardsman, who, face profes-
sionally blank, leaned forward to cut the young man's
bonds and lift him to his feet. Bertaud said, "Enned, son of
Lakas, do you understand what the king has decreed?"

"I—" stammered the young man, who clearly was not
sure. "I know—I think he gave me to you, my lord—"

"I am Bertaud son of Boudan," Bertaud said, striv-
ing, with some success, he thought, for a severe tone. He
tried for the tone Iaor himself used when displeased, and

thought he copied it rather well. The young man seemed impressed, at any rate. "Among my other duties, I serve the king by overseeing the royal guard, to which you now belong. I think you will do well. You had better, because for you there is no return to your father's house. The mercy of the king, while considerable, is not endless. Do you understand me?"

"Yes," Enned said faintly. "My lord."

"You are fortunate to be alive. On your knees, and thank the esteemed Ferris son of Tohanis, who had no duty to seek mercy for you, for your life."

After the merest pause, Enned turned to the judge, dropped to his knees—still awkwardly; he would have to learn better grace—and said fervently, "Thank you, esteemed sir. Thank you very much."

The judge inclined his head. "I will inform your father."

"Thank you," the young man repeated, and looked nervously to Bertaud.

Bertaud crossed his arms forbiddingly over his chest and said, "Now, as you have not yet done so, thank the king."

Still on his knees, Enned turned back to the king and said humbly, bowing his head, "Thank you, your majesty. For your mercy."

Iaor inclined his head by a minute degree, effortlessly royal.

"Now, get up and present yourself to me," said Bertaud, and waited for Enned to find his feet. The young man was flushed, still disoriented by the suddenness and unexpectedness of the king's decision. He probably, Bertaud was aware, had very little idea what the duties of the guard

even were. He looked Enned up and down, maintaining a
stern visage, then glanced at the guardsman. "Annand."

"My lord," said the guardsman.

"Present this man to Eles. If the captain has any questions or reservations about this assignment, tell him he
may apply to me." Bertaud gave the king an ironic glance
on this last, and Iaor crooked a finger across his mouth to
hide a smile.

"My lord," repeated the guardsman, and put a hand on
the young man's elbow to escort him out. Enned went, not
without a wide-eyed backward look over his shoulder at
Bertaud and the king.

Bertaud waited until the door was closed behind the
two men, gently, by the guardsman. Then he let himself
laugh at last.

Iaor, too, was grinning. "You did that well. So stern!
Anyone would quail." He stood up and clapped Bertaud
on the shoulder. "I impose on you, I fear, my friend."

"How could I possibly desire anything other than
what you desire, my king?" Bertaud was having a hard
time finding a serious tone. "No, no. A hot-hearted proud
young fool is meant for the guard—just ask Eles." Eles
was not a man who suffered foolishness from any proud
young men. The captain of the guard certainly hadn't ever
been inclined to suffer it from Bertaud in years past, when
he had already long been the captain and Bertaud merely
Iaor's page and companion. Dour and emotionless, he had
seemed to Bertaud then; only much later had Bertaud
learned to catch the occasional gleam of unspoken humor
in the captain's eye. He hoped Eles would be amused
by this unexpected gift the king and Bertaud had sent
his way.

"So I thought," agreed Iaor. He sounded pleased with himself, as well he might. It was a solution worthy of a Linularinan legist. No one, not even the old Fox, could say the king had passed lightly over the young man's crime; even without imposing an actual *geas*, Iaor might be said to have imposed a rather severe sentence. Or, by taking the young man into his own guard, he had done him honor. And giving him into the hand of the Lord of the Delta was a nice touch: that might be a slight concession toward Linularinan sensibility . . . or a slight insult to Linularinan conceit. Depending on how one regarded it.

Thus, both Feierabiand pride and the king's justice had been preserved, and without doing actionable violence to any legal understanding between Linularinum and Feierabiand. It was an excellent maneuver, worthy of a Safiad. Even so, the king's glance at Ferris was less amused, and less pleased.

The judge saw this change in manner, too. "Your majesty, of course the boy did, without question, offend your law—the law that I swore an oath to uphold. And yet I brought the matter to you. Justly might your majesty rebuke me."

"Am I not the proper authority to hear such appeals?"

"Your majesty cannot have hot-hearted young fools knifing merchants, honest or otherwise, in dark alleys."

"Not even if the young man in question broke my law in answer to a sly slipping of its intentions? Was that not your argument?"

"The misuse of the law to protect dishonest dealing offended me. The boy's honest crime, if I may call it so, offended me less. I did advise him he should rightly have come to me in the first place. It would have been a good deal easier to appeal the matter to your majesty before blood was shed. As you yourself pointed out."

"Mmm." The king was still frowning.

Ferris lowered his eyes. "I am rebuked, then," he said, and formally, "I ask your majesty's pardon."

"Ah. No. I do not rebuke you." Iaor lifted his chin decisively. "Find out the extent of the merchant's losses to the Linularinan merchant. I will pay him compensation for the loss of his son. Out of my own personal monies." He paused.

The judge, reading this pause correctly, bowed. "Perhaps your majesty will permit me to provide that compensation, as it was my decision that led to this expense."

The king smiled, satisfied. "You may pay half. That is only just, I think. Good." He stood, took the older man's arm, and turned with him toward the door. "Walk with me, esteemed sir. I do esteem your judgment, I assure you. I promise you, I have no rebuke to offer. I am glad you brought this to my attention. I am certain Eles desires nothing more than to gain a young hot-hearted fool for his command. Walk with me, if you please, and tell me about the particular intricacies of Linularinan law that allowed this Linularinan merchant to cheat—lawfully!—my honest Feierabiand tradesman."

The judge smiled and said, "Gladly." He appeared resigned to the unofficial fine the king was imposing. At that, Bertaud reflected, even a sizable fine was far less to be dreaded than a royal rebuke.

Bertaud trailed them, sighing. He knew the signs. Iaor had been drawn entirely into kingly concerns. It seemed unlikely he would find time now to ride out with hawks, no matter how tedious his companions might find the threatened intricacy of law. No, he thought, not even if Iaor's young wife greatly desired to try her little falcon.

The trace of jealousy—unworthy, even shameful—in that thought disturbed him at once, and Bertaud called himself to stern order and tried to fix his mind on law.

However, they had hardly got out into the hall before the ring of quick-striding boot heels brought them all to a startled halt. The king released the judge's arm and drew himself up. Ferris cocked his head to one side, looking curious and alarmed. Bertaud himself laid a hand on his sword, ready to draw: Generally, no one ran down the halls of the king's house.

However, this person proved to be a messenger—one of the king's own couriers: a young woman with the king's badge at her shoulder and her courier's wand thrust through her belt. Iaor preferred young women for his couriers, a custom his father had begun; the old king had famously declared that girls rode more lightly and were more careful of their horses than boys, which, as Iaor had once commented, among other effects had ensured that the young men became at least somewhat more careful as well. But the courier-master still accepted more girls than boys for the king's service.

This courier's name was Teien, daughter of Kanes. Bertaud knew that Teien was posted to the south of Tihannad; her rounds included many of the smaller villages and towns along the Nejeied River. She went to one knee and saluted the king carefully. Her breathing was fast, but not desperately so.

"Yes?" said Iaor impatiently.

The woman bowed her head briefly, sucked in air, and said rapidly, "Word from Minas Spring and Minas Ford, your majesty. This is the word: Griffins have come across the mountains. They despoil your country, your majesty, turning good land into sand and sending hot winds across the young barley; they are killing calves in the pasture and game in the forest. Your people ask you for help in their need."

"Griffins," said Ferris, without expression.

"Did you see these griffins yourself?" Bertaud asked the courier.

"Yes, lord: So I could report clearly, I went to Minas Spring and up into the high hills behind the village. There are indeed griffins there. The very rock of the hills has changed its character; it is all red stone and sand there, now. The wind comes the wrong way, from the east, off the mountains. Coming from the heights, it should be a cold wind, but it is hot, and so dry it pulls moisture from the earth—I saw good soil turn dry and crack under that wind. I saw griffins there. I spoke to the folk of Minas Spring and Minas Ford. They say there are many griffins in the hills there, hundreds maybe; that they make all that country their own."

"Hundreds, Teien?" Bertaud said, drily.

"I saw only two," confessed the courier.

"It's more than one or two, to bring the desert wind to this side of the mountains," Ferris observed.

"I would be surprised to learn that there are hundreds of griffins in all the world," said the king. "I much doubt there are hundreds at Minas Spring." He looked seriously at the courier. "Do they kill the people there? Or only calves?"

"So far, they say, only calves and the odd sheep."

"Still," said Bertaud, "we can hardly have griffins settling along in the hills on our side of the mountains, making a desert out of our good farmland. Aside from ruining the land, it would not do to show weakness of either arms or resolve."

The king made a small, impatient gesture of agreement. "Obviously not." He signaled to the courier to rise. "Go find General Jasand and send him to me. Then go and rest. In the morning, present yourself to your captain. I suspect he will have a task for you."

"Your majesty," said the young woman, pulling herself to her feet and departing quickly.

To Ferris, the king said, "Esteemed Ferris, forgive me, but if you will excuse us. Please write me an explanation of the legal matters that created the problem for, ah, Lakas, and send it to me. I assure you I will be interested."

The judge, restraining his interest and curiosity, bowed acknowledgment and withdrew.

Bertaud said, in wonder, "Griffins?"

Iaor began to walk, waving to Bertaud to accompany him. "Teien saw them herself. Do you doubt her veracity?"

"No," Bertaud said. "Of course not. But I don't understand why griffins would leave their own country—and I certainly don't understand why they would go as far south as Minas Spring! If they were determined to cross the mountains, why not simply come straight west through Niambe Pass? That, at least, would make some sense!"

Iaor gave a thoughtful nod. "Perhaps they did not like to fly near Niambe Lake and were willing to go many miles south to the next pass they could find. The natural magic of Niambe Lake would hardly be an amicable magic for griffins. Well, that's a question for mages and we shall pose it to them, but whatever the reason, it's just as well, or we might have the griffins bringing their desert to the shores of Niambe, and all the way to Tihannad, perhaps!"

Bertaud laughed, as his king intended. Feierabiand had never had much to do with griffins, but they both knew it was inconceivable that griffins, no matter how numerous or powerful, would dare trouble the king himself in his own city.

CHAPTER 3

Kes woke as the first stars came out above the desert, harder and higher and brighter than they had ever seemed at home. She lifted her head and blinked up at them, still half gone in dreams and finding it hard to distinguish, in that first moment, the blank darkness of those dreams from the darkness of the swift dusk. She was not, at first, quite sure why the brightness of the stars seemed so like a forewarning of danger.

She did not at once remember where she was, or with whom. Heat surrounded her, a heavy pressure against her skin. She thought the heat should have been oppressive, but in fact it was not unpleasant. It was a little like coming in from a frosted winter morning into a kitchen, its iron stove pouring heat out into the room: The heat was overwhelming and yet comfortable.

Then, behind her, Opailikiita shifted, tilted her great head, and bumped Kes gently with the side of her fierce eagle's beak.

Kes caught her breath, remembering everything in a
rush: Kairaithin and the desert and the griffins, drops of
blood that turned to garnets and rubies as they struck the
sand, sparks of fire that scattered from beating wings and
turned to gold in the air . . . She jerked convulsively to her
feet, gasping.

Long shadows stretched out from the red cliffs, sharp-
edged black against the burning sand. The moon, high
and hard as the stars, was not silver but tinted a luminescent red, like bloody glass.

Kereskiita, Opailikiita said. Her voice was not exactly
gentle, but it curled comfortably around the borders of
Kes's mind.

Kes jerked away from the young griffin, whirled, backed
up a step and another. She was not exactly frightened—
she was not frightened of Opailikiita. Of the desert, perhaps. Of, at least, finding herself still in the desert; she
was frightened of that. She caught her breath and said, "I
need to go home!"

Her desire for the farm and for Tesme's familiar voice
astonished her. Kes had always been glad to get away by
herself, to walk in the hills, to listen to the silence the
breeze carried as it brushed through the tall grasses of
the meadows. She had seldom *minded* coming home, but
she had never *longed* to climb the rail fence into the low-
est pasture, or to see her sister watching out the window
for Kes to come home. But she longed for those things
now. And Tesme would be missing her, would think—
Kes could hardly imagine what her sister might think.
She said again, "I need to go home!"

Kereskiita, the slim brown griffin said again. *Wait for
Kairaithin. It would be better so.*

Kes stared at her. "Where is he?"

The Lord of the Changing Wind is . . . attempting to change the course of the winds, answered Opailikiita.

There was a strange kind of humor to the griffin's voice, but it was not a familiar or comfortable humor and Kes did not understand it. She looked around, trying to find the lie of country she knew in the sweep of the shadowed desert. But she could not recognize anything. If she simply walked downhill, she supposed she would eventually find the edge of the desert . . . if it still had an edge, which now seemed somehow a little unlikely, as though Kes had watched the whole world change to desert in her dreams. Maybe she had; she could not remember her dreams. Only darkness shot through with fire . . .

Kereskiita—said the young brown griffin.

"My name is Kes!" Kes said, with unusual urgency, somehow doubting, in the back of her mind, that this was still true.

Yes, said Opailikiita. *But that is too little to call you. You should have more to your name. Kairaithin called you* kereskiita. *Shall I?*

"Well, but . . . *kereskiita*? What is that?"

It would be . . . "fire kitten," perhaps, Opailikiita said after a moment. And, with unexpected delicacy, *Do you mind?*

Kes supposed she didn't actually *mind*. She asked, "Opailikiita? That's *kiita*, too."

Glittering flashes of amusement flickered all around the borders of Kes's mind. *Yes. Opailikiita Sehanaka Kiistaike,* said the young griffin. *Opailikiita is my familiar name. It is . . . "little spark"? Something close to that. Kairaithin calls me by that name. I am his* kiinukaile. *It would be . . . "student," I think. If you wish,* you *may call me Opailikiita. As you are also Kairaithin's student.*

"I'm not!" Kes protested, shocked.

You assuredly will be, said another voice, hard and yet somehow amused, a voice that slid with frightening authority around the edges of Kes's mind. Kairaithin was there suddenly, not striding up as a man nor settling from the air on eagle's wings, but simply *there.* He was in his true form: a great eagle-headed griffin with a deadly curve to his beak, powerful feathered forequarters blending smoothly to a broad, muscled lion's rear. His pelt was red as smoldering coals, his wings black with only narrow flecks of red showing, like a banked fire flickering through a heavy iron grate. He sat like a cat, upright, his lion's tail curling around taloned eagle's forefeet. The tip of his tail flicked restlessly across the sand, the only movement he made.

You have made yourself acquainted with my kiinukaile? the griffin mage said to Kes. *It is well you should become acquainted with one another.*

"I am *not* your student!" Kes declared furiously, but then hesitated, a little shocked by the vehemence of her own declaration.

She is fierce, Opailikiita said to Kairaithin. *Someday this kitten will challenge even you.* She sounded like she approved.

Perhaps, Kairaithin said to the young griffin, *but not today.* There was neither approval nor disapproval in his powerful voice. He added, to Kes, *What will you do, a young fire mage fledging among creatures of earth? I will teach you to ride the fiery wind. Who else will? Who else could?*

Kes wanted to shout, I'm not a mage! Only she remembered holding the golden heat of the sunlight in her cupped hands, of tasting the names of griffins like ashes on her tongue. She could still recall every name now. She said stubbornly, "I want to go home. You never said you would keep me here! I healed your friends for you. Take me home!"

Kairaithin tilted his head in a gesture reminiscent of an eagle regarding a small animal below its perch; not threatening, exactly, but dangerous, even when he did not mean to threaten.

He melted suddenly from his great griffin form to the smaller, slighter shape of a man. But to Kes, he seemed no less a griffin in that form. The fire of his griffin's shadow glowed faintly in the dark. He said to Kes like a man quoting, "Fire will run like poetry through your blood."

"I don't care if it does!" Kes cried, taking a step toward him. "I healed all your people! I learned to use fire and I healed them for you! What else do you *want*?"

Kairaithin regarded her with a powerful, hard humor that was nothing like warm human amusement. He answered, "I hardly know. Events will determine that."

"Well, I know what *I* want! I want to go *home*!"

"Not yet," said Kairaithin, unmoved. "This is a night for patience. Do not rush forward toward the next dawn and the next again, human woman. Days of fire and blood will likely follow this night. Be patient and wait."

"Blood?" Kes thought of the griffins' terrible injuries, of Kairaithin saying *Arrows of ice and ill-intent*. She said, horrified, "Those cold mages won't come *here*!"

Harsh amusement touched Kairaithin's face. "One would not wish to predict the movements of men. But, no. As you say, I do not expect the cold mages of Casmantium to come here. Or not yet. We must wait to see what events determine."

Kes stared at him. "Events. What events?"

The amusement deepened. "If I could answer that, little *kereskiita*, I would be more than a mage. I may guess what the future will bring. But so may you. And neither of us will *know* until it unrolls at last before us."

Kes felt very uneasy about these *events*, whatever Kairaithin guessed they might entail. She said, trying for a commitment, suspecting she wouldn't get one, "But you'll let me go home later. You'll take me home. At dawn?"

The griffin mage regarded her with dispassionate intensity. "At dawn, I am to bring you before the regard of the Lord of Fire and Air."

The king of the griffins. Kes thought of the great bronze-and-gold king, not lying injured before her but staring down at her in implacable pride and strength. He had struck at her in offended pride, if it had not been simple hostility. Now *he* would make some judgment about her, come to some decision? She was terrified even to think of it.

She remembered the gold-and-copper griffin, Eskainiane Escaile Sehaikiu, saying to Kairaithin, *You were right to bring us to the country of men and right to seek a young human.* Maybe that was the question the king would judge: Whether Kairaithin had been right to bring her into the desert and teach her to use the fire, which belonged to griffins and was nothing to do with men? Escaile Sehaikiu had said Kairaithin was right. But she suspected the king would decide that Kairaithin had been wrong. She gave a small, involuntary shake of her head. "No . . ."

"Yes."

"I . . ."

"*Kereskiita.* Kes. You may be a human woman, but you are now become my *kiinukaile*, and that is nothing I had hoped to find here in this country of earth. You do not know how rare you are. I assure you, you have nothing to fear." Kairaithin did not speak kindly, nor gently, but with a kind of intense relief and satisfaction that rendered Kes speechless.

I will be with you. I will teach you, Opailikiita promised her.

In the young griffin's voice, too, Kes heard a similar emotion, but in her it went beyond satisfaction to something almost like joy. Kes found herself smiling in involuntary response, even lifting a hand to smooth the delicate brown-and-gold feathers below the griffin's eye. Opailikiita turned her head and brushed Kes's wrist very gently with the deadly edge of her beak in a caress of welcome and . . . if the slim griffin did not offer exactly friendship, it was something as strong, Kes felt, and not entirely dissimilar.

Kairaithin's satisfaction and Opailikiita's joy were deeply reassuring. But more than reassurance, their reactions implied to Kes that, to the griffins, her presence offered a desperately needed—what, reprieve?—which they had not truly looked to find. Kairaithin had said the cold mages would not come here. *Not yet*, he had said. But, then, some other time? Perhaps soon?

I have no power to heal, Kairaithin had said to her. But then he had taught *her* to heal. Kes hesitated. She still wanted to insist that the griffin mage take her home. Only she had no power to insist on anything, and she knew Kairaithin would not accede. And . . . was it not worth a little time in the griffins' desert to learn to pour sunlight from her hands and make whole even the most terrible injury? Especially if cold mages would come here and resume their attack on the griffins? She flinched from the thought of arrows of ice coming out of the dark, ruining all the fierce beauty of the griffins. If she did not heal them, who would?

Kairaithin held out his hand to her, his eyes brilliant with dark fire. "I will show you the desert. I will show you the paths that fire traces through the air. Few are the creatures of earth who ever become truly aware of fire. I will show you its swift beauty. Will you come?"

All her earlier longing for her home seemed . . . not gone, but somehow distant. Flames rose all around the edges of Kes's mind, but this was not actually disagreeable. It even felt . . . welcoming.

Kes took a step forward without thinking, caught herself, drew back. "I'm *not* your student," she declared. Or she *meant* to declare it. But the statement came out less firmly than she'd intended. Not exactly like a plea, but almost like a question. She said, trying again for forcefulness and this time managing at least to sound like she meant it, "My sister will be worried about me—"

"She will endure your absence," Kairaithin said indifferently. "Are you so young you require your sister's leave to come and go?"

"No! But she'll be *worried*!"

"She will endure. It will be better so. A scattering of hours, a cycle of days. Can you not absent yourself so long?" Kairaithin continued to hold out his hand. "You are become my student, and so you must be for yet some little time. Your sister will wait for you. Will you come?"

"Well . . ." Kes could not make her own way home. And if she had to depend on the griffin mage to take her home, then she didn't want to offend him. And if she had to stay in the desert for a little while anyway, she might as easily let him show her its wonders. Wasn't that so?

She was aware that she wanted to think of justifications for that decision. But *wasn't* it so?

Come, whispered Opailikiita around the edges of her mind. *We will show you what it means to be a mage of fire.*

Kes did not feel like any sort of mage. But she took the necessary step forward and let Kairaithin take her hand.

The griffin mage did not smile. But the expression in his eyes was like a smile. His strange, hot fingers closed hard around her hand, and the world tilted out from under them.

The desert at night was black and a strange madder-tinted silver; the sky was black, and the great contorted cliffs, and the vast expanses of sand that stretched out in all directions. But the red moon cast a pale, crimson-tinged luminescence over everything, and far above the stars were glittering points of silver fire. Now and again, in the distance, a coruscation of golden sparks scattered across the dark, and Kes knew a griffin had taken to the air.

Kes sat above the world, high atop stone, under the innumerable stars. Kairaithin, wearing the shape of a man as he might have worn a mask, stood at the very edge of the cliff, gazing out into the blackness. From time to time, he glanced momentarily toward Kes and Opailikiita, but he always turned again to look outward. Like a sentinel. But Kes could not decide whether he seemed to be waiting for a signal from a friend—though she wondered whether griffins exactly *had* friends—or from an enemy. She knew very well griffins had *those*.

Kairaithin's arms were crossed over his chest, and now and again when he glanced her way, he smiled slightly—not a human smile. It was even less a human smile, Kes had decided, than his shadow was a human shadow. But she could not decide exactly where the difference lay.

Kes was sitting cross-legged on the stone, leaning back against Opailikiita's feathered shoulder. The young griffin was teaching Kes how to summon fire into the palm of her hand, and how to let it sink down into her blood. *Fire will run like poetry through your blood*, Kairaithin had said to Kes, and she now understood, at least a little, what the griffin-mage had meant. She called the fire out of her body again, set it dancing once more in her hand, and grinned swiftly up at Opailikiita.

Good, said the young griffin, bending her head down to look at the little flame. She clicked her beak gently in satisfaction or pleasure or approval—something at least akin to those things. *Fire becomes part of your nature.*

"Yes, I suppose," agreed Kes. The little flame in her hand was a pleasant warmth. It felt oddly familiar, as though she had spent her life holding fire in her hands—it felt as comfortable as holding an egg, only more lively. More like holding a kitten, maybe. Something small and alive. Something that might scratch, but not seriously. She closed her hand carefully around the flame. For a moment it flickered at her past the cage of her fingers. Then it was gone.

Could you call it back? Opailikiita asked.

Kes looked up at the slim griffin, then down at her closed fist. She opened her hand again, palm up, and drew fire from Opailikiita, from the stone, from the desert air.

The flame bloomed again in her palm. "It's not even hard," Kes said, smiling.

It is always easy to follow your nature, agreed Opailikiita.

"I never knew . . ."

Opailikiita began to answer, but Kairaithin said first, "Every man, and every griffin, believes he possesses a fixed and singular nature. But sometimes our distinctive self proves more mutable than we might suppose possible." He was not smiling now, but Kes did not understand the expression she saw in his eyes. But she did not have time to wonder about it, for then he straightened away from the pillar he'd leaned against and glanced away, toward the east. "The sun rises," he said.

It did. There was nothing of the pearl-gray and lavender dawn Kes might have watched from her window at home. Here, the return of the sun seemed altogether a wilder and fiercer phenomenon. First the merest edge of gold touched the sky over the tips of the mountains, and then the sunrise piled up behind the black teeth of the mountains in towering gold and purple, and then the burning sun itself seemed somehow almost to leap away from the mountains and into the desert sky, fiercer and larger here than it ever seemed in the gentler country of men.

The light was probably gentle and warm in the cold heights, but there was nothing gentle about the sunlight that poured heavily across the desert. Kes thought she could almost *hear* it come, as she might have heard floodwaters roar down from the mountain heights. Heat, thick as honey, filled the air. It was not exactly unpleasant, but it was very powerful. Kes swayed under its force, let the fire she held flicker out, and put her hands over her face to shield her eyes. She blinked hard, expecting her eyes to water in the brilliance, but there were no tears.

"Opailikiita," said Kairaithin in edged reproof, "that is not entirely a creature of fire."

Yes, answered the young griffin, though in a faintly uncertain tone. She stretched out a wing to shelter Kes from the fierceness of the sun. Light glowed through the feathers above Kes's head, but the brilliance was much attenuated.

"Useful as a momentary solution. However, as a permanent resolution of the difficulty, it lacks elegance," Kairaithin said drily. He put out a hand, and stone shuddered around them. A hot wind came up, driving sand whirling about the plateau where they stood exposed to the sky. Opailikiita reached out hastily with her other wing, enclosing Kes entirely in a sweep of rich brown and gold.

Then the wind died. Opailikiita drew her wings away, and Kes, blinking around, saw that tall twisting pillars now stood all around the edge of the flat top of the cliff, crowned with a slab of red stone. The rough hall that was thus formed was nothing at all like anything men would have built. She had not exactly understood before that *making* was truly a thing of men. But this hall—rough, but blatantly powerful—was, she realized, probably as close to making or building as griffins ever came.

She had no time to think about this, however, for into the stone hall, riding on the wind and the light, came Kiibaile Esterire Airaikeliu, Lord of Fire and Air. His name beat like poetry or fire through Kes's blood, overwhelming as the desert sun itself. He seemed huge, much bigger than she remembered; his wings seemed to close out half the sky. The wind roared through his wings; his talons flashed like polished bronze; his eyes were gold as the sun.

To the king's left flew the copper-and-gold griffin, Eskainiane Escaile Sehaikiu, who had told Kes, *When you would set a name to burn against the dark, think of me. Escaile Sehaikiu would burn against the dark like a conflagration*, Kes thought; he blazed with such brilliance that he might almost have been feathered in fire even now. To the king's right flew a female griffin—whose name Kes did not know, as she had never healed her—her red wings heavily barred with gold, lion body gold as the pure metal.

The king came down at the edge of the cliff, tucking his wings in close to fit between the narrow stone pillars and stalking forward with lion grace. He turned his head one way to stare at Kairaithin, then as his companions came under the roof after him, he turned that fierce golden stare on Kes.

His gaze, she found, was less readable than even the regard of an eagle or a lion. Kes wanted to cower down like a rabbit before that proud, incomprehensible stare. But Opailikiita nudged her gently in the back and said softly, her voice creeping delicately around the outermost edge of Kes's mind, *Remember you are Kairaithin's* kiinukaile *and my* iskarianere, *and remember your pride.*

Kes had no idea what *iskarianere* meant—except she did, in a way, even though Opailikiita had not exactly explained it to her. When the slim brown griffin said it to her, something of the sense of the word unfolded like a spark blooming into a flame. Kes put a hand out almost blindly, burying her fingers in the fine feathers of Opailikiita's throat and whispering, "Sister." And though it might not be exactly true in familiar human terms, though she did not really understand what the griffin meant by the word or what it encompassed, Kes was comforted and found the courage to stand up straight.

Human woman, said the Lord of Fire and Air. The king's voice slammed down across Kes's mind like a blow, so that she staggered under it and had to brace herself against Opailikiita's shoulder. The king's voice did not exactly hurt her—not exactly—but it came down on her with the heavy power of the desert sun. He said implacably, *Human mage. And will you become a mage of fire?*

Kes had no idea how to answer.

It seems a small creature, the king said to Kairaithin.

"Esterire Airaikeliu, it will grow," Kairaithin answered, sounding drily amused.

The king mantled his wings restlessly. *Perhaps. But soon enough?*

She made you whole, Eskainiane Escaile Sehaikiu reminded the king. *She found your name in the light and perceived you insistently whole. She is not so small as that.*

The coppery griffin's voice was not at all like the king's: It rang all around Kes's mind as though a brazen gong had been struck, singing with vivid joy. Kes understood that Escaile Sehaikiu had expected the king to die and was passionately glad Kes had saved him—but she thought the copper-and-gold griffin was also by nature expansively joyful.

She will never stand against the cold mages, when they come, said the red-and-gold female griffin. Her voice was swift and hot and bitterly angry, so that Kes stopped herself only with difficulty from taking a step backward.

"*I* will stand against the Casmantian mages," Kairaithin

said flatly. His black gaze passed without pity or fear across the red female and met the king's. "This young *kiinukaile* of mine need merely call into her mind and heart the names of our people and see them whole and uninjured. This she will do, as she has already done."

You will do this, the king said to Kes. It was not a question.

"Yes," Kes said softly. But she was surprised by the certainty she felt. "Yes, lord. If the cold mages come with their arrows. I would not want . . . I would not let them injure your people. Kairaithin says he has no power to heal. I would heal your people."

Indeed. Not so very *small*, said the king, bending low to gaze hard into Kes's face.

Kes longed to back away, but instead she pressed her hand hard against Opailikiita's shoulder and stayed exactly where she was, staring back into those fiery golden eyes.

Your name is Kes? said the king. *That is what they call you, among men? It is too small a name.*

"Kereskiita," said Kairaithin, sounding amused. *For her familiar name? That will do.*

Eskainiane Escaile Sehaikiu said, fierce laughter edging his voice, *Kereskiita Keskainiane Raikaisipiike.*

That is not fitting! said the red-and-gold female griffin, with no laughter at all in her voice. She glared at Kes, so fiercely that it almost seemed her stare could scorch the very air.

The king did not exactly say anything to this, but a forceful, if silent, blow seemed to shake the whole cliff— maybe the whole desert. The female griffin crouched down, snapping her razor beak shut with a deadly sound. But she did not say anything else.

It will do, said the king, and to Kes, *Keskainiane Rai-kaisipiike*. He flung himself back and away off the cliff, his great wings snapping open to catch the desert wind. Little flames scattered from his wings, sparks that glittered into delicate fragments of gold and settled to the sand far below. The other two griffins followed him, Eskainiane Escaile Sehaikiu blazing with glorious abandon and the red female furiously silent.

"She hates me," Kes said shakily, and leaned gratefully against the hot solidity of Opailikiita's shoulder. She stretched her arm as far as she could around the small griffin's neck and pressed her face into the soft feathers. "Why isn't it fitting? The name the king gave me?"

"It draws upon the name of Eskainiane, and upon one of my own names. Nehaistiane Esterikiu Anahaikuuanse objects to both, though especially to the former," said Kairaithin. His tone was distracted; he did not look at Kes but stared after the departing griffins, into the red reaches of the desert. "She is the mate of the Lord of Fire and Air and also of Escaile Sehaikiu."

"Both?"

"Both," said Kairaithin, lifting an amused and impatient eyebrow at Kes's surprise. "She was once wise. But she lost three *iskairianere* to the Casmantian assault and is in no mood to be patient with men."

"Oh . . ." Kes pulled away from Opailikiita again to follow Kairaithin's gaze. "I'm sorry. . ."

That was a night for grief, said Opailikiita, and declared fiercely, *But on the night that comes, my sister, you will burn back the cold.*

Kes wondered if she would.

Kairaithin turned the hard force of his attention back

toward Kes at once. His shadow rippled with flame; its black eyes blazed with a fiery dark like the desert sky at night. He said forcefully, "You must learn the ways of fire. You will have days to do this. It will take days. Do you understand? Thus I hold you here in the country of fire."

"If I do this for you," Kes said slowly, meeting his eyes, "you will be my friend."

"Assuredly not your enemy," said Kairaithin, amused.

But Kes thought he also meant what he said. "You won't harm my people. Or allow your people to harm them?"

"So long as you are my *kiinukaile*, I will see to it that neither your sister nor any of the people of your little town come to harm from fire."

"Then I'll stay," Kes said, and found she felt both glad that she had an unshakable excuse to stop arguing and guilty for the very gladness. She knew she ought to want nothing but to escape the desert and the griffins' dangerous attention. She knew she ought to want to go home— she knew Tesme must truly be desperately worried for her, that everyone would be desperately worried, that their worry would only grow worse if she stayed in the desert for days. But she remembered the strangely comfortable flame dancing in her palm, and there was nothing she wanted more than to stay in the desert and learn the ways of fire.

CHAPTER 4

Reports came in over the course of the next few days, some brought by couriers and some by ordinary folk: Griffins in the countryside around Minas Spring and Minas Ford; griffins settling all through those hills. Hundreds, some of the reports claimed. At least a thousand, asserted the most hysterical.

"Dozens," said General Jasand. "Dozens, I will grant you. A hundred is unlikely. A thousand is beyond any possibility. I doubt there are so many griffins as that in all the world."

The senior of Feierabiand's three generals, Jasand was a tall, grizzled man, broad-built and powerful, twenty years older than Iaor. He was not a personal friend of the king—he had been a friend of Iaor's father. These days, Jasand rarely took the field personally. But his whole career had been spent along the mountain border, and in his dealings with Casmantium he had picked up a good deal of griffin-lore. That was why Iaor had sent for him in particular.

Now the general tapped the table impatiently and added, "Not that we want even a few dozen griffins making themselves at home over by Minas Spring and Minas Ford. They're dangerous creatures, and it's said it takes years to recover decent land from the desert they make where they lie up."

Though no one asked him, Bertaud agreed with Jasand that there could not be hundreds of griffins down at Minas. No one had made a clear count. It seemed that no one, villager or courier or even soldier, quite dared go far enough into the hills to try. But it was clearly unlikely that there should be more than a few dozen of the creatures. All the sweep of history recorded no such invasion. Griffins belonged not to Feierabiand but to the dry eastern slopes of the mountains, the desert north of Casmantium, where rain never fell. They were creatures of fire and air, not earth and certainly not water.

The court mage Diene, the other person Iaor had asked to be present, tented her thin fingers and looked thoughtfully down the length of the table at the king. "As Beremnan Anweierchen of Casmantium famously put it, 'The desert is a garden that blooms with time and silence.' Griffins tend that garden," she observed. "Why have they left it and come to this side of the mountains? The west wind is filled with the smell of the sea: It must work against the wind they bring with them. They cannot be comfortable here."

"Why ever they came, they must not be allowed to become comfortable," the king said firmly. "Let us send them back to their desert. General?"

"A hundred men should suffice to send them off," said Jasand. He sounded confident, as well he might: Those were *his* men, and he had every right to be confident of their capability after years of withstanding the Casmantian brigands that sometimes slipped across the mountains—defying their own king, or so they claimed—to test the defenses of Feierabiand.

"Bowmen," said the general now. "With spears to use up close and swords we'll hope they needn't use at all. But it's surely bow work against griffins. Keep them at a distance and they should hardly be worse than mountain cats or bulls."

"They've magic of their own," countered Diene, putting up a severe eyebrow at this confidence. "They are creatures of fire and air, rather than the good solid earth of men. You've never put your soldiers against such as that, Jasand, and you might find griffins a surprise to men used to fighting other men. Well-made steel-tipped arrows may be—should be—hard for griffins to turn. However, they are *not* mountain cats or bulls. Someone should go to them before Jasand's men and ask them to withdraw."

"*Ask* them," said Bertaud, startled.

The mage turned her powerful gaze to him. Her eyes were the dark color of fresh-turned loam. Her strength was of the earth, to bring forth growing things and coax rich harvests from the land. She was old—the oldest of any of the king's habitual councilors, though not quite the eldest of the mages in Tihannad. Iaor was the third king she had advised. She had taught him his love of flowers, and sometimes regarded Bertaud with disfavor because he had never cared much for her gardens. As a boy, Bertaud had been frightened of her acerbic turn of phrase and stern frown. It had taken him years to learn to see the humor hidden behind both.

She said now, "Griffins are foreign to the nature of men, but they have a wisdom of their own, and they are powerful. Yes, someone should go to them before a hundred young men with bows and spears set foot in their desert."

The king folded his hands on the table and studied the mage. "Someone may indeed go to them. With a hundred young men with bows and spears at her back, to command respect from these creatures of fire and air. I ask you to go, esteemed Diene."

"I?" the mage folded her hands upon the table and judiciously considered this request. She glanced up after a moment. "Men are not meant to intrude into the country of fire, Iaor. But it is said that earth mages find the desert particularly inimical."

The king tapped his fingers restlessly on the table. But he responded at last, "Diene, I confess I had looked for you to bend your wisdom and knowledge to deal with these matters. You do not wish to go? Or you do not find it advisable to go?"

"On the contrary." Diene half smiled. "I would be most interested to study the desert and associated phenomena. I am confident I will be able to endure the desert, however hostile an environment it may prove. I am at least certain that a visit to the country of fire will be a fascinating experience. But I am bound by duty to warn you, your majesty, of the reputed difficulties involved."

Iaor waved a hand, dismissing this warning. "If you are willing to go, esteemed Diene, I wish you to go. One would expect a mage's learning and power to be of particular use in this sort of matter. Or do you feel yourself likely to suffer physically from the task? Perhaps someone more, ah, vigorous might be less troubled by the difficulties to which you refer?"

Diene tilted her head, considering, and Bertaud knew she was telling over the tally of younger mages in Tihannad, and coming up short: Though many people were gifted in one way or another, very few possessed the potential for true magecraft, and of those, fewer still wished to spend years of their lives developing the deep understanding of magic that underlay that craft—and the scholar-mages of high Tiearanan did not accept even all of those for training. "A magical gift isn't sufficient," Diene had commented once to Bertaud. "Gifts are narrow things, though under the proper circumstances and with sufficient effort the right sort of gift may be, hmm, *stretched*, shall we say. But blind desire isn't sufficient, and nor is dedication, though that's important. Magecraft requires a most unusual *breadth* of power."

Bertaud had not understood precisely what Diene meant, but what it came to in practical terms was a general lack of mages upon whom the king might call. There *were* a few young mages in Tihannad, but one was too young and one too rash and one too timid. The only mage more experienced and more powerful than Diene herself was also frail as a wisp of winter-dried barley, and blind besides. Diene frowned, and sighed. "Youthful vigor is all very well, Iaor, but I suspect mature wisdom will be more to the point. I have never encountered a griffin. I believe I would be interested to meet one now. And in any case, you would surely not wish to wait for a younger person to come down from Tiearanan. If it please you, your majesty, I will go."

"Thank you." The king gave a little nod. He turned to Jasand. "General. Select your men. Esteemed Diene, are you able to make yourself ready by the morning after to-morrow?" He accepted their nods and dismissed both general and mage, keeping Bertaud behind with a glance.

Bertaud leaned back in his chair and waited.

"The esteemed mage will go, to lend her learning and wisdom to the task, as I said," Iaor said. "But considering her warning, it is you I would have go, to speak for me."

Bertaud glanced down, then back up, hoping he had not visibly flushed. He turned a hand up on the table. "I am honored that you would send me, Iaor. But General Jasand is far more experienced than I."

"He will guide your judgment. But it is your judgment I trust." The king's voice was grave, measured: This was not an impulsive decision. Even when Iaor decided quickly, his decisions were considered. "I don't know what instruction to give you. So I must ask you to do as I would do, and speak my words to these creatures as I would speak them. Will you do this for me?"

Bertaud hesitated a bare instant longer, then answered, "It will be my honor to try."

Iaor smiled briefly, his father's ruthless smile. But it was also his own, with a quick warmth that the old king had never possessed. Both warmth and ruthlessness were quite real. That, Bertaud thought, was what made Iaor a good king. "Good. I will inform Jasand and Diene of my decision. Thus I will, as ever, take advantage of your loyalty, my friend."

Bertaud answered lightly, but with truth behind the light tone, "That is not possible, my king."

The broad road from Tihannad, paved with great flat stones, crossed a bridge where the little Sef flowed out of

Niambe Lake. On the other side of the Sef, the road was merely packed earth, but it was still broad. Six men could walk comfortably abreast, or four men ride, or one man ride beside a carriage, not that there were any carriages in this company. All the men were mounted, though: General Jasand had selected his men carefully and almost a fifth of them had an affinity for horses. There was no chance, then, that the horses would refuse to go into the desert if Jasand decided that a mounted attack was best, or that they would shy or bolt under the shadow of griffins' wings.

"I much doubt we'll want to take the horses into the desert, but I like to keep plenty of options available," Jasand had commented to Bertaud, and Bertaud had agreed and waited patiently for the general to sort out the men he thought best for this little foray. Three of the men had the much rarer affinities to eagles or falcons and carried birds on their shoulders or on perches behind their saddles. "Even better than dogs for scouting," Jasand had said, and thoughtfully added a man with an affinity for crows because, he said, he wanted at least one bird with brains in the company.

So it had taken longer than Bertaud had expected to put the company together, but they traveled more quickly than he'd anticipated once they got underway. Even Diene rode astride with no thought for a carriage. The hoofbeats on the hard earth of the road seemed to hold muffled words in their rhythm, words that could not quite be made out but held a nameless threat: Peril, they said. Danger. Hazard ahead. Bertaud cast an uneasy glance at Diene, but the mage had her face set sternly forward and did not seem to hear anything amiss in the beat of the earth.

The road past the Sef had been raised above the land,

so that snowmelt drained away to either side and left the surface of the road dry. Casmantian builders had been hired to guide the work on the road. With the magic those builders had set deeply into it, the road shed the rains of spring and summer as though it had been oiled. Thus it was a road on which a company could swing along at a great pace, in good heart, with energy left for the men to sing—which they did: Rude songs that Jasand pretended not to hear, and Diene not to understand. Spearheads flashed and swung above the ranks of soldiers like silver birds; each seemed to call out a single word as it flashed, and the word was *battle*. Most of the men also carried bows, unstrung for travel in damp weather, and the smooth curve of each bow whispered a long, low word of arrow's flight and fall.

Feierabiand was much longer from north to south than it was wide, as though it had long ago been squeezed thin between its larger and more aggressive neighbors. The road from Tihannad ran east along the shore of the lake to the much larger Nejeied River and then turned south along the river; it was raised and broad all the way to the bridge at Minas Ford and then south to Terabiand on the coast, for a good deal of traffic flowed along that route. If one followed the smaller Sepes River straight south from Minas Ford, one would find a narrower, rougher road leading to Talend at the edge of the southern forest. But the forest was not a welcoming place for men, and Talend, perhaps drawing some of its nature from the forest, liked to keep to itself, so that rough track was sufficient for the small amount of traffic that moved along the Sepes.

Bertaud wondered whether anyone in the north would yet have heard a whisper of their coming, if the griffins had crossed the mountains farther south and encroached upon Talend. But then, there was no good pass south of Minas Ford; the mountains near Talend were tall and rugged. And besides, he could not imagine that griffin magic would accord well with the natural magic of the great forest.

There was some traffic here, both on the road and the river, merchants and farmers and ordinary folk about their ordinary business. A courier went past riding north at a collected gallop, her white wand held high in her hand to claim priority on the road. Jasand held up his hand and his men pressed to the left side of the road to let her pass.

"What news, I wonder?" Bertaud said to the general.

Jasand shrugged. "We might have stopped her and asked. But we'll be at Minas Ford soon enough and find out for ourselves."

"You don't want to turn off toward Minas Spring?" Diene inquired, guiding her tall gelding nearer the men.

"Minas Ford is hardly farther. And we can stay on the main road all the way," said Jasand. "Good roads are not to be disregarded, esteemed mage."

"Certainly not by me," Diene said equably.

Jasand grinned at her, so that Bertaud realized the old general was happy to be on campaign again, even a little campaign against griffins rather than a proper company of Casmantian raiders. An open road before him and a hundred spears behind . . . for Jasand, this was a simple vacation from the sometimes tedious court life in Tihannad. His confidence was catching, so that Bertaud felt some of his own tension ease away into the pleasant day. Maybe dealing with the griffins would indeed be that simple; maybe there would be nothing difficult or confusing or controversial about it. He could hope for that, at least.

It was about sixty miles to Minas Ford from Tihannad. Still, if they pressed fairly hard, they should come to
the town of Riamne by evening. Then it would be an easy
enough day's ride tomorrow to Minas Ford, leaving the men
with energy for fighting. If it came to fighting. With luck, it
would not. Better if Diene could speak to the griffins. And
if Bertaud was called on to speak to them himself, in the
king's voice? What, he wondered, would he say? Probably
Jasand had the right of it; probably better to enjoy the ride
and let the coming days arrive at their own pace.

Riamne was a town of timber and brick with cobbled
streets and tall, narrow houses. They reached it just as the
last light failed. It had two inns, both of which were filled
to capacity. Jasand had his men set up their small tents in
a field outside the town, which they had to do by the light
of lantern and moon. The general had his own tent set
up among them. Bertaud displaced a well-to-do farmer
and his family from the best room of the nearer inn and
installed Diene there instead.

"Though I shall go back to the fields myself," he said,
smiling. "Jasand's tent is large enough for two, and if he
will stay with his men, I hardly think I should set myself
up here. Fortunate woman, you are affected by no such
concerns. You will be comfortable here?"

The old mage touched the mattress with one fragile hand
and glanced around at the spare furnishings. She gave Bertaud a caustic glance at his question, though he had made
sure his tone was entirely innocent. "Yes. Certainly. Or, if
not, I should hardly dare to say so after your comment,
young man."

She had been a tutor to both the king and then later to
Bertaud himself, when he had been a boy at the court of

the old king. Then, Bertaud would never have dared predict the familiarity with which he spoke to her now. He grinned and offered a slight bow.

Diene lifted an eyebrow at him, moved slowly across the room, and sank with a sigh into the sole chair it contained. "It needs a cushion," she remarked judiciously. "But it will do, since it is not a saddle. It has been years since I traveled even so far as this, you know."

"I know." Bertaud collected a pillow from the bed and offered it, with courtesy only a shade exaggerated. "Do you need assistance to stand, esteemed Diene?"

The glance this time was even more acerbic, but the old mage suffered him to help her to her feet. Bertaud arranged the pillow in the chair, and she settled back down with a nod of satisfaction.

"I will do very well. Will you join me for supper here? Or do you feel constrained to join the men for that, as well?"

"I think I need not go so far as that." The men carried rations that were adequate, but hardly up to the standards of a good inn. "I shall have the staff serve us here."

"To avoid the curiosity of men," said the mage, her dark eyes sliding sideways to meet his.

Bertaud inclined his head, quite seriously this time. "To avoid the crowd and the noise. You may tell me more about griffins, esteemed Diene, as we in fortunate Feierabiand have never been plagued with the creatures. You may advise me on what the king's voice should say to them, if we should speak."

The mage half-smiled. "I hardly know what advice to give. I will tell you the lines of poetry I know that hold fire and red dust and the desert wind—I hardly expect you will remember anything of your youthful studies, hmm?"

Bertaud flushed and laughed. "Little enough, esteemed Diene, begging the pardon of my esteemed tutor!"

Diene nodded in disapproving resignation. "Young men so seldom care for the poetry and history we so painstakingly draw out for them. Well, I will tell you poetry, then, and you may tell me what intentions the king should have toward griffins."

"Other than that they depart?"

"I hope," said Diene, "that it proves so simple."

So did Bertaud. Fervently.

The village of Minas Ford, when they arrived there, hoped so, too. There was an inn, small but pleasant, and perhaps half a hundred families who lived within a day's walk. Some, wary of griffins, had evidently gone north to Riamne, and others south to Talend or west to Sihannas at the edge of the Delta. But many had stayed. They were happy to see a troop of soldiers with the king's standard flying before them. This was clear even though they refrained from pressing forward toward the new arrivals.

"But a hundred men aren't enough, young lord," the innkeeper said earnestly, holding the bridle of Bertaud's horse with his own hands. "There are a good many griffins in those hills, lord, begging your pardon, and they're big, dangerous creatures."

Red dust stirred under the hooves of the horse as it shifted its feet. It was nervous. Its ears flicked back and forth, listening to sounds a man could not hear. The breeze that moved through the courtyard of the inn had an odd, harsh feel to it.

"The king hopes there are not so many," Bertaud said neutrally, dismounting with a nod of thanks for the innkeeper's assistance. "And we all hope not to fight them, however many there may be. Have you seen them yourself?"

"Not I, lord—that is to say, just as they fly over now and again. But Nehoen and Jos and even Tesme have all been up there looking for Kes, and they say there're a gracious plenty of them up there." The innkeeper gave the horse to a boy to take to the stable. The boy had to weave a path past the onlookers to get it there.

Bertaud tilted his head in interest, glancing out at the crowd. "Nehoen? Jos, Tesme, Kes?" Jasand and Diene had come up silently to listen.

The innkeeper bobbed a quick bow. "Kes was . . . Kes is just a girl, lord. She had . . . she has some skill with herbs, and she can stitch a cut or set a bone. A man came and asked her to come, and she went up into the desert to help somebody who'd been hurt. Before we even knew there was a desert."

Bertaud marked the past tense uncomfortably avoided in this answer. "And she has not returned?"

"No, lord. So we went looking, some of us. All of us, at the first. Tesme—that's Kes's sister, lord—Tesme kept searching. For days. And Nehoen. Nehoen is a gentleman of this district, lord, an educated man, not the kind to stretch the truth out thin, if you understand me. If he says *at least fifty*, he doesn't mean *five and their shadows*, lord. He . . . well, lord, I think he promised Tesme he'd keep looking, so as she wouldn't keep going up there herself. And Tesme's hired man, Jos, he stayed out a long time and went up a long way, but even he, well, I think he maybe doesn't expect to find her, anymore."

"I see." What might pass for educated in a little village like Minas Ford, Bertaud did not inquire. But the innkeeper seemed honest. Bertaud said, "Can you find these good folk for me? We would greatly desire to speak to them before we ourselves go up into the mountains. Which we shall, early tomorrow, I expect. Ah, and I trust there is indeed room in your inn for us?"

"For the lady and some few of your men more, lord, if you please; we've little enough business just now, but, as you see, it's not a large inn. And I'll send my girls out with word you'd like to speak with those as have seen the griffins."

Bertaud nodded his thanks and headed for the welcome comfort of the inn, not forgetting to offer his arm to Diene, who was finding it difficult to walk after two days on horseback but was trying not to show it.

"Fifty?" Jasand muttered on his other side. He shook his grizzled head in doubt. "Do you find that likely, my lord?"

Bertaud shrugged. "Likely? I want to see the men making the claim. You should ask, is it possible? And of course it is *possible*. And if it is true, General?"

"Then I would wish for more soldiers. Though come to it—" Jasand said consideringly, "—even in the worst case . . . I would set the men I brought against even a *hundred* griffins, my lord, if necessary."

Bertaud knew Jasand was right to be confident. The soldiers of Feierabiand had never been able to afford the luxury of incompetence in either their ranks or their officers. Only a clear and continual demonstration of Feierabiand skill in the field, along both the river border with Linularinum and the mountain border with Casmantium, made room for the central of the three countries to remain untroubled. And Jasand did not need to mention his own record or reputation. Though Bertaud might have wished some part of the general's experience had been against griffins. Or that they had, aside from mage's poetry, a Casmantian advisor handy to offer counsel on the creatures. But he said merely, "We shall hope these townsfolk can give us a clear idea of what we shall meet."

And, indeed, the men who came that evening to tell what they had seen in the mountains, Bertaud judged, might, in fact, be credible witnesses. The woman Tesme had not come, but Nehoen and Jos had evidently been close by the inn.

The hired man, Jos, was a plainspoken man who did not seem given to exaggeration or flights of imagination. And by his dress and manner, Nehoen was undoubtedly a wealthy man by the standards of the region and probably an even more creditable witness. Both men were clearly seriously worried about the missing girl and the griffins.

"Kes went up the mountain to assist someone who had been injured," Nehoen said, giving Bertaud the respectful nod due his rank, but with the straight look of a confident man. "The same day the griffins were first spotted, lord. A man came to find her. Seemed to know she has a talent with healing, for all he was a stranger to the district. No knowing who he really was."

"A mage, or so they say," Jos put in grimly, with a wary glance at Diene. "*I* didn't see him." And blamed himself for his absence, by his harsh tone. Or everyone else, for letting her go.

"A mage?" repeated Diene, startled. The innkeeper had not said this.

"Yes, esteemed mage—clearly so," Nehoen agreed, but the emphasis in his voice was clearly for Jos; he was obviously continuing a long-standing argument. "I saw him, and spoke to him, and he was *surely* a mage. A strange, dangerous sort, I would guess. Well, clearly so, or we'd not be missing a girl, would we? Middling age, a hard sort of face, a thin mouth. Black eyes. Hard-hearted, I would say—if I were guessing." The landowner paused, visibly bracing himself. Expecting condemnation, Bertaud realized, for having allowed this stranger to take away one of the Minas Ford girls on some weak pretext. Nehoen added, as much to Jos as to them, "He took her and they just went, like that." He snapped his fingers. "I *swear* to you, it was too quick for any of us to think twice about stopping it! They were just *gone*, right into the air."

Jos set his jaw and looked grim, as though only the presence of the king's servants kept him from a sharp retort.

"Neither of you could have prevented him, if the man was a mage," Diene said firmly. Her mouth had tightened. "You think this man, this mage, took the girl into the desert? To the griffins?"

"Well, esteemed mage," Nehoen said reasonably, "it's a striking coincidence if he didn't, isn't it?"

Diene inclined her head. "By your description, the man is no one I know. And a mage taking a healer girl to the griffins? This is a puzzle."

"I should say so. The *griffins* wanted a human healer? And this mage came and got them one?" Jasand said skeptically—Bertaud could not tell whether he was skeptical of the suggested connection, or skeptical of the whole story. The general frowned at the townsmen. "So you went looking for this girl?"

"A dozen or so folk of this district, yes, esteemed sir. We found . . . we found the desert. It's grown since," Nehoen said, with a simplicity Bertaud found very persuasive.

Jasand continued to frown. "And you've seen these griffins? You, personally?"

The man gave Jasand a nod. "Yes, lord. More than one or two. I'd guess fifty or more. But Jos went farther up than I." He looked at the other man.

"There are certainly dozens of the creatures up there," the hired man said, his tone still grim. "Fifty is a near-enough guess. Not many more than that, I'd say. I walked as close to them as I stand to you, and they did not even seem to notice I was there. They ought never be allowed to rest there on our land."

"They lie in the sun like cats," Nehoen put in. He spoke steadily, but his eyes had gone wide, abstracted with memory. "They ride the still air like eagles. Their eyes are filled with the sun. The shadows they cast are made of light. They are more beautiful . . . I have no words to describe them."

Jos said, even more harshly, "Beautiful they may be, those creatures, but they took Kes and we did not find her."

"I made Tesme stop looking lest we come across her bones," Nehoen said quietly, to Jasand rather than to Jos. "But . . . we didn't find those either. But if there are fifty griffins up there . . . You brought only a hundred men?" He seemed to become suddenly aware of his own temerity in offering criticism to officers of the king, and stopped. Then he said, "Forgive me if I speak out of turn, lord. But it seems to me it would be better to have more."

"A hundred soldiers should do well enough," Jos said roughly. "You clean those creatures out, lord, and you might bid your men, if they find a girl's dry bones in the red sand, they might bring them out of the desert for her sister."

Nehoen bowed his head in agreement, looking from Jasand to Bertaud and then settling on Diene. "If you . . . if you do go into the desert lords, esteemed mage, if you should find her . . . maybe she's still all right . . ."

Jos made a grim, wordless sound that made clear his opinion of this chance. He said, "Destroy them all, lord. That's all you can do for her now."

Bertaud did not know whether he believed a mage had taken the girl—still less whether the mage had been working somehow with the griffins. But he said, "We will certainly bring her out if we find her, even if we find only bones. But we will hope for better." And better still, though he did not say this, if they did not, in fact, require to do battle with the griffins. Whether or not there was a mage, and whatever had happened to the girl.

After the townsmen had gone, Bertaud, Jasand, and Diene discussed the griffins and the proper approach to them by the light of lanterns that threw shadows like half-seen glyphs across the walls of Diene's room.

"A *mage* working with the griffins?" Jasand said, skeptical.

Diene gazed thoughtfully into the air. "One does not expect any earth mage to work with creatures of fire. However . . . there was a mage once, Cheienas of Terabiand, who loved the desert and spoke to fire and creatures of fire. He wanted to ride the hot wind, to catch fire in his eyes and understand it. He vanished from our ken, and it is said he gave away the earth of his nature and became a creature of fire. I wonder if he would strike a man as hard-hearted?"

"Would he be the sort to work against us?" Jasand

asked practically. "And if he is, or if any fire mage is up there and set against us, can you deal with that, esteemed Diene? I've many men with animal affinities . . . but I've no one I'd set against a hostile mage. Mages were not something I expected to encounter."

Diene raised her eyebrows, with an air of faint opprobrium, as though she found this showed an unfortunate lack of foresight. Not that she had suggested any preparations for this eventuality herself before they had left, Bertaud did not point out.

"Then it is fortunate I am here," the mage said. "I expect I would indeed be able to handle Cheienas, if this is he."

Bertaud asked, "And other possibilities?"

Diene considered. "There was a man named Milenne, originally from Linularinum, who lived in the high forest north of Tiearanan. One day he found a golden egg in the forest. Of the creature that hatched from that egg, he wrote only that it was a creature of fire, with wings of fire. What became of it, he did not write. But he left Feierabiand because, he said, it made him want to seek a deeper silence than that found in even the deepest forest."

Jasand waved a disgusted hand. "Poetry and riddles. Golden eggs and wings of fire! Esteemed Diene, if you can handle this mage, whomever he may be, then I'm satisfied. What matters then is how many griffins there are, and how they can be made to go back across the mountains."

"And your ideas about this?" Bertaud asked him.

"Well . . . well, Lord Bertaud, that man Jos only said *dozens*, and he seems to have had as good a look as any. Even the other man guessed only fifty or so. I think maybe we don't need to worry about a hundred of the creatures after all. And then, we brought archers. Arrows are proof against any creature that walks or swims or flies through the air, whether it's a creature of fire or air or good plain earth." Jasand paused, thinking. "We must be certain of our ground. I do not want my men shooting uphill into the sun. If we leave the road—if we divide the men into two companies, say, and go up across the slant, in afternoon so the sun is at our backs—we can set up a killing field between the companies. That should do well enough. At least griffins can't draw bows of their own."

Bertaud nodded. "We might send back to Tihannad for more men if you think that best."

"No," the general answered, consideringly. "No, I think that should not be necessary. It would take time, and what if these griffins begin to do more harm to more than calves while we delay? The core of this company is Anesnen's fifth cavalry."

Bertaud knew Anesnen's reputation. He nodded. "If we must bring the griffins to battle, that is indeed good to know," he agreed. "Especially if there are only a few dozen up there. Still, we shall hope for better than battle. Esteemed Diene, have you given thought to our initial approach?"

The mage glanced up, an abstracted look in her dark eyes. "What is there to consider? We shall be straightforward."

"But prepared to be otherwise," said Jasand.

They were straightforward. But prepared to be otherwise. They left their horses in Minas Ford; neither griffins nor the desert itself would likely be kind to horses. They marched on foot out of the village and up into the hills. The village folk turned out to watch them go, but no one but some of the younger boys ventured to follow. Their mothers called them back before they could follow very far.

"That's as well," General Jasand observed. "In case any of the creatures get past our lines."

Bertaud nodded. The last thing they wanted was to stir up the griffins and then allow one or two to escape to ravage the countryside. "If there must be a battle, we shall hope they are willing to mass and meet us."

Diene gave him a reassuring nod. "You needn't fear they'll avoid us, I think. Indeed, they'll meet us quickly enough, if we walk into their desert. *Griffins* are not likely to avoid conflict, I assure you."

Bertaud supposed that was true enough. He did not find it especially reassuring, however.

They turned around a curve of a hill and, for the first time, found a handful of villagers waiting to watch them pass. Jos, whom Bertaud recognized, and a scattering of grim-looking men and excited older boys. A couple of the men lifted their hands in recognition and salute. Some of the soldiers, pleased to be recognized, returned solemn nods. As Bertaud passed the villagers, he offered a deep nod that was almost a bow, acknowledging their presence and concern.

He remarked to Jasand, "They'll follow, I'm sure, and watch from a safe distance. I trust it will be a safe distance. In fact, I'd send a man to make sure of it, if necessary."

"I hope we'll have plenty of men to spare for all sorts of minor functions," the general answered drily. But he also gave one of his men a glance, and the soldier peeled off from the column and went to speak to the village folk.

The edge of the desert was a remarkably clean line: On one side, the gentle green of the ordinary Feierabiand countryside; on the other, the empty desert. They halted on the ordinary side of the line. General Jasand,

with a nominal glance at Bertaud for approval, divided
his men and began to arrange a company to either side of
the approach he thought most promising for battle. But
for the first hopeful approach, Diene and Bertaud simply
walked straight up the mountain to see what they might
meet. Bertaud gave the mage his arm, which she leaned
on gratefully.

"I'm far too old for such nonsense," she grumbled.
She flinched as they crossed into the heat and drought of
the desert, muttering in dismay and discomfort. Bertaud
found the pounding heat uncomfortable, but from Diene's
suddenly labored steps and difficult breathing, he thought
that the elderly mage was indeed experiencing something
more than mere discomfort. There was a wind off the
mountains that blew into their faces. It was a strange, hot
wind, carrying scents of rock and dust and hot metal—
nothing familiar to a man born on the sea side of these
mountains. There was an unfamiliar taste to it. A taste of
fire, Bertaud thought.

Sand gritted underfoot, on slopes where there never
had been sand before. Red rock pierced the sand in thin
twisted spires and strange flat-topped columns, nothing
like the smooth gray stone native to these hills. Bertaud
glanced over his shoulder to where the men waited, drawn
up in the green pasture at the edge of the desert, and shook
his head incredulously.

A shape moved ahead of them. Not a griffin, Bertaud saw, after the first startled lurch of his stomach. A
man, seated on a low red rock, fingers laced around one
drawn-up knee. He sat there as though the rock were a
throne, watching them approach with no appearance of
either surprise or alarm. His face was harsh, with a strong

nose and high cheekbones. There was a hard, stark patience in those eyes, and also a kind of humor that had nothing to do with kindness. He looked neither old nor young. He looked like nothing Bertaud had ever seen.

"That," said Diene, "is surely the stranger that the man spoke of. And quite clearly a mage." Her voice was flat with dislike. She shaded her eyes with her hand, as though against light.

Bertaud said nothing. He took a step, and then another, feeling heat against his face as though he walked into a fire. The feeling was so vivid he was faintly surprised not to hear the roar of leaping flames before him. He glanced at Diene, but her expression was set and calm. He could not tell what she was thinking or feeling.

The man rose as they approached, and inclined his head. "You were looking for me, I believe," he said. His voice, pitiless as the desert, nevertheless held the same strange, hard humor Bertaud saw in his eyes. "Kes told me I might look for lords of Feierabiand on this road. Your soldiers I saw for myself."

Bertaud tried to focus his thoughts. But a hot wind blew through his mind, shredding his focus. The wind seemed to contain words; it seemed to speak a language he might, if he strained hard enough, learn eventually to comprehend. At the moment . . . it only confused his wits and his nerve. He tried to work out whether this was something the man was doing purposefully or merely a strange effect of the desert, but he could not decide.

"You are a griffin," Diene stated. The familiar human words seemed somehow surprising; they seemed to hold a meaning beyond what Bertaud grasped. The woman stood straight, but there was more than straightness to her posture. She had gone rigid with a hostility that alarmed Bertaud. It was not fear. That, he would have understood. Her feeling appeared stronger and more dangerous.

But the mage's hostility did not appear to be returned. A smile glinted in the powerful eyes; curved, after a moment, the thin mouth. "I have no desire to be your enemy, earth mage. Restrain your sensibility. Have you never before experienced the antipathy between earth and fire? It's compelling, I know, but you need not give way to it, if you will not. I assure you, it *is* possible to rule your instincts—"

Diene shook her head. She broke in, her voice harsh with strain. "I know you are unalterably opposed to creatures of earth. I *know* that. If you would not be our enemies, go back to your own country of fire."

"We cannot."

The woman stared into the austere face. "Then we will be enemies."

Wait, Bertaud wanted to say. Wait. This is moving far too fast. But he could not find his voice. He thought if he tried to speak, the voice of the desert wind would come out of his mouth.

The taut smile became fierce. "If you will it so, then we will be enemies," said the man. The griffin.

"Wait," Bertaud managed, but lost his voice again. The potent stare moved to catch his, and he found he could not look away.

"Man," said the griffin. It was acknowledgment, and something more. "What is your name?"

For a stark moment Bertaud thought he might have lost the ability to speak. But a reflex of pride stiffened his back and let him, at last, find his voice. "Bertaud. Son of Boudan." His tone became, with an effort, wry. "Lord of Feierabiand, Lord of the Delta." And the title that was most precious to him: "Advisor to Iaor Daveien Behanad Safiad, King of Feierabiand. And yours?"

"Kairaithin," said the griffin, with that ferocious hard humor that was nothing like the humor of a man. "If you like. Sipiike Kairaithin. Anasakuse, to those who presume themselves my intimates. Shall we be enemies, man?"

Speaking, Bertaud found, became easier after the first words. A little easier. He shook his head sharply, trying to hear past the high, hot wind that blew through his mind. "Are you . . . are you doing this to me?"

The intensity of that black gaze shaded off toward curiosity. The man tipped his head to the side inquiringly, a gesture oddly inhuman. "I am doing nothing to you. I assure you. Your earth mage would know if fire overreached itself in her presence. But I did not approach you to take hostile action. I put myself in your way only to speak."

"Is something troubling you? Something *else*? What's wrong?" Diene was studying Bertaud with narrow-eyed concentration and an attitude that said, *Whatever it is, it is the griffin's fault and he is lying.*

But Bertaud thought that the griffin spoke the truth. So this strange blurring of his mind was surely an effect of the desert. He shook his head again, stopping Diene when she would have asked again. He tried to think clearly. "You cannot go back to your own desert. Cannot. Why not?"

The griffin mage—Kairaithin—lifted his shoulders in a minimal shrug. "Because we were driven from the desert into the mountain heights, man, and that is no world of ours; because we had no choice but to come down into this humid land where the sea wind combats our own wind. And have no choice but to remain, at least for a time. This country is not ours, but it can be made to serve. We will not give way. We have no way to give. Go back to your king, man, and tell him we have no desire to be enemies of the men here. Tell him he would be wise to make room for our desert."

Bertaud shook his head, drew a difficult breath. Blinked against a haze of hot, red dust. Tried to focus. Asked at last, "Driven by what?"

The griffin's lip curled.

"Driven by whom?" Bertaud asked him. He drew a breath of hot air and tried to think. "Why?"

The griffin held out a hand, a sharp commanding gesture. Bertaud blinked, took a step forward. He almost extended his own hand, as the other seemed to expect. But Diene struck his hand down. The griffin lowered his, slowly. He said to her, "Earth mage, you are unwise. You were unwise to put yourself in my way, and you are unwise now to yield to your dislike for fire."

"Wiser than to trust you." The look in Diene's dark eyes was hostile. "You are a mage. But what else are you?"

"I have been patient," the griffin answered curtly. "You exhaust my patience, earth mage." He shifted his weight restlessly, glancing up the slope toward the cliffs, as though he would go.

"Wait," said Bertaud, faintly. He tried to imagine what an impatient griffin would be like, if this was patience. But the griffin mage, to his surprise, turned back. He was restless, catching Bertaud's eyes again with his as a hawk might catch a hare. But he turned. To meet that hard stare was almost physical pain. Bertaud sustained it with an effort; asking again, "Driven by whom?"

"Casmantium." The expression in those black eyes had gone hard, savage. "Who else?"

Bertaud closed his eyes, trying to think. He breathed the metallic air, listened to the desert wind. The taste of hot copper slid across his tongue. Casmantium. "Casmantium," he said aloud, and opened his eyes again. "Why?"

The griffin's shrug this time was indifferent, edged with a restlessness like fire. "Perhaps Casmantium tired of having our red desert crowd her fair cities." But once again he seemed willing to speak. He took a step forward, holding Bertaud's eyes with his own, and spoke more intensely. "Man, there are some who declare that desert ours, and argue for our return to it. Others say we should make this land ours, and stay. Our . . . king . . . is of the first mind. Therefore, I advise you, go. Leave the desert we make here to the wind of our wings. We will withdraw in time, and then you may reclaim it."

"You have no right to dictate terms to us!" Diene snapped, glaring at the griffin.

"Be *quiet*," Bertaud commanded her desperately. He felt he had been on the edge of an important understanding, and had lost it. He had been so glad Diene had come. He had not wanted to meet the griffins alone, and he had agreed with Iaor that the learning and wisdom of a mage would be valuable in this meeting. But now he would have given almost anything to be rid of her.

"Earth mages," the griffin mage said to him, with an impatient little movement of his head, oddly birdlike. "She should not have come into this desert. Do you not know earth magic is antithetical to fire? All mages experience the aversion, but the stronger the mage, the stronger the aversion. One may make allowances for the effect," he added, his tone edged with contempt, "but your mage does not seem inclined to try."

Diene began to speak, clearly a hostile answer to this statement. Bertaud held up a hand in a gesture so sharp she desisted. He shook his head, trying to shake sense back into his mind, and looked back at the griffin. Kairaithin. "If Casmantium drove you out of your desert, what makes you confident we cannot?"

That strange, harsh amusement moved in the black eyes. "You have no cold mages. Your earth mages here do not study to become cold. Nor, even did you find cold magecraft at your fingers, do we now sleep unaware of human aggression."

Well, that was certainly true. Bertaud drew a breath, let it go. "If you would withdraw into the hills. Leave the pastures. If you would hunt deer and leave be the cattle, I would be prepared to take that as a gesture of goodwill."

"And your king?"

"Will expect some recompense for his generosity to allow your sojourn in his lands. Nevertheless, he will be guided by my opinion."

"Will he? And is your opinion sound, man? We have not hunted *men*. You may take *that* as a measure of our goodwill."

"Yes," said Bertaud. He thought it was. He stared into the austere face. "I will need more than that to take to my king."

"Will you? Then come." The griffin took a step forward, lifted his hand a second time. Not a commanding gesture, this time. Nor the appeal of the suppliant. This gesture held invitation. Or perhaps challenge.

"No!" said Diene.

Bertaud shut his eyes, opened them, and said patiently, "Esteemed Diene—"

"No!" snapped the mage. "Young fool! This creature is nothing you can trust! Put yourself in its power and you may well find it's no power you can put off again. Fool! And you!" She spoke directly to the griffin mage. "Be clear, creature! You say I should trust *you*? What nonsense! Explain what you intend and what you will do, if you will have us trust you!"

The griffin stood with stark patience, waiting, his hand still extended. He did not so much as glance at Diene. His attention, furnace hot, was all for Bertaud.

Diene glared at him, transferred her glare to Bertaud, and drew herself up to her best small height. She was furious, and furiously hostile. But did he, Bertaud asked himself, think his own judgment superior to hers? The heat of the desert seemed to beat against his face like the power of the sun. He knew he could not think clearly. Had not been able to think clearly since he had first found red sand under his boots and looked into the fierce human face of the griffin. If the mage so vehemently distrusted fire, maybe she was right; if earth mages hated the desert, maybe that was a sign it was wise for men to hate it . . .

Young fool, Diene had called him. Bertaud feared that she was right, whether Kairaithin had done this to him purposefully or whether it was merely some strange effect of the desert.

The griffin lowered his hand. He said, with savage

humor and no sign of either disappointment or anger, "Then go. And go, man. Go. Out of this country, you and yours, and back to your king. You may tell him, if he is wise, he will leave well alone. If he is wise, he will heed *that* opinion."

And he was gone. Red dust blew across the place where he had been.

Bertaud was halfway down the mountain before he was aware that he was moving, and farther than that before he remembered Diene.

The mage was with him, struggling to walk over the rough ground, her face set hard as a mask.

Bertaud stopped, offering her his arm. She stopped, too, breathing harshly, and looked him in the face. He did not know what he saw there.

"If you had gone into that power," she said, "I think you would not have come out of it."

Breath hissed through his teeth. But he did not give her the answer that first leaped to mind. He said instead, deliberately, "It's possible you saved my life, esteemed Diene."

The mage blinked, waited.

"Or it's possible you threw it away! We came here to talk to them! Now we will have no choice but to fight. Was that the antipathy? You expected it; did you control it, or did it control you?"

"I expected it—I'd read about it—Meriemne reminded me about it, but I confess it was a stronger effect in the event than I'd anticipated." The lines in Diene's face had deepened; she looked drawn and exhausted and ten years older than she had that morning. "But, believe me, Lord Bertaud, mages' antipathy to fire or no, it's not possible to make peace with those creatures. I know that now, very clearly. Does the wolf lie down beside the fawn?"

Bertaud shook his head, not exactly disagreeing but wanting to disagree. And he did not even know why. He glanced up the mountain, irresolute, ready on that thought to turn on his heel, go back up the mountain, and leave the mage to make her own way down.

Her hand on his arm stopped him. She said, "Lord Bertaud, from the first moment, there was no possibility of avoiding battle. I had hoped—I had thought—but I knew it was impossible when first I saw that . . . when I saw that creature and the shape it had put on. You must surely have known it, too. There is no possible *way* to yield to it! You are not blind. Or I would have said not."

Bertaud wondered if she was right. He said nothing.

Diene waved her hand to indicate the mountains, the heat haze that moved in the silence—a silence vaster and harsher than any that belonged by rights to Feierabiand. "I thought *I* understood what we would face up on this mountain. And I saw nothing any creature of earth will ever understand. Antipathy? How could there ever be anything else between fire and earth?" She was shivering. Even in the heat. She looked small and old and frightened. Despite himself, Bertaud was moved. He let out his breath. Offered her his arm.

This time she took it.

General Jasand, it was clear, was not entirely displeased by the outcome of their first venture up the mountain.

"They must be aware of our numbers," Bertaud warned him. "They can fly—they will know what dispositions we make of our men."

"So? What will they do? Griffins do not use bow or

shield. They can retreat, or they can come down to us. Even if there are a hundred, we'll claim victory. As Casmantium did, by what you say. And we'll then have soldiers blooded against griffins, which can only be useful if we are to have these creatures coming across the mountains once and again."

"Mmm." Bertaud did not feel at all comfortable with that thought. What, would griffins come again and again down from the mountains, and Feierabiand slaughter them over and over? He did not like the idea of Feierabiand being used by Casmantium for any such purpose, if Casmantium had, in fact, decided to rid itself of the desert on its northern border.

But the general did not notice Bertaud's discomfort, or else he attributed it to a different cause. "You may trust our men's training, my lord, and our weaponsmiths. Arrows properly made fly true; spears properly made strike hard. Griffins can hardly be better armed than boar or bear. When all's said, beak and talon are no match for well-crafted steel. With the esteemed Diene to stop any mage from interfering, my men can handle this."

Bertaud, for all his lack of enthusiasm for Jasand's plan, could see no honest reason to disagree with his assessment. Nor did Diene contradict the general's words. The men, drawn up in two orderly companies, looked dangerously competent. The spears and arrows knew what they had been made for; the deadly magic of their making glittered along their edges.

The plan of battle was simple. Bertaud thought the griffins would attack, and he thought there was every chance they would indeed be slaughtered like the animals Jasand was evidently so willing to consider them.

He said bleakly, "If they were boar or bear, any man born with an affinity for boar or bear could turn them and send them into the wild, far from settled land. Would that earth magic ruled these creatures also!"

Jasand only shrugged. "We'll go up there, and there. With your approval, my lord," he added absently. "The griffins are straight up that way." There was no question of that: One could tell by the way the light lay on the land and the taste of the air where the griffins had made the country their own. "If they come straight down, that's fine. If they go after each company separately, that's not as neat, but it will still do. Archers on the inside, you know, and spears on the edge. I can see nothing the griffins can do that will give the men enough trouble to matter. We'll be back at Minas Ford in time for a late supper."

"Yes," said Bertaud. He tilted his head back and stared into the sky. It was blank, giving nothing back. Foreign heat poured out of it. The sun, lowering in the west, cast its light across the face of the hills. He wanted to say, No. He wanted to go back up into the red desert the griffins had made of this country, to find the griffin mage and speak with him again, find some other option. Anything but take Feierabiand soldiers into that desert. Whether it was the men or the griffins who would die of it.

Diene stood to one side, thin arms crossed across her chest, mouth a thin, straight line. Looking at her, Bertaud doubted himself. He could put his judgment above hers, except how could he trust his own judgment? She might have been instantly hostile to the griffin mage, but she had at least been coherent. Fool, she had called him. Perhaps she had been right. He thought of the griffin mage and shut his eyes at the memory of how tongue-tied he had suddenly become in that creature's presence. He was dismayed by his own irresolution. In retrospect, it seemed more and more likely that that had been some subtle form of attack. If it had been, it had worked. How could a man blinded by the power of the desert possibly see what he should do to serve his king?

He said again, reluctantly, "Yes."

Jasand gave a satisfied nod and signaled, and the horns sounded, bright clear notes in the golden afternoon.

The men strode forward, in step. The Feierabiand banner flew above each company: golden barley sheaf and blue river. Spear points glittered and threw back the light. *War*, they said. *War. War.* Bows of horn and wood, light sliding down their sinew strings, were in the hands of the men protected by those spears. Most of the archers already had arrows nocked, ready to draw. Some, those who made their own arrows, were already speaking to the shafts they had crafted, heads bent over their bows, whispering of true flight and blood. General Jasand led one company, one of his captains the other; Bertaud, who might have claimed the honor, stood with the mage Diene on a rock outcropping and left it to the captain, who was a good deal more experienced in military matters.

"If something goes wrong," Jasand had said, "the king will need to learn of it. I certainly won't trust villagers to carry proper word! And we can't leave the mage unprotected." He had given Bertaud a horn, in case a man standing apart might see some urgent necessity those in the thick of battle might have missed. He had not had to say that he expected Bertaud not to use it. Leave the fighting to the soldiers, and keep well out of it—that was the expectation.

Bertaud had taken the horn, and he had not argued. Both points were good. And he thought, though he did not say, that if he went up into this desert, he might find himself unable to think or speak. Where would the men be then? He set his face in the blank expression he had first used to deal with his father and then found useful for tedious or unpleasant court functions. He did not allow himself to pace.

"They'll be perfectly fine," said Diene, tense and straight beside him. He had suggested she sit. She would not.

"Of course," Bertaud said, but wondered whether his tone rang as false as hers.

And the griffins came down. They came straight down the red mountain, straight into the killing field between the two companies, as though they had no fear of bows, or no knowledge men used such things. They flew in irregular formation, some alone and some by threes or fours. Two dozen. Four dozen. Six.

"Earth and iron," Diene breathed. Bertaud was speechless. They were huge, big as the white bulls bred in the Delta, but nothing so tame. They flew out of the light as though the light itself had formed them. Red dust drove before their wind, stinging, whipping into a blinding veil. Bertaud, shielding his eyes with upraised hands, could nonetheless see that fire fell on the wind from their wings and tongues of flame leaped up from the sand beneath them. The griffins, wreathed in dust and fire, stooped like hunting falcons, talons shining. They screamed as they fell, savage high cries that cut through the air like knives.

Men cried out in answer. Bertaud could not blame them. Precious seconds were lost before the soldiers remembered discipline and drew their bows. Arrows rose;

the light that struck off the steel tips was red as flame, and flame fell past the arrows as they mounted. Some of the griffins were surely struck; Bertaud could not tell, but well-made arrows would seek living flesh and turn to find it. Even so, a vicious rain of fire fell into the companies of men, which became suddenly ragged. Spears rose, almost in order despite the flames, and he caught his breath: If the men held, Jasand would be proved right, because even with fire and wind, the griffins would not be able to breach that curtain of steel—not without spilling their own blood out onto the sand. And the men would hold. He was sure the men would hold.

Then griffins came past the rock where Bertaud stood with the mage—griffins with wings folded, moving with great bounds like running lions. Diene cried out, thinly. A passing griffin, powerful muscles rolling under the dark bronze hide of its haunches, turned its head and fixed her with one fierce coppery eye. It went past without pausing.

They would take the men from behind, Bertaud understood at once. The griffins on the ground would come against the soldiers like scythes striking barley stems; hidden by the dust and by the terror of their brethren aloft, they would come and strike below the lifted spears. He found the military horn in his hand with a feeling of surprise, and lifted it to his mouth.

A great white griffin, gleaming even through the veils of whipping dust, cleared the rock where they stood in a bound that was half flight. Talons white as bone closed on Bertaud's arm; a wing like a hammer struck him in the chest. He would have screamed with pain except he could not get the breath to cry out. The griffin's other wing

struck Diene and flung her from the rock; she fell without
a sound, like a child's crumpled doll.

The griffin struck at Bertaud's face with a beak like a
blade, but somehow Bertaud's sword was in the way; he
had no notion how it had come into his hand—his left
hand, for the white griffin had his right pinned in its grip.
He cut at its head, so close to his own, and it flung him
away. He fell hard, to sand that flickered with little ripples
of fire; he rolled fast to get up, beating at a charred patch
of cloth over his thigh, but he made it only so far as his
knees. He could not move the arm the griffin had torn.
White agony lanced through his chest: Ribs were broken.
He could not get his breath, did not yet know if broken
bones had pierced his lungs, could not imagine the pain
would be worse if they had. He had lost his sword in the
fall. The loss did not seem likely to matter. The griffin,
above him on the rock, wings spread wide, seemed immense as the sky. It stared at him with fierce eyes of a
hard fiery blue, and sprang like a cat.

"No," he cried at it without breath, without sound. He
found himself more furious than terrified. He tried to
fling himself to his feet, but his right leg would not hold,
and he was falling already as the white griffin came down
upon him. Darkness rose up like heat, or he fell into it,
and it filled his eyes and his mind.

CHAPTER 5

Despite everything Kairaithin had said about mages and battle, Kes had hoped that perhaps no one would come against the griffins. She had spent days playing with flames, learning to love fire, and if sometimes she thought of Tesme, she found it easier, as measureless time passed, to turn her thoughts away from home, back again toward the fire Opailikiita showed her. But she hoped no one would come. The Casmantian mages would stay in Casmantium, and the griffins would linger here in Feierabiand for a little while and then go home, and Kes would go home as well . . .

But then an army came after all. Word of it came flickering from mind to mind like beacon fires lighting one after another, and Kes spent a tense, anxious afternoon pacing around the edges of the great, high hall Kairaithin had made upon the cliff of the plateau. But the griffins won their fight, so all was well, after all. That was what Kes thought, when Kairaithin came at last to bring her to the field of battle.

But there is little enough for you to do, the griffin mage told her with grim satisfaction. He was in his true form, beautiful and terrible as the embers at the heart of a great bonfire. *Our enemies here do not know how to do battle against us: This time, they came openly rather than in stealth, in the high heat of the day rather than in the dark reaches of the night, and without cold magecraft to shield them or strike at us. Thus, the blood that was poured out upon the sand was theirs and not ours.*

Kes thought, *Our enemies here?* And she wondered why men so little prepared had come against the griffins. But she did not understand exactly what Kairaithin meant until the griffin mage shifted them across the desert and brought her to the place where the few wounded griffins waited for her, and she saw the innumerable dead men lying where they had fallen, all across the burning sand.

They were not Casmantian soldiers. They were soldiers of Feierabiand, and they were all dead. Kes stared out across the red desert where they lay, speechless.

They died well, Kairaithin told her, in a tone of reassurance, as though he thought that this would make it all right that they were dead.

Kes slowly turned her head to stare at him. Looking at the griffin was much easier than looking out at the dead soldiers. She fixed her attention on his fiery black gaze, trying to see nothing else. She found she was trembling, but she couldn't stop.

The worst of our injured lies there. Kairaithin indicated the first of the wounded griffins, a bronze-and-black female who lay beside a low, sharp ridge of stone quite close to the edge of the battlefield.

Kes glanced that way, found her gaze caught by the

abandoned dead, flinched from the sight of the twisted bodies of men, and closed her eyes. She had not previously met the injured griffin. But her name sang through Kes's awareness even from that brief glance: Riihaikuse Aranuurai Kimiistariu. Kes knew she was badly wounded—she already knew that there was a deep cut across her chest and belly. But she did not move. She whispered, "Why didn't you tell me?"

Kairaithin tilted his eagle's head, puzzled. *Did I not tell you?*

"Days of fire and blood, you said!" Kes was not whispering now. She was nearly shouting. "But you didn't say—you didn't tell me—" she gestured blindly toward the men who lay scattered across the sand.

The griffin mage was silent for a moment. He said at last, *I did not mean to do you harm by this. Indeed, I sought to turn the day, for I think it wiser to reserve our strength for use against Casmantium. The King of Feierabiand sent an emissary, which was wise. But the emissary brought an earth mage to advise him, which was not wise at all, for she feared me and loathed the desert and thus he would not speak to me. Thus, the day became a day for blood and fire, and their deaths came upon them.*

Kes stared at him.

But they died well, Kairaithin assured her. *And there is still a need for your gift of healing.*

Kes didn't move. She didn't think she *could* move. She was still trembling. She knew she definitely could not approach the field of battle—no matter how many wounded griffins lay there. And anyway—she asked Kairaithin, hearing her voice shake and not caring, "Should I heal your people? When you kill mine?"

There was a silence. Kes thought that the griffin-mage was not ashamed or even disturbed at what his people had done, that he didn't understand why she was upset, that when he said *It was a day for death*, he meant something other than, and more than, what she heard. She realized that when she did not understand him, he did not know how else to answer her.

But he said at last, *The emissary of your king yet lives. He may die. But it would please me if he lives. I cannot heal his wounds. I do not know whether even you might heal human injuries with fire. But perhaps you may find a way to save this man. Will you try?*

"Of course!" Kes looked around at once, as though she might find the man lying near at hand. She even made herself look across at the field of battle, but flinched again from it—anyway, she could not believe anyone lying there might live. The sand and overpowering heat were already claiming the dead men, who no longer looked as though they'd ever really been alive.

He is not there, said Kairaithin. *I will take you to him. I think you should first remind yourself of fire and of healing. Aranuurai Kimiistariu will die if you do not see her whole. Will you let her die?*

Kes hesitated, looking once more toward the battlefield. She took a step toward the wounded griffin, but stopped. "I can't go over there!"

Kairaithin regarded Kes from the fierce, impenetrable eyes of an eagle. Then he stretched out his wings and brought the wounded female griffin from where she lay, shifting her through the desert afternoon to lie close by Kes's feet.

Riihaikuse Aranuurai Kimiistariu lay almost upright,

in a near-normal couchant position, but her head was angled oddly downward and she panted rapidly. Her eyes were glazed with pain, or even possibly with approaching death. Crimson blood rolled down from savage wounds, scattering as rubies and garnets across the sand.

See her whole, Kairaithin said, *or she will surely die.*

Kes wanted to weep like a child. But weeping would not bring back the dead, and anyway, she found, despite the pressure behind her eyes, that she had no tears. Nor would the death of Aranuurai Kimiistariu bring back the dead. It would be wrong to let her die. Wouldn't it be wrong? Kes hesitated one more moment. Then she let the wounded griffin's name run through her mind and her blood and held up her cupped hands to gather the hot afternoon light. But she did not at once kneel down by the bronze-and-black female, but glared instead at Kairaithin. "You'll take me to the injured man after this? *Next* after this? If he dies before I come to him," she said fiercely, "I won't heal any other of your people! Do you hear?" Even Kes herself did not know whether she meant this threat. But she tried very hard to sound as though she meant it.

Little kitten, you are grown fierce, said Kairaithin. His tone was amused and ironic, but he also spoke as though he approved. *No other of my people are so badly injured that they cannot wait. Make Aranuurai Kimiistariu whole, and I will take you to the man of your own kind. Though it is, in all truth, a day for death, I, too, wish this man to live. An emissary to send to your king is precisely what I desire.*

Kes stared at the griffin mage for another moment. Then she knelt down to pour the rich light she held in her hands out across the griffin's injuries.

*   *   *

The injured man lay high atop the red cliffs, within the pillared hall. The stone roof blocked the direct sun, but the heat even in the shade was heavy—it seemed somehow more oppressive than it had been out in the open light. Opailikiita lay near the man but had, so far as Kes could see, done nothing at all to help him. Kes spared the slim young griffin hardly a glance before falling to her knees beside the man; she was barely aware that Kairaithin followed her, or that he had once more taken the shape of a man so that he would not crowd her when he looked over her shoulder. Her attention was all for the man.

She saw at once that he was badly injured. His arm had been gashed as though by knives; he was still bleeding from those wounds, though fortunately the blood flowed only slowly. Kes thought that his arm was also broken, though she was not sure. She was nearly sure the ankle was broken, though, from the swelling and the black bruising. Worse, the man's breathing sounded shallow and difficult, and there was a bubbling sound to it that suggested to Kes that probably ribs, too, had been broken, and that at least one had pierced a lung.

No one, so far as Kes could see, had done anything to help the injured man. But then, as far as Kes could see they hardly did anything to help one another either, except for lending an injured griffin their company. And Opailikiita had done that, at least. And he was still alive, so maybe the young griffin was actually doing something to help him after all . . .

Opailikiita bent her neck around and down to watch Kes as she opened the man's shirt and touched the terrible spongy bruising across his chest. *I have no power to heal,* she said, not quite apologetically. *I slowed the loss of blood. That seemed the same as for one of my own people.*

"Oh," said Kes, startled and remembering at last that the griffins could at least do that. "Thank you . . ."

"That was well done," Kairaithin said, glancing down at the injured man's arm with a strange kind of indifferent approval. "Another time, you will find that you might also block our desert from drawing the strength of earth from a wounded human. This is possible. One makes the barrier of one's own self."

Yes, said the young griffin, in a tone of surprised comprehension.

"One does not use fire to heal a creature of earth," Kairaithin said to Kes. "But you are uniquely poised between earth and fire. I do not know what you might find to do—either with fire or with earth."

Kes did not really hear him. She was frowning down at the man. She ran her hand across the stone, gathering a little red dust; then she let the dust turn to light within her hand. She knelt, then, holding light cupped in her palm and wondering what, precisely, she could do with it. Nothing of the man spoke to her; though she listened, she could not hear his name in the beat of her blood. She had known that griffins were creatures of fire and that they were nothing to do with earth; she had known that the fire magic Kairaithin had taught her to use was nothing to do with men. But she had somehow forgotten, during these few days in the desert, how very unlike men and griffins truly were. Now she did not know what to do.

The man's breathing had grown more labored, even in this small time. Bubbles of blood formed at his nostrils; blood ran slowly down from the corner of his mouth. He was going to die. If Kes might save him, she would have to do it swiftly; there was no time to think and think again, or to hesitate—and if she tried and failed, he would be no more dead than if she did not try.

Kes took a sharp breath and set her hands on his chest, both her empty hand and the hand holding light. She shut her eyes, listening for his name, for his heartbeat. But no matter how she listened, she heard nothing except his difficult breathing. It was worse still; it worsened every moment. He was surely going to die. Unless Kes could save him.

His blood did not turn to rubies as it fell in droplets to the hot stone; it flowed. There was no fire in his blood. Kes bit her lip and poured fire into his blood, as she had learned so recently to take it into hers. At first, his body fought the intrusion of the fire; he did not wake, but convulsed, and he made horrible, hoarse sounds. Kes flinched. But at least, she thought, he could still *make* sounds. So his lungs were not altogether ruined . . . Opailikiita put out a wide feathered eagle's foot and pinned the man down against the stone so that he would not injure himself further in his agony.

Kes almost stopped, almost drew back. But she knew sometimes a healer has to cause pain in order to heal; and though she hurt this man, she hoped healing might follow. She could not use fire to heal a creature of earth—so he had to stop being entirely a creature of earth, at least for a moment; and if *she* could take on something of both natures, then why not this man? And so she poured fire into him and through him, though he fought it; she made fire run through his blood as she had learned to allow it to run through hers. She altered his very nature, and though his body fought her, she persisted. And he had been much weakened. She felt his resistance break under the relentless assault of fire.

She could feel very clearly that if she persisted he would die, and that if she stopped he would reject the fire and revert entirely to earth, and then he would still die. But for just a moment, caught between those choices, the man held fire as well as earth. And in that moment, Kes poured light over him and through him and pulled him hard toward the wholeness she saw behind the broken body. And, under the touch of her hands and the insistent gaze of her eyes and the fierce pressure of the light, he became whole.

As he became whole, his true nature reasserted itself with violent force, and the fire poured out of him in a fierce blaze that, as Kes lost control of it, might have burned him badly. But Kairaithin reached past her and caught the fire, and sent it elsewhere before it could so much as singe the man's clothing.

The man took a long shuddering breath, but it was a deep and steady breath and there was no blood in it. The wounds were gone; there were not even scars to show where his arm had been torn, nor any shadow of bruises across his chest where his ribs had been broken. He did not open his eyes, not yet. But, Kes knew, he was no longer unconscious. He merely slept.

She stood up, shakily, and put a hand out to Opailikiita. The slim griffin was there, her wing tucking itself under Kes's hand, quietly supportive.

"Remarkable," Kairaithin said. His tone was more thoughtful than approving, and Kes looked at him sharply, but he said nothing else.

Yet he is, in truth, wholly a creature of earth, is he not? Opailikiita said, sounding a little uncertain.

"Yes," said Kairaithin. "Now." His bent a considering glance on Kes. "Will you see the other wounded? There are not so many, and none other so seriously injured. Still, they would benefit from your care. Will you come?"

"Yes . . ." But Kes gave the sleeping man an uncertain look, reluctant to leave him.

"He will live," Kairaithin said. "He will sleep for some time, I think. It is difficult rest you will have given him, *kereskiita*, teaching him to dream of a fire he cannot touch. But I think that will not harm him. You are safe to leave him for a little."

I will stay near him, Opailikiita volunteered, and stretched out like a cat on the hot stone. *I will watch him for you, little sister. I will block the desert from drawing his strength. I think I understand now the way to do that.*

"All right," Kes agreed. She was still reluctant, but she trusted Opailikiita. More, she found, than she trusted Kairaithin. She gave the griffin mage a wary look. "You'll bring me back here?"

"I will assuredly bring you back to this place," Kairaithin told her. "Kiibaile Esterire Airaikeliu will come soon enough to speak to this man. I think when our king speaks to the emissary of the King of Feierabiand, it might be as well if you were here, little fire kitten."

"Oh . . ." Kes winced a little at the idea of standing between the Lord of Fire and Air and the man; only . . . only she liked even less the idea that the man might wake here in the griffins' hall to find himself entirely alone, surrounded by griffins. *That* would be hard. Especially after he had watched the griffins kill all his companions . . . "All right," she said at last. "But I don't know how to speak to . . . to emissaries and great lords."

"You will do well enough," Kairaithin assured her drily. "Am I not your teacher?" He held out his hand.

Kes cast one more glance at the sleeping man and then stepped toward the griffin mage and let him take her hand.

There were indeed not many injured griffins this time. And, as Kairaithin had told her, they were not so badly injured, most of them. They were much, much easier to heal than the man had been; Kes found she barely had to think about what she did. This did not exactly surprise her. It seemed very reasonable that she should find healing the people of fire easy, after the struggle to heal a man of earth.

What did surprise Kes was how many of the griffins greeted her by name—by her fire-name. This time, they did not look through her, nor did any of them strike at her. They were not embarrassed, this time, for her to see them injured and weak—or Kes thought that perhaps that was the difference, or something like it, as nearly as a human woman could understand it. This time, the injured griffins knew her and spoke to her; not only the injured ones, but their *iskarianere* as well. They called her Keskainiane Raikaisipiike in fierce, joyful voices. Kes wondered what *exactly* that name meant. She did not, somehow, like to ask Kairaithin—if it drew partially on his own name, maybe it was too personal a question somehow? Maybe she would ask Opailikiita, later . . .

"When is Esterire Airaikeliu going to go to the hall?" she asked Kairaithin nervously. "Will it be much later than this? Are there many other griffins to heal?"

Kairaithin glanced up at the sun, which still blazed hot and high above the desert, well above the western edge of the desert. "Not so much later," he conceded. "But that was the last."

Around them, the world tilted and shifted. Fiery winds whipped sand through the air, then settled. They once more stood in the hall of stone and sand, high above the desert. The man still lay where they had left him, though now his head was pillowed on Opailikiita's foot. The young griffin had stretched not only a wing above the man, but also a different kind of protection; Kes could see that the desert heat beat less harshly upon the shadowed stone where the man lay.

Along one edge of the hall, with here a foot or there a wing dangling casually above the height, rested the Lord of Fire and Air and his *iskarianere* Eskainiane Escaile Sehaikiu, and the red griffin who was their mate, Esterikiu Anahaikuuanse, and a griffin of pure shining white whose name Kes did not know. They had all been studying the human man. Kes thought Opailikiita was very brave to stay by the man and shield him not merely from the forceful heat of the desert, but also from those powerful stares, which, at least from Anahaikuuanse and from the white griffin held considerable hostility.

Now the king and all three of his companions turned their heads and regarded Kairaithin for a long moment, and then as one bent that implacable regard on Kes. She resisted an almost overpowering urge to step backward and hide in Kairaithin's shadow.

Keskainiane Raikaisipiike, said the king.

"Lord," Kes answered hesitantly, after she found a quick glance at Kairaithin did not yield any guidance.

What is this here? demanded the king, the power of his

voice ringing through the hot air. *Do I understand you bent the nature of fire to repair injury to this creature of earth?*

Kes was too startled by what seemed a rebuke to answer at once. But then she was, to her own surprise, angry. She said, "I bent *his* nature, lord. Since it was fire that injured him in the first place, it seems only fair that fire should repair his wounds!"

The king and the red female both looked angry at this, though whether because Kes had used fire in such a way or merely because of her boldness, she could not tell. The white griffin looked savagely hostile. But Escaile Sehaikiu tipped his head back and laughed—silent, joyful griffin laughter that made Kes want to smile, though she was still angry. It occurred to her that in griffins, anger and laughter might not be so separate as they were in men, but then she did not know what to make of this realization or whether the insight might be important.

The white griffin said in a ferocious, deadly voice, *That is rightfully my prey, and nothing to give to a human woman.*

Kes flinched from its hostility, but Kairaithin said in his driest tone, "If one will make a fire mage of a human, it is hardly just to be astonished when occasionally she acts according to the nature of a human. You may well give up your prey to her and to me, Tastairiane Apailika. Why not? You may surely afford the luxury."

You claim this man, then, said the king, in a hard tone that silenced any response the white griffin might have made.

"I do. Will anyone challenge my decision?" Kairaithin walked across the hall and stood over the man Kes had healed, looking back aggressively at the other griffins.

Opailikiita folded her protective wing and drew away

from the man, coming to join Kes. But her withdrawal was somehow nothing like a retreat; from her fierce stare, it was clear she would willingly take on all four of the larger and greater griffins to protect the human man—for Kes's sake, because Kes had left him with her. Kes buried a hand in the fine feathers of Opailikiita's throat, trying to draw bravery of her own from the brilliant courage of the slim griffin.

"He will wake soon," observed Kairaithin, not glancing down at the man. "And what shall we say to him when he wakes, O Lord of Fire and Air?" He returned the hot stare of the king with effortless power of his own. "Will any here declare that I was wrong to seek out this human woman and raise the fire in her blood?"

You remind us all of your prior right decision, said the king harshly. *Shall we believe that all your decisions are right?*

Kairaithin smiled, a thin, fierce smile with nothing of yielding in it.

At his feet, the man moved at last, groaned, and opened his eyes, blinking against the flooding light, powerful even under the shelter of the stone hall, staring around with a dazed, helpless expression. Without thinking, Kes stepped forward as the man pushed himself up. She knelt to touch his shoulder, that he should not find himself in this place altogether alone.

CHAPTER 6

In the dream, Bertaud had wings . . . cleverly feathered wings that could feel the most subtle shift of wind. He stared into the wind and saw it layered with warmth and greater warmth, heat rising where red stone underlay it. He turned, fire limning each feather of his wings as he curved them to catch the air. Below him, the red desert spread out in all directions: rock and sand, dust and silence; nothing moved upon it but the wind. Both the desert and the wind were his, and he loved them with a fierce possessive love. . . .

He lay upon red stone, in rich sunlight that pooled on the stone like molten gold; he stared into the hot brilliant light with eyes that were not dazzled. The heat struck up from the rock like a furnace, and he found it good. His wings were spread, turned to catch the sun. There could never be too much heat, too much light. . . .

He rode through a storm. The wind roared through his wings. He was flung upward by the violence of the wind;

a wing tip, delicately extended, was enough to send him
spinning sideways into a loop that carried him, at last,
above the storm into clear air. He cried aloud with exaltation. His voice struck through the air like a blade, but
against the bellow of the storm he could hardly hear even
his own cry; yet somehow both his cry and the roar of the
storm were part of the great silence of the desert. It was a
silence that encompassed all sound, just as the violence of
the storm itself was encompassed by the greater stillness
of the desert . . .

He woke slowly. He did not hurt and that seemed strange,
though he did not understand why he expected pain. Trying
to move, he could not understand the response of his own
body. It seemed the wrong body. He could not understand
why he did not have wings and talons. His . . . hands . . . yes,
his hands . . . moved, flinching from unexpected grit and
stone, but he did not know what he had expected. He opened
his eyes, with some difficulty. The lids were gummy, sticky
with . . . blood, he thought. Blood? There had been . . . . there
had been . . . an accident? A . . . . fight?

He got his eyes open at last, scrubbed his arm across
them, and looked up. Memory crashed back so hard it
stopped his breath.

He was lying on stone, high above the world. Pillars
of twisted red stone stood all about, supporting a roof of
stone so that he lay in shade—a hot shade, so hot the very
air seemed like the breath of a living animal. The great
hall surrounded by these pillars was floored with sand;
the desert breeze wandered in and stroked the sand into
patterns on the floor. It was not a human place. He did not
have to be told that it was a place for griffins, which they
had somehow drawn out of fire and the desert.

And there were griffins in it: one that caught his eye immediately though it was not the nearest, dark bronze eagle forequarters merging seamlessly into lion rear, relentless golden eyes staring into his. Anger poured off it, like heat against his face. The anger frightened him. Yet Bertaud did not feel as . . . stifled, as stunned, as when he had first met Kairaithin before the battle. He could think, now. He thought he would be able to speak, if he came up with something worth saying.

Even so, it took an effort to tear his gaze away, to get himself up on one elbow and look around. A gold-and-copper griffin was there, bright as the sun, close by the side of the first. Another griffin, dark red, her feathers heavily barred with gold, lay couchant behind those two males. That one, too, seemed angry. Angry and fierce and ready to kill for any provocation, or no provocation. And a white griffin, quite near, far more terrifying, a griffin from whom Bertaud flinched reflexively before he even remembered why.

Then he remembered. He froze, trying to deal with that memory. The white griffin did not move. Its fiery blue eyes held his, utterly inhuman.

A hand touched his shoulder, and he flinched, turning his head. A woman knelt at his side. No. A girl. Hardly more than a child. *Kes*, he thought. Of course, this would be the girl Kes, who had frightened her family and friends by vanishing into the desert with an unknown mage and had not returned.

The girl's eyes met his with a strange openness, as though she had no secrets in all the world, and yet there was a silent reserve at the back of them that he could not see through at all. A heavy golden light moved in her eyes, a light that held fiery wings and red desert sand, so that it took him a moment to see that those eyes were actually a grayed blue, like Niambe Lake under a stormy sky; the color seemed very strange. He had expected her eyes to be the color of fire.

Then her gaze dropped. Untidy pale hair fell across her delicate face, and she drew back against the . . . shelter, he thought, odd though that seemed . . . the shelter of a slim brown griffin that curved its body behind the girl and curved a wing across her shoulder.

Behind the girl stood Kairaithin. Anasakuse Sipiike Kairaithin. The name slid through Bertaud's mind with a strange familiarity. Kairaithin still wore the shape of a man, yet he did not look like anything human. He stared back at Bertaud with pitiless calm, as though the stillness of the desert had settled in his eyes. He looked . . . satisfied. As well he might, Bertaud thought bitterly. But the griffin mage did not, at least, seem angry.

Bertaud got to his feet, slowly. But not painfully. Recalling his battle, if one could so describe it, with the white griffin, this seemed miraculous. He looked around again, incredulously, at the stone hall, at the waiting griffins, at the girl leaning against the griffin at her back, petting it as though it were a cat . . . at Kairaithin.

"Man," said Kairaithin, and waited, starkly patient.

Bertaud met his eyes with what pride he could find. The griffin mage stared back, something strange and not human in his eyes . . . a kind of hard, fierce humor that was not the humor of a man. Bertaud bent his head slightly before that black stare, acknowledging the griffin's power. "Lord."

Kairaithin tilted his head in satisfaction. "I would have

brought you to this place without spilling blood out on the sand."

"And what place is this?" Bertaud steadied his voice with an effort.

"The hall of the Lord of Fire and Air." Kairaithin walked past Bertaud toward the bronze-and-gold griffin Bertaud had seen first. As he moved, he changed: rising, swelling, extending in all directions, the true form of the griffin emerging from the shape of the man.

He made a splendid griffin: large and heavy, with powerful shoulders and eyes blacker than the desert sky at night. His dark coloring made him yet more impressive: His wings, so heavily barred with black that little red showed through, mantled above a body the color of the dark embers at the heart of a fire. He said to Bertaud, *But here you are come, in the end, are you not, man?*

His voice as a griffin was very much like the voice he had as a man. It had the same hard humor to it. It slid into Bertaud's mind like a lion slipping through the dark.

Bertaud thought of too many things to say, and thought better of saying any of them.

The lord of the griffins stirred, hardly more than a slight ruffling of bronze feathers, an infinitesimal shift of his head. But he drew all eyes. His strength and anger beat through the hot air. He said, in a voice like the sun slamming down at noon, *Bertaud, son of Boudan. Do you serve the King of Feierabiand?*

Bertaud closed his eyes for a moment. He said carefully, "Yes." And added, "Lord."

The griffin tipped his head to one side, unreadable eyes fixed on Bertaud's. *Sipiike Kairaithin considers you might usefully bear a message from me to the King of Feierabiand.*

"I might," agreed Bertaud and, because he did not care to be taken lightly, "If *I* judged it useful; I am my king's servant, and none of yours."

The gold-and-copper griffin tossed its head back in what seemed a silent shout of intermingled laughter and anger; the red-and-gold one was merely angry. So was the griffin king, hard hot anger like a gust from a desert sandstorm.

His own pride held Bertaud still. The girl was not so proud. She drew aside, the brown griffin with her, and tucked herself down into a small space at the foot of one of the twisted pillars. Bertaud was sorry he had frightened her, and at the same time, incredulous that she should be in this place, in this company. He wanted badly to take her aside and ask her a thousand questions. He wished he was certain he would survive long enough to speak to the girl. He was not even confident he would survive the next moment.

Peace. Peace, said Kairaithin, sounding harshly amused, and all the griffins settled, slowly. *Man, take more care.*

"Do you take care for *my* pride?" retorted Bertaud, a little more sharply than he had intended, and made himself stare back without giving ground.

Are you free to come and go in this hall? The griffin waited a heartbeat, pitiless eyes holding the man's. *Then take more care.*

After a moment, Bertaud bowed his head. "Lord."

Your folk died well, said the gold-and-copper griffin by the king. His voice was swift as fire, fierce, proud . . . not kind, precisely. Generous, perhaps. Bertaud stared at him, wondering what death a griffin might find good.

It was a day of blood and fire, said the griffin. He seemed to mean, in some odd way, to offer comfort. *Though they were overmatched, your people fought bravely. You may have my name, to speak as you choose: It is Eskainiane Escaile Sehaikiu.*

"Thank you," said Bertaud, which seemed due. "Did you . . . are they all . . . do any still live?"

Certainly not, said the griffin. Eskainiane . . . Eskainiane Escaile Sehaikiu. His quick fiery voice held surprise, somehow even reproof. *We would not so offend their courage as to leave them living on such a day.*

"What?"

The griffin blinked, a slow sliding of feathered eyelids across amber-colored eyes. *Their dishonored blood would cry out of the sand that drank it in. We would hear their names in our dreams, in the voice of the wind through our wings.*

"Men are not griffins," Bertaud protested. He wanted to shout it. He managed a calm tone, somehow.

The coppery griffin looked at him with unhuman eyes that might have meant well, yet failed entirely to comprehend him. *Blood is blood.*

We have no need to take our counsels with men, the white griffin said, breaking in with angry impatience. His voice came like a knife edge against Bertaud's mind, like fire whipping through the dark—nothing like the blatant power of the king's voice nor the subtlety of Kairaithin's nor the brightness of Eskainiane's.

To Bertaud, this griffin's voice was like a physical assault. He shut his eyes to keep from flinching from it, found his physical balance compromised, and shamed himself by staggering. He steadied himself only with difficulty because there was nothing close enough to catch hold of. It was very nearly as disorienting as his first encounter with Kairaithin, and he had believed himself past that strong a reaction.

We shall do as we please and as we must, and let this human king send men against us if he does not care for what we do, said the white griffin, and again his voice seemed to Bertaud like a blow, although the griffin was not even looking at him.

We would do better, Tastairiane Apailika, to have a care for what men might do, said Kairaithin. *Or why are we here building a desert in this foreign land?*

Peace. The king's powerful voice slammed down across the whole hall, silencing all dissent. Bertaud swayed with the force of it. *Man. Bertaud, son of Boudan. Will you bear a word from me to the ear of your king?*

"Certainly," Bertaud said, staring at him, trying to keep his voice steadier than his undependable body. "If you ask me. What word, O Lord of Fire and Air, would you have me take to my king?"

We forbid men from our desert. We will tolerate no intrusion into the country we have made. In return, we will not hunt men. What will your king say to this word?

Bertaud said honestly, "He will not accept it. He will bring a thousand men against you, or hire Casmantian mercenaries if he must, and drive you back across the mountains."

He expected anger, hotter and more dangerous than before. Strangely, it did not come. The griffins spoke among themselves . . . He could distinguish words and phrases and the odd uninterpretable image. But it was like listening to a quick interchange in a foreign language one barely knew: He knew he missed far more than he understood.

The griffin king said, *What then will he offer?*

It dawned on Bertaud that he was, in fact, negotiating with the griffins . . . just as Iaor had desired, although not from the position of strength they had both expected. But negotiating. He saw that the griffins had made, not an ultimatum, but a first offer. Like merchants bargaining over a length of cloth or a jeweled ring. He was astonished. He said instantly, "My king will forgive your incursion into his land, if you go at once. You may depart in peace."

That is not acceptable, said the griffin king. *We will hold this country hereabout for four seasons, until the heat of the summer rises again, and hunt as we please among the pastures of men and the woodlands of these hills.*

The overwhelming power of his voice made it seem, again, like an ultimatum or a threat. Forcing himself to disregard this impression, Bertaud countered, "You must go south, to the lowlands beyond Talend, where there is little farmland to be ruined. You may stay in that country until the leaves turn, provided you hunt only in the forest and the hills, leaving be the pastured beasts."

There was a short pause.

We will stay in this desert we have made, stated the griffin king. *But we will stay only three seasons, until the light dies and then quickens anew in the rising year. But we must hunt, and there are no desert creatures here for us.*

Unexpectedly, the girl stood up. The slim brown griffin rose with her, gazing at the larger griffins over the girl's shoulder. It seemed the girl, unlike Bertaud, had been able to follow the speech of the griffins, for she said in a low voice that was hardly more than a whisper, "Kiibaile Esterire Airaikeliu, Minas Ford and Minas Spring and Talend—and Bered—all the small towns and villages will give your people a dozen cattle. Two dozen. We will drive them into the high desert you have made and give them to you. So you can leave be the animals we value more." She glanced quickly and nervously at Bertaud. "Lord, it would be better so."

Bertaud stared at her. So did the griffins, but though Kes blushed and dropped her eyes away from his, she did not seem to mind their savage attention.

Six for each month that we stay, said the king of the griffins, to the girl. *And we will not withdraw until the light quickens in the next year.* He swung his fierce head around and stared at Bertaud out of fierce black eyes. *Agree, man, if you are wise.*

The memory of a hundred men butchered like oxen suggested a stiff refusal, followed by a punitive expedition— even if Iaor had to hire Casmantian mercenaries to help deal with the griffins Casmantium understood better than Feierabiand. But the sober knowledge that it was they themselves and none others who had been responsible for leading their men against a foe they had calamitously underestimated, argued otherwise. And he, who might have overruled Jasand, was most to blame.

Kairaithin had tried to bring him here, before the . . . battle. The attempted battle. If he had come—if he had not let Diene's fears overrule his own inclinations— Bertaud deliberately shut down that thought. It was one to endure on sleepless nights. Not, by any means, one to entertain while in the midst of serious negotiations.

He said, "There are small villages and homesteads through all this country."

We will not trouble them, said the griffin king.

"And you have ruined enough land. Your desert is wide enough."

The griffins stirred. The red-and-gold female opened her beak and made a low, aggressive sound. The king did something that was like a silent, motionless hammer blow, and she was suddenly still. All the griffins were still.

We shall contain the desert as we can, said Kairaithin. *It is a considerable concession, man*, he added impatiently. *Agree, if you would be wise.*

Bertaud inclined his head. "Subject to my king's approval, I do agree. However, the king's honor will demand suitable recompense for the damage and trouble you have caused him."

The honor of men, said the white griffin, contemptuously.

"If you seek peace with Feierabiand," Bertaud said flatly, "you will recognize that we have our own honor, even if it is not the same as yours."

Kiibaile Esterire Airaikeliu did not, at least, strike him down immediately where he stood for his temerity. Bertaud thought the white griffin would have liked to. But the griffin king did not move, and Kairaithin said, *We shall consider what you say. Perhaps you may have a suggestion regarding what your king might find suitable remuneration.*

For a moment Bertaud's mind went entirely blank. He could think of absolutely nothing Iaor might consider acceptable that griffins might supply. It seemed, in fact, a question for mages. If a mage could be found who did not despise the desert and actually knew something of its creatures. He said temperately, "I shall inquire. When I bring your word to him."

"Rubies," said Kes, again breaking in unexpectedly. "Fire opals. Sparks of gold."

Bertaud stared at her. But Kairaithin said, *We might indeed part with these echoes of blood and fire, if these would please your king. If he is wise, he will indeed ask for such small tokens. Will you permit me to take you to him? Will you give him this word?*

"Yes," said Bertaud.

At sunset, then. Kairaithin stood and stretched himself like a great cat. He shook his feathers into order. He was suddenly gone: The hot, close air seemed to hesitate an instant before closing into the space where he had been.

One by one the other griffins rose and paced to the edge of the open hall and dropped off the edge of the cliff into the wind. The white griffin went first. Bertaud found himself surprised by the strength of his own relief at that creature's departure. Then the red-and-gold griffin, and the gold-and-copper one, and last the king.

Their departure left Bertaud alone in a hall of twisted red stone and sand, with a girl who spoke to griffins with amazing familiarity and a slim-bodied brown-and-bronze griffin. The relief of the departure of the other griffins was so great that it took him a moment to realize the brown one was still present, for all it was the size of a small horse and undoubtedly capable of tearing an unarmed man in half, if it wished. Which it did not seem to. It stood by the girl like a dog, or a friend. She had her hand on its neck, as though for comfort and support—in fact, precisely as though it were a dog. Or a friend.

The girl did not *look* like a mage. Nor like the kind of

vile, treacherous, death-loving creature who would deliberately let a hundred men go to be slaughtered by griffin savagery and desert fire. In fact . . . in fact, if Bertaud had passed her on the streets of Tihannad, he thought he would not have so much as glanced her way. Though, to closer inspection, she was not without a certain waiflike attractiveness.

She ducked her head as he studied her, closing in upon herself. Her hair fell forward and hid her eyes. The griffin with her stared at Bertaud with pale, fierce eyes, startling in its dark face.

He said, "Kes. Am I right?"

"Yes," she whispered, not looking up.

She was shy. She looked timid as a fawn. And yet she stood in a stone hall above the world with a griffin at her back and had spoken to the powerful, dangerous king of griffins by name.

"Why are you here?" he asked her directly.

The girl glanced up, and dropped her gaze again immediately.

She is a powerful . . . healer, said the small griffin. Its voice was subtle, soft; it came unobtrusively around the edges of Bertaud's mind. *She made you whole.*

Bertaud flashed on the shining white griffin, leaping down from the rock above to come against him after it had cast him down from that height. He had known he was going to die. The memory was vivid enough that he was forced to sit down rather suddenly and lean his head on his hand. He had been badly hurt. He knew that. He remembered a blow that he thought had crushed his ribs, and put a hand involuntarily to his chest. It seemed momentarily beyond belief that he could draw breath, that the bone and flesh under his hand was not even bruised.

And this girl had healed him. So she was a mage, then, after all.

The girl lifted her eyes again, tentatively. "Kairaithin said he wanted you whole. He told me I might use fire to heal you, even though you are a creature of earth. I thought at first I would not find a way to do that. Then I did. It was hard. I thought you might . . . might die of it. But if I hadn't done it, you would have died anyway. And then it worked after all."

"Yes." Bertaud touched his chest again. "Thank you."

The girl gave him a tiny nod. "I was afraid for you. Even after you were whole. Tastairiane Apailika said . . . He said you were his prey. But then Kairaithin made him give you to me."

"He's very powerful," Bertaud said, trying for a neutral tone. "Kairaithin. Isn't he?"

"Yes, lord," the girl answered faintly. "But he has no power for healing. So he told me. He brought me to see the battlefield after the battle was done." She met his eyes with what seemed to be an effort of will. "It was terrible to see everyone dead. I was afraid you would die, too."

But she had healed him. He could not even decide whether he should be grateful. He asked again, trying to sound gentle, "But why are you here?"

She looked at him with a trapped expression. "It would have been wrong to let them *die*. Wouldn't it?"

She was asking *him*? Then it dawned on him what she was saying. "You came up here to heal the *griffins*?"

The girl nodded.

"And now they will not let you leave them?"

"Kairaithin said he thought there would be a battle. I thought he meant with the Casmantian mages. I was . . . I didn't know . . . I think I didn't *want* to know he meant with you. And then he brought me to the place where everyone was already dead. Then I understood. But then it was too late."

"I see."

"All the men were already dead! What good would it have done to let the griffins die, too? How could I let them die?"

Bertaud did not try to answer this.

The girl went on, hesitantly, "Kairaithin told me he tried to talk to you, lord. He said the mage you brought with you hated him. He said you shouldn't have brought a mage. He said she feared him, so that he could not speak to you. Or he would have. I think he would, truly. He brought me to heal you, though he did not know whether I would find a way to do it." She stopped and glanced at him and then away again, seeming afraid that he might be angry.

Bertaud said with difficulty, not knowing whether he believed it or not, "It's not your fault." He walked away, stood at the edge of the hall, looked out over the red desert, and thought about what the girl had said. And what he had answered. He thought it was the truth—both times. What had happened *hadn't* been her fault. He knew whose fault it had been. He should have left Diene with the men outside the desert and walked back into it himself . . . He had not. And so. One dealt with the choices one made. And the consequence they carried with them.

Bertaud sat down next to a pillar at the edge of the cliff, laced his fingers around his knee, and stared out into the air. There were no griffins in sight. Except the one with the girl. The girl . . . "You're from Minas Ford?" It seemed very strange that a powerful mage should also be a timid little girl from a small mountain village.

She nodded.

"Who's your friend? I presume it *is* your friend?"

"Opailikiita Sehanaka Kiistaike. She is my friend." The girl stroked the rich brown feathers of the griffin's neck, and the griffin curved its head around and nibbled Kes's hair gently.

"And Kairaithin?"

"Anasakuse Sipiike Kairaithin . . . is not my enemy."

"No?" He glanced at her sidelong. "You . . . do you speak their tongue, Kes?"

The girl was seeming calmer at last. She came over and sat down near him, her back against the striated surface of the next pillar over. "I understand it a little. Opailikiita is teaching me. She says it is a good language for fire mage-craft. Part of it is the language of fire."

"I didn't know that human mages could be fire mages."

Neither had the girl, or so her quick downward glance seemed to suggest. She glanced up again, though, and said cautiously, "Kairaithin said I would have been an earth mage. Only he showed me fire instead. He said he could do that because the earth magecraft hadn't woken in me yet. He was looking for someone like me, but he said he didn't expect to find anyone. Only he found me, after all. He says I have both natures, now. I suppose . . . no." She met his eyes. "I know that is true, lord. I feel it is true."

Bertaud nodded slowly. He thought he, too, could simply look at the girl and see it was true; he could see the fire in her eyes. "Well, Kes. So what should I tell my king?"

"That they will do as they say," the girl answered at once. "Or . . . as Kiibaile Esterire Airaikeliu says they will. Kairaithin says they would fly in all directions if their king did not choose their direction and call them all to ride the same wind. That's why . . . I don't know. I think that's why he told me it was important to heal the king."

Yes, said the small griffin. Opailikiita. *The people of fire follow the fire. The Lord of Fire and Air and the Lord of the Changing Wind guide the flight of the people of fire.*

"The Lord of the Changing Wind?"

"Kairaithin," explained the girl. "He is the only fire mage they have left. I think mages are as rare among the griffins as among men. And Kairaithin was always the strongest. So he is very important. I wish . . . I wish you had listened to him." She added hastily, "But of course you would trust the mage you brought with you. Kairaithin told me earth mages can't bear fire mages—I suppose he has trouble enduring the presence of earth mages, too, only he's too proud to show it. But if your mage told you not to listen to the griffins, it's not your fault."

It most certainly was. Bertaud did not say so. It was a truth that would return, he was certain, to whisper in his ear in the days to come. "Casmantian soldiers attacked the griffins in their desert and drove them across the mountains. Is that right?"

Yes, said Opailikiita.

"And that is why you have only one mage left?" Bertaud asked the griffin directly.

Yes, she said. *The Casmantian mages of cold earth were very strong. We did not know they came until they were upon us. Our fire mages stood against them to give*

*the people time to fly. The halls broke behind us. The
cliffs fell. The wind blew cold where our desert had once
burned.* She spoke with a simple directness that somehow evoked the terror and grief of that night . . . Bertaud could almost see it, in the dark behind his eyelids:
red cliffs crumbling in a cold gale, griffins pitting the
strength of their fire against the violent cold . . . He
blinked, imagining men cloaked in black walking toward him across sand that froze beneath their feet, hurling darts tipped with ice at blazing griffin mages. Fires
going out in the dark, one by one. He blinked again,
shaking his head, and found both Kes and the griffin
looking at him curiously.

"But you will go back across the mountains," he said
to the griffin, not quite a question. "And face those cold
mages. What *is* a cold mage? A kind of earth mage, isn't
that right?"

Yes, said Opailiikita. *Earth magecraft is always opposed to fire magecraft, and a human mage who truly
sets himself against fire can turn cold. But we must
strike fire through the cold, so Kairaithin says, or perish
in the end. So we will do as we must.* The griffin spoke
very simply, though Bertaud only understood a little of
what she said.

Bertaud thought he recalled one or two glancing refer-
ences he'd seen or heard to earth mages who specialized in
a strange winter magic and drew power from the dormant
earth. It had seemed strange to him at the time. But if an
earth mage should happen to want to fight griffin magic,
the specialty suddenly made sense. And if cold mages
were so strong, he wondered at the griffin's optimism. But
he said only, "I will tell my king what you say."

"Tell him," the girl said earnestly, "that we can spare the cattle. The griffins need to hunt. It's part of . . . part of being a predator of fire."

"He'll make good your loss." Iaor would, in fact, feel bound to, for the sake of his royal honor, if he allowed the folk of this region to feed the griffins until next spring. If he did not decide instead that his pride could not bear them in his country even for so long. Which he might. It was his pride more than any that would be offended by the destruction of his soldiers. "I *wish* it had not come to battle!"

It was a day for death, said the griffin, in a tone that suggested she meant this to be comforting.

Both Bertaud and Kes looked at her. Kes said to him, "Sometimes I don't understand them, either. Most of the time. Almost all the time."

Bertaud nodded.

"But . . . she has a good heart."

He understood what the girl meant, and felt, strangely, that she was even right. But he was not sure why he thought so. He was uneasily aware that this feeling was akin to the impulse he had felt to go with Kairaithin during their first meeting. To trust a creature that he knew was not a man, was nothing like a man . . . a creature of fire, alien to the shape he wore. But then he had doubted all his impulses. And now . . . he doubted them more than ever.

It would not be long until sunset, he thought, looking out into mountains that rose red and dusty in the near distance. He shut his eyes and leaned against a red pillar. And tried to keep images of blood and death from invading the darkness behind his eyes. But the images were persistent, so that eventually he gave up and opened his eyes again. "Why sunset?" he asked, not even knowing whether it was the griffin he asked or the girl, or why he thought either of them would know. Or care to answer.

"Because the shadows are longest then," Kes answered. Her soft voice sounded distracted. She was gazing out over the desert. "Because the wind dies in the evening. The direction of the wind is easiest to change when the air is still."

Bertaud studied her. "Come with me, Kes. Speak to the king yourself. You . . . I think you would be very persuasive."

The suggestion shocked her. Her eyes widened. "I could never . . . oh, no. No, lord. I am sorry. I could never . . . You must understand, lord," she said earnestly, "I could never speak very . . . well."

And if she would change her mind, what would Kairaithin permit? Bertaud frowned at her and leaned back against his pillar. Before them, shadows stretched out across rock and sand. The lower slopes were already in darkness, though the mountains themselves still glowed with a red light, as though lit from within.

Kairaithin returned to the hall on that thought. He came out of the lowering light: a griffin the color of glowing embers, face and wings black as char. The stroke of his wings across the empty desert sky drew fierce music from the wind, which seemed to rise to meet him.

As the griffin mage came down, he dwindled. His wings beat one last stroke, wind singing like a bell through the open stone hall, and closed round him like a cloak. The wind he had brought with him died, leaving behind a silence that felt like the silence after music.

Kairaithin, black cloaked, turned his human face to them. His shadow stretched out long and low behind him, molten as a banked fire. Its eyes gleamed with fire-haunted darkness.

The griffin mage's own eyes were the same: black, secretive, opaque. Bertaud could see nothing in them. Yet he could meet them only with difficulty. He got slowly to his feet.

Kes stood also, with a shy downward glance. Bertaud was shaken by the idea that a girl so fragile and timid should somehow own power. He could not imagine her defying Kairaithin or the griffin king; indeed, Bertaud could not imagine her defying anyone who so much as shouted at her. She would never be able to use her strength for Feierabiand. She would stay meekly in the griffins' desert, and the griffins would rule her.

He said urgently, "Kes. Please come with me to Tihannad. I swear to you, Iaor will be kind to you. We will need you so badly. Who else is there to explain the griffins to us? Please come." He thought perhaps Kairaithin would say something to him then, or to her: a threat, a warning, a simple refusal.

But the griffin mage said nothing. He turned his powerful gaze on the girl and lifted an ironic eyebrow.

Kes only shook her head, leaning back against the dark bulk of her griffin friend.

"She would not be comfortable to do as you ask," Kairaithin said to him, matter-of-factly. And to the girl, "Would you, *kereskiita*? Would you go to the king of Feierabiand, as this lord suggests?"

Kes shook her head, still not speaking.

"You keep her here against her will. To act in your

service, against her own people." Bertaud tried to keep anger out of his tone, to speak as calmly as the griffin.

"We refrain from hunting men here. So," said Kairaithin, tone dry, while Kes looked steadfastly down at the stone where she sat, "do we establish partiality toward our *kereskiita*." The mage held out his hand to Bertaud. It might have been a command, or an invitation. This time, there was no earth mage to warn him against griffin intentions. And nothing to do but yield to them, whatever warnings his own rationality might suggest. Bertaud slowly came forward and took the offered hand.

Kairaithin's thin mouth crooked in austere amusement, or approval, or . . . something else less recognizable. He closed a hand on Bertaud's shoulder, his grip powerful as an eagle's talons, and around them the world moved.

Bertaud staggered. Only the mage's grip on his shoulder kept him on his feet. The air was suddenly much colder; it smelled of moisture and growing things. Even though the sun was not quite below the horizon, it was much darker without the mountains to cast back the late sunlight. Loose water-rounded pebbles made treacherous footing. The gray waters of Niambe Lake washed over the pebbles, running nearly up to their feet, with a low murmur entirely different from any sound of the desert. The unguarded wall of Tihannad rose against the sky less than a bowshot from where they stood.

Kairaithin let him go. Bertaud backed up involuntarily, realized what he was doing, and stood still with an effort. The mage tilted his head slightly. His expression was impossible to read. Bertaud thought that even if the sun had been full on his face, the griffin mage's expression would have been impenetrable.

"Will you think well of us, man?" asked the griffin. His tone, astonishingly, might almost have been wistful.

Bertaud stared at him, taken utterly aback. "How can I?"

"Try," Kairaithin advised. He turned his head toward the west, looked into the last light of the sun, and was gone.

CHAPTER 7

The young lord stepped freely forward into Kairaithin's grip, going to carry word of the griffins to his king. Kes admired him: He was, she thought, not really *so* many years older than she was. But *he* was brave. She knew he was afraid of Kairaithin and she thought that, in his place, she would not have been able to come forward with such courage.

Though she understood that, she did not understand *him*.

He would go to his king . . . her king, too, Kes supposed, but this was so strange an idea that she dismissed it almost at once. He would take to the king his memory of Tastairiane Apailika as well as Kairaithin, and the great Lord of Fire and Air . . . of her, even. And what image of her would he carry to his king? She wondered about that distant king—what was he like? Was he proud? Violent? Did he fear battle, or long for it? Was he clever, or wise? Or neither?

What would this king say to the lord who came to him

from this airy hall? Would the king even listen to a man whom he had sent here, who had lost all his companions and returned alone?

And if he did listen, what would the lord tell him?

If she had gone there, what would she have told the king? Kes sighed. If she had known what to say, perhaps she would have found the courage to go. If Kairaithin had permitted her to go. Kes stared out into the desert night. The wind smelled of hot stone and silence.

Opailikiita's voice slid into her awareness, oddly tentative. *Are you well?*

"Yes," said Kes, quite automatically. Then she asked herself the same question and did not know the answer. She sighed again and stroked the slim griffin's neck, ruffling the feathers gently against the grain so that she could feel them settle back. In the darkness, Opailikiita was perceptible mainly as a stirring of heat, a puff of breath. "Would you take me home?" Kes asked her.

Kairaithin has forbidden it.

Kes hesitated. Yet, somehow . . . she did not feel that this statement, plain as it was, carried quite the force it might have. "Yes," she said. "But would you do it anyway?"

Opailikiita curled her neck around and touched Kes lightly on the cheek with the tip of her deadly beak; it was a caress, and Kes smiled and moved to lean against the griffin's shoulder.

Kairaithin is my siipikaile, said the griffin. *But you are my sister, and I would not hold you here if you did not want to stay. But is the desert not your home? And is Kairaithin not your* siipikaile *as well?*

Kes shook her head, but not exactly in denial. Perhaps

griffin mages never asked whether you were interested in becoming an apprentice, whether you wanted to learn how to make the fire and the rising wind part of your soul, whether you wanted to belong to the desert. Perhaps a griffin only saw that you could hold the power he needed even when you did not know it yourself, and made sure you would learn to use it according to his needs.

Are you angry? Opailikiita sounded curious, but not disturbed by the prospect.

Kes wasn't angry. But longing rose in her, for the simple human house she had shared with Tesme, for the whicker of mares in the low pasture and the homey smells of cut hay and new bread instead of hot stone and dust. She shut her eyes against the heavy darkness and whispered, "I want to go home."

Then I will take you, said Opailikiita. *As far as it is possible to go.*

Riding the griffin was not like sitting on a horse. There was no saddle, no stirrups, but the difference was more than that. The feathers under Kes's knees were soft and fragile. Kes found herself afraid to hold the feathers of the griffin's neck too tightly, lest she harm her.

You may grip tightly, Opailikiita said, and leaped from the rock with a great leonine bound, sudden enough that Kes bit her tongue.

It was not like riding a horse at *all*. The jarring lurch when the griffin opened her wings to the wind nearly threw Kes off. She swallowed a gasp and held tightly with hands and legs.

The high pasture above the house had become desert. The trees that had been there were gone—not dead, but gone, as though they had never grown there. The grass had withered and blown away; even in the lower part of the hill pastures the grass had become sparse and thin. But on the other side of the creek that ran through the midlands pasture, the grass grew thick and green, as abrupt a change in the landscape as though the little creek separated countries that lay a thousand miles apart.

Opailikiita did not cross the creek into that cooler country, but came down to the ground on its desert side. Kes swung her leg across the griffin's neck and slid off her back onto legs that seemed inclined not to hold her; she put an arm over Opailikiita's neck for balance and support.

Can you cross into the country of earth? asked the griffin.

Kes looked at her without comprehension. She straightened gingerly away from Opailikiita's support and walked carefully, then more quickly, to the creek; before she quite came to it, it occurred to her that Opailikiita was not with her, and she turned her head to look inquiringly over her shoulder.

That was perhaps why, when she struck the barrier of cold air at the edge of the creek, it was so unexpected that it knocked her entirely off her feet. She sat, dazed, on parched ground at the edge of the desert and stared, mute with bewilderment, at the water lying inches from her feet.

Kairaithin has put a binding on you, that you shall not leave the desert, said Opailikiita. She did not sound precisely sympathetic. Her tone held something more akin to the satisfaction of someone who has had a shrewd guess confirmed. *You will be angry now. Do not fight him. You do not have the strength.*

Kes was not angry. But she wanted to weep in frustration and disappointment. Looking down the hill, she could see the lights in the windows of the house, small at this distance. She should have been able to walk to it in minutes. It was utterly out of reach. Kes stood up and put out a hand toward the creek. She found that she could not even reach out over the water. The barrier she could not see prevented her.

I will take you to the heights, said Opailikiita. *I will bear you so high you feel the starlight on your shoulders, so high the air shatters and fire comes down to scatter through your feathers. It is very beautiful.*

Kes barely heard her. She looked at her own hand, stretched out toward the creek, unable to reach further. She was aware, faintly, that she was shaking.

Sister, said Opailikiita.

"*You* aren't my sister." Kes turned her back to the griffin and walked away from her, away from loss and confusion, into the stillness of the desert night. When she felt Opailikiita move to come after her, she began to run. She found she *was* angry—angry with Opailikiita, with Kairaithin, with all the griffins, with herself; she hardly knew. Rage, bright and unfamiliar, ran through her in a quick hot wave, like a fire cracking through the dark. The strength of it frightened her. She did not want Opailikiita's company, but it was terror of her own anger that made Kes find a way to shift herself through the world, far from the banks of the creek, into the endless desert silence.

Kes had not known she could do this until she did it, but after it was done it felt as inevitable as taking a step. It was only a matter of understanding the movement of fire. The shifting endless movement of flame through air. That knowledge, which should have been foreign to her, felt as familiar as her own breath. And she found a sure knowledge of what she wanted, which was solitude and quiet.

Solitude Kes found at once. Quiet was longer in coming. The desert itself was quiet; it was within herself that Kes carried a clamor of rage, bewilderment, longing, and terror. She could step from one edge of the griffins' desert to the other; she could step away from the element of earth into the element of fire; but she could not find her way from this emotional storm into calm.

Thoughts of Tesme, of Minas Ford, of the creek she could not cross all beat painfully at her attention. Kes tucked herself down against the base of a great twisted spire of rock and pressed her face against her knees. Her eyes felt hot; she wanted to weep. But tears would not come. Perhaps she was too angry to weep. She wanted Tesme to hold her, to rock her in her arms like a little child. But Tesme was not here. Tesme was at home. Where Kes should be.

Except that, surrounded now by the silence of the desert, Kes felt the storm of anger and longing slowly subside. She thought that all trouble, all emotion, might fade at last into that great silence; that the desert stillness might encompass all things. Kes found in herself a great longing for that silence, and welcomed it as it closed around her. The silence of the desert muted memory and unhappiness. She thought, *The desert is a garden that blooms with time and silence*, but then could not remember where she might once have heard that line, or whether it was from a history or a work of poetry or a story that Tesme, perhaps, had told her long ago. Except it did not sound like it could have belonged to the kind of stories Tesme told.

Time and silence. Time and silence grew through the dark and flowered with a bodiless beauty that seemed almost to have physical presence. Kes stared into the stark desert night and waited to see what would blossom out of it.

That was where the cold mages of Casmantium found her, in the soft pre-dawn grayness that preceded the powerful sun.

The first Kes knew of the Casmantian mages was a darkening of the desert, a shadow that stretched suddenly across the sand, a colder and stranger darkness than the night itself had brought. Then, startled, she saw frost run across the sand at her feet and spangle the stone by her hand.

She scrambled to her feet. Space seemed to close in around her, as though the infinite reaches of the desert had suddenly become bounded. She shuddered and groped at her back for the steadiness of rock, but flinched from the chill of the stone she found under her hand.

A voice out of the dimness spoke words Kes could not understand. Kes could not see the speaker, but turned her head blindly toward him. It was not, to her ear, a pleasant voice. It seemed to her to contain ice and ill will.

Another voice, deeper and harsher and yet not so unpleasant, answered the first. Men loomed suddenly out of the grayed light, closer than Kes had expected. Frightened, it occurred, at last, to Kes to move herself through the world; yet when she reached for that way of movement, for the heat and stillness that balanced motion, she could find nothing. A coldness lay between her and that way of movement. She tried to call out in the manner of a griffin, silently, for Opailikiita or for Kairaithin, but her call echoed back into her own mind unanswered.

The first voice spoke again and laughed. The sound made Kes shiver. She understood suddenly that the cold voice belonged to a mage, and understood as well that she was terrified of him. He was nothing like Kairaithin; though he was a man and her kind, she thought the man infinitely more frightening than the griffin.

The harsh voice answered, and a man, his dark form bulking large against the sky, came forward and laid a hand on her arm. Kes flinched, terrified, from that touch, and at this the grip eased; the harsh voice spoke again, but this time there was reassurance in its tone. Kes could not stop shivering, but her fear also eased and she stopped trying to pull away. When the man put his hand under her chin and tipped her head up, though she shut her eyes, she did not resist. The man spoke, curtly, not to her; then again to Kes. His was the harsh voice, and yet he seemed to be trying to speak gently. He shook her a little, not hard, and repeated himself. She realized, slowly, that the sounds of the language he spoke were not entirely strange, and understood at last that the language the man spoke was the harsh, choppy Prechen of Casmantium, and that he was Casmantian. That all these men were Casmantian.

Other men, farther back in the dimness, spoke—to the man who held her, or to one another, she did not know. The cold one said something, and Kes flinched again and quickly opened her eyes, afraid that she would find the cold man close by her in the dark. But, though dimly visible, he was not too near.

The man who held her answered the cold one, but absently. His eyes were on Kes's face. He gestured abruptly, and torches were lit and brought forward; Kes found her heart leaping up at the friendly brightness of the fire, though she knew her relief was not reasonable. Her shivering eased, and she found herself able to look at her captor more steadily.

He was a large man, not tall, but broad. His hand on her arm was twice the span of hers. He was clearly a soldier. He wore armor—rings of steel showed under his shirt, which was of finer cloth than a common soldier would own, surely. His features were strong, as powerful as his deep voice. He wore a short beard, grizzled with gray where his hair was dark, which made him look somehow harsher still. But his eyes held only interest and a little anger, not cruelty. And the anger faded as he studied her.

He said to her, speaking this time in the language of Feierabiand, "What is your name? How old are you?" He spoke carefully, awkwardly, with a strong accent, so that at first Kes did not understand him. But he repeated himself patiently. She was surprised, even in her fear, at his patience.

"Kes," she whispered at last. "Fifteen, lord. Fifteen this spring."

Heavy brows lifted, and the man said something in Prechen, sounding surprised. Then he said to her, speaking carefully, "A girl. A child." And something again to the cold mage at his back.

"She is a mage, my lord, no matter her age; make no mistake about it," said the mage. He spoke quickly and easily, his Terheien effortless. The light of the torches showed that he was an unusually small man; indeed, he was hardly taller than Kes herself. Yet he did not seem young—nor precisely old. Kes thought he seemed somehow ageless, as though passing years had touched him only lightly. He might have been forty or fifty years old— or a hundred, or a thousand. Kes would have believed he had lived a thousand years; there was a depth in his pale eyes that whispered of long years and hard-won power. His features were fine, almost delicate; his hair, worn much longer than the soldiers wore theirs, was frost white.

Despite his small size, the cold mage seemed very much assured. He was smiling. Kes would have shied away from that smile, only the other man held her so she could not. "A fire mage," said the mage. "So they found a child on the cusp of power who might be turned from earth to fire. Who would have thought it?" He reached to touch her face.

Kes shrank with a gasp against her captor, hiding her face against his chest from the threatened violation of that touch.

The lord of soldiers held still an instant in clear astonishment. Then he closed a powerful arm around her shoulders, gently, and said something terse in Prechen to the cold mage that stopped the other man in his tracks.

The mage spoke in Prechen.

The big man shook his head at whatever the mage had said, then shook it once more, a curt gesture, when the mage spoke again. He said something to the mage in his turn, and then again to the other men in a tone of command. The men fell back and turned away, making ready to go . . . somewhere.

"Come," the man said to her, but kindly. His grip on her arm eased and finally fell away. "Will you come? Not try to run? I not—I will not hurt you." He added as an afterthought, "My name is Festellech Anweiechen. My honor would broke, would be broken, to hurt little girls."

His clumsy Terheien was oddly reassuring. Or perhaps, Kes thought, it was the careful way he tried to reassure her.

"All right," she whispered, and took a step as he directed.

They took her high into the mountains, out of the desert. Her promise notwithstanding, Kes looked for a chance to break away from the men and flee into the desert, but her captors were careful and no chance came. There were horses waiting with more men a little distance away. Kes thought she might be able to get away when she saw the horses, but she was not given one of her own. She was lifted instead to sit in front of the lord. Kes did not protest, but inwardly she felt despair; she knew she was trapped as surely as any rabbit in a snare. She would never be able to leap from the horse without the lord catching her, and even if she did jump all the way down to the sand, she would never be able to flee on foot from men on horseback. She could do nothing but make herself small and quiet and hope to see the bright, clean flight of a griffin across the brightening sky. But she saw nothing.

It seemed to Kes that they rode for a long time, always up and farther up, but she thought afterward that it could not have been so long, for the dawn had not yet fully arrived when they reached the place where the desert border lay against the mountain country. The cold boundaries around her mind seemed to close her in upon herself, so that she found it hard to think. But she knew that the binding Kairaithin had put on her must have been broken, and this cold binding put in its place. She knew the little mage must be very powerful, and she was more afraid than ever.

When the hoof falls of the horses changed from the soft muffled thud of hooves falling on sand to the sharper metallic ring of shod hooves on stone, she looked up. The air had seemed cold to her since the men had found her in the shadow of the red cliff. But the cold was different now, seeming deeper, more a true part of the world. The cold mage sat back in his saddle, small hands letting the reins fall loose on his horse's neck, seeming to relax from a tight-held tension Kes had not recognized until it vanished. Everyone seemed relieved. Men all around her laughed and spoke among themselves. They took cloaks from their saddles and put them on. Festel-lech Anweiechen threw his cloak around Kes without a word, riding bare-armed himself. Kes slowly pulled the cloak around herself. One kind of cold eased. The other kind did not.

They had come much higher into the mountains, she understood, and had crossed beyond the farthest edge of the griffins' desert into country no one, neither griffin nor man, claimed. There was even snow, glimmering white in the pale morning light. Kes had longed to wrench herself free of the desert, but she had wanted to go home, not be forced to ride up to a snowy pass in the high mountains. Now she longed for the desert, but it was behind her, and felt miles farther with each step the horses took.

At last they came to a camp. They rode past rank after rank of tents without slowing, and she saw that it was very large. The tent they came to at last was three times the size of the others and had men standing before its door,

which was folded open to the night. They stopped in front
of this tent. Lord Anweiechen dismounted and held up his
hands for Kes as though she was a much younger child.
She bit her lip and took his hands carefully, allowing him
to catch her as she slid down the horse's shoulder. He took
her into the tent, seeming oblivious to her nervousness.

More men came in—some who had come with them
on the ride, and others, she thought, who had not. The
cold mage was one who came in. Kes recoiled from him,
but he did not approach her. She found herself whisked
instead to one side, to a pile of cushions thrown across a
thick carpet on the floor of the tent. Someone went around
the tent lighting lanterns. Someone else passed around
mugs of hot spiced wine, giving Kes a mug with a matter-
of-factness that made her take it. She sipped it carefully.
The spices were not the ones her sister would have used,
and a sharp homesickness, distinct from the fear that had
begun to ease, went through her. She bent her head over
her mug, blinking hard. Men spoke among themselves
and to Lord Anweiechen, who answered them cheerfully.

Then another man came in, and Lord Anweiechen rose
to greet him with a quick attentiveness that caught Kes's
attention. In fact, everyone rose, orienting to this man as
naturally as flowers turn toward the sun. He was younger
than Anweiechen, but not a young man: There was no
gray in his beard, but he was thickset and powerful. He
was clearly a soldier, metal showing at wrist and throat;
he was tall as well as broad, with a heavy, rugged face that
nevertheless did not seem cruel. Anweiechen spoke to
him, and he answered in a friendly tone and clapped the
man on the shoulder. So they were friends, Kes thought,
and this newcomer was also surely a lord; indeed, every-

thing about him proclaimed it. The cold mage inclined his head and said something to him, and again the man answered cheerfully, this time glancing aside at Kes where she sat among the cushions.

She could not understand them, and found herself looking down at the carpet on the floor. Except then nervousness made her look back up to make sure the little mage was not coming near. He was not. He had taken one of the chairs to one side of the tent, near a long table, and sat there, imperturbably smiling, with a mug of hot wine in his hand. He was not even looking at her. He laughed at something one of the other men said to him. Kes could not help shrinking from the sound of his voice.

The new lord noticed. He came over to her and stood frowning. Kes looked down. He said abruptly, in harshly accented Terheien, "I am Brechen Glansent Arobern. Do you know me?"

Kes mutely shook her head.

The lord tossed a wry look to Festellech Anweiechen and said something in Prechen. The older man grinned. Then the lord said to Kes, speaking slowly, "I am King of Casmantium. Do you understand me?"

Kes nodded cautiously, staring at him. He looked, she thought, like a king. There was a power to him like the power of the king of griffins. The other men in the tent moved around him with the same kind of awareness the griffins had for the Lord of Fire and Air.

"This *child* is a fire mage?" another man said, in slightly better Terheien. He also wore a beard—rare in Feierabiand—but his was brown verging on red, and considerably thicker than those of the other men. As though to balance the beard, his head was bald. Then Kes, blinking, saw that he did have hair, but that it was shaved very short all over his head. She realized she was staring, blushed, and looked down.

"So Beguchren assures me," said the king.

The man made an incredulous sound.

"She is indeed a fire mage," said the small mage, coolly, in his smooth Terheien. "Though new to it, I judge, and with nothing of the customary mage's training. The human training. A griffin mage must have woken fire in her when she was just on the verge of coming into her proper magecraft. He preempted the magecraft of earth before it could rise properly. Look at her shadow."

They all looked. Kes looked also. Her shadow, dim in the light, had been thrown out in several different directions because of all the lanterns. It swayed and flickered as the lanterns moved. Yet even Kes saw that it was edged with flame, that it stared back at the cold mage with eyes more fiery than lantern light. She blinked in surprise.

"So," said the king, in a thoughtful tone.

"I thought the griffins had no mages left," said Lord Anweiechen, his tone faintly accusatory.

"I, also," the frost-haired mage said mildly. He said to Kes, regarding her with composed curiosity, "Whoever he was, the griffin mage did you no favors, child. Did he tell you what would happen to your shadow if you reached out your hand to the fire?"

Kes did not try to answer. She looked helplessly down at the carpet, feeling very small, like a rabbit surrounded by wolves.

The king said something to the mage.

"Of course," he answered the king, but in Terheien. "I am not merely an earth mage, but a cold mage. Mages of fire and earth have a natural aversion toward one another at the best of times, but this girl has a greater antipathy toward me than she would even toward an ordinary mage of earth. She would fear and dislike me under far kinder circumstances than these, lord king." He hesitated, and then shifted to Prechen and spoke again.

The king frowned. He said to Kes, quite kindly, "Rest, child. Sleep a little, if you can. No one will hurt you. Certainly Beguchren will not." Then he turned away and went to the table, where some of the men joined him. An-weiechen took another of the chairs. Some of the other men did the same. Other men received orders from the king—that was clear from his tone and attitude—and left the tent.

One man came and stood near Kes. Like many of the other men, he wore a brown shirt with a black badge on the shoulder; metal links showed where the shirt laced up at the throat. He had a short sword at his side. He rested his hand on its pommel absently, but he did not look threatening when Kes glanced at him timidly. He gave her a brief smile, crossed his arms over his chest, and looked away. The understanding that he was a guard set on her by the king dawned on Kes slowly. But he did not seem unkind. Ignored by all the men, she even began to relax a little. Later still, she slept, and dreamed of flying through brilliant skies on pale wings that flung fire into the air with each downstroke.

CHAPTER 8

Bertaud found Iaor in his private parlor with his queen and only the barest handful of attendants.

The king gave Bertaud one assessing, incredulous stare and rose from his couch. Eles, behind him, cocked his head to one side and looked warily interested. Bertaud waited as the king murmured a word of apology to his little queen. He whispered something to her that made her blush and giggle, and she went out happily. She smiled at Bertaud as she left the room, a smile untouched by any faintest shadow of worry. She looked very young.

Keenly aware of his own youth and inexperience, Bertaud glanced after her. He found himself faintly aware of surprise that he had ever managed to be jealous of this girl, whom Iaor petted and reassured and dismissed like a child; the king had never treated him so—even when he had been a child. Now, far worse than the intrusion of the new young queen into Iaor's life was the new question of how much of Iaor's favor had ever been merited by a man incompetent enough to lose a hundred men and a mage in a single day's disastrous campaign. How much would be left, after this?

Gathering his courage, Bertaud told the king, in a few terse words, what had occurred in the griffins' desert, and how he had come to return to Tihannad alone. Eles, standing stolidly behind the king, jerked his head at a guardsman, who went out quickly. Eles folded his arms and looked grim.

The king, schooled from childhood not to wear his thoughts on his face, nevertheless looked stricken, to a man who knew him well. He slowly sat back down on the couch. Leaning his elbow on its arm, he looked at nothing for a long moment.

Bertaud hesitated, ashamed to ask for reassurance and yet unable to keep still. "Iaor . . . this isn't news I wanted to bring you."

The king glanced up. "Bertaud," he said after a moment. "I don't think you, or poor Jasand, can justly be held responsible for failing to anticipate what happened. It was I who sent a hundred men with spears and a mage, when it appears I would have perhaps done better to send you alone."

This was a far kinder judgment than Bertaud had expected, or was due. "I could have overruled both Jasand and Diene. I should have done."

"Why didn't you?" The king's tone still did not hold condemnation, only query.

"Iaor . . . I did not trust my own judgment in the matter." Bertaud hesitated, not knowing how to explain the confusion that had afflicted him in the griffins' desert. Not certain he wanted to try. No. He was certain he did not want to try. What he wanted to believe was that he wasn't obligated to try. But . . . Iaor would need to know what he faced.

After a moment, he said reluctantly, "That is not a comfortable desert for men. It is hard to think clearly with the red wind blowing. I mean that literally. I felt— I thought—this isn't easy to describe, but I didn't trust my own thoughts or feelings. The problem seemed—it seemed worse for me than for Jasand. And worse, or at least different, for me than for Diene. And as Jasand and Diene were in accord, it seemed better to trust their opinion than my own."

Iaor nodded slowly. "I will send you to Meriemne. She may understand the affliction you describe. Will you go to her?"

Bertaud hesitated. Diene had been . . . implacably hostile to the desert and the griffins. He found in himself a strong reluctance to face the eldest mage of Feierabiand and see in her seamed face the same hostility. But . . . the suggestion was only one step from a command, and if he didn't comply willingly with the one, he had no doubt the other would follow. He bowed his head obediently. "Of course, Iaor."

The guardsman returned, escorting General Adries, who had clearly been told the news. The general nodded grimly to Eles and took a quiet place to one side. The king acknowledged Adries with a glance, but spoke to Bertaud. "And so, now? What do you advise me to do?"

Alarmed, Bertaud shook his head. "Please. Don't ask me. I don't . . . I don't trust my own judgment even now. Truly, Iaor."

The king's eyes narrowed.

"You know what I will advise you," Eles said to the

king, and asked Bertaud, "How many men would it take to do the job right and have it done?"

Bertaud felt a strong reluctance to even address this question. But he had no choice, and answered slowly, "I certainly saw more than a hundred griffins. I would not be surprised if there were several hundred there. If we expected them to be clever as well as big . . . a dozen companies ought to be able do it, with mages to keep the fire and wind away from the men. If your majesty," he added to the king, "thought that wise."

Iaor propped his chin in his hand and gazed at them both. "Bertaud," he asked again, deliberately, "what is it that *you* advise me to do?"

In a way, this insistence could only be seen as flattering. But Bertaud dropped his eyes, for once uncomfortable with the trust Iaor showed in him. Since the king demanded an answer, however, he tried to form one. He thought of Kairaithin saying, *Agree, man, if you would be wise*. He thought of the great force contained, barely, within the powerful griffin king. He thought of fire falling from the air like hail, and the flame-edged flight of griffins across the dust-veiled sky.

He thought of Kes, her hand on the shoulder of her friend, saying, *I don't understand her, but she has a good heart*. He thought of Kairaithin asking, oddly wistful, *Will you think well of us?*

He asked, "What will your honor endure?"

The king, relentless, returned the question. "What should it endure? What will you advise me?"

Bertaud let his breath out and spread his hands. "Leave them be for their year. That desert can be reclaimed by time and rain. The land won't be lost forever."

"Is that what you advise me? Shall I take the rubies I am offered and let men say I traded the blood of my men for a handful of gemstones?"

Bertaud winced, though he had expected precisely this reaction. He thought of the blood of a hundred men poured out on the red sand. He thought of a frail, elderly mage, flung through the air by a careless blow from a great white wing.

He thought also of Feierabiand, with sly Linularinum on one side and aggressive Casmantium on the other, and how both neighbors would surely think, *How strong can Feierabiand be, if Iaor Safiad makes accommodation with invading monsters and will not fight them even when they take his land? If Feierabiand will not guard its borders from griffins, perhaps it will not guard its borders from us?*

He thought of the rumors that must already have run to the Fox of Linularinum and Brechen Arobern of Casmantium, and knew Feierabiand was endangered by the presence of the griffins in the heart of their country, even aside from the damage done by the desert they had brought with them.

Against this there was nothing but the voice of an unlettered village child, saying helplessly, *But it would be wrong to let them* die.

Bertaud pressed the heels of his hands over his eyes, sighing. Then he dropped his hands and looked up. "My king . . . I see that you have no choice but to drive them out. But *I* wish you would let them be."

The king sat back in his chair, looking subtly dissatisfied.

"Iaor . . . I understand that Feierabiand must not appear weak, lest Casmantium or even Linularinum become overexcited. But I don't . . . I don't think you should take what happened with the griffins as provocation, or see their simple presence as affront, or necessarily go to great trouble to be rid of them. It was our fault. My fault. It's no reason to spill living blood after dead."

"Theirs was the provocation."

"They couldn't help it, Iaor."

"They could certainly have acted with greater restraint once they arrived in our lands. *We* are not the ones who drove them from their own country. Their arrogance here does them no credit."

Bertaud made a frustrated gesture. "You asked my opinion, Iaor. I told you I did not trust it. But I would not wish . . . if you will permit me . . . I would not wish to make the desert our enemy."

"Is it not our enemy now?"

"Not yet."

The king conceded this possibility with a slight tilt of his head.

"I am sorry to disagree with the esteemed Bertaud, but if these creatures make desert of our lands or kill the cattle of our people, then they are our enemies. And if we permit them their depredations, we will look weak," Adries argued, contributing to this debate for the first time. Adries was a younger man than Jasand, a quieter man, less experienced in the field, not given to braggadocio or showy gestures. But he had a gift for keeping a great number of details in mind at once, and so was trusted by Iaor to keep track of all the military matters that concerned both borders. He added now, "Save if they yield a great tribute to your hand, my king; and even if they did, could we trust them? They are not creatures of earth. They are foreign by their very nature."

Iaor Safiad glanced at Bertaud and turned a hand palm up. "My friend, you must know this is true."

Bertaud nodded. He did know it. Bitterness filled his mouth; he did not even clearly understand why. "I never guaranteed them peace from you."

The corner of Iaor's mouth twitched up. "I should think not."

"I had simply hoped for it."

"I am sorry, then, that I cannot follow that course. I will send General Adries south. I must. Nor, though I regret this as well, will I ask you to accompany him when he goes."

And Bertaud knew that the king's regret was real. Not that it made the slightest difference. As a true Safiad, once decided on a course, Iaor committed himself fully. General Jasand was dead, but Adries remained. Iaor would send the younger general south, and spill blood once more to water the thirsty desert sands. Adries, warned by Jasand's example, would be cautious, but he would be determined: it was not likely to be only human blood spilled, next time.

Bertaud was grateful not to be asked to lead, even nominally, this second force. Grateful not to even be accompanying it. He *was* grateful, most determinedly. He would not allow his exclusion to feel like a slap; had he not repeatedly questioned his own judgment? How then could he blame Iaor for questioning it, too?

So he pretended to a calm he could not feel, and outlined the weapons of the griffins for Adries. Wind and fire; dust that stung and blinded . . . surprise.

"We shall have to summon a mage or two from Tiear-anan," Adries said, acknowledging this warning with a serious nod. "And I shall ask several of the mages here to accompany us. I think that will reduce the effects of wind and sand. And surprise is a weapon you yourself give to your opponent. We shall endeavor not to give the griffins that weapon a second time."

Bertaud tried not to read this last comment as yet another judgment on his own recent performance. He knew Adries did not mean it so. He was simply a straightforward, quietly competent man who was determined to redeem the honor of Feierabiand. Bertaud understood perfectly. That he could not desire the general's success with a whole heart was not Adries's fault.

Bertaud understood very well whose fault it was. He was furious with himself for allowing the singing clarity of a griffin's flight across a lucent sky to echo in his memory. But that night, he dreamed that he rode on outswept wings across fiery winds. In his dreams, he let exultant storms of sand and wind sweep him up to crystalline heights so dark and pure that even fire froze and shattered like glass . . . He woke in the morning startled by the earthbound heaviness of his own humanity.

Meriemne, eldest of all mages of Feierabiand, found his stumbling descriptions of the desert and the griffin and his dreams both interesting and troubling. She gave him tea and made him sit on the floor by her feet so she could rest the tips of her thin fingers on his cheek. Bertaud sat patiently, leaning his head against her knee. He felt as though time had scrolled backward and he had returned to this court as a boy of ten. Or as though that boy sat next to him, filled with fear and despair and barely acknowledged hope, not yet confident of the strength and constancy of Prince Iaor's protection. But in time, powerful bonds of loyalty and trust had grown between them . . . Had the man finally lost the trust with which Iaor had honored that boy? He tried not to even think about that question, focusing rather on the details of his encounter with the griffins.

Meriemne listened intently to Bertaud's recounting of what had happened in the desert, her blind old eyes aimed at his face as though she could see. She acknowledged, when Bertaud asked her, that a budding earth mage might, if caught just as her power began to flower, be twisted into other channels. "At least in theory," Meriemne said thoughtfully. "One can see how such a thing might be possible. That is technically quite interesting, but it *is* hard on the poor child. Does she know what long-term effects this, ah, alteration of her nature is likely to have?"

Bertaud had no idea what Kes knew, and could only guess what Meriemne meant. He shook his head. "I don't know, esteemed Meriemne. If it's true that earth and fire mages have a strong aversion to one another, then one would imagine it might be uncomfortable for a girl to be made into a fire mage when she ought to have been an earth mage?"

"Oh, the aversion is real enough," Meriemne agreed absently. "Natural affinities and antipathies are not unusual, you know. As the aversion of a songbird to a serpent, or the affinity of a raven to a wolf: There is a similar affinity between earth mages and young people growing into a gift for magecraft, you know; that's often the first hint of the coming gift. And then there is this deep aversion between mages of earth and those of fire. But no, I don't believe it will be uncomfortable, as you say, for the girl herself. More for those who love her, who find she has become something they cannot recognize . . . and a shame to lose her," the mage added more prosaically. "We can always use another earth mage."

But what had happened to Bertaud in the desert, Meriemne did not recognize.

"Not a deliberate attack," she said thoughtfully. Her fingers, cool and dry, moved across his face and drew away as she straightened in her chair. "Or I think not. It seems more an intrinsic response in you to the fire of the griffin. As the antipathy poor Diene experienced was intrinsic in her, and a mercy it is that only mages suffer such an aversion."

"I saw no sign that the griffin mage returned Diene's aversion," Bertaud said, suddenly realizing that this was true. "Or is it only earth mages who suffer it, and not mages of fire?"

"Oh, no, young man—the antipathy is a knife with two edges." Meriemne paused. "Hmm. This was an experienced mage, then, to rule his own reaction so well you did not even perceive it. Well, you say he took on human form. I wonder whether he is very experienced indeed with moving through the country of earth? Perhaps he has learned to recognize and compensate for the aversion? I would almost," she said thoughtfully, "wish to meet this creature. Though, on further consideration, perhaps not . . . You yourself did not suffer from the classic mage's aversion? No, indeed, what you describe is entirely distinct. Tell me, esteemed Bertaud, are you gifted at all? Have you an affinity for an animal? Or are you a maker? A legist?"

"No, esteemed Meriemne. Those of my family are rarely gifted." Though his father had held an affinity to hawks and falcons, and had been furiously angry when Bertaud showed not the slightest trace of any affinity of his own. Bertaud, wincing from the memory, did not mention that.

"Hmm." Turning her head, the mage stared into his shadow with her blind eyes. What she saw in it, if anything, she did not say.

"But the dreams?" Bertaud pressed her.

"Certainly the dreams you describe are unusual," the mage conceded. "I shall search in my books for such reactions."

With no guarantee she would find anything this year or next. And in the meantime—"What shall I tell Iaor?" Bertaud asked her.

"Hmm. Well, child . . . do you love the king better than you love the desert?"

"Of course!" he snapped, and then wondered at the instant offense he'd felt. Was it too sudden? Too sharp? A defense, perhaps, against his own heart? He dismissed the doubt at once, yet it returned, slipping uncomfortably around the edges of his thoughts.

"Then trust yourself," Meriemne advised serenely, either missing or ignoring this uncertainty, and he could not bring himself to give it voice and ask her advice. A baseless concern, anyway. An impossible doubt. Surely.

And so Bertaud went through the next days, and attended his king, and tried not to find the fixed stolidity of stone walls disturbing.

Three days after Bertaud's return from the disastrous field of battle, Iaor Safiad declared himself satisfied with the preparations for the second attempt to clear the desert from Feierabiand. But on that third day, Bertaud found, to his astonishment, that the griffins had not waited for soldiers to come to their desert. Kairaithin came to Tihannad.

Kairaithin came, unannounced, into the large conference chamber where Iaor and his advisors and General Adries and Meriemne and one of the younger mages in Tihannad were all gathered, discussing last-minute details of the impending military exercise.

It was dusk. The desert wind, Bertaud thought, had no doubt died . . . From the heart of that stillness, Kairaithin stepped into human time. His black eyes, pitiless as fire, swept across all of them, checked for the space of a breath on Bertaud's face, and settled on the king.

"Iaor Daveien Behanad Safiad," he said, and took a short step farther into the chamber. He bowed his head infinitesimally. "May I speak?"

The king was startled, but not, Bertaud saw, afraid or angry. He said, "You should have given your name to my steward. Did no one stop you as you looked for me? This is a private meeting. You should have been told the proper day and manner in which to seek an audience."

At first bewildered, Bertaud finally understood that the king did not understand that the man who had come so precipitously into this conference was not a man. He could not see, or had not yet seen, the fire in those inhuman eyes; he had not yet noticed that the shadow the lanterns cast back from his visitor was made of fire . . . He was blind.

It slowly occurred to Bertaud that all the men in this

room were similarly blind; even the mages were blind. The younger was looking with growing dislike at the stranger who had come into their presence, but Bertaud saw no sign in his face that he understood what he saw or felt. Only Meriemne, for all she was truly sightless, turned her head toward the griffin with a slow awareness in her old face. *She* looked, as yet, less hostile than simply distressed.

Rising so sharply his chair fell backward onto the stone floor, Bertaud found himself standing between his king and the griffin mage with no clear memory of having moved and no notion at all what he would do if Kairaithin intended harm to Iaor, or to any of them.

"Son of Boudan," Kairaithin said to him, pitiless amusement moving in his unhuman eyes. "So you have regained your place."

"Anasakuse Sipiike Kairaithin," Bertaud answered, and was surprised to find his own voice steady. "Why are you here out of yours?"

"Peace, man," the griffin mage said, turning empty hands forward. "I followed the path you made for me to speak to your king, if he will hear me."

Iaor had not risen, but his whole body had tightened. General Adries was on his feet, as were several of his officers. They were armed, and Bertaud could only hope they did not draw their swords and, with that, Kairaithin's enmity.

"The path I . . ." Bertaud cut that startled question off short, and said instead, "Iaor, this is the greatest of the griffin mages come to speak to you. I would suggest—"

The young mage, his face twisted in an expression of fear and aversion, rose suddenly and flung a binding of stone and earth at Kairaithin.

Kairaithin, not even blinking, sent the binding awry in a shower of sparks. He said patiently to the king, ignoring the mage, "King of Feierabiand, I have come to this place to speak to you on a matter of importance to us both. If you are wise, you will hear me."

Iaor gripped the arms of his chair hard. He was meeting Kairaithin's eyes, and even if he did not see the griffin behind the man, he would have had to be dead not to feel the power rolling through the air around him. He drew breath to speak.

Before he could frame a word, Meriemne shut her sightless eyes and turned her frail hands palm up on the table. The full gathered weight of the earth fell down upon Kairaithin as irresistibly as a landslide.

The griffin, evidently taken by surprise, had only a fraction of a second to react, and it was not enough. Then the stolid power of the earth rolled over him and crushed him to the floor. Even his fiery shadow was pressed out; it went out like a snuffed candle. Helpless, bound by the power of stone and earth, his restless shadow quenched and his black eyes closed, Kairaithin had never looked more human.

"Meriemne?" the king inquired.

"That," said the oldest mage, "is an unbearably dangerous creature, Iaor. Even from the esteemed Bertaud's descriptions, I had no idea . . . Do you not perceive it?" Her voice was the husk of a voice, barely audible. She had turned her face toward Kairaithin as though she could see him.

"He only wished to speak to you!" Bertaud exclaimed.

Meriemne turned her blind gaze toward him. A line appeared between her brows; she tilted her head intently to one side. She whispered, "I would not wish to . . . Iaor, I might bind this creature. Then you might speak to him safely . . ." her voice trailed thinly off as though she had simply lost the strength to speak.

Iaor looked from the mage to him. "He may speak to me," he answered at last. "Once he is bound. Bertaud— would you expect me to leave this powerful creature unbound in my presence? In this company? In this house? Will you say Meriemne was unwise to do as she did?"

"Not unwise," whispered Bertaud, and added more strongly, almost despite himself, "but wrong."

The king hesitated. "Do you trust your own judgment in this? Shall I trust it?"

Bertaud could not prevent a slight flinch that said as clearly as a shout that he did not know.

The king shifted his attention to Meriemne. "Will you release this creature from your hold without binding him? What is your advice?"

The mage opened a frail hand. "This creature is opposed to earth, Iaor. It cannot help but be opposed. I am afraid it would pull every stone of this hall down on every other stone, and burn your hall to ash. The stones want to fall just for its presence here. The very air wants to ignite. Can you not feel this?"

Her fragile voice held conviction. Bertaud shook his head. "That's the aversion speaking—she can't help but feel that way, Iaor—"

"Do you advise me from uncontrollable antagonism?" the king asked Meriemne. "Is your advice sound?"

The mage hesitated. "I think it is sound," she whispered at last. "I think so, Iaor. I know this creature is horribly powerful—and unalterably opposed to earth. I *know* that."

Bertaud stood wordless and helpless when his king looked deliberately back at him. What could he say? That the oldest and wisest mage in Feierabiand was wrong even in her certainty? What possible reason could he give Iaor to think so? He tried, nevertheless, to find words that might persuade him, persuade them all. None came to him.

The king looked back at Meriemne. "You can bind him?"

"Oh, yes," the mage whispered. "I will make you a chain with the power of earth and of made things in it; it will not be broken by anything that is not of earth. It will bind fire and air and the changing wind. With that chain, you may hold this creature safely in your hand."

The king nodded. "Make your chain."

She made it. She shaped the chain link by link out of a sword one of the guardsmen gave her, and out of the stone table itself. She made a link out of a delicate porcelain cup and another from a copper bangle one of the soldiers gave her, and another from a string of polished wooden beads. Into each link she put a power of solidity, of holding, of weight.

The younger mage took the chain reverently from Meriemne's hands when she was finished making it. It looked like an ordinary chain, but from the manner in which the young man lifted it, it contained the weight of the world. He fastened it around Kairaithin's wrists and stood back.

With a tiny gesture of her hand, Meriemne released the griffin mage from her hold. Then she leaned back in her chair and tucked her hands in her lap, trembling in exhaustion or in the sudden chill that seemed to invade the room.

Kairaithin lifted his head and got his hands underneath his body, drawing himself slowly to his knees. He looked at the chain that bound his wrists without expression, almost as though he could not actually see it. But when he got to his feet, he moved as though he felt its weight dragging at him. His shadow was . . . gone. Though the lanterns threw light across the room, and all the rest of them cast shadows . . . Kairaithin's shadow was not among the rest. Bertaud could not have said why he found this so deeply disturbing.

Kairaithin did not look at Bertaud. Nor did he look, even for an instant, at Meriemne. He turned his head slowly and looked straight at Iaor.

"If you have something to say to me," said the king, "say it."

Kairaithin's mouth crooked in an expression that might have been humor. "Now? Now I have nothing to say."

The king stared at him. "Griffin. Fire mage. Kairaithin— is that your name? What greeting was it you looked for from me?"

His answer was a slight lift of austere brows, and a dry, "You have there a man who has seen the heart of fire. You should listen to him."

"Bertaud?"

Bertaud gave his king a helpless shrug, unable to find words to express his belief that his king had made a terrible mistake in his—surely perfectly reasonable—defense of his own person and his people. He could ask only, "Let me take the chain off, Iaor."

He knew this was out of the question when he asked it, and was unsurprised by the judicious tilt of the king's head, *No.* It might even have meant, *I'm sorry, but no.* But it did not offer any yielding.

Bertaud turned to Kairaithin instead. "If you came here to speak to the king, then speak! Is your pride worth sacrificing the chance?"

Kairaithin returned him only a blank, incredulous stare.

"Take him," the king said to General Adries, "to the tower room; hold him there." And to the griffin mage, he said, "When you would speak to me, I will hear you."

Kairaithin stopped the general in his first step with merely his fierce stare. He said to the king, "Very soon you will have no choice but to hear me. But, I warn you, by then it will do you no good to listen."

Iaor's mouth tightened, and he waved sharply to Adries.

"Didn't you *hear* him?" Bertaud cried in frustration and inexplicable terror.

"Yes," the king said. "Tell me clearly what I should do to make him speak. Or do you truly believe I should release this dangerous creature in my hall? Everything he has said to me so far has had the tone of a threat."

I don't know! Bertaud wanted to shout.

He did not shout. He merely plucked the nearest soldier's sword from the man's hands, stepped forward, and brought the blade slashing down between Kairaithin's wrists, where it cut the mage-wrought chain that bound him as though the links had been made of grass stems. They spilled away in all directions, shattering into bits of metal and stone and porcelain.

Kairaithin did not watch the descent of the blade, but had stood quite still and gazed at Bertaud instead. His eyes held an odd expression, as though he had, for once, been taken by surprise and was having difficulty deciding on a reaction to the experience.

It seemed to Bertaud that everything was happening very slowly: That it had taken an hour to lift the sword and step forward, that it had taken a day for the sword to fall and free the griffin mage, that it had taken a year for Kairaithin to lower his arms to his sides. The eyes of the griffin mage held his, so that his vision swam with fire, its black heat all he could see. It filled his mind: a fiery silence as perfectly free of thought or emotion as the sun.

Then Iaor shouted and that odd sense of timelessness was shattered: Meriemne bent slowly forward in her seat and rested her forehead against her fragile hands. She did not try to renew any attack on Kairaithin. Neither did the young mage; he stepped back, and back again, face white.

Adries drew his own sword and lunged forward to put his own body before that of the king. All the officers had their swords out. Bertaud shut his eyes for a moment, his mouth dry. He let the sword he held fall from fingers that had gone suddenly numb. It rang on the stone like the stroke of an iron warning bell, sending echoes all through the room.

"Stop," the griffin mage advised them all, his tone not loud, but deadly serious. The general flung up his hand and all the movement of his officers halted, men stopping where they stood.

Iaor's eyes were on Bertaud's face. He did not speak. He looked far more astonished than angry.

For his own part, Bertaud did not think he *could* speak. He certainly could not think of anything to say.

"Ask me for protection," Kairaithin advised Bertaud. "I will grant it, if you ask me."

Bertaud moved his gaze from Iaor's face and stared at the griffin.

"Ask," said Kairaithin.

Bertaud swallowed. He looked again at Iaor. The king's face had gone stony, impossible to read. He looked at Adries, and the general's face was very easy to read. He shut his eyes, but nothing came to his mind save the desert and the brilliant sky.

"Yes," he whispered.

And the world tilted and widened; the walls fell away to an immense distance, and the fierce living heat of the desert crashed down around him.

Heat beat up from the stone underfoot, into a darkness ornamented but not brightened by stars: A desert darkness that had nothing to do with the lantern-lit halls of men. Kairaithin's strong hand caught Bertaud's elbow when, disoriented, he staggered. The grip steadied Bertaud until he had regained his balance, then released him.

Kairaithin, disembodied in the powerful darkness, said quietly, "I have been surprised many times by the unpredictable actions of men; not least tonight."

"Yes," Bertaud said, his throat tight. "I, as well." He wanted to weep, not for fear of the griffin, but for loss and grief. Iaor's face came before him in the blind darkness, set and hard; but the king's eyes were not angry, only astonished. Iaor had simply not believed Bertaud's treachery.

For, though Bertaud had not thought of it that way in the moment—he could hardly have been said to be thinking at all, in that moment—how else could his actions be described, save as betrayal? Bertaud thought he might dream of that look in Iaor's eyes for the rest of his life. He turned sharply away from the griffin, lifting his hand to his face to hide the shine of tears.

There was a short, tense silence. The griffin said finally, "I did not ask you to free me. I admit I expected you to speak for me to your king. I judged him by you and did not expect him to be a fool."

"He is not." Bertaud took a breath and tried to think past what he supposed, with some dispassionate part of his mind, to be shock. He said at last, "He did not trust you—your intentions, or your power. What man would?"

"You, evidently," Kairaithin answered drily. "I find that curious."

Bertaud said, "You've surely given no reason for trust. To Iaor, or to me." He turned and walked blindly several paces, until a sense of space and shape he had not known he possessed told him suddenly that the stone before his feet fell away into emptiness. He could not even find room in his heart for wonder at this strange perception. He asked the night, not turning, knowing the griffin mage watched him patiently from the powerful darkness, "Why did you go there?"

Kairaithin said, "I would have told your king that Casmantium has come into his kingdom. The Arobern of Casmantium waits in the hills just there, above our desert."

Bertaud, incredulous, turned. He took a step back toward the griffin. "What?"

"Brechen Glansent Arobern of Casmantium," Kairaithin said patiently. "And five thousand soldiers. Just there." He nodded to a point in the mountains, visible as a bulk against the stars. "It is as well the Safiad did not hold me, as I think he will have enough to trouble his days without my people striking as the mood takes them all through his lands, as Airaikeliu and Eskainiane would not be able to prevent them without my support. So you did well to free me, man."

Bertaud took a deep breath, let it out in a slow trickle. Then, unable to contain himself, he drew a second breath and shouted, "And you did not *tell* him about Casmantium?"

The griffin did not answer. He was not visible in the darkness, and yet Bertaud knew where he stood, even knew the hard, pitiless look that would be in his eyes, if he had been able to look into them. Bertaud shut his own eyes. He whispered, "You did not even tell me?"

The quality of the silence changed in some indefinable way. "I should have come to you, perhaps, man, and asked you to speak for me to your king," said Kairaithin. "That did not occur to me. And then your king offended me. I am sorry for that."

"Sorry!"

"Yes," said the griffin. "I am sorry for it, because my young *kereskiita* has gone into the cold hand of Casmantium, and I do not know now how I may get her out of it."

It took Bertaud a long moment to understand this. He said at last, "Kes?"

"Kes. Yes," said Kairaithin, and there was something in his voice that was not exactly grief, not precisely fear. "I did not know in time that she had come to the attention of the cold mages, and then it was too late. Now she is beyond my reach." He came forward and stood near Bertaud at the edge of the cliff, gazing out into the dark and up at the bulk of the mountains that rose above the desert.

"What . . . will that mean?"

"I hardly care to guess what it may mean." But the griffin's voice was weary, shadowed by something that sounded very close to despair. There was a short pause, and then Kairaithin touched Bertaud's shoulder—a light touch, oddly tentative. "You are tired." A low sound, not quite a laugh. "As are we all. Rest, then. Perhaps the light of the sun will bring clarity."

Bertaud could only hope it would. He had little hope of it.

CHAPTER 9

Kes woke, confused and afraid, nestled into a bed of cushions, with shadows swinging dizzyingly around her as quiet-footed men took down the lanterns and carried them away. She had slept, she understood, though surely not for very many hours. But the tent was filled with daylight. It was also nearly empty of men: Her guard was there, and the king, sitting in a chair with his long legs thrust out before him and a scattering of papers across the table at his side. The door of the tent was open, light and cold air spilling in across the carpeted floor. The light was nothing like the hammering brilliance of the desert. Kes looked at it, feeling lost and somehow bereft.

The king looked up as Kes straightened in her nest of cushions. He smiled, shoved some of the papers out of the way, and held out a powerful hand to her, indicating a chair near his. "Come," he said in Terheien.

The King of Casmantium looked younger in daylight, and yet somehow larger than ever, even though he was sitting down. He had clearly not slept himself, but energy radiated from him as heat from the sun: When he looked at Kes, his attention was powerful as a griffin's.

He was no longer wearing mail. His shirt was a soft ivory color that made the blackness of his hair and beard more stark by contrast. His hair was very short, but his head was not, at least, shaved completely, as some of the Casmantian soldiers seemed to do. He was not wearing any kind of crown, but he had a thick-linked chain of gold about his throat. It seemed somehow to suit his heavy features.

Kes climbed stiffly to her feet, brushing wrinkles out of her clothing as well as she could with her hands. She wanted a bath, a comb, and a change of clothing. There was no sign that she was to be given any of these things, at least not immediately. But it seemed the King of Casmantium did mean to offer her breakfast. Kes looked at the platters of rolls and sliced fruit on the table without interest and settled gingerly into a chair a little farther from the king than the one he had clearly meant her to take. She folded her hands in her lap and looked at the table.

"Kes," the king said affably. His voice was still harsh and guttural, but he could not help that, and he seemed to want to be kind. "Where is your home?"

Kes found her voice after a moment and whispered, "Minas Ford."

"You are fifteen, Festellech Anweiechen informs me?"

She nodded.

The king grunted and shoved a platter of rolls her way. "You look twelve," he said bluntly. "It is the shy way about you, I suppose. My mage Beguchren Teshrichten says you

are becoming a fire mage. He says you are half fire now. I
suppose that is true."

Kes supposed it was.

"Eat," ordered the king, frowning at her. "You are all
bone. That makes you look young also."

Kes obediently took a roll, nibbling it without appetite.

The king took one also and ate it in two bites, continuing to frown. He asked abruptly, "Why were you alone in
the desert?"

Kes had no easy answer for this. But she was afraid not
to answer. She said, ashamed of the timidity of her voice,
"I . . . I was walking. And . . . and thinking."

"Walking and thinking," repeated the king. His eyebrows had gone up a little, but he did not seem to find this
answer incomprehensible. "Humph. Minas Ford . . . are
there king's men at Minas Ford? Feierabianden soldiers?
I hear there was a battle and many soldiers of Feierabiand
were killed, yes? Did any survive, do you know? Or did
some stay in Minas Ford, or others come after?"

Kes blinked at him and shook her head.

"Humph." The king continued to study her. "Is Iaor
Safiad content to have *malacteir* in his land, then? Griffins, yes?"

Kes did not know what to say, or whether she should
say anything at all. It seemed best perhaps to say nothing,
but she was afraid silence would make the king angry. Besides, he looked at her so expectantly and so forcefully that
she felt she had to find some kind of answer. At last she
answered cautiously, "There . . . there was a battle. Yes. I
saw the place, after. It was . . . it was horrible. I suppose
there might be more soldiers there now. I don't know."

The king's eyebrows went up again. "Huh." He did not

say anything more for a little while, gesturing instead for Kes to eat.

Kes was not hungry. She made herself eat part of the roll, to make the king happy, and a small slice of white cheese. She did not want even that. Because the king did not seem unfriendly, she nerved herself to ask, "What . . . what is it that you want . . . in Feierabiand . . . lord?"

"A port city with a good harbor," he answered promptly, taking Kes utterly by surprise. "And if I can win one, perhaps a new province for Casmantium, hah? Terabiand has a good harbor. Your kings have always charged very high to use it. And the tolls on the mountain road are, ah, an insult, you know? Always the tolls go up, and the road is not even good."

Kes stared at him. "You can't . . . you can't just *take* Terabiand."

"I think I can," said the king mildly, or as mildly as his heavy voice would allow him to say anything. "And all that country between Terabiand and Casmantium, maybe all the way up to Bered and Talend. That would make a very good province. It would rival Meridanium, which my great-grandfather won, hah? You, well, you may be a problem, yes."

Kes looked down at the table, at the bread she had been slowly pulling to pieces with her fingers.

"Do you know . . . *did* you know that the *wanenteir*— the fires-mages of the griffins, you understand? — were making you into a *sandicteir*, a creature of fire? Did you know you must stop being a *sandichboden*, a creature of earth, to become a creature of fire? You would lose your *festechanken*, your human-ness, the part of you that is part of the earth. You would not be able to get it back." The king had tilted his powerful head to the side, frowning again, angry . . . on *her* behalf, Kes understood suddenly. She remembered being angry herself and wondered if she should be again, but the anger was dim now. Fear of the cold mage suffocated even the memory of anger. She only felt cold. She said nothing.

"My mage, Beguchren Teshrichten, you know? He says you are not all the way *sandicteir*. Not yet. He says he could clean the fire from you, he and my other cold mages. But you would fight him, very hard. So hard you might die of it."

Kes stared at him, horrified. The thought of that small, white-haired mage touching her in any way whatsoever made her feel ill.

The king propped his head on one hand, looking at her closely. "You would fight him, yes," he concluded. "You do not like my cold mage, yes? He does not like you either, little fire mage. He says it is a natural . . . what is the word . . . dislike, but stronger. Yes? So Beguchren is wise enough to leave you to me, which is best. I am not a mage at all. I like you, little *festechanenteir*. I do not like what the *wanenteir* did to you. Do you like it?"

Kes hardly knew. She knew that what the king said was true, that Kairaithin had indeed made her into something other than she had been. It felt natural to be as she was, to long for the sun and the clean desert, to reach for the stillness that lay at the heart of the flame . . . She reached out, on that thought, and flinched away from the cold barriers the Casmantian mage had put around her mind. She huddled instead into her chair.

"You should help me," the king said persuasively. "Against the *malacteir*, not against your own people; I would not ask that. But against the *malacteir*, why not? You have family, yes? A lover waiting for you, maybe? The *malacteir* would take those things from you. Did the *wanenteir*, the mages who began this change, did they warn you what they did? Help me against the *wanenteir* and at least the change will not go further. If you wish, if you want enough to be human, my mages can give you back your *festechanken*. They could take the fire out of you. You could endure their touch if you wanted it enough. Yes? I think you could. I think you are very brave."

Kes did not know what to say. She was afraid that everything the king said was true, and she did not want it to be true. She did not feel brave at all.

"Yes?" the king urged her.

Kes thought of Kairaithin, of the sweep of powerful wings against the hot blaze of the desert, the griffin mage's mastery of fire and air. His power. His austere voice, saying, *You are a gift I had hardly hoped to find.* He had made her feel . . . had made her know . . . had made her understand . . . her thoughts stuttered to a confused halt. Kairaithin was too difficult to think about. He had bound her so she could not go home, so she had to stay in the desert. She had been so angry.

Now she was too frightened to be angry. The cold binding Beguchren had put on her seemed so much worse than anything the griffins had done, even if it hurt her only because of what Kairaithin had done to her first. It might not be sensible to be more frightened of the cold mage than of Kairaithin; in fact, it might be *sensible* to do as the King of Casmantium said and ask his mages to tear the fire out of her blood—but it wasn't a matter for sense and Kes couldn't help what she felt. And what she felt, she realized bleakly, was that she would rather die than let Beguchren touch her. Except, if she could never go home again, that would be *like* death, wouldn't it? And would she *truly* rather accept that than let the cold mage take the fire out of her blood?

She did not even know. She whispered, almost blindly, "Why did you have to drive the griffins into Feierabiand?"

The King of Casmantium regarded her through narrowed eyes and did not answer.

Kes answered her own question. "Because you *wanted* them to make their desert in Feierabiand. So we would worry about them and not see you. But you thought you had killed all their mages. No wonder . . . no wonder you want me to help you. And then stop being . . . being a mage myself." She stopped, looking suddenly and fearfully at the king.

He had his chin propped on his hand, and he was smiling. That smile would have looked threatening, except for the rueful expression in his eyes. "Well," he said. "Not so much a child, are you? So you think behind those fire-lit eyes, yes? So, Kes, you must understand . . . if you will help me against the *malacteir*, that would be good, but I can do without this." He paused, and his expressive eyes hardened. "If you will not, well, I must have my own mages free to help me and not spend all their attention to guard me against *you*. So if you will not do as I ask, I will have Beguchren take the fire out of you. I think that is what I must do. Do you understand?"

Kes understood. She shrank into her chair.

"I am sorry," the king told her.

Kes knew that he meant it. And that he had meant

the threat he had made as well. She could not move. She longed, suddenly and desperately, for the brilliant silence and layered time of the desert—and then realized that she ought to have longed for her own home. But all she saw when she closed her eyes was the stark beauty of the desert. She tried again to cry out within her mind for Kairaithin, for Opailikiita. But her voice echoed within the barriers the cold mage had closed around her and she knew they would never hear.

"All your choices are hard," the king said, and sighed sympathetically, but with no suggestion he would change his mind. He stood up and gestured curtly toward the soldier who still guarded her. "That is Andenken Errich. He will stay with you, yes? He will not harm you. He speaks Terheien, a little. He will bring you water to wash, food if this does not please you. You may stay here or go out of the tent, walk around—Andenken Errich will go with you, you understand? No one will harm you."

"Except you," Kes whispered.

"Except me," the king agreed. "So think hard, little *festechanenteir*. Walk and think. I will send for you at dusk and ask you again. You understand?"

Kes nodded. Her throat felt thick, her eyes dry and barren of tears, yet she thought if she tried to speak she might weep like a child.

The king, frowning again, shook his head. Then he went out.

Kes looked cautiously at her guard.

The soldier looked sympathetic. He said in bad Terheien, "Would go out? Would walk? Is cold."

Kes thought of all the tents in this camp, of all the Casmantian soldiers there. Of how they would all look at her if she went out. They would all know she was the human fire mage their king had caught—the king's mage had caught, netted like a fish out of a stream. She felt as much out of her element as that fish. She wanted to cry. Her throat swelled; she blinked hard and shook her head.

But then the confines of the tent seemed suddenly as unbearable, and she jumped to her feet after all. She took a step toward the door and, hesitating, turned back to the safety of the tent—knowing it was not safe, that nothing was safe, but it felt safer than the outside world. She could hear the voices of men, the clatter of activity all around her. It frightened her. Yet she could not bear to stay still. She looked in appeal at her guard.

He seemed to understand what she felt, although Kes did not understand how he could. He went to the door of the tent and held the flap back for her. "Come," he said— not a command, but an invitation.

The guard took her first to his tent—she thought it must be his own, from the way the soldiers there greeted him. They called him Errich and laughed at him for being so lucky as to escort a pretty girl—Kes did not have to understand their language to understand that. He blushed, looking younger than she had thought him, and they teased him harder. But when Kes also blushed, they stopped teasing and became very solemn, although their eyes still laughed.

There were four of them besides her guard. They were all young, all earnest, and all very polite. Young men in Minas Ford would never have been kind enough to stop teasing just because a girl blushed—that would only have made them tease harder. Or, well, maybe they, too, would be gentler, with a girl they did not know, a prisoner whose language they did not speak.

Either way, because they had hardly any language in common, Kes didn't need to speak, and the young soldiers couldn't think her strange for her silence. *They* did not know she had been made into something not entirely human, Kes realized, and on the heels of that thought found it surprising that they couldn't see the fire in her eyes. She could see the earth in theirs.

They offered her bits of dried fruit, clearly the choicest food they had, so that she blushed again and, although she wasn't hungry, made herself nibble what they gave her. They brought her water to bathe, which was wonderful, and stood careful guard over her privacy while she washed. Kes washed very quickly, but though she half expected one or another of the young men to peek in at her past the cloth they'd hung up, none of them did. One of them had given her a clean brown shirt to wear after she'd washed. The shirt was much too big for her, coming down past her knees, making a kind of short dress. Kes looked doubtfully down at herself after she put on the shirt. It was certainly a *strange* kind of dress. She knew she must look ridiculous wearing it. Gathering enough courage to put back the cloth took longer than the bath itself. But what choice did she have? She couldn't hide in this tiny corner of the tent for the rest of the day. Could she? The idea was tempting. But, no, Kes decided reluctantly. Really she couldn't.

But when she at last came out into the tent, the young men didn't seem to think Kes looked ridiculous. They hid smiles at how far she had to roll up the shirt's sleeves, but that wasn't the same, and their glances were admiring as well. Although she blushed again, they didn't make Kes want to hide. One of them—the tallest—found a thin strip of leather and gave it to her for a belt, because all their belts were too big. Then all the young men went off somewhere, with much teasing back and forth, except Errich, who watched them leave and then gathered up his sword and a spear—Kes could not imagine he thought he would need them, but he took them anyway—and led her to the edge of the camp.

It took a surprisingly long time to go all the way to the edge. It was hard for Kes to guess how many soldiers there might be in this company. A lot, she thought, but she had no clear idea how many that might really be. The camp was far larger than Minas Ford. Most of the men had gone somewhere else—Kes could hear them in the distance, a shout of command and roar of response, and supposed they were doing something soldierly and probably violent. So there was no crowd of soldiers in the camp. That made it easier to look curiously around, to examine in wonder the neat rows of tents—for everything was neat and orderly, despite the rugged land in which the soldiers had been forced to camp.

From the edge of the camp, she could just see the desert. She longed for its heavy golden light. But of course Errich wouldn't let her go that way. She sat on a rock and just looked at it, as a little crippled sparrow might have looked at the wide sky it could not reach. Errich stood nearby and gazed down at the desert as well, a slight worried crease between his eyebrows: Was he thinking of marching down into it to face the griffins? Or of coming out the other side to strike into Feierabiand? What did simple soldiers think about when their king took them off into battle? Kes couldn't imagine what that might be like. She shivered.

Think hard, the king of Casmantium had advised her. Kes found it hard to think at all. She sat on the gray stone with her arms wrapped around her drawn-up knees, the sleeves of her borrowed clothing rolled up around her wrists, and stared at the boundary between the human world and the world of the desert.

Errich leaned on his spear a few paces away and waited patiently. Occasionally a soldier jogged past about some fathomless errand. None of them even seemed to notice Kes. They all looked the same to her—large young men in brown and black, with metal showing at neck and wrist, carrying swords or spears or bows. None of them looked worried. They all looked depressingly like they knew exactly what they were doing and what their place was in the world. Maybe Errich had only been thinking about Kes, who had been found in the desert and who so clearly wanted to return to it—was it clear to him? Probably. She hadn't tried to hide her longing.

The sun climbed higher, shedding little warmth across the mountain heights. Errich had found a place near Kes to sit down. He still seemed patient. He simply rested, his spear leaning against the rock where he sat, his hand casually resting on the hilt of his sword. But he was alert enough. Kes knew that if she got to her feet and started to walk down the mountain, he would stop her.

Men came and went in the camp at their backs, sometimes many men and sometimes only a few, according to some pattern of activity that doubtless made sense to Errich but that seemed completely random to Kes.

A soldier came up during one of the quiet periods, a big man like any of the others; Kes did not look at him. He said something to Errich, and her guard laughed and agreed. The soldier smiled. He started to go, turned back, said something else, and both men laughed. Then, leaning smoothly forward with a casual air, the soldier drew a knife swiftly and competently across Errich's throat.

Kes, shocked, leaped to her feet.

Errich, his eyes wide with horror and amazement, made it to his knees before the other soldier thrust him back and down. He could not cry out; with his throat cut, he could not even whisper. The blood ran down his chest. He made an awful choking sound as the life went out of his eyes.

The soldier bent down and closed the young man's open eyes, speaking again, a low phrase in Prechen. At that moment, the Casmantian language did not sound coarse or harsh at all. It sounded like a language meant for grieving, for sorrow. For loss.

Kes had not made a sound. She stood with her hands clenched in front of her mouth, her eyes wide, staring.

The soldier who had killed Errich straightened and turned toward her. She thought he would kill her next and knew she should run away, except he would catch her, and besides she couldn't move. Then their eyes met. For a long moment she did not know him, even then. But then she did. The big soldier—wearing the clothing of a Casmantian soldier as though perfectly familiar with it, with a sword at his side like it belonged there and a shirt of metal chain under the one of brown cloth—was Jos.

He said, "There is a horse," and nodded back the way he had come.

For another long moment, Kes was completely incapable of movement. Or speech.

He said impatiently, almost harshly, "We must be quick."

She shaped his name, without sound. But then she took the hand he held out to her and went the way he indicated.

There was indeed a horse, a very good one, black with three white feet and a narrow white blaze. It waited, ground-tethered, around the curve of the mountain, not forty feet from where Kes had sat with Errich to look at the desert. Jos gathered up its reins and mounted, and held down a hand to help Kes up in front of him. He was clearly tense, but also clearly far from panic. He had a plan. He meant to fold her up into it and . . . what? Take her back to Minas Ford and Tesme? She should want that.

Kes glanced over her shoulder at the camp, which was stirring briskly. No one, as far as she could tell, had yet noticed . . . anything amiss. She said, barely above a whisper, but clearly, "The desert. The desert is close, Jos."

Jos put the horse into a brisk trot north and west, angling down and across the slope, not quite parallel to the distant edge of the desert, but nearly. "We'll cut around above Minas Spring, avoid the desert—they'll be sure you went straight down into it. They won't think so quickly to search this way."

Kes rested her hands on the neck of the horse; its muscles moved smoothly under her palms. She had a strange feeling it should be feathers under her hands. "They will . . . will they not see us?"

"Men see what they expect to see," Jos said, his tone grim. "I have given them a thing they think they understand, and so they do not see anything else."

Kes didn't understand, but she nodded. She thought of Beguchren, waiting with his imperturbable smile and ice-pale eyes to take the fire out of her heart, and whispered, "I want to go to the desert."

"You don't," Jos answered flatly. His arms around her were tense. She felt him move to look back over his shoulder, then shift to face forward again. "You must not go back into the desert; I know it looks like the quickest way, but the *malacteir* will only find you again if you go there. They'll take you back into their power. You need to get home. You and Tesme—you can take horses, ride west. All the way to Sihannas, if necessary. You'll be safe there."

Safe, thought Kes. *Sihannas?* It took a moment for her to understand what Jos had said, as though he had expressed an idea so strange she could not wrap her mind around it. She opened her eyes at last, turned her head warily. The camp was still there, on their right, stretching on—a little farther away, but only a little. There were men moving briskly about, and yet no one had challenged them. She did not understand how they could slip so invisibly by the camp. She looked at Jos's mailed wrist, at his Casmantian uniform shirt. But if he looked like he belonged to this camp, surely she did not? But she did not ask. She only reached out to take the reins in her own hands and turned the horse firmly south, straight toward the desert.

Jos started to speak, a muffled exclamation.

"The desert," Kes said tensely. "The desert. Beguchren—Beguchren put a cold binding on me. The sentries don't matter—the men don't matter. Only Beguchren. Only the desert. Please. I have to go into the desert. The griffins—they will not harm me. You—you don't have to come. But I have to go."

He started to shake his head, a movement she sensed rather than saw.

"Jos," she said.

He stilled, his hands quiet on the reins, not fighting her. Then he shifted in the saddle. "What are you to the *malacteir*, Kes? You were a prisoner there! Were you not? Shall I not take you home?"

Kes started to say that she had not been a prisoner of the griffins. But she could not say that. It was not true. And yet it *felt* true. She knew perfectly well that she felt this way only because of what Kairaithin had done to her, teaching her to use fire, making her into a fire mage. But even though she *knew* this, she still felt, all through her bones, that fire was a natural and normal element for her, and that Beguchren's cold magecraft would destroy her. And besides—

She whispered, "They need me. They need me so much. And besides—" she touched her chest—"The cold. *Whatever* else is true or might be true, I can't bear it, Jos. I need Kairaithin to break the cold binding. Or Beguchren will find me. He'll know as soon as he begins to look for me where I am—" She shuddered helplessly. "I couldn't stand that. I couldn't. Please. *Please*, Jos."

Jos muttered a curse under his breath, turned to look carefully behind them, and nudged the horse into a slightly faster gait. Down the mountain this time, along a rough path that led almost straight for the desert. Kes shuddered again, in an agony of anxiety lest someone should shout behind them. No one did.

They came around a turn in the rugged path they were following and a man—two men—rose to stand in their way. One of the men had a bow, with an arrow already nocked, though not pointed at them. Kes uttered a small scream, but Jos seemed perfectly unmoved. He drew the horse up and spoke briefly to the men in Prechen, his tone matter-of-fact.

The men looked at Kes with covert interest, but their answers seemed respectful and somehow perfunctory. The one with the bow slipped his arrow from the string. Jos said something else, and the men laughed. Then, nudging the horse, Jos sent it on past them.

"Why—why don't they stop us?" Kes asked him, when she thought she might be able to speak without her voice shaking.

It took Jos long enough to answer that she thought he was not going to. But he said at last, "This is Lord Anweiechen's horse. Men know this horse. And I am wearing his badge. So they think I am his man, on his errand, and that is what they see."

Anweiechen's horse. The lord who had come into the desert with Beguchren to capture her. Hadn't that been Lord Anweiechen? Kes said doubtfully, "You stole Lord Anweiechen's horse?" After a moment, she added, her tone rising incredulously, "You knew his horse, to steal it? You knew his badge, to wear it? You have a Casmantian uniform. And you speak—you speak Prechen. I don't—I think I don't understand anything."

There was a silence, long enough for the desert to grow measurably nearer. But finally Jos said, harshly, "I am Casmantian."

"Yes," said Kes. That much was obvious, though inexplicable. "But . . ."

The horse tossed its head as Jos's grip on the reins tightened. Jos muttered a word under his breath, but he eased his hands and the horse pricked its ears forward again and quickened its pace. Jos said, in a tone flat and hard as the gray mountain stone, "I am—I was a Casmantian spy."

This didn't make sense. Kes blinked. She turned her head, trying to look at his face. She didn't understand what she saw: The glimpse she got of his expression was . . . different. It didn't even look like him, but like some bleak stranger. She said tentatively, "But . . . you worked for us. For Tesme. For years."

"Minas Ford," Jos said, in that precise hard voice that seemed so little like his, "boasts one of the finest inns between Terabiand and Tihannad. A small inn, but still. Men stop there. Merchants, petty lords, everyone. And they talk. To one another, to Jerreid. Jerreid can draw out anyone. He doesn't really listen to their private business when travelers confide in him. But I do. Did. Minas Ford is a good place for a spy."

Kes, unable to think of anything to say, said nothing.

"I knew when the Arobern brought his army across from Casmantium. I encouraged that young lord from Tihannad to do battle with the griffins; I watched the battle and saw that little army destroyed, exactly as the Arobern wished. I meant to bring the news of that battle to Anweiechen, who is master of the Arobern's spies. I did bring that news. But once I came here, I also heard of you."

And had freed her. Killing a man to do it. A countryman, impossible though that seemed. Kes shook her head slightly, incredulous.

"I—" said Jos, and stopped.

Kes could not imagine what he might say. Apparently, neither could he, because he did not finish his thought, but only pressed the horse to greater speed. When Kes looked cautiously back, she found that the Casmantian camp was no longer visible; it had been lost behind them among the gray stones and snow. She relaxed a little. For a few moments, there was nothing but the sound of hooves on stone and rough ground, the feel of the horse between her thighs, the solidity of the man behind her. Whom she had thought she'd known.

Jos had never pressed Kes to speak; silences between them had always been easy. Companionable. But this time, his discomfort seemed to radiate outward from his body like heat. He fidgeted in the saddle, turning his head to look behind them—there was still no sign of pursuit—then turning again a moment later. His hands shifted on the reins, then shifted again, until the horse tossed its head uncomfortably.

"You came for me," Kes said, not turning. And he was taking her toward the desert, even though he didn't want to go there or take her there, even though he couldn't understand why she insisted that she must go there. She had never understood gratitude, she thought, until this moment. She said again, "When I was a prisoner, and alone, you found me and freed me, when I thought no one would."

The quality of the silence behind her eased.

Before them, the red desert grew closer, until she thought she could feel its presence like a hot wind against her face, though the air was still.

CHAPTER 10

Bertaud did, despite all, rest a little. There was no place to sit or lie down other than the open cliff. He sat on the stone, leaned against more stone, and shut his eyes.

He did not dream of Iaor, which was a mercy and yet dismayed him even as he welcomed the fierce griffin dreams that came to him. He dreamed of rivers of burning liquid rock that ran across a jagged iron-dark land and cast droplets of fire into the air where it broke against stone. The air smelled of hot brass and burning stone. Soaring across a last ridge of broken black rock, he found before him a lake of molten fire; a violent joy consumed him, although he did not know why. Sweeping back his wings, he plunged into a steep, fierce dive straight for the heart of the fiery lake, knowing that when he entered it . . . when he entered it . . .

Bertaud woke, heart pounding, with red light in his eyes. He moved, startled, murmuring, and a hand closed on his shoulder. It took him a moment to understand that the hand belonged to Kairaithin, and that the griffin mage had stopped him from moving too near the edge of the cliff where he had slept. The red light was the dawn, the sun burning down across the slopes where the red desert rose to the heights.

He was, Bertaud realized as he pulled himself slowly out of his dreams, stiff and hungry and desperately thirsty.

Kairaithin did not look like *he* was stiff or hungry. He stood on the edge of the cliff, his face toward the rising sun, light and heat seeming to pour out of him as much as out of the sun. His shadow, the shadow of a griffin, molten and hot, shifted like a live thing across the stone, and fixed Bertaud with fiery black eyes.

Kairaithin turned, and his eyes were the same as his shadow's; he gazed at Bertaud with an air of surprise, as though taken aback to find a human man here beside him on this red desert cliff.

"You are thirsty," he said then, and a wry look came into his eyes. "I am not accustomed to providing for the needs of men."

"Is there—surely there is no water in this desert?"

"No." Kairaithin did not quite smile. The sunlight poured across the desert and lit an aureole behind him. His outline seemed to shift, or his shadow had risen up and stood beside him; he seemed now man, now griffin. He said, and Bertaud was not certain whether he heard his voice in the ordinary fashion or merely within his mind, *There is no water nor hope of water in this desert.*

Bertaud suddenly felt twice as thirsty. He shut his eyes.

Come, said Kairaithin, and the world tilted and moved.

The air was suddenly much colder—cold and fresh, with a clean living scent to it utterly unlike the smells of hot stone and metal that filled the desert. It struck Bertaud like a bucket of icy water. He gasped, opening his eyes.

The stone was gray and smooth underfoot rather than jagged. Twisted mountain trees clung to the thin soil captured by hollows and pockets of stone. Snow lay tucked into shadows and crevices. A thin trickle of clean water ran down a sheer stone face and gathered at its foot into a small pool.

Bertaud blinked at this startling, chilly world, and turned his head.

Kairaithin, in griffin form, lounged in pouring golden light not twenty paces away. Red sand flickering with delicate tongues of flame spilled out from the shadow of his wings. The desert stretched out behind him, running down the lower slopes of the mountain and vanishing in a bright hot horizon.

Bertaud looked back at the icy pool, and then lifted his gaze, following the sweep of the mountains up to the cold heights where the edges of gray stone blurred into a pale sky. He shook his head, bemused, and went forward to drink. The water from the pool was so cold it hurt his teeth. It tasted of the living earth and the promise of growing things.

Bertaud straightened, feeling that he might never thirst again. He dipped his hands in the water idly once more, and walked back toward the griffin and the desert with droplets of icy water spiraling around his fingers and sparkling as they fell to the stone.

Quite deliberately, Bertaud stepped from the pale light of the mountains into molten summer. The water on his hands evaporated instantly.

Kairaithin waited. His taloned front feet were crossed

lazily, one over the other; his haunches were tucked to one side like a great indolent cat. A slow breeze stirred the fine feathers of his neck and the longer ones across his shoulders. He looked very much part of the desert, as though it had brought him forth from red stone and golden light and the blackness of the desert night. His head turned to fix Bertaud with the quick unhuman movement of an eagle. But his black eyes were exactly the same.

Bertaud cleared his throat and gestured up the mountain. "Is that where the Casmantian troops are?"

Kairaithin tilted his head a little to the south. Light slid across his beak as over a sword blade. *There.*

Bertaud eyed the steep land the griffin had indicated. It did not look like it hid thousands of men. A close inspection yielded a suggestion of haze in that area that might have been the smoke of cooking fires. Or might have been simply haze. "The *King* of Casmantium is there? The Arobern himself?"

Do you doubt me?

Bertaud looked back at the elegant form of the griffin, at the fierce eyes. They were harder to read, set in the face of an eagle. He thought he saw a familiar hard humor in them. He did not see deception. He could not imagine a reason for this particular deception. "No."

You should not. Shall I send you back to your king to tell him so?

Bertaud thought of the look on Iaor's face when he had brought his stolen blade down across Kairaithin's chains and winced. And he had left his friend and his king for the desert, at the urgent demand of a griffin. "I don't . . . I doubt . . ." He did not know how to finish his thought, and fell silent.

*If I sent you to speak for me to the King of Feierabi-
and as my agent . . . as the agent of the Lord of Fire and
Air, if you would prefer . . . the human king could not lift
his hand against you. And then you might speak to him of
Casmantium. I might suggest such a course of action.
Would he hear you?*

"He did not hesitate to raise his hand against *you*."

He would not perceive you as a threat.

That was certainly true. Bertaud let his breath out
slowly. He did not want to go back to Tihannad to face
Iaor. He very passionately did not want that. He turned
the idea over in his mind, and said at last, "If I go back to
Iaor, it will most certainly not be as your vassal. Or as the
vassal of any griffin. Meaning no offense, O Lord of the
Changing Wind." On the other hand . . . he could not help
but realize that the griffins did most desperately need an
emissary. He winced slightly, thinking about that.

Kairaithin merely watched him, without sign of either
offense or understanding. Waiting, Bertaud understood,
for something more: something, perhaps, that he would
be able to understand.

He sat down on the hot sand and wrapped his arms
around his knees. "Perhaps . . . I don't know. Perhaps I
might agree to speak for you. As your . . . I don't know.
Not your vassal. I should never have let you give me your
protection. Potent though it undoubtedly is."

It seemed expedient at the time, Kairaithin said. *If I
misjudged and did you harm, I regret it. That was not my
intention.*

"You are not at fault," answered Bertaud, and sighed,
feeling the weight of guilt. He tried to think. "Maybe as
your advocate."

Casmantium is dangerous to my people; Feierabi-and is dangerous. Kairaithin turned his head, stared out across the reaches of the desert as though he tried to gaze through possibility and chance to see what he should do. For all the griffin's undoubted power, Bertaud understood that he, too, felt the press of limited, difficult options.

I must reclaim my little kereskiita, said the griffin, in the tone of one acknowledging stark necessity. *With her, we have choices; without her, we have nothing. You must help me regain her, man, and then we will talk further of human kings and armies.* Kairaithin rose to his feet, scattering sand; when he shook himself, the movement of feathers settling into place made a sound like the hissing of fire.

Bertaud, too, stood. He said, "But—"

He did not know what he might have said. A horse bearing a rider came at that moment around the curve of the mountain, checked nervously at the sight of sand and griffin, and then came on slowly.

The feathers on the back of Kairaithin's neck rose into a stiff mane; he opened his fierce beak a little and clicked it shut again, with a noise of bone against bone. He said, *Kes.*

"What?" Bertaud was startled. It was obvious to him that the rider on the horse was far too big to be Kes—too big to be any woman.

Kes, said the griffin. *And a Casmantian soldier.* His beak clicked again, a sharp aggressive sound.

"What?" said Bertaud, in an entirely different tone, finding this hard to credit.

But, as the horse drew closer, he saw that Kairaithin was right. A Casmantian soldier sat in the saddle, with

Kes, in an outlandish brown dress rather too short for decency, perched on the animal's withers in front of him. She sat with her hands resting on the horse's neck, leaning forward eagerly, like she might at any moment slip from the saddle and run to the desert.

Though she did not hold the reins, it became clear as they neared the desert boundary that it was Kes who chose their direction. When the soldier eyed Kairaithin and even Bertaud askance, it was Kes who touched his arm and spoke to him, and he—reluctantly, Bertaud thought—directed the horse directly toward them. And when the animal tossed up its head and balked at the searing, dangerous scent of the griffin, it was Kes who slid down to the ground, Kes whose word to the soldier drew him to dismount after her.

The soldier released the horse, which backed nervously, spun, and cantered back the way it had come. The soldier cast a glance after it as though he thought of following its example, but then he looked down at the girl at his side and followed her instead.

Kes showed no uncertainty at all. She ran forward, crossing the border between natural mountain and desert with the urgency of a drowning swimmer coming to the surface of the water and a lifesaving mouthful of air. She was barefoot, but showed no sign of discomfort, though the sand should have burned her feet. Barely seeming to notice Bertaud, she went straight to Kairaithin. Her pale hair was tangled and her eyes huge in her small, delicate face; she looked like a tiny child next to the griffin. Kairaithin bent his head down to her like a falcon bending over a mouse. Their shadows lay across each other on the sand, the griffin's made of fire, the girl's fire-edged.

The Casmantian soldier crossed the desert boundary more slowly, with far less enthusiasm. He looked at Bertaud, oddly, with more trepidation than he seemed to hold for the griffin. His face, coarse featured and broad, was perfectly inexpressive. Passing him in the streets of a town, one would perhaps think him simple. Bertaud sincerely doubted this was the case.

Kereskiita, said Kairaithin, ignoring the soldier completely, and stroked her face lightly with his beak.

"Anasakuse Sipiike Kairaithin," answered Kes, in her timid little voice, and reached, not timid after all, to lay her hand on the griffin's face just behind that dangerous beak. Then she drew back. "This is my friend Jos," she said simply, indicating the soldier, who glanced uncomfortably away from the searching look Bertaud gave him. Again, he seemed less worried about Kairaithin.

Bertaud found it difficult to imagine what Kes was doing, running from the Casmantian army in the company of a *Casmantian* soldier. Even if he could have thought of a way to ask, he doubted he would get an answer.

If he brought you out of the grip of Casmantium and back to me, I am grateful to him, said Kairaithin. The look he bent on the man was severe, dangerous, forcefully attentive. The soldier—Jos, if that was his right name— swayed under the force of it, going ashen. He did not look away from the griffin's stare; perhaps could not. For the first time, he appeared more impressed by the griffin than by Bertaud.

"He did."

Then I am grateful. The griffin had not glanced back at Kes, but continued to fix the soldier with his hard, black stare. He said to him directly, *I am in your debt. What will you ask of me?*

"Nothing," said the man, in a deep, quiet voice. "Lord."

Wise. Kairaithin's voice glinted with humor. He turned again to Kes. *You are well? I see you are bound.*

"Free me," whispered Kes.

Whose binding? Do you know his name?

"The little one. The white-haired one, with ice in his eyes and his blood. Beguchren, Beguchren Tesh— Teshrichten, I think."

Yes, said Kairaithin. *Beguchren. I know him. I know his work. He is very powerful, but now that you are come back to me, I can break his binding. Come here to me.* He lifted his head, his wings; fire ran suddenly across his wings and filled his eyes, his open beak. Fire ran down the fine feathers of his throat and fell, like the petals of some strange flower, to the sand. It burned bright and clean, without smoke; it made a sound like the hissing of wind-caught sand.

The Casmantian soldier stepped back hastily. Bertaud, too, backed away.

But Kes lifted her hands to the griffin's fire. She took fire into her hands, into her mouth; fire ran across her skin like water, blossomed in her eyes. There was a hissing sound, as fire meeting frost might hiss: Mist rose around the girl in a thin, drifting veil. She made a small sound that might have been surprise or fear or even anger, though Bertaud had never seen Kes angry.

The air chilled suddenly. Frost ran across the sand at the girl's feet, flashing brilliantly white in the stark desert sun. Kairaithin leaned forward and reached deliberately into the cold air with a feathered eagle's leg. He touched

Kes's face with a single talon. The sunlight that surrounded him seemed to gain body and spill from the air like liquid; it roared like a bonfire. Both Bertaud and the Casmantian soldier took another step back.

Again, Kes made a wordless sound, this one definitely both angry and frightened. She had crouched a little, and now sank down to her hands and knees and buried her hands in the red sand. Fire hissed across the sand and rippled up along her wrists. She bowed her head over the flames as a normal girl might bend over a friendly little campfire. Kairaithin made a sharp gesture with his head and flexible eagle's neck as though he were throwing something into the air from his beak. He *had* thrown something, something small and bright and—Bertaud thought—deadly. Whatever it was, it left a delicate trail of tiny sparks as it flashed away, back the way Kes had come. Sparks fell glittering to the ground, sparkling now as they became—Bertaud looked more closely—minute fire opals and specks of gold. He took a deep breath of the hot air and looked up again.

Kairaithin was standing perfectly still, looking not after the thing he had cast away, but at Kes. The girl was still kneeling on the ground, her face tilted up to the sunlight. Light poured over her, thick and golden as honey. She swayed suddenly and shut her eyes, then opened them. They were filled with light; tears of fire ran down her cheeks, but she did not seem to be in distress. In fact, she shivered all over and then smiled and sat back on her heels.

Beguchren has lost his binding, said Kairaithin. He folded his black-barred wings and sat down on the sand with a satisfied air.

"I know," answered Kes. She looked away, up the mountain, gray and cold, to where the snow lay on heights. "He will know it, too."

Oh, yes. The griffin's tail lashed across the sand, one quick motion.

"Soldiers," the Casmantian said suddenly, jerking a hand toward the boundary between the normal mountain chill and the desert.

There were: To his chagrin, Bertaud had not seen them until the Casmantian had pointed them out. They were far away, but coming fast. Quite a few men. *That* was not good. And neither he nor—he looked quickly—Jos had anything more than a knife.

Beguchren Teshrichten is among them, said Kairaithin.

"Then why are we still here?" Bertaud asked urgently. The Casmantians had put their horses into a gallop; he saw arrowheads glitter in the pale morning light. The first arrows arched high and began to fall.

There will be an accounting between us, said the griffin. *But you are correct, man. It cannot be yet.* The world tilted dizzyingly around them—then tilted back. Bertaud flung a hand out for balance, staggering. He had expected Kairaithin to move them far back into the desert, but when his sight cleared he found that they were still at its very edge. And the Casmantian soldiers were moving even faster now, if that was possible.

Beguchren prevents me, said Kairaithin.

An arrow whipped past Bertaud's face and buried itself for a third of its length in the sand at his feet. He took an involuntary step backward and cursed, shaken. Nearby, the Casmantian, Jos, drew his knife as though he seriously meant to face down several dozen Casmantian horsemen with nothing but that. Other arrows fell around them, though none so close as the first. Then arrows started bursting into flame as they flew, burning to ash and blowing away on the hot wind.

Well done, Kairaithin said to Kes.

"Five minutes and they'll be on us," said Bertaud to the griffin mage, drawing his own knife. "Or less."

"Less," said Jos, tersely.

Kairaithin half spread his immense wings. Flames rose, pale in the brilliant sunlight, at the edge of the desert. The racing horses, almost too close to the fire to stop, shied away to either side so violently that two of their riders fell. One fell into the flames and sprang up instantly, running blindly toward them, his clothing on fire, screaming in a horrible high-pitched voice. Kes covered her eyes, crying out herself, and the man crumpled almost at their feet, no longer burning.

Jos, without a word, took the man's sword. There was no sign now that the man had ever been burned, though his uniform was charred. Kes knelt on the sand near Kairaithin, eyes wide with terror, looking tiny and young and entirely helpless.

Kairaithin said, *Beguchren is trying to smother my fire*. The griffin had ringed them with fire, a towering but thin circle of wavering flames. As Bertaud watched, the circle narrowed perceptibly. The heat pouring off it was incredible. If they hid behind its protection for very long, he doubted either he or Jos would survive the experience.

"Who is stronger? You or Beguchren?" Bertaud asked Kairaithin.

In this desert, I. But if I set myself against the cold mage and break his hold, I will not have sufficient attention to spare to prevent the men from coming against you. And I will be too busy with Beguchren to defend either you or myself from them.

"Then you'll have to let them past and hope we can keep them off you long enough. It would be nice if you didn't take too long with Beguchren." Bertaud stepped forward to put himself shoulder to shoulder with Kes's Casmantian friend, in front of Kes and Kairaithin. He added, "I'll need a sword."

"Yes," said Jos.

The circle of fire died. Bertaud could tell which of the men outside that circle was Beguchren, not only because the cold mage, small and white haired and finely dressed, looked nothing like a soldier, but also because he stopped in midstep and put his hands over his face, looking like a man under a terrible strain.

Besides, he wasn't carrying a sword. Well, so slight a man wasn't likely to do well in a sword fight, but he wasn't carrying even a bow. No doubt being weaponless was less of a handicap for the cold mage than for Bertaud.

The first three Casmantian soldiers came in at them in a rush: Swords, not arrows, which was good; so Kes had done that much for them by burning the earlier arrows.

Bertaud threw his knife at the first man, and a handful of sand at the second—Jos lunged forward and killed the first man as he ducked away from the flung knife, and engaged the other two while Bertaud got the first one's sword; Bertaud flung himself down, rolling under a stroke from a fourth soldier and barely making it back to his feet in time to block a slashing blow from a fifth.

The fifth soldier was a heavily built bald man with tremendous reach and plenty of weight to put behind his attacks. He also proved to be, unfortunately, extremely fast on his feet and uncommonly good with a sword. Bertaud backed up rapidly, half running, trying to prevent the rest of the Casmantian soldiers from coming at his back while he worked to keep his opponent from eviscerating him, and also tried to draw the soldiers away from Kairaithin. He was peripherally aware of Jos at the center of a knot of Casmantian soldiers, he had lost track of Kes entirely, and what *was* Kairaithin *doing*? The griffin mage seemed to be taking an unconscionable time about getting them all out of this.

The attempt to draw off the Casmantian soldier had certainly worked . . . a little too well. The bald soldier was backed up by two others, both uncomfortably skilled. The bald man aimed a slashing blow at Bertaud's face, then brought his sword around in a smooth arc, terribly fast, in a reversed cut at his chest while his companions circled in either direction around Bertaud. Bertaud blocked both attacks, the second one just by a hair, and attacked straight ahead to get out from between the other two soldiers. The bald Casmantian met his attack without giving back more than a step or two; the force of their swords clashing together reverberated through Bertaud's whole body.

He feinted at his opponent's lightly armored legs, tried a real thrust at his belly, and was forced to leap sideways to avoid the aggressive attack of one of the others, a much younger man with silver-chased armor—he dropped to one knee under a wickedly fast attack of the young one, swept his sword in a circle to force all his attackers back, lunged to get to his feet, and the bald Casmantian made a quick sideways rush, and this time Bertaud did not manage either to block or avoid the blow.

It was like a kick from a horse against his side: There was no sense at first of being cut. That would, Bertaud knew, come. He felt no pain, yet. That would come, too. He tried to get back to his feet and found no opposition—a measure of how badly he was hurt, that his opponents backed away and did not try to re-engage. Another, that he could not after all manage to get up. He found, to his surprise, that he no longer seemed to be holding his sword. He touched his side and felt moisture; he could not bring himself to look down, and looked up instead.

He saw Kairaithin, surprisingly close, rearing up, his red-chased black wings immense against the brilliant sky. He was aware of Kes, huddled by the griffin's leonine feet, looking tinier than ever. He thought Jos was still fighting—good for him—although he was aware of a faint and foolish embarrassment that he'd gone down before the other man. As though that mattered. He wondered whether Kairaithin was still too much engaged with Beguchren to protect himself from the soldiers. Bertaud had not managed to do much to reduce that danger. Nor would Jos, probably. Bertaud could not see the cold mage anywhere. Was that a good sign? It was obvious that neither Bertaud nor, soon, Jos was going to be able to protect the griffin or Kes much longer.

He thought he saw Kairaithin come down to all fours, wings spreading out to cover the whole sky, darkness blotting out sun and light and heat alike . . . and then the light returned, pouring across him with an intensity that was almost pain. He was blind with light, filled with light and heat, he felt his very bones had turned to light and burned through his body. Gasping, he lunged upward and found himself caught and held. For an instant, remembering battle, he tried to fight. A voice, soft and delicate, spoke words he did not at once understand, and the constraint disappeared. So he got an elbow under himself and pried himself up at least far enough to look around.

Kes, sitting back on her heels beside him, sighed, relaxed, stretched, and got to her feet.

Bertaud blinked, and blinked again, trying to clear his eyes of light enough that he could see. The measureless desert stretched out in all directions. Red cliffs and spires twisted upward all around them, reaching narrow jagged fingers to the hard sky. Heat poured down upon them so forcefully that it might have possessed weight and body.

If Bertaud was disoriented, Kes was not. She now stood poised, looking at once timid and confident, close by Kairaithin's side. Her fine soft hair fell around her face, sun glowing through it; it might have been spun of pale light. A warm light seemed to glow through her skin, as though it contained fire rather than flesh. Possibly she would have been an earth mage save for Kairaithin's intervention, but she looked now as though she had always been meant to be a mage of fire. She looked, in fact, as Kairaithin did when he wore the form of a man: like nothing that had ever been human.

Jos sat on the sand near Bertaud, in the shadow of a twisted red rock, not looking at any of them, but outward at the desert. Bertaud followed his gaze.

All around them, among the spires of rock, lounging on the hot sand or on rugged ledges, were griffins. Golden and bronze, warm rich brown and copper red; pale as the edges of a candle flame or darkly red as the last coals of a smoldering fire, they sprawled in the sun like cats and stared into the brilliant light with eyes that were not blinded. Only a few appeared to acknowledge the arrival of Kairaithin or Kes or human men in their midst.

Kes looked at Bertaud, glanced at Jos, shook her head, and raked her fingers absently through her hair. They moved again, the world tilting around them. Bertaud realized with a shock that it was the girl and not the griffin mage who had moved them this time. That she had done it as a griffin mage would: With a thought, with a shifting of the stillness of the desert. They stood suddenly in the stark black shadow of a broken cliff. The contrast of the shadow with the relentless pounding sun out in the open was dizzying.

Bertaud gasped, catching his balance with an outflung hand against the stone wall. He did not try to get up, but leaned his head back against the cliff wall and shut his eyes.

The Casmantian soldier, who had gotten to his feet, sat back down as well, with slow, careful movements.

Kairaithin lay down, stretching out like a cat. He appeared amused, although Bertaud could not have said why he had such an impression. Bertaud asked him, "Beguchren?"

Retreated, answered the griffin, with obvious satisfaction. *This day was mine*. And, after a moment, with a little tip of his fierce eagle's head, *Ours*.

Bertaud nodded back to him and said to Kes, "That's twice you've saved my life, I think. Thank you."

Kes gave him a quick shy smile, but she seemed more edgy and nervous now than she had during the fight. She paced hurriedly from one edge of the shadow to the other, unable to settle. She said, "I used fire. It was much easier this time."

Of course, Kairaithin told her. *You do very well, kereskiita. You are quick to learn and powerful in your gifts.*

Kes turned to the griffin. "The Casmantian king said I was—was—I don't know the word—*festech*-something."

"Festechanenteir," said Jos, not looking up.

"Yes—*festechanenteir*. That means a fire-mage who is also human. Isn't that what it means?"

Yes, agreed the griffin.

Near Bertaud, Jos glanced up at Kes and then looked away again. Her friend, she had said, with no explanation of how she had made a friend of any Casmantian soldier. The man did not seem inclined to explain.

"My heart is turning to fire, my bones to red stone. Why didn't you *tell* me?" Kes asked Kairaithin. Her voice rose; she might have been happy to get away from Begu- chren and back to the desert, but now that she felt her- self safe, and despite her apparent shy timidity, she was clearly angry. "I knew you were teaching me to love fire. But I didn't know you were teaching me to forget earth! Why didn't you *tell* me what you were doing to me?"

Jos turned his head away and shut his eyes. Bertaud, though most of his attention was on the girl and on Kairaithin, studied the Casmantian curiously.

Should I have? Should I have said, "You should be an earth mage, you would wake into your power at a touch, but if you reach for fire now, you will become fire? Your heart will become fire, your breath will become desert wind?"

"Yes!" Kes cried. "Shouldn't you? Why should you not?"

Think, said Kairaithin, patient and pitiless as the sun. *I might have told you, "Take what I give you, do as I teach you, and you will lose what you are and become something other." You would have fled me and fought me and wasted your strength struggling against the fire, until I would have been forced to compel you by threat to obey me. I would have killed your sister's horses, one by one. And then I would have killed your sister's servants. And then I would have killed your sister. Would you have withstood all that I would have done?*

Kes stared at him, her anger smothered by shock and fear. She should have been weeping. Her eyes were dry as the desert. She whispered, "I would not even have been able to bear the horses."

So. And then you would have become fire all the same.

Bowing her head, the girl whispered, "I would rather have known what it was I was losing."

You do know, now. Does this knowledge please you? Kereskiita, you will become other than human. Already fire rather than earth sustains you. You have no thirst, no hunger; though you may be weary, it is not with the weariness of men. Does it profit you to know this?

Kes did not answer. Perhaps she could not. She looked down at the sand beneath her feet, her breath catching. Tears fell at last, flashing in the sun and rolling in the sand, fire opals and carnelians. Kes dashed jewels away from her face and turned her back on them all.

I would give you a choice, if I could.

Unexpectedly, Jos moved. He got up and took a step forward, coming up close behind the girl. With startling familiarity, he laid his broad hands on her shoulders and turned her to face him, giving her a little shake to make her lift her head. With unexpected eloquence he said, "Kes, this *wanenteir* would have you believe you have already given up your humanity. But you have not. You use fire; fire flows through your hands and your eyes and your heart and you think you are made of fire. But you are not. You were born to use the magecraft of earth. You should gather earth into your hands; you should use earth and metal and human magecraft until there is no room left in your heart for fire. You can do this. Would you abandon earth? Forget Tesme? She certainly won't forget you. She thinks of you all the time, she watches the hills all the time, she still hopes you will come back to her. What you choose now is what you will become. But it is still your choice. Won't you come back?"

Kes stared up at him.

Kairaithin said, *You are mistaken, man. Have you not been listening? She has no choice, for I will give her none.*

Jos didn't even look at the griffin, but only at Kes. He said, "You need her. You need her goodwill, lord *malacteir*. Or how should your people stand against even Feierabiand, far less Casmantium? You found her and you made her and you intend her now to be your weapon, but if she will not, then you are lost. I know this, and you know it, and if *Kes* understands it, she will be proof against any threat you can make—"

Be quiet. Or it is you I will kill, said the griffin.

"No," said Kes. Her voice was thin and shaky, but she turned quickly to stare at Kairaithin, and her eyes, though enormous in her delicate face, held in them a resolve that Bertaud had not expected.

Kairaithin tipped his head to the side, studying the girl out of one fierce black eye. His expression was not readable. But he did not threaten Jos again. He said to Kes, *In a hundred years perhaps you will have the strength to challenge me. But I assure you, you do not have that power today, and you will do as I choose and not as you would choose.*

"I trusted you," Kes whispered.

Do you not understand that my need is too great to allow me to be trustworthy? I will permit neither Casmantium nor Feierabiand to destroy what remains of my people. The choice you have is whether to suit your power to my need by your own choice or by mine. That is all the freedom you have. Kairaithin paused. No one spoke. The desert wind brought the dry scents of dust and stone and heat into the dark shadow of the cliff.

It is not a terrible thing, to be a creature of fire, the griffin added, his tone almost wistful. He angled his head sharply downward; his beak opened and clicked cleanly shut. Fire ran through his eyes, and he went suddenly elsewhere, leaving three humans who should never have been in this foreign desert to stand alone in the shadow.

Kes sighed sharply and sat down rather suddenly, her legs folding under her. Her thin hands trembled. She closed them into fists and stared blindly at the sand. The Casmantian soldier sat down more slowly next to her, and she leaned against him and turned her face into his shoulder.

"Who *are* you?" Bertaud asked him, bewildered anew by the familiarity between the soldier and the girl.

The soldier sighed. "No one," he said.

Kes straightened and wrapped her arms about her drawn-up knees. She said, in a small, weary voice, "He . . . he works for Tesme. My sister. But . . ." Her voice trailed off.

"I was once a soldier of Casmantium," the man said. He met Bertaud's eyes, flatly refusing anything further.

Then his eyes dropped back to rest on the girl's face, and he shook his head. "Better I had left you with the Arobern. He would not have harmed you."

"He would have," Kes whispered. "Don't you understand? His need would have been too great to allow him to be kind." She shut her eyes.

"I—" said Bertaud. "You—"

Neither of them even glanced at him. Jos touched her chin with a fingertip, turned her face up toward his. The girl opened her eyes again, surprised. Jos said gently, "He would have made you human again, and that would have been a good thing. Kes, that creature was trying to frighten you, and I suppose he did—he frightened me— but, look, he can't force you to use fire. To become a creature of fire. Either you will or you won't, and truly, the griffin's need is a weapon in *your* hand. Why else should he have tried to silence me? All you require is the courage to use your own strength."

Kes gazed at him wordlessly.

Jos dropped his hand to rest on his knee. But he spoke with even more intensity. "You've always been braver than anyone would think, to look at you. Braver than you've thought yourself. You can make them believe no threat will move you, if you try. The *malacteir* need you. You don't need them. The sword is in *your* hand."

"But threats can move me," whispered Kes, "if they are the right threats." She sounded very tired. "And, Jos . . . what if I want the fire? I ought to want to go home, and sometimes I do want that, but the fire is so beautiful. What if I forget to want anything but fire?" She closed her eyes and tipped her head up toward the hard sky. Again Bertaud thought there should be tears; he heard them in her voice. But this time no tears glittered into jewels down her face.

The man gripped her shoulder, giving her a tiny shake. "And Tesme? Meris? Nehoen? All those who searched for you when you vanished into the desert? *They* are your people. Minas Ford is your home. Would you turn away from them forever?"

"I don't know," the girl whispered. She paused and then confessed in an even smaller voice, "Sometimes I forget even *Tesme*. I'm sorry, I'm sorry she's worried for me, I knew she would worry, I don't know how I can forget, but sometimes . . ."

"Then I'm sorry, too." Jos touched her cheek with the tips of two fingers, then dropped his hand again, slowly.

Bertaud came a step forward, dropped to one knee to put himself at the girl's level, and asked her quietly, "And Casmantium?"

Kes opened her eyes. Both she and Jos looked at Bertaud as though he had spoken words in a foreign language neither of them understood.

"An army of Casmantian soldiers in the mountains, poised to come down across Minas Ford and all Feierabiand? Is this not a matter of concern? Do you not wonder about Casmantium's intentions?"

"Oh," said Kes. And answered very simply, "No, I know what Casmantium wants. The king told me. He wants a new province. He wants a port city with a good harbor."

"Terabiand," said Bertaud, appalled.

Kes nodded. "And not to pay the toll on the road. And he says the road is bad. But I think really what he wants most is Terabiand. And as much other land as he can take."

"And all Iaor knows is that griffins have made a desert

here. He will come down from Tihannad, expecting nothing but griffins, and he will find the desert on one side and
Casmantium on the other."

"You can warn him," the girl said, not understanding. "Kairaithin would take you to him, I think. He
would . . . surely he would rather soldiers of Feierabiand
fought Casmantian soldiers than came against his own
people. Or I . . . I could ask Opailikiita to take you to him,
if Kairaithin will not. I think she would, if I asked her."

"I think," Bertaud said bitterly, "that probably if I have
the temerity to approach Iaor after the way I left him, he
will have me arrested."

The Casmantian soldier gave Bertaud a narrow look at
this, but Bertaud did not care. He was consumed suddenly
by a disbelief in all the events of the past hours. It seemed
incredible that a griffin should have come to Tihannad,
that in order to free him, Bertaud should have renounced
the loyalty that meant more to him than life itself. Again,
the image of Iaor's face in that moment of betrayal came
before his eyes. He flinched from that image, staring instead out into the desert, trying to let the brilliance drive
that memory away. Despite everything he could do, it
lingered.

Though . . . if he had not freed Kairaithin . . . he
would still be in Tihannad, and no one in Feierabiand
would know yet that Casmantium had come across the
mountains. It was clear what Brechen Glansent Arobern
intended: to let Feierabiand commit its strength against
the griffins and then come hard against them from behind
when they were exhausted with fighting fire. Was not the
chance to prevent that worth anything? Bertaud pressed a
hand over his eyes and tried to believe this.

Kes, too, rubbed her thin hands across her face. Then she asked, "But won't he listen to you before he arrests you?"

Bertaud sighed and stood up. He stared out across the stark, beautiful desert, where light pulled fire out of the sand and spilled fire down the red spires of rock until the brilliance of it became painful to gaze upon. He said, reluctantly, because it was not arrest he feared but the look in Iaor's eyes, "Yes. Yes, I suppose he will." He looked back at the girl, incredulous all over again at her smallness against the strength and power of the desert. "And what shall I tell him you will do?"

"I don't know," she whispered.

"You must do as *you* choose," said Jos, his deep, slow voice sounding very certain.

Bertaud answered him sharply, "Sometimes circumstances choose for us." He turned urgently back to the girl. "I shall go to Iaor and hope he will hear me. And you . . . Kes, the griffins must support Feierabiand against Casmantium. Is not Casmantium inexorably their enemy? Have they not proven so? *We* need not be their enemies. We might even be allies. Do you understand?"

"Yes," the girl whispered.

The Casmantian soldier had a grim look to him; he, too, understood what Bertaud was saying. He said nothing.

"Can you make Kairaithin understand? And the rest of them?"

She only shook her head, clearly not knowing.

"You must," he said intensely. "You must. We must not allow Casmantium a free hand here. That will be no benefit to the griffins or to us." He gave Jos a hard look. "Will you say otherwise? Whom do you support in this?"

The soldier only shook his head. "I chose . . . when I killed that boy and took Kes out of the Arobern's hands; again when I fought against the king's mage and his men. That was my choice then, lord. Do you think I can go back now?"

Bertaud gave a slight nod, not really satisfied. But it was all the assurance he was going to get, clearly. He said to Kes, "Then will you get your friend to take me to the edge of the desert? As far north as she can?"

And so Kes called Opailikiita.

CHAPTER 11

Bertaud found Iaor, this time, in the better of the two inns in Riamne, with a very respectable army spread out in an encampment half a mile below the town, along the Sepes where the smaller stream divided from the larger Nejeied and quickened its flow between steepening banks. That Kes's griffin friend had known where the king of Feierabiand rested this night . . . that carried its own uncomfortable message.

Opailikiita had brought him to Riamne by that strange folding through air and time that the griffin mages seemed able to do, but Opailikiita did not linger in Riamne; she brought him to its walls and immediately took herself away again. Back to Kes, who was her friend? Back to Kairaithin, who was, Bertaud understood, her master? If she went to Kairaithin, would she tell him where she had taken Bertaud? If she did, and if he was angry, it would be a problem for Kes to deal with. Could she?

Whether or not, there was nothing he could do about

it. Standing outside the town's open gates, Bertaud gazed at the diverging rivers that ran past the walls. He wanted, suddenly and intensely, to walk away again and never turn his head to see what he was leaving. The water slid steadily past on its way south to the sea. He might follow it south to the coast. Or he might go west to his own estates in the Delta. That would certainly surprise his uncles and cousins there.

He turned back to the town instead, deliberately, and went through the gates, threading his way through its streets to the inn.

The inn was a brick edifice, three stories tall, with balconies outside the highest rooms and flowers on the balconies. Bertaud knew where the king would be: The best suite the inn offered was on that top floor, with rich furnishings and a private bath and rooms for servants the lord who guested there would bring. Iaor would have taken that whole floor for himself and his military advisors and senior officers, and for Meriemne if he had brought her with him, as seemed likely. Possibly the king's entourage was ensconced all through the lower floors as well.

What Bertaud did not know was how best he might now approach the king. His own nervousness appalled him, but he couldn't help it. The thought of Iaor's face when Bertaud had defied him came back to him again, starkly. And if he had lost the king's trust and regard, perhaps forever? What would be left for him then? His father's house in the Delta? He grimaced.

Deliberately, he put that thought aside. If he'd lost the king's esteem . . . at least, Bertaud thought, surely Iaor would listen to him before he sent him away, or had him arrested. And so the king would know that a Casmantian army was in the mountains behind the griffins' desert, with Brechen Glansent Arobern at its head. That news would surely buy forgiveness. But, Bertaud thought, probably not a return of the easy trust, the certainty that he and Iaor had once had between them.

He sighed and stepped toward the inn's main door, wanting now primarily to get this whole encounter behind him.

A soldier was posted there, not a guardsman whom Bertaud would have known, but a man in the colors of some western-border company whom Bertaud had not, to his knowledge, ever seen before. Bertaud began to speak to him, but the soldier unexpectedly laid a hand to his sword without waiting, moving quickly to block the door to the inn and raising his voice in a shout.

Startled, Bertaud began to protest, then paused. He might not know this young man, but surely there was no chance that the soldier did not know him. Had his captain set orders that Bertaud was to be arrested on sight? Had a general given such orders? Adries, perhaps?

Had Iaor given that command himself? Bertaud thought, heart cold, that after the way he had fled Tihannad with the griffin mage, this was all too possible. He wondered now why he had not expected it; why he had imagined to be able to walk straight into the king's presence. Perhaps, indeed, Iaor would refuse to speak with him.

Or if this command had been given by some general or courtier who had been his rival in the court, perhaps Iaor would not even be told that he had come back.

It was this last thought that sent Bertaud's hand to catch and hold the soldier's before the young man could quite clear his sword from its scabbard. The soldier tried to break his grip, so Bertaud caught the man's wrist in his other hand, even knowing how stupid this was, knowing that he had lost this encounter the moment he'd allowed it to become a physical contest. Other soldiers were coming . . . He saw no guardsmen, no one he could expect to listen to him over whatever order they'd been given. He could not fight the soldiers; he could not command them. What else was left? Bertaud let go of the soldier's wrist and stepped back, hoping for inspiration. It did not come.

Another soldier, some lieutenant he didn't know, as he did not know any of these men, grabbed Bertaud's arm and stepped behind him to pinion him. For a moment there was quiet. Bertaud opened his mouth to speak, but found he did not know what to say.

A young guardsman, undoubtedly drawn by the commotion, came out of the inn. He looked curious and half alarmed. The young man was faintly familiar . . . Bertaud had thought he knew all his guardsmen well, but this one . . . He recognized him, then, and was all but overcome with a sudden unlikely desire to laugh. It was Enned son of Lakas, whom he had reluctantly accepted as a guardsman . . . what, seven days ago, eight? Enned recognized him, too. The young man's eyes widened.

Bertaud started to call out, but the lieutenant jerked his arm sharply upward and he desisted, trying not to gasp in obvious pain. "If you please, my lord," said the lieutenant, like an order. "You'll come with me, quietly now, my lord."

Enned ducked silently back into the inn.

"I must see the king," Bertaud began.

"That's for my captain to decide, my lord."

"I'll take him," said a new voice, much deeper. Eles came out through the doorway of the inn, having to duck his head slightly to clear the lintel. The guard captain turned a grim stare on the lieutenant, who looked unhappy. There were a dozen soldiers in the yard of the inn, now, but three or four guardsmen pressed out of the inn after their captain. Though, with Eles present, the numbers would not matter: The captain would not likely allow this encounter to become a physical confrontation between soldiers and guardsmen . . .

The lieutenant tightened his grip. He looked as though he would have liked to countermand Eles's order, but knew he did not have the authority to do so. He said, "His lordship is to be brought to my captain, sir, and smartly. That's my orders."

"I'll take it up with your captain," Eles said curtly, and the lieutenant hesitated. The man might not have served in Tihannad, but everyone knew Eles. Indeed, sometimes Eles's reputation served him better than his actual presence. Although Bertaud was glad of his presence at this moment.

"You'd best come along with me, my lord, according to my orders," the lieutenant said at last, and shoved. Bertaud set himself and resisted.

Eles shook his head and sighed, a slow exhalation that carried a startling menace. "Lieutenant. Mennad, is it?"

The lieutenant stopped again, looking uncomfortable.

"I," said Eles, "will take this up with your captain, lieutenant. Sebes," he said to one of his own aides, "if you would escort his lordship."

Sebes, a dark, thin man with an even more dour look than the guard captain, came forward and laid a matter-of-fact hand on Bertaud's arm. "If you will come with me, my lord?"

"My *orders* . . ." began the lieutenant, weakly.

"The responsibility is mine," said Eles, without any special emphasis. Bertaud would have liked to be able to create that quality of grim certainty with so little effort, but it did not seem to be reproducible.

The lieutenant, yielding at last to the inevitable, opened his hands.

The second floor of the inn, it was evident, belonged to the guardsmen. At least they all came up the stairs with their captain and Bertaud, and none of the soldiers followed. No one laid a hand on Bertaud once they were clear of the soldiers. But once they were up the stairs, Eles himself turned back to face Bertaud, who perforce came to a halt. For a moment, the two men regarded one another in silence. Around them, the other guardsmen were uncomfortably silent.

"Lord Bertaud," Eles said at last, with a hard look. "And have you brought . . . anyone . . . with you?"

"No."

Eles studied him. Bertaud had never been confident of his own ability to read the guard captain's face: When he had been a boy, he had thought there were no emotions behind the captain's inexpressive face to be read. He did not know what he saw there now.

"You want to see the king?" Eles asked Bertaud at last.

"Yes," said Bertaud. Neither demanding nor pleading. Just a neutral statement. "It's urgent that I should, esteemed captain."

"Urgent," repeated the captain. "Is it?" He regarded Bertaud for another moment. "Are you armed?"

"No, esteemed captain."

Eles gestured. One of his men—Sebes again—came forward, expression neutral, and with a murmur of apology proceeded to search Bertaud. Bertaud felt his face heat. But he lifted his arms and stood still, suffering the search without comment.

Finding nothing, Sebes took a step back and glanced at Eles.

"Wait there, if you please, my lord," Eles said briefly, tilting his head to indicate the nearest room. "I will speak to his majesty and find out whether he will see you."

"Thank you," said Bertaud. And added after the slightest hesitation, "If he will not, Eles ... esteemed captain ... I ask you: Speak to me yourself. It is indeed extremely urgent information that I bring you. His majesty must hear it, from you if he will not hear it from me."

The guard captain nodded briefly, and Bertaud relaxed a little.

"If you would care to sit, my lord," said Sebes, once they had gone into the room to wait. Bertaud obediently sat down in the closest chair, folded his hands across his knee, and waited. Sebes stood behind him with two other guardsmen, including, Bertaud saw, Enned. They all waited, as patiently as was possible.

Bertaud said, after a moment, to Enned, "Well done, to go for the captain. Thank you."

Enned looked uncomfortable. "I . . ." he glanced at Sebes, hesitating. The older man lifted an eyebrow but did not rebuke the young man for speaking to Bertaud. So Enned continued. "It was my duty, my lord, but also my pleasure. I think . . . I did not thank you, my lord, that day. I never . . . and then, later, I thought I would be glad of the chance to do so."

"You have well repaid me," Bertaud assured him. He was again half inclined to laugh. Then the thought of Iaor made the inclination die a quick death. For all he feared what the king's reception of him might be, he could hardly bear to wait.

But, in fact, the wait was not very long at all. Eles returned mere moments after he had left, and, Bertaud saw, discomfited, Iaor himself accompanied the captain.

Bertaud first stood, startled, then quickly dropped to one knee and bowed his head. He glanced up covertly from beneath lowered lashes, trying to discern Iaor's mind behind the mask of his face, but found that he could not.

"Bertaud," the king said. Bare acknowledgment.

That coolness was hard to face; as hard as Bertaud had feared, surely. A dozen apologies and justifications, explanations, and excuses battled suddenly for primacy within him. He set his teeth, fixed his mind on the needs of the moment, and said, as crisply and cleanly and briefly as he knew how, "Brechen Glansent Arobern has five thousand men in the mountains above the griffins' desert, poised to come down upon you like a hammer against the griffins' anvil. The Arobern has been heard to say he wants Terabiand as the cornerstone of a new province, but I doubt he expects to get it without taking a certain amount of trouble."

The king stood very still. He said at last, "Valuable word. Well done, to bring it to me." He hesitated, then asked in a warmer tone, "Was it for this purpose . . . was it to get from the griffins the word they would not give me that you went with their mage?"

Yes! Bertaud wanted to cry. It would have been the best possible explanation, indeed: a noble risk, undertaken for loyalty and duty. But . . . it would be a lie. And where would loyalty and duty be then? He gave Iaor the truth instead, painfully. "I did not know why I did anything I did that night. I still don't know." He looked up to meet the king's eyes, afraid of what he would see there . . . Doubt? Mistrust?

What he saw was . . . both of those, he estimated, and bowed his head again in pain.

"You told me you did not trust your own judgment," the king said quietly. "I did not understand then what you were trying to tell me. Perhaps I understand it better now."

Bertaud looked at him helplessly.

The king came forward, laid a hand on Bertaud's shoulder with unexpected sympathy, urging him to stand. "Up," he said softly. "Up. All aside . . . I am glad you have come back to me. I confess I did not know whether to expect it. Up, I say. I am grateful for the warning you have brought me. But are *you* well?"

Unable to find an answer to that question, Bertaud only shook his head. He got to his feet rather shakily, finding Iaor's hand under his elbow in swift support.

"Sit," said the king, indicating the nearest chair. "Sebes . . . wine. Eles."

The guard captain came forward a step. "Your majesty."

"Go confer with Adries and Uol. Begin to develop alternate plans we might use in this exigency. Frontal attacks up into the teeth of the mountains are probably not the tactic of choice. Do think of some alternatives."

Eles bowed and went out. The king waved the other guardsmen out after him and dropped into a chair of his own. He picked up his cup of wine, though he did not drink. He looked instead at Bertaud. "Well? Tell me everything. Begin . . . try to begin with why you freed the griffin in my hall, if you can. And then go on from there."

And was this, then, forgiveness? It was not, Bertaud judged reluctantly. Not quite forgiveness and not quite absolution, though it might perhaps grow into either. It was better, even so, than he had had any right to expect.

He drank off his own wine in one quick draught and set the cup down on the arm of his chair with a small decisive click. And groped slowly after impressions he had been trying for a long night and a day to pull into some coherent order. He found, with some surprise, that stumble though he might, it did not actually take all that long to lay out the events of the prior hours. Not days. Only hours, though that seemed unbelievable. So little time to go from knowing your own place in the world to . . . knowing very little with certainty, it seemed.

Iaor was silent, thinking. Of many things, probably: deserts and fire, Casmantium and cold . . .

"I think . . . that Kairaithin sincerely does not want battle with you. With us. And that if he is not with his people, his opinion is not likely to carry the moment. I think that without strong leadership, the griffins will take all courses of action instead of just one, and become very dangerous. Kairaithin told me . . . that he came to Tihannad to warn you of Casmantium."

"But he changed his mind."

Bertaud spread his hands. He was baffled by the griffin mage's behavior himself, and had no idea how to explain it to Iaor. He said tentatively, "You hurt his pride, I think.

I don't know! I don't know. He seemed . . . I believe he was honestly distressed to leave you uninformed. For his own purposes, if not for your sake . . . I think he meant to use Feierabiand to try to get his little fire mage back from the Arobern."

Iaor put his cup down again, still untasted. He shook his head, incredulous perhaps at the shape of the world, so different than it had seemed so few days earlier.

Bertaud found himself tapping his fingers nervously on the arm of his chair and folded his hands firmly in his lap. He glanced at the king, and away. And, reluctantly, back, gathering his courage. "Iaor?"

The king glanced up.

Bertaud met his eyes, with an effort. "Iaor . . . I'm sorry."

"I am not certain you have reason to be. The news you have brought me has great value."

Bertaud shook his head. "All else aside . . . I asked protection from another lord, against you. That was . . . I don't know what I was thinking. At the time, I don't suppose I *was* thinking; not clearly. I . . . well. I am sorry, Iaor. My king. I most earnestly beg your pardon."

Iaor was still for a moment. Then he nodded. He said nothing, but . . . Bertaud thought some of the edge had gone from the king's manner. The king said, "I was also at fault. Another time I will listen more closely to what you try to tell me. As I have tried to listen tonight. I ask for your advice. If I go south, can I depend on your Kairaithin to hold back his people? It should be Casmantium against which the griffins rage, not Feierabiand. What say you? Is there a way to speak to the griffins, to win their quiescence, if not their aid? Or if they should aid us, they may have their desert, and welcome. Would they be amenable to this suggestion? Can I find this Kes, could she perhaps make my desire clear to them?"

"Kes would be the one who might well go between you and the desert," Bertaud agreed slowly. "I have told her so, and told her to seek you out, though . . . I don't know that she would have the nerve. She is a timid creature, and herself half fire, now. Or, failing the girl, you might try to speak to Kairaithin yourself. If he will speak to you. I do not know what to advise you, my king. Except, do not send a mage to speak to the griffins. I don't think earth mages understand how strong the antipathy will be until they experience it. I am the last person who should speak, I know, but . . . I truly, truly do not think you should trust the opinions of a mage when it comes to dealing with griffins."

"I might send you," Iaor suggested. "If you thought you might trust yourself."

That question, not quite asked, was hard to face. Bertaud thought of Kairaithin saying, *I could send you as* my *agent* . . . He had instantly rejected that idea. But neither was he confident that he could act as Iaor's agent against the griffins.

"Shall I trust you?" Iaor asked him. He asked as a friend. And as a king. "You chose the griffin over me in Tihannad. If it came to that a second time, whom would you choose? If your Kairaithin bids you against me . . . are you certain what choice you would make? Can I be certain?"

Bertaud knew, to his dismay, that he could not answer this question.

It was Iaor, his friend, who looked at him with sympathy. But it was the Safiad, King of Feierabiand, who said,

"I will consult with Meriemne. I will take counsel of my generals and my advisors. But, my friend, I think we will be riding south tomorrow, and I think that you will stay here, under guard. I beg you will not think less of me."

"No," Bertaud whispered.

The top floor of the inn held five rooms. The best of these was actually a suite, containing a sitting room and servants' quarters as well as a bed chamber. Soft rugs covered the wooden floors, chairs with scrolled arms stood by small decorative tables, and a rather good painting of the town hung opposite the curtained bed. The walls were white, the wood bleached pale, the rugs and curtains the color of pale ivory; the effect was one of spacious light, though none of the rooms was large.

Wide windows, shutters thrown open, offered an impressive view over Riamne's low walls to the river. The afternoon sun struck the water to gold, as though it were molten fire that flowed there. Bertaud shifted uneasily and tried to see the river as simply water. On the road that ran alongside that river, a long column of two thousand men was slowly passing away to the south.

The king, with his banners and his retinue, was already out of sight. It would take an hour, probably, for the tail end of the column to pass out of view. Bertaud, his hands resting on the broad sill, watched their slow movement. For a very little, he would have gone out the window, found a horse, and followed them.

He knew what he wanted: to ride after the king, ask for a different decision, for leave to ride with the army. He understood there was no point. He had not remonstrated with the king's decision. He had not allowed a whisper of resentment, of bitterness, to inform his manner or his leave-taking with his king. If that leave-taking had been strained . . . that was nothing for which Iaor could be faulted. He believed that.

And now there was this window, with guards below— Bertaud did not have to look for them to know they were there—and the slow procession, of which he was not part. He paced unhappily from the window to the door and back to the window: Both would be guarded. By men who kept him here by order of the king they all served, whom he did not wish to defy.

He paced again, from window to door, from sitting room to bed chamber, back to the window. The column of soldiers was still in sight, and still moving so slowly a brisk stride might well carry a man to its head before the last of its baggage tail was well in motion.

Which, of course, he could not prove himself. In disgust, Bertaud flung himself into one of the fine chairs and stared sightlessly at the wall, refusing to look again out the window.

The quality of the light flooding the room changed slowly, so that the plaster of the walls turned from white to cream to the palest gold and then to a more luminescent gold, tinged with the red of the lowering sun. Shadows crept slowly into the room, dimming its light, and the breeze that wandered through the window became uncomfortably cool . . . time passing, carrying them all forward with it, he feared: The king riding endlessly through this suspended moment into the south and the new desert; and the Arobern, hidden with his army in the stillness of the mountains above that desert; and the griffins contained within it, building it out of themselves. All, all of them, separated by distance, but all contained in the identical moment. Until the moment should break, and they all crash together into disaster . . . He could all but see it, a fast-approaching moment toward which the inexorable wind of time carried them all . . .

A hand was set firmly on his shoulder, so that Bertaud jerked upright and spun sharply. Yet he was somehow not surprised to find it was Kairaithin who stood over him, in the form of a man, with his shadow the shadow of a griffin. "Earth and iron," he breathed, and dropped back into the chair.

"You called me," Kairaithin said, rather harshly. His face was not clearly visible in the dim light, but his eyes blazed with fire that made their blackness somehow only the more absolute.

"I?" Bertaud said blankly.

"You." Kairaithin gave him a long stare. "Well? Will you tell me you had no intention to call?"

Ignoring this baffling question, Bertaud instead leaned forward and said urgently, "Kairaithin, when Feierabiand comes into your desert, you must pretend to do battle. *Tell* Iaor what you will do. Go to him—or take me to him and I will speak for you. We can arrange it all. Then you and he can *both* turn against the Arobern when he comes down out of the mountains, and all will be well!" And the disaster toward which the wind carried them all would fail, and Feierabiand remain as it should be: Peaceful and green and in no way broken by griffin fire or Casmantian ambition.

The griffin mage turned his fierce, proud face toward the window and the sky beyond.

"Well?" Bertaud asked him urgently. "Well?"

"Tastairiane Apailika has persuaded Eskainiane Escaile Sehaikiu of the efficacy of a different course," Kairaithin said. His black eyes shifted from the window to Bertaud's face. "And Escaile Sehaikiu has persuaded the Lord of Fire and Air. We shall draw both Feierabiand and Casmantium into our desert, Feierabiand by pretended aggression and Casmantium by the hope of easy victory; yet both shall be illusion. Thus, once the Casmantian force has destroyed the soldiers of Feierabiand, we shall come down upon it in its turn, and Casmantium will not be able to stand before us. Thus the men of Casmantium will follow those of Feierabiand into the red silence, and my people shall be secure."

Bertaud stared at him, appalled. He got to his feet, took a single step forward. "Is this what you want?" he whispered.

The fierce eyes held his, without a shadow of apology or regret. "I argued for the calling up of a different wind. But no one has more influence with Kiibaile Esterire Airaikeliu than Escaile Sehaikiu; they are *iskarianere*, closer than brothers. The argument did not go my way. And, in truth, man, this plan will do well enough."

"Not for Feierabiand," Bertaud said sharply. "Not for Iaor."

"No," agreed the griffin, but not with sympathy. Only with frightening indifference.

Bertaud moved to the window and looked sightlessly out into the dusk for a moment. Then he turned back toward Kairaithin. "Casmantium beat you before, drove you from your own desert, destroyed all your mages but one. Why should you believe you can face the Arobern now? Even wearied by battle against Feierabiand?"

"I have no power for healing," stated the griffin. "But Kes does."

The implication stood starkly in the silence between them. Bertaud said at last, "Then you should not need to blunt the Casmantian spear against a Feierabiand shield."

Kairaithin tilted his head to the side, a slight gesture somehow more like the movement of an eagle than of a man. Fire seemed to burn just out of sight beneath his skin; his black eyes were filled with pitiless fire. He said, "While Casmantium battles Feierabiand, I shall hunt the cold mages. They will discover that the roused desert is more powerful than they had imagined. Thus when the battle of men is over, my little *kereskiita* will be neither wearied nor opposed. Thus she may do her work well during the battle between Casmantium and my people. Thus will the Arobern learn that the People of Fire and Air are not to be lightly offended."

"No," Bertaud whispered, without strength.

Kairaithin's stare held . . . regret, possibly. But still no hint of apology, or yielding. He said, "You will not need to call me again." The world shifted, tilted . . .

"No!" Bertaud shouted, not disbelief this time, but out of desperate need and horror. And found, to his astonishment, that that strange shift of space and time did not continue, that the world and the room steadied, that the griffin had stayed after all.

Kairaithin seemed exasperated, but he remained. "Cease," he said sharply.

Bertaud stared at him. The fire shone just below the surface of the griffin; for a moment, he saw neither the man-shape Kairaithin wore, nor the true griffin beneath that shape, but only fire—contained and channeled and ruled by will, but fundamentally wild.

He seemed to hear it, roaring high in its burning; he felt its searing heat against his face. It was fierce and merciless, wild and beautiful, passionate and joyous. It spoke, and its voice was the voice of the griffin. It spoke of the hot wind, of the desert storm, of stone that melted and flowed like water.

He was not, Bertaud knew distantly, dreaming. Though his eyes, it occurred to him, were closed. He opened them.

Kairaithin was standing very still in the center of the room, watching him. His proud, austere face showed very little. And yet Bertaud knew that the griffin was afraid. And he knew why. Impossible though it had seemed. Impossible though it seemed still.

He said, "You came when I called you. Can you go, though I refuse you leave?"

"You would not be wise to challenge me," Kairaithin said. He did not move, did not even blink, but a hot wind sang tensely through the confines of the room; sand hissed across the plaster walls and drifted on the rugs.

"Stop," Bertaud commanded him.

The wind died.

"Man," said Kairaithin, "I warn you plainly. You do not know what you are doing. Cease this foolishness. I *will* go. Be wise, and do not challenge me." The room shifted, tilting underfoot.

"Stop it!" snapped Bertaud, catching his balance on a windowsill that seemed, under his hand, to want to become twisted red stone.

And the room stilled, with both of them still within it.

"I do know what I am doing." Bertaud tried to steady

his voice, which kept wanting to rise into a shout of incredulity. He tried to steady his hands, which were trembling. "Though I . . . did not know it was possible for a man to hold the affinity to griffins."

"It is not possible." Kairaithin blazed into griffin form and then into fire, a savage red fire that cast its own shadow, which was golden and shaped like a griffin. The fire roared up, red and gold, flames running along wooden tables and thick rugs, across the wooden floor and up the plaster walls. Somewhere, distantly, there were shouts.

"No," said Bertaud, and fought the fire. It only roared the more passionately until he stopped fighting it and let himself love it: its passion, its fierceness. "No," he whispered, and quieted it.

His eyes were shut again. He drew a breath of air that tasted of fire, and opened them.

Kairaithin stood in the center of the charred room, in the form of a man. His eyes, filled with fire and rage and a bleak awareness of his own helplessness, were fixed on Bertaud. It hurt to see that bleakness where there should be exultant power. It took a wrenching effort of the heart not to cry *Go, then!* and free the griffin of all constraint. Even knowing that, freed, Kairaithin's first act would certainly be to strike down the man who had constrained him. That knowledge alone would not have been enough to hold Bertaud back. But his own safety was far from the most important consideration, now.

"I offer you a new plan," Bertaud said.

"You do not command me."

Bertaud paused. He took a breath, made his heart iron, and said, carefully and ruthlessly, "Kneel to me."

The griffin's human face tightened. He fought the command. Bertaud simply waited; there was no effort in the compulsion he imposed on Kairaithin. It was not like a mage using the power of the earth to overcome the power of fire; it might have been something more akin to the compulsion of the Casmantian *geas*. Bertaud had always found the idea of the *geas* repellent. But the reality of this affinity was worse. The compulsion it let him impose did not require a battle of skill or strength. For Bertaud, though it twisted his heart, it was not a battle at all.

Kairaithin, with a low sound of effort, went to his knees on the charred floor. His quick breaths hissed like blowing sand.

"I do command you. You do not have the power to resist me. So you will do as I choose and not as you would choose."

Kairaithin brought his gaze up to meet Bertaud's. He said in a harsh, level tone, "I acknowledge your power, man. I acknowledge your strength. You are wrong to use it."

Bertaud agreed completely. It felt normal and right to understand the fierce mind and heart and will of the griffin. It felt horribly, devastatingly wrong to coerce that fierceness. He truly understood for the first time in his life why a man who could command the deer would not call them to the huntsman; why a man who could compel wolves to leave a village's flocks alone would slaughter his own sheep for them in a hard winter. He hated what he did. And yet . . . he lifted his hands, palms up. "Is not my need too great to allow me to choose what is right? I must choose what I must have. You *will* yield to me."

There was a pounding, sudden and loud, on the smoke-stained door. Both of them, startled, flinched. Kairaithin also used the moment of startlement to try to break Bertaud's hold, to fray into wind and fire and try to fly back to the desert.

Bertaud, after the first instant of surprise, stopped him. It did not even take a word. Only a thought. Only a thought to force the griffin back into human shape, to pin him to the charred boards, to force that proud face to the floor. As a man with the gift to speak to cattle might bring an enraged bull to instant docility, so he forced compliance from a creature not meant to yield to any compulsion.

Kairaithin fought him. To no effect.

"Yield to me," Bertaud insisted, furious and frightened and sickened all at once. And, as the pounding at the door suddenly took on a threatening force, "Keep them out!"

On that, they were in perfect accord. A blazing sheet of fire sprang up all around them. Without the room, there were sudden cries and then silence. The fire died. Kairaithin, as though obedience to the one command carried a yielding to both, slowly and deliberately relaxed the muscles in his back, in his neck, in his arms. He said, muffled against the floor, "I acknowledge that you are stronger than I. I could not possibly mistake it."

Bertaud eased the compulsion. He was shaking. Kairaithin, gathering himself slowly to his knees and then to his feet, was not. He was angry, with an anger deep and unrelenting as molten stone. Shamed and frightened and angry. Bertaud knew everything the other felt, recognized the shame and fear and anger, understood the source of those emotions and their power.

Kairaithin bowed his head, brought one long hand up, touched his own human face, his own eyelids. He looked, with that gesture, very human. Seeing past all outward

appearances into his heart, Bertaud saw the griffin behind the human form and the fire behind the griffin.

Looking up, Kairaithin met Bertaud's eyes. "You are
wrong to do to me what you have done."

"I know," Bertaud whispered. And then, more strongly,
"I could not possibly mistake it. Were you right to cast
Kes into the fire and make her your tool? Is my necessity
less dire than yours?"

Kairaithin did not look away, but neither did he answer.

"Tonight," Bertaud said, "or tomorrow, Iaor will lead
his two thousand into your desert. And . . . everything
will go as it will go, from there. You have told me what
your king expects. Here is the new plan: Your people will
pretend to engage mine in battle, but both sides will understand this is pretense. Iaor will affect to be hard-pressed
and ignorant; he will set his men with their backs to the
Arobern. When the Casmantian army is lured down from
the mountains, both your people and mine will fall upon
them and destroy them."

Kairaithin heard this without expression. Inwardly, he
was raging still, and afraid, and in neither his rage nor his
fear was he human. He was something other, that should
have been incomprehensible. And yet Bertaud looked past
his form and understood his heart.

The face the griffin showed outwardly was calm. "This
is not the intention of the Lord of Fire and Air."

"*Make* it his intention!" Bertaud said, his voice rising with anger and self-loathing. He caught himself, and
continued more quietly. "You say you did not favor the
current plan, that's all very well, but did you care enough
to fight against it with all your strength? Now you must.
Remind your king that it is Casmantium that is his enemy,

that Feierabiand and your people have a common enemy in this. Suggest to him that if the Arobern's ambition is not curtailed now, Casmantium will only become more aggressive and more dangerous. Is that what your lord would desire? Is there not natural reason for alliance between your people and mine? Can there not be lasting advantage in an understanding between Feierabiand and the desert?"

Kairaithin did not answer. But at least he did not instantly decry these suggestions.

Bertaud warned him, "Or we shall see whether I am strong enough to force all your people at once to my will. I have never heard that there is a limit to how many animals a man can rule, who has the affinity for that animal."

"The People of Fire and Air are not to be called to heel like dogs."

Bertaud stared into the griffin's fiery eyes. "To me, you are."

Kairaithin closed his eyes against a visible leap of fury, clenched his teeth against the first violent words that came to his tongue. A moment passed. Another. Mastering his own rage, the griffin said, forcing his tone to a temperance and restraint with an effort Bertaud felt wrench his own heart, "You must not do that, man. Lord. You must not reveal to any other of my people even the merest shadow of the power you have shown to me." His black eyes met Bertaud's with a caution foreign to his nature, a trepidation that hurt them both. He said, harshly, "Do you not know what you would do to them? I will beg, if you demand it. I will kneel willingly."

Bertaud was so horrified by this suggestion he actually recoiled backward. "I have no desire whatsoever to, to . . . command *any* of your people. I promise you. *You* must see to it that my necessity does not encompass any such act. I want only what I have said."

Another pause. Kairaithin bowed his head, again with that clear effort. "And if I am not able to persuade him? Lord, you must not set such a penalty on my failure—"

"You will persuade him. You *must*."

Another moment. "Let me go, then," the griffin said harshly. "And I will see to it that all occurs as you require."

Bertaud nodded. "I will follow you in my own time, and expect to see that you have. You won't fail. I have," he said quite sincerely, "great faith in your strength and cleverness, once you put everything you have of each into this effort."

Bitterness shifted through Kairaithin's heart, hidden behind the mask of his face, but clear to Bertaud. Turning toward the window, the griffin let go of his human seeming and reached after the desert wind. It came to meet him, the world tilting as it came, and Kairaithin touched the boundaries of the desert. He made as he did so one last effort to reach also for freedom.

He did not succeed. Bertaud contained the griffin's shifting form, his tilting location, his fast flight into the dark and his fierce, sudden lunge against the binding that held him. It did not break. Distance thinned it to a thread. But if he called Kairaithin again, Bertaud knew, the griffin would have no choice but to come. And he knew Kairaithin knew it, too.

This awareness was both reassuring and deeply disturbing.

Bertaud stood for a long moment, his mind following

Kairaithin south. Then he collapsed in the fire-damaged chair and put his face in his hands, struggling against overwhelming reaction: He wanted both to laugh hysterically and sob like a child; he wanted to spread great wings with feathers made of fire, to turn his body into fire and blaze like a torch through the sky. All those dreams, explained. And the explanation was nothing he had ever imagined or desired. An affinity for griffins! He felt as though the affinity, woken at last—undoubtedly by Kes, when she used fire to heal him—well, however it had happened, the affinity completed something in his heart that he had never even recognized was missing. A new depth informed the whole world. It felt wonderful. It was horrifying. If Kairaithin was again before him, he knew he would constrain the griffin exactly as he had done before; yet he could hardly believe even now that he had ever twisted the affinity to such a use.

He found that he understood far better than he ever had just how divided Iaor was between his two roles, both man and king. Of course, Bertaud had always understood this. But he understood it much better now. He understood it *intimately*. He had known that power requires to be used; that the world compels the exercise of power if one possesses it. And that necessity constrains what one may do with power.

The last shreds of resentment he had harbored against Iaor shredded in the face of this understanding; *of course* the king had left him in Riamne. What else could the king have done? This, too, though Bertaud had already understood, he understood much better now.

Even so, Bertaud knew that he could not possibly stay in Riamne now. He got to his feet . . . stiffly. He felt stiff all over, as though he'd pressed his body to its limits, rather than his heart. But stiff or not, he made his way across the fire-scarred floor to the door. How long would it take to get a horse and start after Iaor? Longer, he supposed, if men felt required to try to prevent him . . . He laid his hand on the door, took a breath, and shoved it open upon charred boards and the smells of smoke and burning.

CHAPTER 12

Kes watched the King of Feierabiand approach the desert from a high perch on an outcropping of red stone. She had one arm thrown lightly over Opailikiita's neck. Jos sat uneasily some distance away on her other side. It was not the height that made him uneasy, Kes knew. It was Opailikiita. Or perhaps it was Kes herself. She would not have blamed him.

At the edge of sight, where the northwestern border of the griffin's desert met the gentle country of river and field, lay the road that ran past Riamne, which Kes had never seen, all the way north to Tihannad, where she had never even imagined going. The King of Feierabiand was on that road. The dust of his army made a haze in that direction. So she knew he was there, approaching the country the griffins had made theirs.

And to her other side, beyond the desert, hidden within the smooth gray stone of the mountains, was Brechen Glansent Arobern and Beguchren and thousands of Casmantian soldiers. When the Feierabiand soldiers had met the griffins in the desert, they had all died. And when more soldiers of Feierabiand met that Casmantian army? They would all die. The griffins would let that happen. Even Kairaithin, though he had argued against it. Even Opailikiita, though she would be unhappy to make Kes unhappy.

Kes rested her face against her drawn-up knees, wanting to hide from the world, from her own thoughts, from everything she knew. She no longer exactly wanted to run home to Tesme. She could neither imagine leaving the fierce desert nor wishing to leave it. But at the same time, grief shadowed the brilliance of the desert. She longed for a simpler, gentler time, for the girl she had been and the life she had owned before the griffins had come. A time when the only choices she had to make were simple, because they did not *matter*.

Nothing was simple, now. She wished she could be angry about that. She should be angry—with Kairaithin; with the Lord of Fire and Air; with Brechen Glansent Arobern, the ambitious King of Casmantium, who had driven the griffins out of their high desert as a tactic against Feierabiand. And she *was* angry. But her anger only flickered around the edges of her fear.

Against her side, Opailikiita stirred. The griffin turned her head to look at Kes out of one golden-brown eye, a fierce attention that drew Kes all but involuntarily back into the immediate present. The stroke of gold through the feathers above the griffin's eye gave her a ferocious look. And she *was* ferocious. But . . .

"Sister," said Kes, and smoothed those soft feathers with the tip of one finger.

The griffin closed her eyes and tilted her head against the delicate caress; if she had been a cat, she would have purred.

Kes stared into the desert and thought about fire, and earth, and sisters. What, she wondered, would Tesme make of the red desert? Of the fire-eyed griffin? Tesme would be horrified by both, Kes was nearly certain. She would be afraid of both. And either might kill her, the griffin almost as indifferently as the desert. Though Opailikiita would not want to make Kes *unhappy*. But she might kill Tesme anyway and say in surprise when Kes protested, *But it was a day for blood*.

A day for blood.

Blood would surely water the desert, soon. It would flood forth abundantly. And what would bloom of this gathering storm? And what would it cost to turn that storm? If she could. Could she?

And if she could, would she be glad afterward? Perhaps she would say, *But was this not a day for blood?* and wonder why she had troubled herself. Kes pressed her hands over her eyes, trying not to think about losing herself to the desert, of letting it change her not only into a different person but into an entirely different kind of creature. But even if she refused to think about this, she knew it was possible. More than possible. She almost longed to pour fire through her heart to her hands, to scatter fire across the wind right now, just so that change would *happen*, would be *done* with, so she could stop agonizing over the prospect. Afterward . . . afterward, what would she think? Or feel?

Did it matter what she thought afterward? Or felt? Did it matter, what she might lose by what she chose, when she had no choice, really? Did it matter what she might gain?

Kes said to Opailikiita, "You know the binding Kairaithin put around me."

I know, the slim griffin said.

"I can't leave the desert. But you could help me. You could push the desert . . . out." Kes gestured vaguely.

The griffin turned her head, closed delicately feathered eyelids half across her golden-tawny eyes. *Where would you go?*

In a way, Kes wanted to say, Home. She shut her eyes, trying to think about the comfortable house where Tesme would be waiting for her. Worrying for her. Wondering where Kes was, what she might be doing, whether she was safe. But images of the desert intruded on memories of her home: flames rippling in the wind and licking out of the sand; the merciless sun blazing above red cliffs, stark shadows stretching out beneath . . .

She blinked, and blinked again, and stared away north and west, toward the dust haze that marked the road and the king. "There."

At her side, Jos stilled attentively.

What would you do there? asked the griffin.

"Find the king. And tell him . . . tell him . . . everything, I suppose." Kes contemplated this feat, now that it was laid out plainly in words, with extreme disquiet. She shivered. *Could* she walk into the presence of the King of Feierabiand and tell him anything at all?

Tears pressed at her eyes, or a pressure and heat that should have been tears. If she wept, she knew that fire opals would scatter across the sand. She blinked fiercely, not wanting to see jewels where there should be tears.

She had bravely enough declared what she wanted to do. But when she stood in the midst of a crowd of soldiers and courtiers and strangers, she knew she would stand mute and helpless until, defeated by her own inability to speak, she was forced to retreat again to the silence of the desert.

And yet, if she could not believe she would find the courage to stand and speak, could she not at least find the courage to try for the first small step in that direction?

Opailikiita, fearless herself, did not understand fear and would not have comprehended Kes's anxiety even had she tried to put it into words. But she understood peril and prudence. She said, *The Lord of Fire and Air would be very angry.*

Kes knew this was so. She asked cautiously, "But . . . do you care?"

And it seemed she correctly understood the heart of the griffin, because where a human woman—or a human soldier—would have cared, and cared deeply, Opailikiita said simply, *No.*

Jos stared at her. At them both.

Kairaithin would also be angry, said Opailikiita. *His opinion, I do care for.*

Kes looked into her fierce tawny eyes, and beyond them into the ferociously independent, unconquerable heart of the griffin that would not bear any kind of mastery. "Kairaithin has imprisoned me here. He leaves me to choose only what he would have me choose. Is that right?"

No, said the griffin, definitely.

"Then," Kes asked her, "would you not help me choose as I would choose?"

Yes. If you ask me. You may ask.

Kes rose to her feet, standing on the edge of the cliff, at the edge of space; she blinked and stared into it, looking for the layers of heat and motion that a griffin would see. She perceived only space, however fire-touched her eyes. And, to the west, the haze of rising dust. Where the king would be. She did not let herself think of him. She thought only of the desert and the red cliff and the dizzying drop into space. And of Opailikiita, who was her friend and her sister and who understood space and movement.

Jos stood up and moved a step closer to her. "And me."

"Of course," said Kes, surprised, and put out a hand for his.

And the world shifted around them.

The edge of the desert was a sharp, clean break. Red sand and heat lay at their backs, an austere splendor ruled by a merciless sun set in a sky that was a hard and brilliant white. But before them, soft greens and grays and browns ran down the gentle hills into the more verdant green where the river ran. The light itself lay tenderly on the young green of pastures and woodlands, and the sky before them was a soft, delicate blue.

The king's camp was not in sight. Kes could see where the road must be, from the shape of the land; she knew there was a great host strung out along it from the dust and the distant sounds of many men.

And she knew, without even needing to put it to a test, that she could not step from one land to the other. Kairaithin had set the desert's boundary in her mind, or her heart. She could not pass through it.

Even if she found him, probably the king would not listen to her—why should he? He was not her friend, as Jos was. There was not, Kes thought, really much point to trying to speak to him. She could go back into the silent reaches of the desert and sit with Opailikiita and Jos on a high cliff and watch events unfold and there would really be nothing, nothing at all, she could ever have done about any of it.

She sighed. Then she said to Opailikiita, "I can't leave the desert, but you could move it." She gestured outward with both hands as though shooing the desert forward. "If the desert comes to the king, then I can speak to him and yet not break past Kairaithin's boundary."

Opailikiita said, *Yes.*

"I know it will be hard," Kes said apologetically. The griffins spun the desert out of their own hearts; the desert wind came into the world through their own souls. She did not quite know how she had such temerity as to ask Opailikiita to spend her own self and strength on a task that the griffin did not even value—that might even be dangerous for her. She started to say, No, never mind, don't worry about it, let's go back to the high desert and listen to the sun striking the red stone—whatever will happen, let it happen.

Before she could, Opailikiita half opened her wings and leaned forward. A hot wind blew past her, or out of her; it came from the shadow under her wings and stirred the green grasses of the pasture. The grasses withered at that sere touch, an alarming thing to watch. Sand blew gently across them, catching in the yellowing blades. The strength of the sun came down, and the grasses dried and crumbled and blew away on the parched wind.

Opailikiita took a step forward. And another.

Behind her, Jos swore softly and fervently.

Kes closed her eyes and followed Opailikiita blindly. She did not need to look where she walked: She walked in the desert and her path was always the same no matter where she set her foot.

A Feierabiand soldier spotted them before the camp itself came into their view; his shout of amazement and alarm made Kes open her eyes. She stretched her stride to come up beside Opailikiita and put a hand on the griffin's slim neck, hard-muscled under its soft feathers. She said worriedly, "If there are arrows—"

You must catch them, said Opailikiita, a little breathlessly. *They move in the air, they fly, they belong to the air. You can catch them with fire if you are quick, or turn them with wind. Remember, men make them so they will try to strike you. A wind must be very strong to turn them aside.*

Kes had burned arrows before; she knew she could be quick enough to catch them with fire. If there were not too *many* arrows. But what if there were too many? If an arrow struck Opailikiita, she thought she would be able to heal her. But what if an arrow struck her own body? Or Jos? Her steps slowed. It would be so much easier just to go back . . .

"They are not shooting," Jos said, and laid a hand on her shoulder. He meant the touch for reassurance, she knew. It felt like a pressure at her back, shoving her forward.

The one soldier had been joined by others, a few at first and then more. But the shouts ceased. Men drew aside into two companies, one to either side of the path Opailikiita was making; they were close enough now that Kes could make out bows in some hands and spears in others.

"You can see they will let us come right in among them," Jos said. Again in his deep voice Kes heard not reassurance, but warning.

She said worriedly, "Is the king there?" She did not know what she would do if the king was not there. Who else should she speak to? Who might carry her words to the king, and would they sound persuasive in someone else's mouth?

Would they, in hers?

Jos peered ahead. "Just there, I think."

Kes looked at the man he indicated: Standing between the two armed ranks of soldiers, with others close by him. He looked grim and authoritative and sure of himself, thoroughly intimidating. He was like a lion, she thought, with a broad, assured face and muscled arms and sun-bleached streaks in his thick tawny-colored hair. He wore no crown, but nevertheless he looked very much a king.

And what would this man see when he looked at her?

Closer yet, and the nearest soldiers were close enough to have almost touched Opailikiita with their spears. They didn't, however, but stood still, in straight ranks, with their spears grounded on the earth at their feet and their eyes straight ahead, except for little covert fascinated glances at the griffin, and at Kes and Jos.

The king, close now, was also standing patiently. There was a man at his side—not Bertaud, and Kes was sorry, she would have trusted Lord Bertaud far more than these strangers. There was a very old woman seated in a chair, with woman attendants about her. Her eyes were closed, but she turned her face toward Kes with an awareness that went beyond sight. Kes knew by the sudden twist of dislike she felt that this woman must be a mage and flinched uneasily away from her strong awareness.

Opailikiita stopped and sank down couchant upon the sand she had brought with her; her beak was slightly open and she panted with rapid shallow breaths. Kes laid an apologetic hand on her shoulder, cast one despairing glance back along the narrow tongue of desert they had made, and turned slowly and reluctantly to face the king.

He looked stern, she thought. Forbidding. She wondered if he ever smiled. Now that she was so close, she could see that his eyes were dark: not measurelessly black like Kairaithin's eyes, but dark as fresh-turned earth, with a power to them as the earth possessed. He did not have the presence of the Lord of Fire and Air. But he had a presence of his own.

Words deserted her. Just as Kes had feared, she did not know what to say, and stood tongue-tied and clumsy in the midst of a hundred men. She edged closer to Opailikiita, trying to draw strength and courage from the griffin, who possessed both in such generous measure. But Kes still felt neither herself. She was horrified by the possibility that she would not be able to speak after all, that the day for blood and death would come and she would not even have been able to *try* to prevent it.

The king came forward one step, and another, waving away the concern of the men who pressed forward anxiously at his back. His dark eyes looked into hers, and Kes wondered what he saw in them, and thought that if he was perceptive he would see fire. His own were filled with curiosity.

Then he brought his attention back to her face, looking her over quickly from the top of her head to her bare toes.

"Kes, I presume," he said, and the laughter she had not seen in his face was suddenly perceptible at the edges of his voice.

Kes blinked. She nodded hesitantly.

"And who is this?" The king was looking in open wonder at Opailikiita.

Kes followed his gaze, and managed to smile, because the griffin was so magnificently unimpressed by men with spears, no matter how numerous, or by kings, no matter they were kings. Opailikiita arched her neck a little so her feathers ruffled into almost a mane; sun glinted off her feathers as though each one had been pounded separately out of bronze and had fine gold scrollwork inlaid across it. The muscles in her slim lion rear shifted powerfully as she eased herself to a sitting posture, and her tail, wrapping neatly around her talons, tapped gently on the sand.

"Opailikiita Sehanaka Kiistaike," said Kes, finding her voice after all. "She is my friend, and brought me here because I asked her to. She is not—well, she is dangerous, but not to you, um, your majesty, unless you try to shoot her. She only came because I asked her to make a path for me."

"She is welcome," said the king, and looked curiously at Jos.

"That is—"

"No one," Jos interrupted harshly. "Except her friend."

Kes looked at him in surprise.

"That is a Casmantian uniform," noted the king, in a mild tone.

Jos shrugged.

Kes did not want to say anything about Jos to the King of Feierabiand. She asked instead, "Did, um, did Bertaud, did Lord Bertaud, did he tell you . . . about the Casmantian army?" Her heart sank: What if, for whatever reason, Bertaud had *not* told his king about Casmantium? Why ever should the king then believe anything *she* should say about that threat?

"He told me," the king said reassuringly.

"Well," Kes said, and nervously stroked Opailikiita's neck, trying to draw courage from the griffin's hot presence under her hand. She tried to look only at the king, to pretend that no one else was there, only she and the king. Who was not, after all, a very frightening man. Not nearly so frightening as Kanes the smith, really, she told herself. He hadn't shouted even once, yet. She took a shallow breath and looked at her feet, trying to think what to say.

"Bertaud advised me very strongly that I should listen to you, if I was lucky enough to meet you," the king said gently. "What is it you came to tell me?"

Kes glanced up to meet his eyes, glanced down again. She said unhappily, "Kiibaile Esterire Airaikeliu—that is, the Lord of Fire and Air, the king of the griffins, you know—he has decided to, to . . . make you come into the desert and fight Casmantium there. And when Casmantium has destroyed you, he will bring his people down against Casmantium while they are still in the desert, and destroy *them*. It is," she explained earnestly, "a very simple plan, because you have to fight the griffins. And the King of Casmantium has to fight *you*, or why did he bring his army here? And he won't know the griffins are as dangerous to his men as to yours because he thinks his cold mages can keep the griffins from harming his men. He doesn't know—he doesn't know about me. Or . . . he knows I am here, but he doesn't know . . . we think he doesn't know what I can do."

The king stood very still, his eyes on her face. But Kes thought that he was seeing, not her face, but battles hidden just around the next corner of time. He said at last, "And if we will not fight this battle to please the griffins?"

Kes nodded hopefully—maybe he could find a way not to fight—but Opailikiita said, *The Lord of Fire and Air will see to it that you must fight.* Her graceful, unobtrusive voice slid delicately around the corners of the mind, but many of the men still flinched in surprise. Some swore, though quietly. The old earth mage recoiled slightly, looking like she was struggling between offense and fascination. The king's eyes widened briefly. He said to the griffin, with careful courtesy, "How would he do this?"

This land knows us, now. The desert we have made out of our hearts is ours. Your earth mage will not break its power, though she may try. The King of Casmantium does not yet understand that his mages cannot break its power, either. So you will understand you must fight within the reaches of our desert.

The king stared at her. His face tightened; he looked suddenly stern again. "And if I take my people back up the road to the north?"

If you retreat, you will cede all this country to Casmantium; if you go south to block his move there, my people will put the desert under your feet and hold you. If you stay where you are, then the Arobern will press you against our desert and destroy you and still claim all this land.

"And what do you suggest I do to preserve my people against destruction, then?" the king asked her.

There is nothing you can do, Opailikiita said, with a strange griffin satisfaction.

"Split your force," suggested Jos. His deep voice carried an odd, reluctant kind of assurance. "If you must take part of it into the desert, do so, and use those men as well as you can. You will lose most of them, probably. But also send men to cut around through the mountains and come down on the Arobern from above. Even a small force can have a great impact if it's used well. That way you may save something from this battle. If you send word to the west and the south now, at once, then what you do here may at least hold the Casmantian army long enough for the rest of Feierabiand to prepare."

Everyone looked at him. He shrugged, looking half apologetic and half defiant.

"You're a soldier," the king said at last. "To be plain, a *Casmantian* soldier."

"Not any longer."

"No? Then where is your loyalty now?" the king asked him.

Jos grimaced, nothing that could be called a smile, though he might have intended it that way. He tilted his head toward Kes. "With her."

"You were a spy," said one of the men with the king, his expression neutral but his tone flat with distaste. The man turned a hand palm up when they looked at him, and shrugged. "Or so I surmise." He seemed to consider this for a moment and then added to his king, with sudden urgency, "We need this man."

Kes flung a worried glance up at Jos's face and put a hand anxiously on his arm.

Jos looked down at her, touched her cheek with the tips

of two fingers, and took his hand away in a gesture like a farewell.

"No," said Kes.

He said, "It was a choice . . . to come here. It was for this I made that choice."

"No!" said Kes, sure, if she was sure of nothing else, that she could not let Jos go into the hands of men who . . . men who . . . She did not know what soldiers might do to a captured spy, and she did not want to find out. Opailikiita, probably understanding nothing of the specific accusation, nevertheless understood that Kes was upset. She stood up, half lifting her great wings, fire limning the brown feathers with gold. Half the soldiers present lifted their bows, steel arrowheads flashing like ice in the sun.

The king flung out his hands in urgent command, compelling all to stillness; remarkably, all were still. Even Opailikiita.

It was to Kes the king spoke. "No one will harm him, you know—for your sake, if there were no other reason. Is it not his choice? Did he not make it when he suggested a plan against his own people?"

Kes, struck mute by her own words in this king's mouth, could not find an answer.

Jos could. He stepped off the narrow line of desert Opailikiita had made for them, walked the few paces necessary to come to the king, gave him a brief nod, and turned toward the officer. He was pale. But no one could miss the deliberation of what he did.

"He is yours," the king said to the officer.

Jos bowed his head and allowed the officer to lay a hand on his arm.

Opailikiita, perhaps baffled by these strong human emotions, or perhaps merely disliking the way the arrowheads caught the light, said, *We should go back to the desert. Are you satisfied with the warning you have given, sister? Do you not desire to return to the heart of fire?*

Kes blinked. She looked at the king, who gave her a brief bow and a murmur of gratitude. A brief worried glance at Jos saw him stolid and uncomplaining, with a stubborn look on his face that she knew was meant for her. She took a small step toward him, though she could not leave the desert. "But I don't understand," she whispered. "Why would you want to do this?"

Jos said gently, "Kes . . . you are still partially a creature of earth. But if this battle takes place as your friend describes, what will you do?"

Kes said helplessly, "You know I can't let them die."

"Which? Your people . . . or the griffins?"

Either. Both. Kes could not speak.

"If I help your king against mine, there is a chance . . . a poor one, yes, but a *chance* . . . that Feierabiand will be able to turn Casmantium back without the griffins coming in at all. That, even if the griffins come in, they will not need you to keep them in the battle. However poor, this is the one chance that the griffins will not after all carry you with them into their world. If you do not use fire, you will still have a way back to earth."

Kes shook her head.

"A poor chance, I said. Can you see any other?"

They looked at each other, Kes tongue-tied and silent, Jos stubborn. He said at last, "Don't use fire, Kes. Don't let that Kairaithin force you to it. Don't be drawn into this battle. It will burn out your humanity. You know that is true. This is the griffins' battle, and a battle for men. It's nothing for you."

"I think—Jos, I think it's not so simple—" Kes turned and put her hand almost blindly on Opailikiita's shoulder. She thought of the exaltation of flight when the slim griffin carried her, the warmth of Opailikiita's voice when she said *sister*. It occurred to Kes that she had ceased questioning the word. It was a truth, now. But she thought it could not be a truth unless she lost *Tesme* as a sister. Learning to love the desert would mean turning away, once and for all, from human love. And she realized she couldn't bear to give up either her earth nature or her fire nature. "Maybe I can keep them both," she whispered. "Can't I just stay in between? Can't I keep both worlds?"

Jos, his mouth set in a hard line, started to come back toward her.

"If you will all please wait," cut in an austere voice that Kes knew instantly, and everyone turned hurriedly: Arrowheads and spear points flashed again, light striking off metal in quick, hard glints.

Kairaithin was there, in a little space that cleared about him instantly simply because of the barely leashed force that seemed to radiate outward from him like heat from the desert sun. He was in human form, but he had never looked less like a man. The harsh features of his human face barely hid the eagle's fierce eyes and savage, predatory beak; his long hands might as well have been talons. His shadow was entirely that of the griffin: Insubstantial feathers ruffled in the wind, and the shadow stared out upon them all with fiery eyes.

The slim bar of sand and heat Opailikiita had made swept out in both directions to make a much wider extension of the desert; a hot wind carried red dust whispering across the earth. Kairaithin stood on sand; the wind stirred his clothing and whipped with sudden strength through his hair. It reached the king, and the king blinked and lifted a hand to shield his eyes against the dust; men all through the company were doing the same as the desert suddenly encompassed the land on which they all stood. The air smelled of hot metal and molten stone. Opailikiita shook herself, stretched, and lay down on the sand, looking much more comfortable. Kes understood how she felt. It seemed to her also as though the world itself had suddenly widened.

The old mage with the king shifted in her chair.

Kairaithin rounded on her instantly, small flames springing from the ground at his feet and ruffling his black hair. His power, grounded in the desert, thundered soundless and potent through the air; the very air tasted of fire. "Do *not* press me!" he snapped at her. "This is *not* the time. Fire and *air*, cannot you earth-mages rule your own inclinations?"

"Yes," answered the woman without apparent offense. "If we have sensible reason to do so. I am not challenging you. Can you not tone *your* power down a little, griffin mage?"

The taut line of Kairaithin's mouth did not ease, but the wind died slowly and the fire at his feet ebbed like water back into the sand. He turned his back to the woman and the king, came to Kes in three long strides, and took her by the shoulders. Some of the men shifted—Jos clearly wanted to come back to her side—but the king lifted a forbidding hand and none of them moved to interfere.

Kairaithin was, Kes understood, very angry. Very

angry. She wanted to shrink away, and could not. She wanted to hide herself away in any small shadow that might offer sanctuary, and could not. She stared into the griffin's fierce eyes and tried not to flinch visibly.

"You are everything," the griffin told her harshly. "You are my hope of deliverance for all my people. And I find you here! Within the reach of powerful earth magic; within the reach of human kings! What would you have done if this earth mage had cut across your little strip of desert and trapped you here in the cold?"

Unable to speak, Kes only shook her head.

The tight line of Kairaithin's mouth eased unexpectedly. He released her and shifted back a step, giving her a little space. She was shaking. He frowned at her and half turned, to take in the king as well. But most of his attention was still for her. "If you would have men and griffins together lay an ambush for our common enemy, we shall do so. Do you understand me?"

"I had been told," said the king warily, "that this was not your intention." He, too, must have felt the barely contained rage that burned within the griffin, but he met his eyes steadily.

"Your man Bertaud son of Boudan persuaded me of the justice of your cause," Kairaithin snapped. "Do *not* press me, king of men; I am not yours to rule. I will tell you what you will do: Go into the desert when the opportunity is offered, and the Lord of Fire and Air will make a pretense of battle; both your men and my people will bring the Arobern down into the desert and there destroy them, and them alone."

The king studied him; one sun-streaked eyebrow lifted. "Is that how it will be?"

Kairaithin's thin mouth tilted into a hard smile; he looked taut and dangerous and like nothing human. He said to Kes, "If you face Esterire Airaikeliu and tell him that you will make whole no injuries of griffin-kind, save if he and his protect and aid your people, he will have no choice but to do as you require or else give way before the armies of men. And he will not give way, nor would he long rule my people if he attempted it. Yours is indeed the will that may rule here, *kereskiita*. Our need for your goodwill is greater than your need for ours."

Among the Feierabiand soldiers, Jos gave Kes a slow nod, meaning, *Is that not what I said? Do you see now that you do in truth hold the sword in your own hand?*

"But—" whispered Kes. "Tesme? And everyone?"

"The Lord of Fire and Air will be angry," Kairaithin acknowledged, meeting her eyes. "His mate Esterikiu Anahaikuuanse will be angry; Tastairiane Apailika will be very angry. You must withstand all their anger, all their threats. I suspect that Eskainiane Escaile Sehaikiu will support you. But it does not matter. If they would carry out their threats, *I* will prevent them, and you must trust me for that. I promise you, no harm will come to your sister, nor to your little village of men. Will you trust me to do as I say?"

"Isn't your need too great to allow you to be trustworthy?"

"You will have to decide whom you will trust."

Kes nodded, slowly.

"You taxed me previously with unjustly withholding choice from you. I give it to you now. There is a cost. You will pay it either way. You will ride the fiery wind and be changed by it, and achieve triumph for us all. Or you will refuse to become fire, and your people will be crushed by the strength of Casmantium. You wished me to be clear with you. Am I clear?"

He had unbound her. Kes could feel the difference, as though her awareness of the desert had suddenly expanded and clarified. She whispered, "Yes."

Among the men, Jos came half a step forward and then stopped as he met an officer's forbidding hand. He said furiously, "No! How dare you steal her from earth, how dare you make her a fire mage and force her to do the work *you* ought to do—"

"If she will be a fire mage, it's not in the way a griffin is a mage!" snapped Kairaithin. "*I* have no power to heal. It's not your choice, man! Nor even mine." Kairaithin turned his proud stare upon the king, who met it and did not even visibly flinch. "And you, king of men? You are the other one here to have a choice: to battle griffins in the desert, and then Casmantium when the Arobern comes down from the heights, or to trust my intentions and my skill and reserve your strength for Casmantium alone. Do you understand what it is I will do for you?"

"I think I do," said the king. He looked deliberately at Kes. "Shall I trust this creature? What say you?"

Kes shook her head, found her voice, and whispered, "You should trust me." She looked at Jos. "You . . . you told me that the . . . the sword was in my hand. I didn't think so. But it is. You were right. I see that, now. I won't let them harm you. But you know I will have to use fire. I will have to, Jos."

He started to answer, to come back to her, but the king shook his head, and the officer stopped him with a hard grip. Then the king glanced at the woman in the chair. "Meriemne?"

The woman's strange clouded eyes might be blind, but they still saw more, Kes thought, than the surface of men; she looked down, feeling exposed and very small.

"She has given her heart to the fire," the woman said to the king, her fragile voice nevertheless perfectly clear in the quiet. "But she has not yet forgotten how to love the earth. She will try hard to do what she has said she will do."

"And the griffin?"

"Ah." Ruthless discipline struggled with dislike in those old eyes. "There I can't well judge."

"Wise," Kairaithin said to her, at once harshly furious and amused. He looked at the king, waiting.

"I am inclined," said the king, "to follow your script, griffin mage."

"Wisdom is showered like fire across the earth!" exclaimed Kairaithin, with more bitterness than humor. And laid a hand on Kes's shoulder, and moved them all, Kes and Opailikiita and himself, back into the heart of the desert.

CHAPTER 13

The Lord of Fire and Air was very angry. His anger beat through the air as though the sun itself raged across the desert. He was angry with Kes, but he was angrier still with Kairaithin.

This is your kiinukaile, he said to Kairaithin, his powerful voice slamming down around them like silent thunder. *This is* your *little kitten. You set yourself against me—you set this little earth-creature before you and set yourself in its shadow!*

Do you believe so? For this battle, Kairaithin had taken his true form. He matched the king glare for glare, but he sat poised and still, like a cat, ostentatiously unconcerned with any threat. He said, with a disdainful, contained fury of his own, *Will you say that I keep to the shadow of any creature? Of earth or fire or both at once? Do you declare so?*

Shall I? demanded the king.

Little flames licked up and down Kairaithin's black

wings. *I declare your intention is ill-conceived. And will you nevertheless hold to it, in the face of the necessity I perceive?*

Lord of the Changing Wind, will you claim to be Lord of Fire and Air?

There was a short pause. Kairaithin did not drop his gaze as a man would have before his king; he did not look away or bow himself down or make any gesture that recognized the griffin king's threat or challenge or reprimand or whatever it had been. He merely said, *No.* Just that, flatly.

Having considered the direction of the wind, I *decide how the People of Wind and Fire shall follow it,* the king said, and the whole desert seemed to shudder with the force of that assertion.

Having found the direction of the wind unsustainable, I alter its direction, Kairaithin answered, still in that flat tone.

You are influenced by your little kiinukaile, said Tastairiane Apailika. The white griffin lounged in a pose that mimicked relaxation, but he was not relaxed. Kes heard the tension in his voice; it sang in the wind that ruffled the shining feathers around his fierce eagle's head and neck and shoulders. When he shifted a forefoot, he tore deep gouges through the red stone with his eagle's talons. He said contemptuously, *Your* kereskiita *maintains attachment to its mud-people, and you are influenced by its attachment. There comes a wind of blood and fire; we may mount the heights to ride this storm. We have this chance to rid ourselves of both kinds of human creatures and claim this land. And you would* change *this wind, Sipiike Kairaithin?*

It is an error to set trust or good regard into the keeping of any human, added Nehaistiane Esterikiu Anahaikuuanse, mantling her red-and-gold wings and glaring at Kes. *You would distinguish between the human creatures here and those who came into our great desert to destroy us, but this is a false distinction. We had much better destroy them all. Have you not fashioned this human woman into a creature of fire for this exact purpose?*

Kes, horrified, said, "I won't!"

For a terrible moment, all the griffins stared at her. The combined ferocious power of their regard nearly drove her to cower away from them. Kes closed her hands into fists, shut her eyes so she would not have to try to meet all those furious unhuman glares, and concentrated on standing up straight. She said again, "I won't! You want to *kill* everyone? You say the—the Lord of the Changing Wind made me into a creature of fire to *destroy all my people*? Well, maybe I've learned to love fire, but I remember my people and it doesn't matter what you do! I won't ride *any* wind of death that comes against my people!" Then she had to open her eyes again, trying not to flinch.

Esterikiu Anahaikuuanse, glaring more ferociously than ever, began to answer.

Eskainiane Escaile Sehaikiu interrupted the red female. *It's a brave little kitten*, he declared approvingly, *and it knows its own mind and heart*. He turned to the king. *I watched this little one make you whole, my brother, when she was still almost entirely a human woman and hardly knew fire. Even then, that was nothing any of us could do, and who but her teacher might guess what she might have become since?*

Exactly so, said the red female sharply. *Thus—*

She's not of our kind, said Eskainiane, and turned to nudge Kes with the tip of his beak, a gesture that was not *exactly* friendly, but something very like. He said to the other griffins, *If she was, what reason would Sipiike Kairaithin have had to seek her out? If she casts herself free of one wind for another, then if the wind changes, I might let slip the one wind from beneath my wings and ride the other.*

There was a pause. Esterikiu Anahaikuuanse still looked furious, but the king now seemed more thoughtful than angry. It was his decision that mattered, and he did not speak.

She is determined on her course, Kairaithin said in a hard voice. *She is adamant. She will yield to no threat.*

If you would begin to carry out *the threats you have made so liberally, she would cower at your feet*, Tastairiane Apailika said, his voice whipping through Kes' mind like a thrown knife.

I am satisfied you are mistaken, said Kairaithin. *And who perceives the hearts of men more clearly, you or I?*

The white griffin had no answer for that.

And if you are wrong, said Kairaithin, *and no threat nor punishment will move her, and we lose her gift and her skill, then what will we do when at last a more powerful Casmantium settles its strength and strikes against us? As it will. Do not mistake the Arobern's intention: He will not suffer a desert to exist in the midst of his new lands. And Feierabiand, though weakened and angry, will in the end join with Casmantium against us, for all human peoples are natural allies when fire strikes against earth. You believe that with my* kiinukaile's *skill and gift, we can destroy anything of humankind that comes against us, but the strength of earth is far less exhaustible than you imagine. And who would know better than I?*

A deadly pause spun itself out. Tastairiane Apailika began to answer.

Kes drew courage from Kairaithin's strength, from Opailikiita's warm support, from bright Eskainiane's amused approval. Eskainiane Escaile Sehaikiu was wrong: She was not brave. She did not know how to make powerful speeches. She was too afraid of the white griffin to even look at him. But she said swiftly to the Lord of Air and Fire, before the white griffin could speak, "I might cower at your feet. Maybe I will. But I won't . . . I *won't* make right any harm that comes to any griffin. If you harm people of Feierabiand. I won't. Nobody of Feierabiand has harmed *you*. What business is it of yours to do them harm?"

Eskainiane Escaile Sehaikiu laughed, quick and confident and brilliant and pleased by courage wherever he found it—even in her. Even when she opposed his own plan.

And the king, always inclined to be swayed by his *iskarianere*'s opinions more than any other, allowed himself, at last, to be amused as well. He said, *We will consider this new wind you propose. Sipiike Kairaithin, you may make it plain to us, and we shall consider it.*

Kairaithin inclined his proud head at last, small flames rippling through the delicate black feathers of his throat. He said, *It will please you well enough, O Lord of Fire and Air—or so I believe. And if it will also please my little* kinukaile, *shall we not be generous to please her?*

Perhaps we shall, said the king, and Kes knew they had won after all—won a changed direction for the wind, and life for her people, and a chance for safety for all of Feierabiand. She moved quietly to one side, joined

Opailikiita, and leaned against the young griffin, catching her breath and trying to believe that they had won and that everything would be all right.

Iaor Safiad of Feierabiand engaged Casmantium in the midst of the desert, as everyone, Kes supposed, had at one time or another intended, although for wildly differing purposes. But they did so under conditions designed to favor Feierabiand. Or Kes hoped that was so. Kairaithin said it was. Opailikiita said so, too, an assurance Kes trusted more than the griffin mage's.

When the army of Feierabiand came bravely into the desert, the griffins flew to meet them with every appearance of violent intent, but without harboring such intent in their fierce unhuman hearts—or so Opailikiita assured Kes.

Kes tucked herself between Opailikiita's wings when the young griffin took to the wind: She clung hard to handfuls of feathers, trying not to think about how far below the sand lay. Opailikiita turned in slow spirals through the hot air, above even most of the larger griffins, and slowly Kes relaxed a little. Opailikiita lay so still on the wind, with only the slightest shift of feathered wings to adjust her course, that it began to be easy to feel safe. Kes leaned what seemed perilously far over to peer across the griffin's shoulder.

The griffins rode the hot winds below Opailikiita. They soared in small groups or alone, forming slow patterns in the air as groups overlapped and parted and merged and parted again: bronze and gold, red and brown, and copper and black. White Tastairiane flew fiercely alone, sliding through the patterns other griffins made, and the rest made way for him. The only griffin Kes could not find below her in the sky was Kairaithin, and she knew where *he* was and why he was not with the rest.

She followed one griffin and then another with her gaze. She knew all their proud, violent names. She knew the feel of each one's voice, fierce or subtle or sharp as wind-honed stone. She would have known each from all the others just from the tilt of a head or the fiery glance of an eye. Their names thundered in her blood and rolled across her tongue, each one distinct. She knew she would feel injury to any one of them as a break in the natural flow of fire through this desert. She knew that she would be able to channel fire into such injuries and make them whole.

And she knew that doing so would mold her own body and soul into the shapes of fire. She would fly with Opailikiita and call fire through the air, pour it through her hands; fire would run through her veins like blood and she would become a creature of fire. She knew this. She thought, briefly, of shifting herself off Opailikiita's back and far away. Of leaving this war between men and men, between men and griffins, between earth and fire to be fought by someone else, its cost borne by someone else. Anyone else. She could do that. Kairaithin did not bind her. Nothing bound her. She might find herself outside Tesme's house, with her sister's voice calling to her . . . What would Tesme be saying? She found she could not imagine any possible words.

Far below stood the men, far away and small, impossible to tell one from another. The heads of their spears flashed like silver droplets of water in the desert; the strings of their bows and the heads of their arrows flashed silver. They stood in precise ranks, lines of men and more lines beyond them: Kairaithin had said the King of Feierabiand had brought only a small army with him into the desert, but to Kes it looked like a very large army. She wondered whether they might actually turn against the griffins, and if they did, what would happen.

They have a magic of their own, which they bear with them, even into our desert, Opailikiita commented. *Those arrows are not earthbound. They, if not their makers, may fly to meet a griffin in the air. Men are very dangerous. And the spears make it hard to come against men on the ground.*

"You did not . . . the last time, you did not seem worried about the spears?"

There are many times as many men here now. And this time they would expect blinding dust and sand, and falling fire, and attacks from any direction. See how they have angled their companies to guard one another.

Kes could see nothing of the sort. She asked tentatively, "What would you do if I were not here?"

Were you not with us, said Opailikiita, *we would have a difficult battle, so few of us against so many men. Though the desert itself is our element and will fight for us and carry our power, still there are earth mages to hinder us. Even so, you will see today, when the Arobern comes onto the sand, how the desert is our ally and our tool, we who have no other gift for making.* She sounded fierce and joyful and proud; she sounded like she was looking forward to it.

"You are sure the . . . the Casmantians will come into the desert?"

Are you not? Yes, little sister, they will come. You see how the Safiad sets his people so that they would be vulnerable to attack from out of the mountains. The Casmantians will see it also, and they will come to that opportunity, as an arrow in flight would be drawn to its target. Well you are with us, my beautiful sister, for if not my people would be as vulnerable as the men of Feierabiand.

Below, men lifted twisted horns of brass; long golden notes rolled out over the desert. Soldiers halted and turned; spear points dipped and rose again, flashing. Men in the center of each formation lifted bows, strings flashing silver, and nocked arrows. Horns rang out again, rich and mellow and sounding to Kes like slow summer days and harvest festivals and not like war at all.

Above the men, bright Eskainiane Escaile Sehaikiu swept a long, fierce trail of fire through the hot air. Esterire Airaikeliu, Lord of Fire and Air, darker and more terrible than his companion, curved suddenly out of a spiral and fell after his *iskarianere*, with a shrill piercing cry like a stooping falcon: His cry struck fire from the air. Above him, other griffins shrieked and flung back their wings and stooped, and fire fell from the wind that roared past the long feathers of their wings.

Below the griffins, men cried out in fear and shouted urgent commands: Arrows rose suddenly in a silver rain.

Kes covered her eyes and bowed low over Opailikiita's neck.

No. Look, said Opailikiita, and Kes peeked timorously from between her fingers. Arrows did not reach their targets but burst into flame in midflight. Griffins, striking, came down savagely upon the . . . sand, between companies of men, outside of spear's reach. The beating of their wings flung up red dust and sand until Kes could see nothing clearly. Men shouted. Metal crashed against metal, with a horrible clatter of ringing and shrieking.

But spears did not strike griffins, nor did griffins strike men. The fire that burned across the sand guttered in the stiff wind and went out.

Good, said Opailikiita. *They are brave.*

Kes did not know whether she spoke of the griffins or of the men. But she thought the men were very brave. Their horns sang through the thick dust, and the long notes were valiant and clear.

Casmantium, Opailikiita said, in a tone of satisfaction.

Startled, Kes followed the direction of the griffin's gaze. There, where the mountains came down and met the edge of the desert, men were coming out from around a corner of smooth gray stone onto the red sand. Men and more men, and then more yet, in ranks that formed quickly and instantly broke into motion: brown and black, with silver spears and bows that caught the light like griffins' beaks.

See, said Opailikiita, still with satisfaction, *they think the Safiad is ignorant of them still. Possibly they even believe* we *are ignorant of them.*

"Yes," Kes said nervously. It seemed to her to be taking a very long time for the Casmantian army to cross the sand and close up behind the Feierabiand soldiers. And, if she could trust Kairaithin and Opailikiita, they would find themselves in a terrible trap. Of their own making. Yet she could not watch, and covered her eyes.

Then she could not bear to be blind, and looked after all.

The first part of the Casmantian army struck the rear of the Feierabiand army, and there was suddenly a vast confusion all through that region: Kes could find no order to any of it.

But Opailikiita said fiercely, *Thus we strike down those who would destroy us.*

Kes said nothing. A griffin's name rolled through her mind suddenly: Esheteriu Nepuukai, a young griffin, copper-bright wings and golden lion pelt, bright and passionate. She knew as though she stood beside him that he lay in the sand with a terrible wound across his chest and a spear through his foot, blood pouring out of him, shattering into garnets and rubies as the sun struck it. She knew when the spear was wrenched out and drawn back for another thrust. She thought of Tesme, fleetingly, but there was not time to think or worry or be frightened, because the spear was already stabbing out once more. Before the strike could be made, Kes made the young griffin's body whole, and watched with her mind's eye as he hurled himself forward. She felt as though she flung herself forward with him, exaltation spilling like fire through her own wings.

Shaistairai Kaihastaikiita fell through the brilliant air, arrows in her side and flank; the arrows were tipped with ice and ill-intent. Kes burned through them with clean fire and closed the wounds with fire; the griffin fell through sheets of fire, caught the wind with powerful wings, and flung herself straight down in an explosion of joy and fury, an explosion that burned through Kes as well.

The Lord of Fire and Air himself took an arrow in the throat. Kes burned it out and left him surging forward straight into a thicket of spears. They tore him open, face and chest and sides, and Kes, his name pounding like the sun through her blood, made him whole again. And again. Until the wounds ceased to come.

Is it hard, my sister? asked Opailikiita, turning in her slow spiral path to carry Kes back across the battleground.

"No," whispered Kes. It was not hard. But it swept Kes's attention inward, where griffin names sang like poetry in her blood.

She had no attention to spare any longer to look from above at the battle. She felt she was in it herself: a battle to repair tears in the natural order of the world, to weave wholeness through ragged injuries. Once or twice a cold malaise seemed to touch her, crept like ice across her fingers where she gripped Opailikiita's feathers in her hands. But each time the cold fell away almost before she knew it was there, and she forgot it instantly in the rolling thunder of fire that filled her eyes and her heart. At last all she saw was fire, until she became fire and burned with Opailikiita, who turned to fire beneath her and laughed with fierce joy.

Kes did not notice right away when the frequency of injuries pressing themselves upon her attention slowed, and slowed . . . Eventually she found she had time to find herself riding the wind, griffin back, in human form again, uncertain whether she had ever truly left it. She had time to lean over Opailikiita's shoulder and stare into the burning dust below, time to try to see the shapes of men and griffins hidden by that red dust. She did not fear to fall, now. She thought that if she leaned too far and fell, she would simply fall into fire, turn into fire and blowing sand. But she did not fall. Nor did she speak. It seemed to her that she had forgotten the sounds of human language—that if she spoke, flames would fall like jewels from her tongue.

Opailikiita, too, seemed disinclined to speak. An

awareness of her filled Kes, because she was so near or because she was so closely allied: She seemed not only a slim brown griffin, but also equally a streak of bodiless fire falling out of the molten sky.

Below, the dust was settling. Sunlight poured through the dust and turned the air the color of blood or fire. Small griffin fires burned here and there in the sand, leaving flecks of gold and fire opals and carnelians to glitter where they burned out. The darker garnets and rubies of griffin blood sparkled in the sand where the griffins had fought and bled for this victory.

The griffins themselves had drawn aside, going up into the red spires that were their halls and their homes. Few remained among the men, and those were reaching out with immense wings and pulling themselves, one after another, back into the sky.

Weary men moved slowly across the sand, heavy earthbound creatures, nothing that belonged to the desert, though some of them were gathering the jewels that blood and fire had spilled out across the sand. Kes understood: Thus they would keep a small piece of the desert with them when they departed, as was only right. Their own blood had flowed like water and left only stains little redder than the sand.

The victors wore the undyed linen of Feierabiand uniform and the vanquished wore the brown and black of Casmantium, so she could tell the difference between them. Men were putting up awnings to shield the wounded from the hammer of the desert sun, and passing out skins of water and watered wine. Men of both countries bore injuries, but these did not call themselves to Kes's attention as griffin wounds would have done. There were not many men in brown left alive, Kes saw, which was only as it should have been: It had been a day for death, and their deaths had been good. The exaltation of the fire had ebbed, but she was still very happy.

She looked for the King of Casmantium among those who had survived, but she could not find him. She found the King of Feierabiand, however, in the shade of a great twisted tower of stone. She slipped down from Opailikiita's back and went toward him.

He was limping, she saw, and he looked very tired, but also deeply satisfied. He clapped another man on the shoulder as Kes approached, sending him off with a word that made the man laugh, though wearily. Then he turned to Kes with a quick nod of greeting and satisfaction. "Well done!" he said. "Your griffins turned the day handily, young Kes. We, now—we have wounded, though nothing like so many as we might have had facing the Casmantians alone. Can you heal them as you healed the griffins?"

"I could heal them, I think," Kes answered, feeling fire roll within her blood, desiring to spill flames across the world. She could loose it, she thought, and stitch with flames ragged patterns that should be smooth. She wanted to. It would be pleasant to run fire through her hands. Even for men.

"I don't think that would be wise," Meriemne answered, from a cushioned chair in the shade where Kes had not noticed her. "Men are not meant to be filled with fire."

Kes looked at the mage, whom she had not realized was there, first with startlement and then with dislike and confusion. Meriemne did not seem as unpleasant and frightening as Beguchren had when he had caught her in the desert and trapped her with his cold bindings. But she simply did not *like* her. The instant warmth of the smile the king turned toward the old woman confused and upset her.

"Fortunately," added the old mage, "I can heal them myself. Once they are out of this atrocious desert. No offense, fire child," she added to Kes, who only blinked at her in a confused muddle of aversion.

"Yes," the king began to say to the mage, but interrupted himself at the shout of one of his men and looked out across the desert where the man was pointing.

Kes backed quickly around Opailikiita to put the griffin between herself and Meriemne, and looked too. *Can you see?* she asked her.

A feather's weight of men, Opailikiita answered. She tilted her eagle's head and studied the approaching riders. *One of them is the lord of men who is beholden to Kairaithin—Bertaud son of Boudan.*

"Bertaud?" said the king, in a pleased tone. "Well, and timely arrived, for all I left him sternly in Riamne. Still, of course, he would know I would welcome him now. Well, well . . . he can join us at least for the ride out of this terrible desert. No offense," he added to Kes, who gazed at him in confusion.

They come in haste, Opailikiita observed, her attention still on the handful of approaching riders.

"Do they?" the king shaded his eyes and stared hard at the approaching riders. "So they do. They are not pursued? You see them in no difficulty?"

I see only those men, King of Feierabiand. If there is difficulty, I do not see it.

"Well, we shall discover the reason for their haste

soon enough," the king said, faint unease in his tone, and turned to speak to officers of his men. Kes did not listen. She was looking across the desert at the men. They came slowly, slowly, until she wanted to blaze a path for them through the sand that would bring them directly to this one point of sand in all the vastness of the desert. It seemed momentarily strange to her that she should be impatient, she who had always been by nature patient; but then Opailikiita called to her and she turned back to the griffin.

Kairaithin summons me.

Then go, Kes said. *But listen for me.*

Your voice is in my blood, said the griffin, and shifted herself away through the desert in the manner of griffin mages.

The men came at last into the Feierabiand company and were temporarily lost from sight behind the awnings set up for the wounded men. The king turned expectantly, smiling, to greet the new arrivals; his smile faded as they came back into view and rode up. Kes, her eyes on the distressed, blowing horses, did not at once look at the men. But then the king's attention pulled hers after it at last, and she lifted her eyes to the strained face of the riders.

"Bertaud!" The king strode forward to greet them.

One of the men murmured something about water and took the young lord's horse as he dismounted, leading it and the other animals away to be walked and watered.

Lord Bertaud strode rapidly to the king. He said sharply, urgently, "I could not stay in Riamne."

"No, I understand so—your friend Kairaithin found me and said, what was it, something about how you had persuaded him of the justice of our cause. Well done, well done, my friend! I would have sent for you then, but there seemed no time—we would have had a hard time of it without griffin assistance—"

Lord Bertaud seized the king's arm, fierce as a griffin in his urgency. "Iaor. I might not have been in time for the battle, but I saw part of it from a high cliff. Answer me this. Where is the Arobern? Captured? Killed?"

The king shook his head, studying the other man in obvious concern. "No, no—we did not see him. A griffin took him, I suppose. The Casmantian army was a good deal smaller than I'd feared—it seems your report was overanxious—"

"Overanxious?" Lord Bertaud gave a short, harsh laugh, looking more tense and strained than Kes had ever seen him. "Overanxious! No, Iaor! The rest of the Casmantian army is simply somewhere else. *And* the Arobern. I will lay any wager for it. And where else would he be but slipping down the edge of this terrible desert to strike unopposed as he sees fit?"

The king stared at him. He, too, clearly saw the truth of it at once—now that he had the leisure to think on it. "I should have realized."

"You were occupied."

"Yes, as the Arobern intended. Earth and iron! That man is far too bold. And now we shall all pay the cost of our own lack of imagination. How many men do you suppose he has with him? Three thousand? More?" He turned, shouting for his officers—one came up hastily from somewhere and said rapidly, not waiting for the king to speak, "Your majesty, that spy who came to us—he tells us we should have faced twice as many men here."

"So we have been discovering," said the king, and he gripped the man's arm, giving him a small shake. "Go get the best information you can about the number that should have been here. See if the man has any guess about what the Arobern might have done with the rest."

Bertaud, for his part, shouted for Kairaithin while Kes was still distracted by the mention of Jos.

The griffin arrived even before the officers, falling out of the red sky, half fire and half griffin: He reared up as he struck the ground and his wings, streaming behind him, were sheets of flame. Men fell back from him, shouting in alarm. Horses reared and wanted to scatter in panic; horse speakers ran to take lead lines and bridles, calming them and holding them still. Kes thought it was a pity no one could do the same for the men, but at least none so forgot themselves as to loose arrows at the griffin.

What? the griffin flung at Bertaud, rage blazing within as he burned with fire without. *Well? And do you not find this outcome satisfactory, man?*

Kes stared, shocked at the naked violence of Kairaithin's manner, of his voice; so much more ferocious than even when he had been angry at her for defying him to go to the king.

"Where is the Arobern?" Bertaud shouted back at him, appearing, to Kes's astonishment, neither surprised nor cowed by Kairaithin's violence.

Kairaithin stared hard into the man's eyes. His own were filled with rage and, strangely, something stronger, which might have been despair. But a more rational thought crept into them as Kes watched, and she was no longer certain what she had seen at first.

He gathered himself into a form winged with feathers

rather than flames, and settled more solidly to the sand. *Is he not here?*

"No!"

"Nor is Beguchren," Kes added.

I will seek the cold mage, said Kairaithin, and flung himself back into the sky.

"But what about the Arobern?" Bertaud shouted after him.

Wincing at his shout, Kes shook her head and laid her hand on the lord's arm. "Let him go. Let him go. He will look for Beguchren."

"Forget about the cold mage," snapped the king, leaning forward intensely. He had the reins of a horse in his hand and was clearly preparing to mount. "Bertaud is right—it's the Arobern who concerns us now!"

Kes shook her head again, but she also called into the silence of the desert, so little disturbed by the shouts of men, *Eskainiane! Eskainiane?*

And the copper-and-gold griffin, riding the winds of the burning heights and resting as griffins rest, answered. He plunged from the wind to the red sand, from the side of the Lord of Fire and Air to Kes's side, so that the king's horse reared and had to be calmed by a horse speaker who ran hastily to it.

Kereskiita, Eskainiane said joyfully, ignoring man and horse and king. *Well flown, on a fierce wind! Do you call me? I declare I will hear you!*

Kes laughed and lifted her hand to touch the side of his beak, a gesture he returned by turning his head to brush her palm lightly with the cutting edge. He was still exultant from flight and battle, passionately joyful with victory and the speed of the wind. And he had come, as he said, to answer her call, though he was brother and more than brother to the Lord of Fire and Air.

Kes had known that he would. After this day's battle, where she had come to know them all, she loved this griffin above any other save only Opailikiita. Powerful and brilliant and generous, she trusted Eskainiane Escaile Sehaikiu to come to her call out of that open-hearted generosity and listen to her. *Eskainiane*, she said. And aloud, after the manner of humankind, "Eskainiane, where is the King of Casmantium? Would you ride the wind and search for an army that did not come into the desert? Would you send your people to look to the north and the east and the south, beyond the sand, where men might have gone and we not known?"

For you, kereskiita, *we will fly beyond the powerful sun and search*, answered Eskainiane, and touched her face with his beak in a griffin caress. *All will search: I will ask Kiibaile Esterire Airaikeliu to send all save Kairaithin, who is about business of his own, and after this day, I tell you, Kiibaile will hear your name in the wind through his wings*. The griffin flung himself back into the sky.

"Kiibaile—what?" asked the king, bemused.

"Kiibaile Esterire Airaikeliu," Kes said absently. "The Lord of Fire and Air. *You* shouldn't call him by his first name. That's for his *iskarianere*—his intimate . . ." she began to say *friends*, but that wasn't quite right and she stopped, frowning.

"Well, whatever his name, if he will set his people to searching, that will do," said the king, reaching again for his horse's reins once the griffin was gone. "Thank you, Kes. We will not wait. I want out of this desert, and if the Arobern did not watch from above and take himself back off across the mountains, it's to the east he'll be. Where is your horse, Bertaud? Has the creature a run left in it? How fast do you suppose we can make it out of this savage desert? And be in decent shape to fight? If we can find the Arobern to give him a fight! How can I have been so blind?" He paused. "I wonder if Eles found him? Earth and iron! I didn't give Eles half enough men to face any such threat!"

Lord Bertaud took a step forward, looking surprised and cautiously relieved. "Eles?"

The king frowned at him. "Well, what else was I to do when I must ride into a trap but make provision? It did not seem wise to leave all Feierabiand to depend only on my army. Eles was to get me another, as many men as he could, and to come south on his own, and on any account to stay out of the desert. I meant to keep him safe from the griffins and safe from the first thrust of the Arobern, but now I do not know where he is or what he may have met on his road."

For the first time, the tension that had tightened the lord's face and manner eased. He laughed and clapped the king on the shoulder. "My horse will have to do," he said, and beckoned to the man who had taken it away.

CHAPTER **14**

The desert was as cleanly and elegantly beautiful as any airy palace or many-towered citadel built by men, Bertaud thought. But it was not a place meant for men, or for any creature of earth. Its starkness invited meditations on mortality and on the silence that lay behind life; the voice of the wind that sang across its twisted sharp-angled spires offered a suggestion of that greater music that lay behind the ordinary melodies of men. Its fierceness encompassed the fierceness of the griffins that made it; the passionate beat of its light and heat echoed the passion of griffin nature. Bertaud could imagine griffins emerging directly from the red silence of sand and stone, engendered by that powerful light, carved into shape by that ceaseless wind.

But it was not a place meant for men. It was drawing the very life out of them as they stood within its boundaries, as the sand might absorb blood spilled out upon it. And, it was clear, not even the earth mages, not even Meriemne, could resist that power. Not while it surrounded her, binding her strength and cutting her off from the living earth.

So there was a confusion and a haste that seemed utterly out of place in the patient desert: haste to load wounded men into litters and shaded carts, to cover dead men and lay their bodies out in other carts; haste to form men already fainting with heat and dazed by light into company ranks and send them east toward the cool country that waited so little distance away. Haste to lay plans for what they might find when they came there.

Iaor rode back and forth, with the vanguard for a short length and then back to the rear to check on the slowest of the carts. Here, he leaped down from his horse to lend a hand with an awning that would not stay up; there, he gave watered wine from his own supply to a wounded man. That was a king's task: to be seen everywhere, to inspire. Bertaud left him to it and made his own slow way through the company, studying the men.

Two thousand and more men, he knew, had ridden south with the king from Riamne. Some, probably, had gone with Eles when Iaor had divided the army. Most had followed the king into the desert, and though Casmantium had not broken them, nor the griffins flung fire down upon them, still the battle, and even more the desert, had taken a toll. For every man struck down by spear or sword or arrow, Bertaud estimated, likely two had collapsed from heat and lack of water—though the army had carried a great deal of water, a man could not fight and drink simultaneously, and exertion under the pounding sun had sucked the moisture out of them.

Of whatever number had come into this desert with the king, perhaps a thousand remained strong enough and with heart enough for battle . . . if they should get out of the desert and into the green country and have time to rest and recover a little from the desert.

Kes rode with the army, perched high on the shoulders of the slim brown griffin who was her constant companion. Of them all, Kes rode with her face turned up to the sky as though she could not get enough light. She still wore the short brown dress she had made out of a Casmantian soldier's shirt, and with her skin ruddy with sun and her tangled hair down her back like a fall of pale light, she looked little more human than the griffin. And yet in a strange way her very unearthliness seemed to suit her, as though she had somehow always been meant for fire.

Kes brought her gaze down from the brilliant sky when Bertaud looked at her. She smiled at him, a sweet, perfectly human smile, but her eyes were edged and lit with fire. When she slid down from the griffin's back and ran across the sand to Bertaud's horse, men shied out of her way. She did not seem to notice this, either, but turned to walk beside his horse and lift trusting, unhuman eyes to his. If she had not clearly been able to see, he would have thought her blind.

"Yes?"

Bertaud strove for a neutral tone. "Eskainiane Escaile Sehaikiu?"

"Yes—Eskainiane." Her voice lingered over the name as though she spoke poetry. Her voice was not really a human voice any longer, although Bertaud could not have said precisely where the difference lay. Even the girl's steps seemed to have lightened, as though at the next step, or the next, she might walk right off the ground and into the air. "Eskainiane Escaile Sehaikiu . . . he will find them.

Indeed, I think he has found them. You know," she said earnestly, patting the horse's neck, "you can trust Eskainiane. He is open-hearted and . . . not kind, exactly . . ."

"Generous," said Bertaud.

"Yes—generous. He will send . . . ah." She said then, in a different tone, "He has sent Kairaithin, I think."

The griffin mage came this time in a long, slow, smooth flight that carried him easily over the column of men and left him walking, in the shape of a man, beside Iaor's horse. He did not even glance at Bertaud, who was forced to take a moment to put down a violent and extremely stupid surge of jealousy.

"Esteemed mage," Iaor said to Kairaithin, with a nod.

Kairaithin gave the king a taut smile. "There is battle," he said. "Beguchren Teshrichten is with the Arobern, and both are with the main part of their army outside the town called Minas Ford."

"Minas Ford?" said Kes, much like someone told that the town of her childhood, distantly remembered, lies just beyond the next turn in the road.

"Eles *engaged* him?" Iaor said, in a completely different tone. "There is battle *now*?"

"The griffins must aid us again, then," Bertaud said, trying for no tone at all.

Kairaithin turned to him swiftly. "I have destroyed the cold mages sent against us here. But outside this desert, I cannot match Beguchren. And would you have us come down outside our place of power, with our fire turned all to ash, upon soldiers armed with cold steel? Bows made with purpose to kill creatures of fire? No, man. We would be destroyed, and is that your desire?"

Iaor said, "We haven't enough men to face down another army the size of the first—and our men spent with heat, and his men near fresh? Esteemed mage—"

"They *will* help us, my king," said Bertaud with resolve, and stared into fiery black eyes.

Kes gazed, clearly curious and alarmed, from him to Kairaithin.

Kairaithin did not glance at her. His attention, hot as the savage desert, was narrowed to Bertaud. "I will find a way," he said, straight to Bertaud, "if you will trust me for that, and do nothing on your own account." There was no anger in the griffin's voice, belying the anger in his eyes and his heart: He was, Bertaud understood, making a fierce effort to keep his tone neutral. It was, perhaps, the closest Kairaithin could publicly come to a plea.

Bertaud hesitated. He could imagine no greater dereliction of his duty to Iaor and Feierabiand than to allow the Arobern to strike through Minas Ford and then, unopposed, for Terabiand on the coast. Nor did he believe Iaor had any real chance of turning the Arobern from that purpose with a bare thousand sunstruck soldiers.

Yet at the same time he could imagine no greater wrong than to compel the wild, brilliant-hearted griffins to the service of men. No matter how desperately Feierabiand needed their service. He had dreamed of violent winds and lakes of molten stone: What would his dreams contain if he broke the griffins to harness like oxen? Or if he drove them all to their deaths in a cool green country where their fire could not burn?

He said at last, "Who could do so better than you, esteemed mage?"

Kairaithin inclined his head, backed up a step—waiting, Bertaud saw, to see that he would indeed be allowed to go—and then folded himself through space into the far heart of the desert.

Bertaud let his breath out. He said casually to Iaor, just as though nothing untoward had taken place, "He will do his best, I think, if only to humble the pride of Casmantium. I think he resents how his people were used as tools against us."

The king nodded sharply. "I should certainly think so." He glanced ahead and added with a good deal more interest, "Earth and iron, is there no *end* to this cursed desert?"

Kes, who had been gazing at Bertaud with alarming intensity, shifted her attention to the king. "You see that flat-topped spire? That one, with the double arch on the eastern side? The boundary is just there." She added at the king's raised-eyebrow look, "I always know." Her tone was almost wistful. "But cannot you see it? It is dark, like the edge of night against the day."

Bertaud thought he could. Iaor only shook his head.

"It is not far," said Kes, and walked away toward her griffin as though simply forgetful of the king, or of his rank. But she moved with that odd lighter-than-air grace, and Bertaud thought she had not so much forgotten Iaor's rank, as become, griffinlike, disinclined to care for it.

The creature had waited for Kes patiently. She lowered her beak to brush the girl's hair and turned for her to mount, then spread dark wings and reached for the heights. Bertaud watched them go. He knew, uneasily, precisely what it was like to spread wings and mount the sweeping stair of the wind. Precisely what it was like.

"I wish we might fly, and spare our feet," grumbled Iaor. "Or that the horses might, and spare their strength.

Just there, is it? Well, I suppose I do see it, as the girl said. About time. Pass the word, Bertaud—men to form up once we cross that line. Water all around, and we'll try to get the sun-dazed men back on their feet, but with Eles possibly pressed by whatever the Arobern has with him, we cannot delay."

"Leave the sunstruck to guard the Casmantian prisoners," Bertaud advised.

The king nodded sharply. "Yes, that will do. That's a duty for which they should be fit. The horses—I think they will have done what they can merely to get us to the boundary. You have ridden this recently. How far from the boundary to Minas Ford?"

"Half an hour's ride, no more."

"And the griffins? *Will* they aid us?"

"Yes," Bertaud said fiercely, but then more moderately, "I think they will, my king."

"Well, we must not depend upon it. We must have surprise, if we can keep it—find Uol and have scouts sent ahead to see what waits for us—if we can find the disposition of men, that at least may favor us—earth and stone, Bertaud," Iaor added in a different tone, "how can a worn and paltry thousand stand against all the Arobern undoubtedly has brought to this war? Who ever heard of such a war as this, pulled out of a peaceful summer without a whisper of warning? *Can* the griffins aid us when we stand on good earth and not on their burning sand?"

Bertaud opened his mouth to say that he was sure they could, and closed it again. He did not know. He said at last, "I think they will try. As we will. The men know what this battle is for."

Iaor lifted one hand and rubbed his face; he looked

suddenly as though the past days had suddenly caught him up. Then he let his breath out, dropped his hand to his horse's neck, and straightened in the saddle. "Well, if we dare not lose, then we must win, griffins or no," he answered his own question, and pressed the horse into a canter.

Bertaud did not follow. He, too, looked along the slow-footed column of Feierabiand soldiers and wondered what these men would be able to do at the end of a day such as they had had.

The leading edge of the column turned around the spire that Kes had pointed out, and suddenly the pace picked up; the men in front did not spare breath for shouting, but nonetheless as they found the desert boundary in sight before them, their weary relief was transmitted instantly straight through to the men at the very rear. Even the Casmantian prisoners matched that pace; even the horses drawing the carts of the wounded and dead stepped out with a will. Bertaud's horse lifted its head and flared red-rimmed nostrils, sensing that ahead lay air that did not burn with fire; it wanted to run, and after the briefest moment he gave the animal its head. It leaped forward over the sand as though flung like a spear.

The line between desert and ordinary land was sharp and clear as though lain down by a deliberate hand. On the other side of that line, it was raining.

Bertaud stared at the rain, coming down slantwise and heavy through the air; at the heavy skies above; at the water washing downhill past living trees and over living earth, and he laughed out loud as his horse broke from a canter to a stretched-out gallop. It shot across the boundary and tossed its head up, shying sideways as the rain came down against it. It was, after the desert, like charging into an icehouse and being pelted with sleet. Bertaud flung back his own head and opened his mouth, eyes closed, rain running down his face like tears. But he could not have said himself whether they were tears of grief or joy. Both, perhaps.

Probably no soldiers anywhere had ever been so glad to form up in the rain. Men shouted with the first shock of cold—then adjusted to the coolness that was, after all, no colder than usual for summer rain, and stripped off their helmets to let rain pour down their necks. The awnings on the carts suddenly became useful for keeping rain off the wounded, while Meriemne swept back the curtains of her litter to let the rain fall on her wrinkled face. She was already sending her bearers straight for the carts, and Iaor rode past and dipped to take her hand and kiss it, laughing: one more worry off his mind. Bertaud only hoped the earth mage could help the sunstruck also.

General Adries rode by at a smart pace, causing scattered soldiers to leap to order by his mere presence. The men should have had an hour to rest, hot food, wine— but there was no time, or so Iaor clearly feared. Bertaud feared it too. There were great holes in the ranks. Officers were working hastily to merge tattered companies into solid units; sergeants moved through the lines, taking out a man here or moving one to fill a hole there, making sure bowmen were protecting their strings, issuing orders for the men to sit down right in their ranks and get what rest they could. Baskets of hard bread and dried fruit were being passed down the ranks. It was raining harder now, hard enough for the drops to sting, but no one complained about the rain soaking the food. They were too glad for the extra moisture in their parched mouths.

Bertaud found Iaor speaking with his senior officers at the edge of the small army, all of them looking off down the hill as though they expected to see the Casmantian army right down there.

"Ah, Bertaud," Iaor said, catching sight of him. "We'll move out on the quarter hour. We'll cross through the pastures, come down the hills through that wood over there. If the Arobern has men posted to watch for us, that's where they'll be; at least, that's where I'd put them if it were me, so I'll want a dozen or so men to go down quietly in front of us and see what there might be waiting. This rain is luck for us."

Bertaud nodded. The rain would kill alertness, mute sound, restrict visibility.

Iaor frowned in thought. "We've got about eight hundred men fit to march—that'll have to do, no matter if the Arobern has two or even three thousand, as the spy tells us. We can hope Eles has blunted his teeth a little." He did not put into words what they both knew: that if Eles had put whatever force he had gathered against the Arobern, probably he and all his men had already been butchered.

"So . . ." Bertaud said instead, "we captured a Casmantian spy?"

"Not captured, precisely. He came with the girl and put himself in our hands—gone over to her side, I gather, if not precisely to ours. I gave him to Emend, you know, one of Moutres's people."

"Ah." Moutres was Iaor's master of spies. And the man, then, was the Casmantian soldier who had brought Kes out of the Casmantian camp. That he'd been a spy was very believable. That he'd entirely thrown over his own people for Kes . . . that, also, remembering him with her, was perhaps believable. Though one trusted turned spies not at all, and depended on their information as little as possible—but Iaor would know that, and at least there was little doubt he'd truly turned.

Iaor ran a distracted hand through his wet hair and glanced at the sky. "Luck for us, as this rain is—luck comes in threes, or we shall hope it does. I know what I want from it: quickness and surprise. Time?" he asked one of the officers.

"Twelve minutes, your majesty," said the man.

Iaor gave a curt nod and strode urgently off with a handful of officers trailing him.

Bertaud watched them go and then walked away, to the edge of the woods and then in among the trees. Rain beat down on the leaves overhead, a comforting sound that quickly muffled the noise of soldiers and horses behind him, until he might almost have been alone in this countryside. His shirt was soaked through . . . not unpleasant, after the desiccating wind of the desert. He stopped at last, his hand against the bole of a slim tree, and called into the rain, "Kairaithin."

As though he had been waiting for that call, the griffin mage was there. Maybe he *had* been waiting; he had come so quickly. He stood in the shadows of the trees with his shadow smoldering dimly behind him, as banked coals may glow faintly through thick ash. His eyes, Bertaud fancied, smoldered as well.

Bertaud said, "This rain—"

"My people cannot fly in this wet," said the griffin harshly. "Do you understand, man?"

Bertaud said nothing.

"You must not call us. If you call, we shall be compelled to come. And in this rain, we shall be helpless against Beguchren—against the cold arrows the Casmantian archers possess. Do you understand?"

The griffin's tone was abrupt, just short of savage; his face rigid. He was trying, Bertaud thought, to overcome his vast pride enough to plead. He was going to manage it in another moment. Bertaud said quickly, to forestall him, "Do *you* understand what will happen to my people, if yours will not aid us? You are asking me to sacrifice my people for yours—perhaps more: Perhaps my king. Perhaps Feierabiand entire." His voice fell to a whisper. "How can I fail to use all the weapons I possess, when the alternative is such profound betrayal? Do you deny that your griffins would still be a useful weapon in our need, even pulled out of the desert and weakened by rain? That your people might still help me save mine?"

Kairaithin came forward a step and half lifted a hand, only to let it fall with whatever gesture he had begun unfinished. He said nothing, perhaps because he could not fathom what argument might move a weary human heart in this exigency. Even silent, the griffin's presence beat against Bertaud like the heat of a great fire, though one banked and dim.

Bertaud ran his hand slowly down the smooth bark of the tree and tried to think, through the distraction of the rain—heavier now—and the fierce pressure of the griffin's presence so near at hand. He could not.

Distantly, he heard the shouts that told him the Feierabiand soldiers, what poor remnants of them remained, were forming up into ranks and prepared to march. They would move quickly, he knew, coming into this wood: There was not yet any need for stealth. He need not rush back to join the Feierabiand army. It would come here, to him. Indeed, he thought he could already hear the sounds of its approach.

He said harshly, hardly knowing what he said, "I won't call you."

Kairaithin met his eyes, waiting, expressionless.

Bertaud thought—knew—that the griffin did not yet believe him. Kairaithin expected some impossible demand to be laid on him, on his people, which they would not be able to refuse and which would destroy them. He repeated simply, not knowing of any complicated oath that would create belief, "I won't call you."

The griffin mage tilted his head to one side, a gesture startlingly like that of a bird. He started to speak.

Behind them, a voice called urgently, "My lord!" A young man came through the trees, riding a horse of his own and leading Bertaud's. "The king is asking for you," said the man.

Bertaud took the reins and turned back to look for Kairaithin. But the griffin was gone. A sharp sense of loss went through Bertaud like an arrow, and a sense of release; he understood that the griffin mage was gone, indeed, and would not return. This would be a battle between men. There was every chance Feierabiand would lose. But the griffins would not, at least, be pulled down with Feierabiand. Bertaud swung up into the saddle without a word to the young man—he felt wholly unsuited, just now, for speaking to men—and went, as directed, to find his king.

There were Casmantian sentries in the wood. "Three of them," Adries reported. "I hope that was all there were, for that's all we found."

By that time, the sounds of battle were faintly audible even over the sounds of rain and wind coming through the trees.

"Eles is holding?" Iaor wondered aloud. "How?" He sent Bertaud a sharp look. "Could your griffins have come there before us and reinforced him?"

Bertaud shrugged. He could hardly explain why he was certain they had not. So he said nothing, and wondered bleakly how he had come to keep such secrets from his king and his friend.

Minas Ford was not, of course, walled. It was far too small to bother defending, and all its wealth—in land and crops and livestock—would have lain outside any wall anyway. There were no more than a few dozen cottages in the village proper, all made of white stone and dark timber, with a single cobbled street and a broad green in the center. The Arobern's army pressed close on all sides. But the army had not yet entered the village: It had been stopped at its edges.

Defenders used the cottages themselves to fill out their lines: They had ranked themselves between ready-made walls. Even so, their lines were frighteningly thin, and growing thinner as Bertaud watched. They were mostly using swords, and mostly against spears, a desperately uneven match, especially with the vastly disparate numbers. Grunts of effort were audible, panting cries of anger or pain from both sides, the ring and scrape and crash of metal against metal . . . Orders, shouted in sharp, high voices to carry above the clamor. The scream, somewhere, of an injured horse, piercing and innocent as the cry of a child. And over all, the constant steady rush of the rain, pouring and pouring out of the heavy sky . . .

Men also were within the houses, shutters thrown wide so they could shoot out at the Casmantians. At first, Bertaud thought those within the buildings were all soldiers, but then he saw, from the way they cast back the dim watery light, that the arrowheads were the slim copper-tipped ones used for hunting and not war, and after that he saw that many of the defenders shooting from the windows were simply villagers. Of course, the Casmantians were shooting back, though it was harder for them, out in the weather as they were, to keep their bowstrings dry. But some of them were clearly managing the trick. When a defender, struck, cried out, it was a woman's high voice Bertaud heard. He flinched from the sound of it.

"Eles did well, and does well," Adries commented, coming up beside Bertaud. "That's more than a hundred men he has there, I expect—more nearly two, if you count the civilians. Women, too—yes, you heard that, too, did you? He might hold another quarter hour, even half, before the Casmantians break through that line somewhere. Then it'd be all over, of course . . . Well, we'll see if we can't beat that moment."

Adries did not put into words the obvious, which was that whatever they might do to relieve Eles and his men for a moment or an hour, it would nevertheless not be possible to win. Unless the griffins came in. *Kairaithin*, Bertaud thought, longing for the power of the griffin to reinforce the men of Feierabiand, but he did not call. The rain fell steadily, as though it had always fallen and always would, as though rain was an intrinsic quality of the air on this side of the boundary. Earth magic brought it, he was increasingly certain: the cold earth magic used by Casmantium, utterly antithetical to griffin fire . . . If he forced the griffins to fight, Bertaud thought, they would only come to be slaughtered, and what good would that do any of them? He did not call.

"We won't be sounding horns. You'd best take your position, my lord."

Bertaud, mouth dry despite the rain, nodded and reined his horse back to look for Iaor.

The king, helmed and armored, held a spear across his knee; his sword was sheathed, ready for a quick grab. He held no bow: He would not hang back in the rear to shoot, but ride with the vanguard. As would Bertaud, of course, to guard him as he might during the crush. He said, for Iaor's ears alone, "If we broke off and pressed hard for Terabiand, we could organize a welcome there that might be more a match for the Arobern than anything we can manage here."

The king gave him a quick edged smile. "Buying that chance with Minas Ford and the blood of all its defenders? Is that a price you would willingly pay? Or one you would expect me to pay?"

"No," Bertaud admitted.

"Of course not. I did," added the king, "send men south. The Arobern will have his welcome even so. If we bleed him heavily enough here, it may even be enough. And your griffins?" the king asked again, not with much hope.

Bertaud shrugged. "In this rain? It's a mage-crafted rain, I think—meant expressly to keep the griffins away."

The king smiled again, fierce as a griffin himself.

"There can't be more there than three thousand or so. We need only kill three of them for every one of us that falls."

"An even match," Bertaud said, in a deliberately serious tone, finding himself despite everything falling back, at last, into the manner they had always had between them.

"Exactly," said the king with a brief grin, and turned his horse to ride quickly across the ranks, gathering the attention of all his men. He did not cry out the words of any fine speech: Such would only be heard by the men below and give everything away. He only met the eyes of one man, and another, and another. Then he turned his horse, gathered it, and sent it suddenly racing down the hill straight at the rear of the Casmantian force. Which turned, awkwardly at first but then more smoothly, to face them: The Arobern, clearly, had posted men to watch for such an attack. Or sentries had gotten away from the Feierabiand scouts. Or the Arobern was just that able, and watched all directions at once, rain or no rain.

There might have been a thousand Casmantian soldiers on the east side of Minas Ford: They were strung out more widely than the Feierabiand column, but until the armies should crash together that was an advantage to the Casmantians, who could shoot from both ends of their line into the Feierabiand advance. The arrows did not fall as thickly as they might; the rain thinned the volleys. The hundred or so Feierabiand bowmen who still had both dry strings and arrows fell back, halted their advance, and began to provide covering fire. The rest pressed forward as quickly as they could. The small horse contingent, including the king with Bertaud at his back, went before the foot soldiers, meaning to open a gap in the Casmantian line if they could.

Casmantian horns called, called again, and mounted Casmantian soldiers swept around from the other side of Minas Ford since they could not go through, rushing to reinforce their lines. From Minas Ford itself, a small force surged forward suddenly, trying to weaken the Casmantian line so the Feierabiand horse could break it. Rain fell, harder now, and colder.

The Arobern himself, marked by his sheer presence as much as by his banner, flung forward to meet the Feierabiand charge, and suddenly Bertaud was battling madly, his sword crashing against defending swords—he cut at a man on foot, did not know whether he hit the man or not—cut at a horse, which reared, screaming—fended off a spear that might have taken him in the side and sent his horse leaping to cover Iaor's side, where another spear threatened the king. He had lost sight of the Arobern. He tossed his head to clear rain from his eyes and pressed his horse sideways to stay with Iaor, and they were no longer moving forward; they were halted, or nearly, and that was not good—an open space appeared before them, and he shouted and sent his horse for it, Iaor right beside him—and they were jolting forward again, men at their backs—Feierabiand men, Bertaud fervently hoped—and men before them, and Iaor shouted and flung up his sword, and everyone swept sideways and forward again, and the hooves of the horses rang suddenly on cobbles.

They were *in* Minas Ford, on its one street. They had gone right through the Casmantian line—Bertaud understood suddenly that the Arobern had let them through, the better to have all his opponents bottled up in one trap.

Iaor, he saw, had understood this at once; beside him, the king was cursing steadily.

"He let you through," Eles snapped at Iaor, coming suddenly from among the defenders of Minas Ford to set a hand on the bridle of the king's horse. He and all his men, guardsmen and soldiers and townsfolk alike, looked as hollow-eyed and desperate as though they'd been under siege for a week rather than, at very most, a few hours. And those who had meant to be their saviors looked very nearly as badly off.

"I know it," Iaor agreed, and gave up cursing in favor of a swift examination of the village and its defenders. A dismayingly small number, they seemed to Bertaud, to hold ground against the Casmantian army outside the village. And too many of them wounded already, and all of them exhausted. Soldiers and guardsmen had quietly gathered around Iaor, rivalry forgotten in this moment, looking to the king to come up with some miraculous deliverance for them all. A village woman with a hunting bow and a drawn expression had a place with archers in the uniform of regular soldiers; men in rough-spun village clothing had found swords and filled out ranks of infantry. Bertaud spotted Enned son of Lakas among the rest and was absurdly pleased the boy yet lived. Though that was no guarantee he, or any of them, would see the coming dusk or the dawn that followed it.

"Well, well . . . Minas Ford may be a trap, but it may still close in both directions," said the king. "He daren't leave this town unsecured at his rear. With the men I brought, we can hold it a while yet, I should think, and I've sent men to raise the south. Eles, man . . . you did very well to pin him down here."

The guard captain gave him a dour nod. "I sent men west to Sihannas and Eheniand. And Keoun of Sihannas does have a brain. He'll have a thousand men on the road by tomorrow afternoon at the latest. Much good it will do *us*," he added, with a glance back toward the Casmantian lines.

"In the end, the Arobern will have to come to terms. And he'll have to do it with me, and he must know that by this time. He won't take Terabiand with three thousand men, and we may thank the griffins he so kindly sent us he does not have more. For all the griffins' absence now, they have saved us by what they did in the desert." Iaor, too, sat back in his saddle, stretched, and turned to study the Casmantians.

"How about . . . more nearly seven, perhaps?" Bertaud asked, and jerked his head toward a great dark mass moving slowly down the distant slopes of the mountains. It was hard to see through the rain-hazed air . . . but the glitter of thousands of spear points was unmistakable.

Eles drew a slow breath between his teeth. Iaor did not make a sound, but his face, grimly satisfied a moment earlier, went still.

The Casmantians, too, had seen that force: Their shouts rang like horns, hailing their victory.

"He knew he would need more than five thousand men to take Terabiand, of course," the king said after a moment. "And so kept his force divided. To keep some of his people out of the desert, perhaps. Or to get me to underestimate him and commit myself to an indefensible position. Either way . . . well. How long, do you suppose, for him to get those men around the desert?"

"If they force the pace . . . they will be here before dawn, certainly."

"They won't stop here," said Adries, riding up and drawing rein near them. He looked perfectly disgusted. His wet hair stuck to his neck and clung to his mail. He stripped off his helmet and rubbed a hand impatiently across his face. "They'll go straight south, while the force already here holds us in place. I would lay odds. They could be in Bered by midnight, and in Terabiand by noon the next day, long before anyone there expects them. Meanwhile, the Arobern will finish us off this afternoon, rest tonight in Minas Ford, and take his men with him, come the new dawn, to meet any men coming east from Sihannas or Eheniand. Or so I would do, in his place."

The king looked at Bertaud. "We must have the griffins. And that girl to keep them flying."

"Yes," said Bertaud. He thought, *no*. He had made his decision earlier, and he kept to it now, desperately: There was no possible way to demand that of them. He said after a moment, "Only, outside their desert, my king . . . I think they will find themselves unable to be the weapon that turns this tide for us. And I can't think why they should fly to their own deaths in an attempt to protect us. Especially when they must ultimately fail."

"They could take word for us south to Terabiand. They could take word all across the south and the west. Would they do that for us?" Iaor asked. He glanced around as though half expecting Kairaithin or Opailikiita to suddenly loom up out of the rain and then glanced, frustrated, at Bertaud. "Or they could, if they would and if they were *here*. But we have no way to even ask them to do this for us."

Bertaud said nothing. He could call Kairaithin, breaking his word; he would even have done that, in this extremity. Except he knew, he was *sure* that this rain had been brought by the cold mages—by Beguchren. If he called Kairaithin into this mage-crafted rain, the griffin would surely fall to the cold mage, and what would be the good of that to any of them? Under these conditions, he could not, *must* not call. He thought, briefly, of trying to set a compulsion on all the griffins to fight Casmantian forces, not here at Minas Ford, but rather as and where they could . . . only he knew *exactly* how compulsion would ruin them, and in any case the compulsion would cease at his death. So he could not do that, either. Which was, in its way, a vast relief.

"Then if we have no help from the griffins, we are lost," Adries summed up, eerily as though he had been listening to Bertaud's thoughts. But the general went on with heavy decisiveness. "And I cannot imagine we will have such aid. That second Casmantian force will stay well clear of the desert, depend upon it, and I think we may be sure that there will be more cold mages accompanying it." He looked to the king. "Your majesty . . . despite everything we have done here, I doubt we can weaken this force enough to give the griffins a chance against that one, even if they should trouble themselves for our sake. Nevertheless, we could fight here as long as we can stand to battle. If you ask it. Or we could break a path through the Casmantian lines for you. You could get out and away toward Eheniand and so keep out of Casmantian hands yourself. Or," he added, his voice dropping, "you could ask the Arobern for terms. You will have to deal with him in the end, and he'll know that you will know that by this time."

Iaor's hands had tightened on the reins; his horse twitched its ears back and mouthed the bit uncomfortably. The king's grip eased, and he patted its neck in absent thought. Rain blew through the air, cold against their faces.

"Form up the men," Iaor said to Adries. And to Eles, "Integrate yours with his, if you please, my friend. Wounded . . . we have no earth mages with us here. Have you?"

"No," Eles said quietly.

"Casmantium is a civilized nation, at least," said Iaor. "And the Arobern, by all accounts, a generous man." He, too, took off his helm and ran a hand through his wet hair. His look was bleak. "Well, Bertaud? Shall I break out toward the west and run like a stag before the hunters' horns? Or form up the men and bravely make a stand? Or go out to face the Arobern of Casmantium and see what terms he will give me?"

The secret Bertaud was concealing seemed in this moment an enormity. He wanted to drop his own gaze; he wanted to blurt out, *I have an affinity for griffins, I can call them whether they will or no, and even now we may turn back the Arobern.* But he knew, he *knew* that summoning the griffins would do nothing but destroy them, and without saving anything from the wreckage of this day. He met Iaor's eyes steadily and, unable to find any honest advice to offer, said nothing. He wondered what the king was thinking: of his own pride, and failure? Of Feierabiand, which all the Safiad kings had always kept safe and independent, and a large piece of which he might be losing at last to Casmantium? With a sudden startling pang, Bertaud thought of the pretty young queen waiting

with confidence in Tihannad. It seemed incredible now
that he had ever been in the least jealous of her. Looking
into the king's set face, he wondered whether Iaor was
thinking of her, too.

He wanted to say, *Go, get out. How can you think of
surrender? How do we know what the Arobern will do
with a Safiad king once he gets one in his hands?* If Bertaud could not lay a victory at Iaor's feet, he might furnish
at least momentary hope. But what he said, at last, was,
"I certainly . . . can desire nothing but what you desire.
My king."

"Yes," said Iaor, and tried to smile. He took a deep
breath. He started to speak again, and stopped. He asked
instead, "The griffins will not come, you think? They can
do nothing for us?"

"I don't see how they possibly could, my king."

"No," said Iaor, and sighed again. "Well—" he said,
and turned his horse toward the end of Minas Ford's one
street.

The Arobern of Casmantium had drawn most of his
men up in close order there, barely out of bowshot from
the houses. He was there himself. Not inclined to press
an attack, evidently. Waiting, rather. Bertaud could see
him, sitting a big bay horse before his men, the banner at
his side limp in the rain his mage had made. His face was
turned toward Minas Ford. His whole attitude, even from
this distance, was clearly one of patience.

Iaor rode as far as the last house and halted his horse
there. Bertaud rode at his side, and Adries at the other.
They halted with him.

"Well?" said the king to them.

"The decision," his general said without looking at the king, "is yours, your majesty."

"Bertaud?"

"I will bear your word to him, Iaor. Whether that is a gauntlet flung into his face, or . . . or the other."

"Yes," said the king, and let his breath out slowly. He straightened his back. "Tell him . . . tell him . . . My friend, you must tell him that I understand that continuing this battle now will do nothing but spend all the lives of my men, and to no purpose. Ask him . . . ask him for—"

The rain stopped. It did not slow or taper gently to a halt, but stopped all at once.

The wind turned. It had been blowing in ragged gusts from the west, a heavy moisture-laden wind. It turned now to come from the south, and it carried with it scents of sand and fire. This wind was so dry that it sucked moisture from the air and from the slick cobbles and from the very clothing men wore. Bertaud lifted a suddenly unsteady hand to touch his hair, which, cropped short, was already dry.

The clouds shredded on that wind, not blowing away so much as simply disappearing. The sky turned a deep sweet blue . . . then paled, and paled further, taking on a hard metallic tone. Heat came down across Minas Ford like a hammer dropping on an anvil; Bertaud almost thought he could hear the ringing blow as it struck.

And the griffins came. They rode their desert wind out of the south, their wings flashing gold or copper or bronze. The Lord of Fire and Air led them, fire falling from the wind of his wings; on one side of the griffin king flew white Tastairiane and on the other the blazing copper-and-gold Eskainiane. Bertaud looked for

Kairaithin among that host, but could not find him. Men
shouted, with joy in Minas Ford and with dismay among
the ranks of the Casmantian army. Bertaud, too much
stunned for words, made no sound. He could not imagine the power it had taken the griffins to force their desert through the rain and the cold. He could not imagine
the cost they had taken on themselves to bring it here to
this field of battle.

And then he found he could indeed imagine that cost.
Because, as the griffins approached, it became possible
to see the increasing raggedness of their flight. Where a
formation of five griffins flew, fiercely splendid, one and
then perhaps another would suddenly rip apart into a blast
of fire and red sand. The desert wind came from this,
Bertaud understood. They made the desert out of themselves. He had never before realized that if a griffin gave
too much strength to the desert, it might unmake itself.
But that was what they were doing. He could not bear to
watch, but equally he could not look away.

The new desert, following the harsh dry wind, struck
across Minas Ford and an instant later across the Casmantian army. Sand hissed across the cobbles. Red dust
rode the wind, tinting the air the color of blood. The
griffins flew low, well within bowshot, directly over the
Casmantian ranks. Men cried out in alarm, lifting their
bows. Arrows rose, striking griffin after griffin. Griffin
after griffin faltered . . . then caught its balance and regained its place in the sky. Far above the battle, far out
of bowshot, Bertaud found a single dark griffin wheeling
in slow circles, and knew that though a griffin might tear
apart into fire and air, no griffin would die by arrow or
spear this day.

At the forefront of the Casmantian soldiers, the Arobern turned to the small figure beside him. The cold mage Beguchren, for it could be no one else, lifted his hands, fighting the desert. Bertaud did not know whether he truly felt the man's cold power struggle against the fire or whether he only imagined he felt it.

From the first ranks of the griffins, Eskainiane suddenly cast back his bright wings and stooped like an eagle. Bertaud thought the griffin meant to strike down the mage bodily, but he did not. Instead, he cried out, the long piercing shriek of a hunting eagle, and burst violently into flaming wind.

The cold mage put his hands over his face and staggered; if he made a sound, it was lost beneath the cries of the griffins. The Arobern supported his mage, and though Bertaud could not see his expression, the Arobern's attitude had now become one of furious acknowledgment of defeat. He turned and shouted to his men, waving his arm in urgent command, and as his officers picked up and repeated that command, the flights of arrows ceased.

The griffins wheeled slowly above the Casmantian army. They did not descend to strike, but slid through the hot air to spiral around Minas Ford, coming lower still, sunlight flashing from their savage beaks and pooling in their molten eyes. Griffins landed on rooftops, talons and claws tearing gouges through wooden shingles, their outspread wings tilting for balance. Others stayed in the air, sweeping slowly in a wide spiral out across the village and back over the Casmantian army; a long narrow line of fire followed their curving flight, leaping up all around that army and then dying back, leaving little tongues of flames flickering in the red sand.

A single griffin, gold and red, slanted down across the
light toward the Arobern. It landed, light as a cat, directly
before him. The King of Casmantium, as any of his opponents knew, did not lack boldness. He stepped forward
to face it.

"Nehaistiane Esterikiu Anahaikuuanse," said Kairaithin, suddenly standing beside Bertaud's horse. The horse
shied; all the horses were suddenly shying and trying to
rear, and Iaor and Adries and Bertaud found it simplest to
dismount and send them away.

"She was the mate of Eskainiane Escaile Sehaikiu and
of our king," continued Kairaithin as though he had not
noticed the disruption. "She has lost yet another *iskarianere* today. Now that Escaile Sehaikiu is no more, it falls
to her to carry our word to the King of Casmantium. He
had best be courteous. She will bitterly mourn her mate."

"And what is that word?" Iaor asked him. He was pale,
but his tone was bland. He had clasped his hands behind
his back, Bertaud saw, and thought probably they were
shaking. He knew his own were.

Kairaithin's smile had nothing human about it: It was
like the smile of the desert, utterly pitiless. "We will not
be lightly offended," he said, and his smile tautened. "We
will *ring* his army—both his armies—with desert sand, if
we must; we will lay the desert beneath his boots and beneath the boots of his men and hunt them like earthbound
cattle across the red sand. Let Beguchren Teshrichten
challenge *this* working. He has already found it is beyond
him."

"Why did you do it?" Bertaud asked in hushed tones.

"Many of us ceased to exist," the griffin said, and harshly,
"But we will not be the tools or playthings of men."

It was to Bertaud that the griffin directed that furious statement, he knew. But Iaor did not know that. The king said quietly, "For breaking the Arobern's power, I thank you, even if you did not do it for us."

Kairaithin's lip curled. He barely glanced at the king. "It was well done, to show Casmantium our strength . . . so. Esterikiu Anahaikuuanse has given the Arobern our terms. He will deliver himself and all his men into your hands, Safiad king—for men to deal with men—or we will go to whatever lengths we must to destroy them ourselves." His black eyes glanced sideways at Bertaud. "What will he choose?"

"You ask me?"

"A man to judge what men will do. Well?"

"He will yield," Iaor said quietly. "When he sees that continuing this battle now will do nothing but spend all the lives of his men, and to no purpose. He will yield."

CHAPTER 15

The King of Feierabiand took the formal surrender of the King of Casmantium an hour before dusk, seated in the best chair Minas Ford had been able to provide. The chair was not particularly fancy. Iaor made it a throne simply by his presence in it. His face was drawn with the strain of the long day, his eyes bruised with weariness, and he had elected, for convenience as much as effect, plain soldierly dress. Bertaud saw that now, for the first time, there were touches of gray in Iaor's lion-colored hair. This only made the older man look more than ever like a king.

The chair had been set beneath a hastily erected pavilion by the bank of the river, with the lowering sun at the king's back. This was not the harsh sun of the desert. The red desert had engulfed Minas Ford, but it had not quite come down to the river. Thus the pavilion, set out of the sand in the cool evening.

Iaor's small army had been drawn up to his left; Eles's guardsmen and the people of Minas Ford had a place of honor before the pavilion. The Casmantian soldiers, those who had been with the Arobern, stood in their ranks, disarmed and under a light guard, to the right. The other Casmantian army, receiving a messenger the Arobern had sent to them, had not come farther into Feierabiand, but rather had held its place on the far side of the desert.

Kairaithin, in griffin form, sat near Iaor's chair on one side, and Bertaud himself stood on the other.

The king of the griffins was not present, but the savage white griffin, Tastairiane Apailika, sat a little beyond Kairaithin. Bertaud did not know what the attendance of these particular griffins signified. Kes probably knew why Tastairiane Apailika in particular had been sent to watch these proceedings, but she sat on the ground between Opailikiita's feathered forelegs, her own arms around updrawn knees, and looked not at all approachable.

The girl's hair had been brushed out—it was the first time Bertaud had ever seen it free of tangles and knots—and braided with a strand of honey-colored beads. And she had finally changed out of her makeshift Casmantian dress. She wore a plain pale-yellow gown that had no adornment at all. Bertaud suspected that Kairaithin had found, or perhaps made, the clothing for her; it seemed to him a detail that would matter to the griffin mage, though he could not have said why.

Kes looked older and less waiflike, but still not very human. Her feet were bare, her skin nearly transparent; she seemed barely to contain an internal light. She had not shown any desire to put herself in the company of the Minas Ford people. Most of those folk looked at Kes, quick anxious astonished looks, with a great deal more intensity than they spared for the king. She did not look back. She had her head tilted against Opailikiita's leg, and her own attention seemed reserved for the Arobern.

Brechen Glansent Arobern walked forward between the two armies, past the townsfolk and the griffins, and stopped before Iaor's chair. He had not been bound— "No," Iaor had said, undoubtedly thinking how nearly this moment had gone the other way, "let him keep his pride. We will see how little else we can leave him." So the Arobern was not chained. He had only been disarmed. He looked intent, energetic, not in the least humbled; his focus was not inward, on his own defeat and humiliation, as one might have expected, but outward, on Iaor.

He walked forward quite steadily, a big man with powerful shoulders and a face that was strong, even harsh. His dark beard accentuated the strength of his jaw and made him look stubborn, which he probably was; his eyes were quick and brilliant and utterly redeemed his heavy features from any appearance of dullness. When he got to Iaor, he did not kneel, but bowed, and then studied his conqueror with every appearance of lively curiosity as he straightened. He was tall enough, and arrogant enough, to make it seem by his attitude alone that his was the predominant will in all this company.

Iaor smiled. It was not an amused smile. He had not wanted to humble the Arobern, but, Bertaud thought, he had rather expected the Arobern to show a certain humility of his own accord. That was lacking. Iaor did not demand it. He only said, with a mildness Bertaud recognized as his father's, signalling dangerous temper, "Brechen Glansent Arobern. Your country and mine were not, I thought, at war. And yet here we are. Why is this?"

The Arobern lifted powerful shoulders in a shrug.

"Well. I thought it would work. Yes?" His Terheien was harshly accented, but perfectly understandable. "I thought I would come across the mountains and take your Bered and Terabiand, yes, and all that country to the east of the river, and make a new province for Casmantium. Then the road through the mountains might be made better, and Casmantium could profit from Terabiand's harbor. You understand, I did not think the *malacteir*, the griffins, I did not think they would fight for you. I thought the other way: That you would fight them and so be made weak."

His eyes went to Kes, where she sat at the feet of her griffin friend. She looked back at him with eyes that were filled with fire and the memories of the desert.

"I did not expect the *malacteir* to find a girl like that one. And then when I caught her, I did not think the little *festechanenteir* would slip my hand. And then she came into her power. So all I meant to do turned and went another way, yes? The *festechanenteir* turned the weapon I thought I had set against you so that it came against me instead. So I was wrong," he finished simply, and turned his attention back to Iaor. "So you have the day, yes? What will you do, Iaor Safiad?"

It might have been a humble question. The Arobern did not ask it humbly.

Iaor tapped the arm of his chair in a gentle rhythm. He said, even more mildly than before, "Naturally, I wish to restore relations between Feierabiand and Casmantium to their former amicability. I am certain you share this desire, Brechen Glansent Arobern. A reasonable indemnity will do. I presume your brother will pay it. Of course, it is one of your brothers you left holding your throne?"

"Yes. He will pay. For me. For them." The Arobern nodded over his shoulder toward his men.

"You are fortunate in your brothers."

"Yes," agreed the Arobern, very simply.

"And when next you conceive a plan to acquire a new province? I wonder whether your brother is perhaps less ambitious than you are, Brechen Glansent Arobern. I wonder if perhaps I would be wiser not to send you back to Casmantium, whatever price your brother offers me for you?"

The Arobern tilted his head back, assured and arrogant. "It would offend Casmantium if Feierabiand held her king beyond the time it takes to gather the indemnity. I do not think you should do that, Iaor Safiad."

"Don't you? Well, I will accept an indemnity for the damage you did to my lands and my people, and an indemnity for your men. But I think it only just to give your own person to the griffins, whom you wronged first and more grievously. And your remaining cold mages, of course."

This was a surprise. Bertaud blinked, wondering whether Iaor had come up with this idea on the instant. It was not, perhaps, a terrible idea. It would be impossible for Casmantium to argue that the griffins did not have a claim. And certainly no one would expect an offense against griffins to be paid off with gold; no, if they were to collect an indemnity, in what other coin would they take it but in blood? And Iaor might very reasonably be thinking of ways to keep the griffins well-disposed to Feierabiand. *That* would set Casmantium well back. *And* Linularinum. Both countries respected ruthlessness. They would no doubt be very impressed if Iaor could persuade the griffins to become Feierabiand's allies. Especially if he purchased this alliance with the blood of a rival king.

The Arobern, taken initially by surprise, quite obviously also concluded that this was a course of action Iaor might reasonably pursue. He glanced at the griffins, then back at Iaor. Iaor merely looked blandly courteous, an expression he did extremely well. The griffins were hard to read, but they certainly did not look courteous. Tastairiane Apailika opened his beak and clicked it shut again, producing a small deadly sound. Kairaithin tilted his head, a gesture that expressed, Bertaud thought, perhaps a kind of humor. Kes, tucked against Opailikiita's legs, looked very small, very young, and not at all human. She, Bertaud was disturbed to see, was smiling.

The Arobern said slowly, "You will do what you will, Safiad king." He looked faintly nonplussed, as though he had thought he had known how this interview would go and was taken aback to find his predictions overset. Bertaud might have told him that Iaor, when truly angry, was likely to become both quiet and creative. The King of Casmantium went on, slowly, choosing his words with care, "But I will ask you do it to me and not to my people, yes? My mages only did as I bade them, you understand?"

"The People of Fire and Air spent themselves recklessly this day. Shall I not acknowledge their cost?"

Kes stood up. All eyes went to her, though she did not appear to be trying to draw attention. A woman among the Minas Ford folk edged out toward her and then hesitated—her sister, Bertaud realized, though he could see no resemblance between them whatsoever.

Though she left one hand on Opailikiita's neck, Kes edged forward a step. She did not glance toward her sister, but said to the kings, in a small voice that was nevertheless surprisingly audible, "They don't want him. Or even Beguchren."

Iaor, clearly taken aback, lifted his eyebrows. His hands stilled on the arms of his chair as he tensed, waiting to hear what the girl would say so that he could try to fit it into his own plans. The Casmantian king tilted his head quizzically to the side. Even Bertaud was startled. But he felt Kes was right as soon as she had spoken.

"They don't want vengeance, you know," Kes said, glancing from one man to the other. "They don't . . . they don't think that way. They kill things, too, you know. They don't hold it against the King of Casmantium that he was fierce. Ferocity is something they understand. It's not vengeance they want."

Iaor gave her a questioning glance, not wanting to ask out loud what they did want and thus admit that he was as surprised as anyone else at what Kes had said.

Kes looked quickly at the griffins. Neither Kairaithin nor Tastairiane Apailika spoke, but only regarded her from fierce eagle's eyes. They were both sitting very still. They looked massive and powerful and thoroughly ferocious themselves, although neither of them moved. Kes turned her gaze back to the king, and then to the Arobern. "They want Melentser."

"They want what?" said the Arobern, in a startled tone.

Kes repeated, "They want Melentser."

Melentser was not merely a town. It was a small city near the edge of Casmantium's border with the desert.

"Melentser is ours." The Arobern now sounded rather blank. "My mother's mother was from there. It has been part of Casmantium for more than a hundred years."

"Well, before that, it was part of the desert," said Kes. She stroked her hand through the feathers on Opailikiita's shoulder, and the slim griffin bent her head around and brushed Kes's face with her beak. Kes smiled. She said, "The desert will take it again, King of Casmantium. That is what the People of Fire and Air want."

"I will not agree, *festechanenteir*. My brother will not agree. You set your indemnity too high."

"King of Casmantium," said Kes, "the desert here is new and it cost the lives of many griffins to make. But sending the great northern desert to take back Melentser will cost less, because no one will be fighting the desert when it comes. And no one will fight it. You will yield it. Or the Lord of Fire and Air will ask the King of Feierabiand to give all your people to the desert, those here and those in the mountains. And the King of Feierabiand will do it."

Kes paused, giving the Arobern a careful, assessing look. Then she added, deliberately, "Tastairiane Apailika wants to kill you all. He says he could do it by himself, if I am there to keep him whole. I would do that, if I had to. And then the desert will reach out to Melentser all the same, and your brother will find he is not wise to fight against sand and stone. Because I can defend the People of Fire and Air against anything he can do, and Feierabiand will be here at his flank, and Casmantium will be weak after losing all those men."

The Arobern regarded her with patent astonishment. He took a breath.

"Or you may simply yield Melentser as a proper indemnity," Iaor interrupted him easily, his tone perfectly matter-of-fact, just as though he had known all along what the girl was going to say. It sounded very smooth. "Casmantium can afford it."

The Arobern transferred his attention to Iaor.

"Melentser to the desert, a suitable indemnity to Feierabiand, and we may all go on with our lives," Iaor said to him. "With, of course, some form of reassurance that you will not think again of fashioning new Casmantian provinces out of my country. I believe you have a son, do you not, Brechen Glansent Arobern? Twelve years old, is he not?"

"You want my son as hostage?" The Arobern hesitated, now clearly off his balance. He ran a hand through his black hair, a frustrated gesture that made him look suddenly younger and much less arrogant. "No. I may yield Melentser. But not my son. What else would you take instead?"

"I am not negotiating." Iaor leaned forward in his chair. "I am telling you what I require. Melentser to the desert. An appropriate indemnity for the trouble to which you have put Feierabiand. And your son, as a guarantee of your future restraint. All this before I will return you to your kingdom, King of Casmantium."

The Arobern listened to him carefully. He nodded, not in agreement, Bertaud thought, but only to show he understood the terms demanded. Then he came forward a step and sank down to one knee in front of Iaor. His harsh features were not made for humility, but he was now clearly trying. "But I will ask you not to do this, Safiad. I acknowledge you have won everything. You have won, yes? Casmantium will yield everything. As you have said, yes? I know you have made alliance with the *malacteir*. I know your little *festechanenteir* gives the *malacteir* a strength I cannot challenge. Is that not enough assurance?"

"No," said Iaor. He sat back in his chair, hands relaxing. His chin tipped up in satisfaction. He had wanted the Arobern to humble himself, to ask for mercy. But now, having forced the other king to submit, he was willing to be kind. He said, "I will hold your son only eight years. Then he may return to Casmantium."

The Arobern did not rise. Evidently perceiving the satisfaction but not the inclination toward generosity, he said harshly, "You will not take vengeance on my son for your offense at me. I will not put him in the way of Safiad anger in a hostile court."

Iaor, startled, cast a brief involuntary glance at Bertaud, who lifted an eyebrow, trying to keep his face expressionless. Then the king said violently to the Arobern, "Do you think such things of me, Brechen Glansent Arobern? Your son will serve me as is appropriate for a young lord—he will be well-schooled at my court and treated as befits a prince. I assure you. Then he may return to you."

Some of the Arobern's tension eased. He nodded, and hesitated. "The years from twelve to twenty are long years. Yes? You will take a boy and teach him to be a man. At your court. If not to fear you, you will teach him to love you. Will you not? To love Feierabiand. That is what you mean."

"That is exactly what I mean," Iaor agreed.

"Yes." The Arobern bent his head, accepting this assurance because he had no choice. "The Safiad kings are clever. I knew this, but I thought I was more clever. Very well. I will take your word and do as you say."

"I was lucky," Iaor admitted. He paused, and Bertaud

knew that the other king's submission had again inclined Iaor to generosity. He said slowly, "If Feierabiand was confident of Casmantium's intentions, there would be no intrinsic reason why mutually beneficial terms might not be worked out regarding the harbor at Terabiand and the eastern road. I find no compelling reason to reconsider the harbor dues. But we might discuss improvements to the road."

"Hah." The Arobern stared at Iaor. "Well." He got to his feet, managing a smile. "Mutually beneficial. Yes. If Casmantium is not beggared by the indemnity you set, Safiad king, we might well wish to make improvements to the mountain road. Our builders would be pleased by the challenge, I think. Maybe it might be widened. Maybe to twice its present width. It might even be paved, yes? And bridges put in, yes? Then the toll ended to compensate Casmantium for the expense. That would be fair, if Casmantium provides the builders."

"We will discuss these matters," said Iaor, and lifted his hand a little. General Adries gestured to the Arobern, and the Arobern bowed, rather more profoundly than he had initially, and suffered himself to be led away.

Iaor sighed, and leaned back in his chair. He glanced at the griffins, who did not now seem very interested. Kairaithin tilted his head, and was gone, with Tastairiane Apailika. Kes, not glancing around, appearing utterly unconcerned about anything creatures of earth might choose to do, put an arm around Opailikiita's neck and also vanished. She left behind only a breath of stone-scented wind and a scattering of sand. Her sister took a hesitant step toward the empty place where she had been, looking bereft.

Bertaud glanced away, reluctant to intrude on such personal grief. But then he found his eye caught by Iaor. "Well?" asked the king, making a private moment out of the general movement of men all around them scattering about evening duties and business.

Bertaud let his breath out. He shook his head. "What do you mean, well? Are you asking my opinion? I don't think . . . I don't think I would dare offer one."

"I will stop the toll on the eastern road," Iaor declared. "And Brechen Glansent Arobern will put an end to Casmantian tariffs on our goods. *And* he'll pay the harbor dues, and like it."

"I've no doubt you'll teach the Arobern not to bite," Bertaud agreed.

The king gave a satisfied little nod. "I doubt I can make a personal friend of the man, but perhaps I can do something with his son. Perhaps I'll reduce the dues in eight years, as a going-home gift for the boy."

"Well," Bertaud conceded, "I admit, that would be a good thing, if you could make an ally of Casmantium for a generation or two. And . . . I, of all men, don't underestimate your ability to make boys into your friends, Iaor."

Their eyes met, and after a moment the king said gently, "This has been hardest on you, perhaps. You seemed to me . . . You dealt well enough with the desert, this time, did you not, my friend?"

"Yes," Bertaud agreed without explanation. "I think my . . . susceptibility to the desert was a temporary problem. It seems to have passed off."

Satisfied, Iaor clapped him on the shoulder. "And so we have an agreeable end to the day, after all," he declared. "Earth and stone, I at least am glad for dusk and an end to this particular day, though I suppose we had luck riding our shoulders throughout it."

Bertaud met his king's eyes. "You made your own luck, Iaor."

"The griffins made it for me. Through your good governance, not mine, as I well know." The king shook his head in wonder. "You will have to tell me someday how you persuaded that terrifying mage of theirs to come in on our side. Well, and yet we have everything we could desire. With the possible exception of being rid of this desert on our doorstep. Though there are compensations, to be sure." He cast a wry glance over the displaced people of Minas Ford. "Some of the indemnity must go to these folk."

Then something about the quality of Bertaud's silence caught at the king's attention. "And you?"

"My king?"

"I am asking," Iaor said patiently, "whether you, too, are satisfied, my friend. Or whether there is perhaps something I have missed?"

Bertaud produced a smile that was, unexpectedly, almost genuine. "Iaor. What could I possibly desire, save what you desire?"

Iaor grinned suddenly and clapped Bertaud on the shoulder. "If something occurs to you, you must certainly let me know."

But what Bertaud wanted, he knew, was nothing Iaor could give him. This was a new thought, for he had always depended on Iaor to give him . . . everything. But now . . . the fire in his heart had burned high during the course of that last battle, as the griffins had unmade themselves to defeat the Casmantians. Now, when he longed for its heat, it was all but guttered out to ash. Yet he knew, with an odd, unaccustomed assurance, what he must do. Not to bring the fire back to life, but to . . . bank it properly.

The camp settled, Feierabiand soldiers and Casmantian prisoners housed alike, with few amenities and far too weary to care. Fires sparked in the twilight, friendly little fires that seemed to have nothing whatsoever in common with the red desert. Some impulse led Bertaud to look for Kes's sister, but the people of Minas Ford had all gone away somewhere—certainly not back to their lost village. Probably to some outlying farm they knew and strangers to this district did not. Likely they wanted the comfort of familiar walls and of one another's company, and no blame to them.

Bertaud did not want company, nor walls. He walked slowly up the road away from the river, toward the new desert, and then left the road and struck more directly up the sloping ground, welcoming the effort, the numbness of exhaustion that clung to him. The damp grasses yielded gently under his step, and he passed the small close-pruned trees of someone's orchard. Stripped of fruit now, he guessed, by soldiers only too glad to supplement their hard bread and dried meat with better. He would give long odds someone had found the energy for that.

Beneath his feet, the soft grasses suddenly gave way to sand. A heartbeat later the heat hit him, forceful even in the dusk, striking upward from the sand. Bertaud hesitated. Then he went on, walking more slowly still. He came to a low wall made of flat, rounded stones, tumbled and cracked now as though time and sun and the power of the desert had worked on them for many years rather than a single afternoon. He put a hand on top of the wall and clambered stiffly over. He felt as though he'd aged a score of years in this one night, and might have rested on the wall for a moment. But in the end, he couldn't settle: When he tried to sit still, he had too much time for thought. For the slow creeping terror to press through his weariness. So he went on quickly, looking for . . . he hardly knew what, or why one place would be better than another, for what he had in mind. Perhaps he was simply searching for a certain slant to the lengthening shadows. Or for an excuse to delay the closing moments of this interminable day.

In the end, he found himself walking down Minas Ford's one street, its cottages bulking to either side. Sand had covered the cobbles. The houses that had stood so bravely against the Casmantian army had been broken by the desert the griffins had made with their last effort: Here a wall had buckled as stone shifted beneath it, there a roof had fallen . . . Bertaud walked slowly through the village and at last discovered the gate to the inn's yard. He went through the gate. Tables still stood in the abandoned yard. Several had vases still poised on them, all their flowers dead and dried, at once absurd and desolate.

Bertaud sat down at a table. The light had nearly gone, now. The ageless stars shone overhead, hard and brilliant, with little of the trembling sparkle they would have had in a gentler sky. Bertaud looked up at them, somehow comforted by their timelessness. He found himself thinking of the stars above the lake at Tihannad and then, for some reason, of the wide sky of the Delta where he had spent those grim years of his early childhood. He had not thought of the Delta much at all in these latter years; he had quite deliberately refused to think of the Delta or his father's house. Even after his father's death, somehow even then he had not let his thoughts turn that way. Now he found he regretted that studied indifference. He wondered, for nearly the first time in his life, what he might have made of his inheritance if he had devoted himself to the Delta and not to Iaor's court, and it seemed both amazing and reason for grief that now he would never have the chance to find out.

It was perhaps a little late to entertain such thoughts. And he could hardly regret the place he had made for himself with the king—or Iaor had made for him—or they had made together. In the end, that place had survived . . . everything. *That* awareness, for all he had been compelled at last to walk out alone into the desert, was surely of infinite worth. Bertaud looked deliberately down from the sky, focused on the surface of the table between his hands. He called, "Kairaithin?"

Then he waited.

The griffin came. He was hardly visible in the night, and yet his wings seemed to reach across the sky. Starlight slid off his beak, his talons; his eyes, filled with fire, shone more brightly than the stars. The rush of air through the great feathers of his wings made a sound like sand across stone.

As he came down, he took on human form so smoothly that at no point was Bertaud certain where griffin became man. But it was as a man that he walked forward, and as a man that he faced Bertaud.

"Anasakuse Sipiike Kairaithin," Bertaud said softly.

The griffin considered him in silence for a moment. He said at last, "You did not call us to your battle. As you promised. Though you were defeated and faced death, or worse than death."

Bertaud did not ask him what a griffin would consider worse than death. He already knew that it was the defeat, and the shame attending that defeat. He understood how a griffin might flee before superior force, but would never yield. This seemed perfectly natural. The griffin heart informed his own, so that it had become difficult to distinguish one from the other.

"I have been surprised many times by the actions of men," Kairaithin said softly. "Not least this past day. Why, in your extremity, did you choose to loose my people from your hand?"

"If I had known that your people might have saved us, I might have called you," Bertaud admitted. "But I thought it would cause your destruction for, probably, nothing . . . I did not know you could bring the desert with you through all that cold rain, not with any sacrifice. So it seemed insupportable to demand your help."

Kairaithin lifted one narrow eyebrow. "And now?"

"Now . . . it seems still more insupportable to do anything whatsoever. I called you . . . to assure you that I will not call again. Not you nor any of your people."

"What?" said Kairaithin drily. "In no exigency?" He paused. "Do you know, man, what will happen to my kind if they discover that for you they are only animals? That they may be commanded as easily as dogs or horses?"

"Yes," Bertaud said.

"They would fight you to their deaths, if not to yours."

"I know."

"And if by some chance any of them survived it, and you not, they would spend every remaining spark of their lives doubting their own hearts and souls, which might be compelled to the will of another. Unlikely though it might be that another man with so unusual an affinity would have it woken by fire as yours was, they would fear that. So they would turn to hunting men, to their own eventual destruction."

"I know. You must make very certain Kes does not heal any other men. Just to be sure no one else with this peculiar affinity is brought to this . . ." He hesitated. It hardly seemed a gift. "Power."

"I shall. You may be quite confident. I shall tell her the truth, I think. That will constrain her more strictly than any limitation I might otherwise employ."

Bertaud nodded. "I called only you. I constrained only you. None other guessed?" he asked, to be sure.

"No, man. So you may be easy," the griffin said, with some irony. "Only I have been brought to heel by the strength of your command."

Bertaud tried not to flinch visibly. He said after a moment, "It's in the nature of a horse to yield to its rider. It's even in the nature of a wolf to respect the limits a man may put on its hunting. But I know . . . to submit to anyone's rule is utterly against the nature of your kind. Do *you* understand . . . how terrible a thing it is for a man to force against its nature a creature of his calling?"

"Is it?"

"It would break my heart," said Bertaud, very simply.

Kairaithin's proud face tightened. "So I should be glad to trust my freedom and the freedom of the People of Fire and Air to your gentle sensibilities, man? Is that what you expect of me?"

"No," said Bertaud. "I don't expect that at all. I know

very well that you would spend the long years of your life doubting your own heart and soul." He met the griffin's fiery black eyes. "You should take your true form," he added after a moment. "I think you would be quicker so. You will need to be quick. Because if I . . . if I feel the blow coming, I don't think I will be able to let you deliver it."

Kairaithin stared at him.

Bertaud shut his eyes and waited.

A long moment passed. Far longer than should have been necessary. Bertaud opened his eyes.

Kairaithin sat before him in griffin form, like a great cat, lion tail wrapped neatly around taloned front feet. His neck was arched, his head tucked in toward his chest, his ferocious beak pointed at the ground. The feathers behind his head ruffled in the desert breeze. He looked massive and dangerous and heraldic and, somehow, indecisive.

"Do you think," Bertaud asked him, "that this is an offer I will make twice? Do you think I have endless nerve? Because I promise you, you are mistaken." His voice shook; he bit the last word off sharply.

No, said Kairaithin, softly. His voice slid delicately around the edges of Bertaud's mind. *I do not expect that at all.*

Bertaud stared into the griffin's eyes, then looked away. His hands, lying empty on the table, moved slowly across its gritty surface. He gathered up a small handful of red dust and let it run through his fingers. For a moment, he looked only at the faint glitter of dust in the starlight. He did not speak. He could not think of anything to say. The infinite sky arched over them both.

I will trust your sensibility, man, Kairaithin said. His

tone was harsh and proud, as though it was defiance he expressed. *You will not call. You will not put your will upon me. Upon any of my kind.*

"No," said Bertaud.

I will spend the years studying ways to kill you, in the case you should prove false.

"I'm sure you will."

The griffin said, more gently, *I will not expect you to call. I will not wait for the moment. I will not live in dread of the sound of your voice speaking my name.*

Bertaud bowed his head. Then he looked up. "I won't speak it. I swear to you. I won't see you again."

No.

"That will break my heart. But in . . . in a better way." Bertaud opened his hands, a gesture of release.

Kairaithin was gone. The night seemed suddenly, bitterly, empty.

But Bertaud still lived to endure it. So even the bitterness, he thought, was something to cherish. And the promise of years to come during which the bitter loss might—would surely—transmute to a gentler memory. He took a slow, deep breath of the dry desert air, and left the ruined inn to the sand and the sleepless wind, to go back to life and to his king.

CHAPTER 16

Jos found her sitting on a twisted red rock where the highest pasture had once been. There had been a tree where the rock now stood; there had been a spring that had welled from the earth and spilled away toward the lower pastures. Neither tree nor spring remained.

Kes was sitting with her knees tucked up and her arms wrapped around them, looking into the desert sky. Its beauty pierced her like a spear; she wanted to mount the heights and fly through air so crystalline and pure that the light of the myriad stars might shatter it. She wanted to fly west until she overtook the sun, then pour herself into its molten light; she wanted to shred her body into fire and wind and dissolve into the desert. But she stayed where she was. She had not known why she waited, until Jos came to her.

He came forward and stood at the base of the rock. He was tall enough, and the rock short enough, that their faces were nearly at a level. His eyes shone with starlight. Kes knew that her own glimmered with fire.

"You always liked this place." Jos glanced around, sighed, and leaned against the twisted rock where Kes sat. "Now only the lie of the land is the same. You can't even tell where the spring used to be."

"I still like it."

"Do you? Is it the same in your eyes?"

"No. Not the same."

"No." He paused. "I have brought your sister to see you. I thought . . . it seemed like a good idea. She doesn't . . . You know, Kes, she hasn't seen you since, well. Not from the time you went into the desert, till the Safiad's little play this evening. You might . . . try to be kind."

Kes slipped off the rock, blurring through the little distance that separated its top from the sand. She noticed only afterward that Jos had put a hand up to help her down; he lowered it slowly.

Then Tesme came forward out of the dark, walking carefully over the unfamiliar ground, and Kes had attention only for her.

"Kes?" Tesme said. She did not run forward to embrace her sister. Her tone was tentative, almost doubtful. She was wearing a plain undyed dress, the sort of thing she might have worn to visit the horses and would not normally have put on to go away from the house; her hair was bound back with a simple twist of wooden beads. Her face was thinner than Kes remembered, with faint new lines at the corners of her eyes. There was a bandage around her left wrist, and she moved stiffly. She did not smile. "Kes?"

"Yes," Kes said. But she did not step forward.

"Kes?"

"Yes," said Kes patiently.

"You look . . . so different."

"Do I?" Kes thought about this. She thought she did feel different, within herself. But it was hard to think about what she had been like, before. When she reached after memories of herself, she could find nothing but fading echoes of a person who seemed only vaguely familiar. A shy but laughing child, a shyer and more silent girl . . . loves and sorrows and memories that seemed, now, to have little to do with her. The person she remembered had been a creature of earth, a person whose needs and desires and emotions she could not now readily understand. When she reached after memories of Tesme . . . those memories carried regret, even something like grief, though she did not really understand why they should. "I think I am different."

"Can you . . . can you . . . change back?"

"No."

Jos, watching them both, asked, "Do you want to change back to what you were before?"

Kes glanced at him, surprised. "No."

Tesme bowed her head a little.

"I'm sorry if you are hurt," Kes told her. "I do remember you. I haven't forgotten anything. It's just . . . it's different when I think about things now. I remember you. But it's like remembering a language I used to speak and have forgotten: What I remember doesn't feel . . . real. I'm sorry," she added, because an expression of regret seemed somehow appropriate.

Tesme's tears were real, and fell like drops of rain to the sand. She said in a low voice, "Jos told me. But I didn't understand what he said."

"I'm glad he brought you to see me," Kes said. "I see now I should have come to see you. I didn't think of it."

"I see you didn't," Tesme answered. Her head was still bowed, her shoulders rounded.

"You should probably go back to your own kind."

"Yes," Tesme whispered. She came forward suddenly and reached out, quickly at first but then more tentatively, to take Kes by the shoulders. She folded her into an embrace, fierce and longing and sorrowful all at once. After the first startled moment, Kes returned the embrace, bending her head against Tesme's shoulder as she had when she was a child needing comfort; it felt very strange.

"Are you happy?" Tesme asked. She eased back so that she could look into Kes's face.

This was not the sort of question a griffin would ask. Kes had to think about the answer. But she said at last, "Yes. I am happy. I don't think there was any other choice to make. But it was a right choice, all the same."

"I love you. But you'll never come home again."

"I will be glad to remember you. But the desert is my home now."

Tesme nodded, and let her go. She was trying to smile. "I know you're not alone. I hear you have a new sister."

"Opailikiita."

"I hear she's very beautiful. Does she love you?"

Kes could not even think about the question in those terms. But she said, "We are *iskarianere*—I think that is like love, for a griffin."

"You aren't a griffin, Kes."

"But I'm like a griffin now," Kes said, trying to make her tone kind, trying to remember exactly what kindness was, so that she might be kind to this human woman who had been her sister. She remembered that men valued kindness, that once she herself had needed people to be kind to her.

Tesme looked searchingly into her eyes. "Are you? Are you?"

"Yes."

Tesme's shoulders slumped again, and then squared as her head came up. "All right," she said. She might have meant to speak firmly—her attitude was firm—but the words came out in a thread of sound. "Be well, Kes. Wherever you go, into whatever strange country. Be happy."

"I will be," said Kes, and watched the woman who had been her sister walk away. Tesme looked back once. Then she turned her face forward and disappeared into the darkness.

"You did not ask how *she* was," Jos commented.

It had not occurred to Kes to do so. She looked at him wordlessly.

"She went to Nehoen's house. Everyone from Minas Ford did, except the badly injured. His house and most of his lands are still outside the desert, you know."

Kes did know this, when she thought of it. She knew where the boundary of the desert lay, and though everything beyond that boundary seemed dim and distant, her memory of the land told her where Nehoen's property lay.

"He has been courting her. Ever since you . . . left. I think he had her in his eye before that. He's been a great oak for her to lean on, this summer. I imagine that when everyone else leaves his house, she will stay."

"Oh," said Kes. She was glad, in a distant sort of way. She thought she had once liked Nehoen. He seemed old for Tesme. But then . . . perhaps Tesme was not so young as all that, really. "Good."

"You should be pleased." Jos regarded her with an expression she could not read. "The match will be good for both of them. Especially Tesme. She wore herself out with worry about you. Nehoen is the romantic sort. He'll be just what she needs now."

Kes had no feel for such matters, but she presumed he was right.

"They won't stay around here, you know," Jos added. "Tesme . . . well, Tesme hates the very sight of the desert. She was talking about Sihannas. That's good country for horses, and she and Nehoen will easily be able to afford the move, what with the king directing a good chunk of the indemnity to the folk of Minas Ford."

Sihannas. Sihannas, at the edge of the Delta. Kes had never even dreamed of going so far from home. And now she had gone so much farther, even standing in this high pasture so near the ruined village. She smiled slightly, feeling the desert wind tug at the edges of her soul.

"You don't mind that she will go so far?"

Kes blinked, recalled to the moment. "Everything in the country of earth is far, for me." Then she asked, the question slowly welling up in her mind, "But where will you go?"

Jos regarded her with an odd, intent expression. He said at last, "Not to Sihannas. The Safiad wants me either under his eye or out of his country, and who can blame him? Not to Casmantium: How could I face the Arobern? Not to Linularinum: I hate all the sly maneuvering that's lifeblood to everyone on that side of the river."

It had not occurred to Kes that Jos, of them all, faced

the greatest dislocation. For her, there was the desert; for the folk of Minas Ford, all of Feierabiand; everyone else could hope to return eventually to their homes and their people. But she could not imagine where Jos would go.

"I thought," he said, his eyes on her face, "that I might go with you, Kes. That I might remind you, from time to time, what it means to be human."

Kes did not understand him. "There is no place in the desert for a creature of earth."

"There are places where earth borders fire, Kes. Where the mountains meet the desert, north of Casmantium . . . there are places there a man might live. Or—" and he took a deep breath—"for you it was different, I know. But maybe your friend Kairaithin might find a way to make an ordinary man into a creature of fire."

Kes stared at him, taken utterly by surprise. "Why would you want to do that?"

Jos took a step toward her, took a breath, started to speak, and stopped. Then he said, with careful restraint, "What is there for me in any of the countries of men? Hear me out, Kes. You may no longer be human, but among the griffins you will still be alone; you are not one of them, either. Think of that. You may learn to take the shape of a griffin, but you won't ever really be one, any more than Kairaithin is a man when he takes the form of a man. Will you endure a lifetime of loneliness? Of being one alone among many?" His voice had quickened as he continued, until his words tumbled over one another at the last and choked him silent; he was still, then, his eyes on her face.

Kes said slowly, "I would have been an earth mage.

Kairaithin redirected what I should have been and made me a creature of fire. You are not a mage of any kind."

"He'll find a way. Or you will. If you want to."

Kes took a step forward and lifted her hand to touch his face. She found she was smiling. She did not know what a creature of earth would feel at such a moment. But what *she* felt was a kind of fierce possessive pleasure, something like the *iskairianaika* she shared with Opailikiita, but not the same. She was pleased Jos had made this unanticipated offer. Loneliness was not something she feared; she feared very little, now. But even so . . . "Yes," she said. "I would like your company in the country of fire. I think I would like that. Yes, I would. Yes." And she folded both of them into a sweep of shifting time and silence and took Jos away with her into the heart of the desert.

extras

www.orbitbooks.net

about the author

Rachel Neumeier started writing fiction to relax when she was a graduate student and needed a hobby unrelated to her research. Prior to selling her first fantasy novel, she had published only a few articles in venues such as *The American Journal of Botany*. However, finding that her interests did not lie in research, Rachel left academia and began to let her hobbies take over her life instead. She now raises and shows Cavalier King Charles Spaniels, gardens, cooks, and occasionally finds time to read. She works part time for a tutoring program, though she tutors far more students in math and chemistry than in English composition. Find out more about Rachel Neumeier at www.rachelneumeier.com.

Find out more about Rachel Neumeier and other Orbit authors by registering for the free monthly newsletter at www.orbitbooks.net

interview

Have you always known that you wanted to write novels?

I always made up stories in boring classes—as far back as I can remember. (Doesn't everybody?) And I was never interested in short stories. Novel length is the only length that works for me. Or longer! It was *hard* to learn to write *short* novels.

After a hard day of writing, is there anything you like to do in your free time?

It would be nice if I could read, which has always been one of my favorite things. But when I'm actually involved in writing a book of my own, I read very little fiction. I read nonfiction, or cook, or work in the garden, or take the dogs for a walk, or if I have a show or obedience trial coming up I might work on, say, teaching one of my dogs to stand beautifully or heel backing up or something. Of course, if I work with one dog, they all want in on the fun, so training sessions can take a while.

Do you have any particularly favorite authors who have influenced your work?
Certainly! I love Patricia McKillip and Robin McKinley. And Patricia Wrede, Diana Wynne Jones, CJ Cherryh, and Lois McMaster Bujold, in no particular order, and I'm sure I've missed a couple of my favorites. But I have to say that I can only hope Patricia McKillip has influenced my writing; I think she writes the most perfect stories, in the most beautiful language.

The connection between the desert and griffins is a unique take on griffin mythology. Where did you draw your inspiration from?
Nowhere. It just happened. I didn't have that connection in mind at all. I like griffins and wanted to do something with them, but I had no idea there was going to be a connection between griffins and fire. Then I wrote the very first paragraph, and boom, there it was, right out of a, so to speak, clear sky.

Do you harbor a secret preference for any one griffin?
Actually, yes, not that it's secret. Eskainiane, the griffin who at the end—well, that would be giving too much away, I suppose. But to me, Eskainiane really exemplifies what the ideal griffin should be—generous, joyful, passionate, courageous, even exuberant. We don't see too much of him, but he's the sort of griffin who would make you think, Hey, being a griffin might be pretty neat.

The subtle, earth-based magic is seamlessly woven into the fabric of Kes and Bertaud's world. Was this an idea

you had from the outset or did it develop over time?
It was a necessary part of the structure of the world as soon as griffins became connected to fire. I immediately saw that fire should be intrinsically opposed to, or at least foreign to, something else, something human. The something else became earth. The exact nature of human magic developed and changed a lot over time, though, and is actually still changing now as I finish book two and think about book three.

What's in store for the next novel of the Griffin Mage series?
That would be telling! Oh, okay, it's set in the country of Casmantium, it concerns the ongoing problem of imbalance between humans and griffins, and it develops a different aspect of earth magic than we see in the first book.

Finally, what has been your favorite part of the publishing process?
You'd think it would be seeing the book actually on the shelf in real bookstores, wouldn't you? But actually, by the time the book hits the shelves, I'm pretty accustomed to the idea that it's going to. (Not that this isn't still a fine thing!) No, the *best* part is when you *first* hear that an editor at a good publishing house loves one of your books and is making an offer.

The funny part about LORD OF THE CHANGING WINDS is that I had *just* moaned to a friend that this book hadn't found a home and I was starting to be afraid it wasn't going to—twenty minutes later, I got the good news from my agent. That is a thrill that isn't going to get old anytime soon.

if you enjoyed
LORD OF THE CHANGING WINDS

look out for

THE MAGICIANS'
GUILD

book one of the Black Magician trilogy

by

Trudi Canavan

CHAPTER 1

THE PURGE

It is said, in Imardin, that the wind has a soul, and that it wails through the narrow city streets because it is grieved by what it finds there. On the day of the Purge it whistled amongst the swaying masts in the Marina, rushed through the Western Gates and screamed between the buildings. Then, as if appalled by the ragged souls it met there, it quietened to a whimper.

Or so it seemed to Sonea. As another gust of cold wind battered her, she wrapped her arms around her chest and hugged her worn coat closer to her body. Looking down, she scowled at the dirty sludge that splashed over her shoes with each step she took. The cloth she had stuffed into her over-sized boots was already saturated and her toes stung with the chill.

A sudden movement to her right caught her attention, and she side-stepped as a man with straggly grey hair staggered towards her from an alley entrance and fell to his knees. Stopping, Sonea offered him her hand, but the old man did not seem to notice. He clambered to his feet and joined the hunched figures making their way down the street.

Sighing, Sonea peered around the edge of her hood. A guard slouched in the entrance of the alley. His mouth was curled into a sneer of disdain; his gaze flitted from figure to figure. She narrowed her eyes at him, but when his head turned in her direction, she quickly looked away.

Curse the guards, she thought. *May they all find poisonous faren crawling in their boots*. The names of a few good-natured guards pricked her conscience, but she was in no mood to make exceptions.

Falling into step with the shuffling figures around her, Sonea followed them out of the street into a wider thoroughfare. Two- and three-storey houses rose on either side of them. The windows of the higher floors were crowded with faces. In one, a well-dressed man was holding up a small boy so he could watch the people below. The man's nose wrinkled with disdain and, as he pointed his finger down, the boy grimaced as if he had tasted something foul.

Sonea glared at them. *Wouldn't be so smug if I threw a rock through their window.* She looked about half-heartedly, but if any rocks were lying about, they were well hidden beneath the sludge.

A few steps further on, she caught sight of a pair of guards ahead of her, standing in the entrance to an alley. Dressed in stiff boiled-leather coats and iron helmets, they looked to be twice the weight of the beggars they watched. They carried wooden shields, and at their waists hung kebin – iron bars which were used as cudgels, but with a hook attached just above the handle, designed to catch an attacker's knife. Dropping her eyes to the ground, Sonea walked by the two men.

'—cut 'em off before they reach the square,' one of the guards was saying. 'About twenty of 'em. Gang leader's big. Got a scar on his neck and—'

Sonea's heart skipped a beat. *Could it be . . .?*

A few steps past the guards was a recessed doorway. Slipping into the shallow alcove, she turned her head to sneak a look at the two men, then jumped as she saw two dark eyes staring back at her from the doorway.

A woman gazed at her, eyes wide with surprise. Sonea took a step back. The stranger retreated too, then smiled as Sonea let out a quick laugh.

Just a reflection! Sonea reached out and her fingers met a square of polished metal attached to the wall. Words had been etched into its surface, but she knew too little about letters to make out what they said.

She examined her image. A thin, hollow-cheeked face. Short, dark hair. No-one had ever called her pretty. She could still manage to pass herself off as a boy when she wanted to. Her aunt said that she looked more like her long-dead mother than her father, but Sonea suspected Jonna simply did not want to see any resemblance to her absent marriage-brother.

Sonea leaned closer to the reflection. Her mother had been beautiful. *Perhaps, if I grew my hair long*, she mused, *and I wore something feminine . . .*

. . . oh, don't bother. With a self-mocking snort, she turned away, annoyed at herself for being distracted by such fantasies.

'—'bout twenty minutes ago,' said a nearby voice. She stiffened as she remembered why she had stepped into the alcove.

'And where are they expectin' to trap 'em?'

'D'know, Mol.'

'Ah, I'd like to be there. Saw what they did to Porlen last year, little bastards. Took several weeks for the rash to go away, and he couldn't see properly for days. Wonder if I can get out of – Hai! Wrong way, boy!'

Sonea ignored the soldier's shout, knowing that he and his companion would not leave their position at the entrance of the alley, in case the people in the street took advantage of their distraction to slip away. She broke into a jog, weaving through the steadily thickening crowd. From time to time, she paused to search for familiar faces.

She had no doubt which gang the guards had been talking about. Stories of what Harrin's youths had done during the last Purge had been retold over and over through the harsh winter of the previous year. It had amused her to hear that her old friends were still making mischief, though she had to agree with her aunt that she was better off keeping away from their troublemaking. Now it seemed the guards were planning to have their revenge.

Which only proves Jonna right. Sonea smiled grimly. *She'd flay me if she knew what I was doing, but I have to warn*

Harrin. She scanned the crowd again. *It's not like I'm going to rejoin the gang. I only have to find a watcher – there!*

In the shadows of a doorway, a youth slouched, glowering at his surroundings with sullen hostility. Despite his apparent disinterest, his gaze shifted from one alley entrance to another. As his gaze met hers, Sonea reached up to adjust her hood and made what would be taken to be a crude sign by most. His eyes narrowed, and he quickly signed back.

Sure now that he was a watcher, she made her way through the crowd and stopped a few steps away from the door, pretending to adjust the binding of her boot.

'Who're you with?' he asked, looking away.

'No-one.'

'You used an old sign.'

'Haven't been about for a while.'

He paused. 'What you want?'

'Heard the guards talking,' she told him. 'Plan to catch someone.'

The watcher made a rude noise. 'And why should I believe you?'

'I used to know Harrin,' she replied, straightening.

The boy considered her for a moment, then stepped out of the alcove and grabbed her arm. 'Let's see if he remembers you, then.'

Sonea's heart skipped as he began to pull her into the crowd. The mud was slippery, and she knew she would end up sprawling in it if she tried to brace her feet. She muttered a curse.

'You don't have to take me to him,' she said. 'Just tell him my name. He'll know I wouldn't mess him about.'

The boy ignored her. Guards eyed them suspiciously as they passed. Sonea twisted her arm, but the boy's grip was strong. He pulled her into a side street.

'Listen to me,' she said. 'My name is Sonea. He knows me. So does Cery.'

'Then you won't mind seeing him again,' the boy tossed over his shoulder.

The side street was crowded, and the people seemed to

be in a hurry. She grabbed a lamppost and pulled him to a halt.

'I can't go with you. I have to meet my aunt. Let me go—'

The press of people ended as the crowd passed and continued down the street. Sonea looked up and groaned.

'Jonna's going to kill me.'

A line of guards stretched across the street, shields held high. Several youths paced before them, shouting insults and jibes. As Sonea watched, one threw a small object at the guards. The missile struck a shield and exploded into a cloud of red dust. A cheer erupted from the youths as the guards backed away a few steps.

Several paces back from the youths stood two familiar figures. One was taller and bulkier than she remembered, standing with his hands on his hips. Two years of growth had erased Harrin's boyish looks but from his stance, she guessed that little else had changed. He had always been the undisputed leader of the gang, quick to smarten up anyone with a well-placed fist.

Beside him was a youth almost half his size. Sonea could not help smiling. Cery had not grown at all since she had last seen him, and she knew how much that would annoy him. Despite his small stature, Cery had always been respected in the gang because his father had worked for the Thieves.

As the watcher pulled her closer, she saw Cery lick a finger and hold it high, then nod. Harrin gave a shout. The youths pulled small bundles from their clothes and hurled them at the guards. A cloud of red billowed from the shields, and Sonea grinned as the men began to curse and cry out in pain.

Then, from an alley behind the guards, a lone figure stepped into the street. Sonea looked up and her blood froze.

'Magician!' she gasped.

The boy at her side drew in a sharp breath as he too saw the robed figure. 'Hai! Magician!' he shouted. The youths and guards straightened and turned towards the newcomer.

Then all staggered back as a hot gust of wind battered

them. An unpleasant smell filled Sonea's nostrils, and her eyes began to sting as the red dust was blown into her face. The wind ceased abruptly, and all was silent and still.

Rubbing tears away, Sonea blinked at the ground hoping for some clean snow to ease the sting. Only mud surrounded her, smooth and unbroken by footprints. But that couldn't be right. As her vision cleared, she saw it was marked with fine ripples – all radiating out from the magician's feet.

'Go!' Harrin bellowed. At once the youths sprang away from the guards and fled past Sonea. With a yelp, the watcher pulled her around and dragged her after them.

Her mouth went dry as she saw that another line of guards waited at the end of the street. This was the trap! *And I've gone and got myself caught with them!*

The watcher pulled her along, following Harrin's gang as the youths raced toward the guards. As they drew close, the guards lifted their shields in anticipation. A few strides from the line, the youths veered into an alleyway. Following on their heels, Sonea noted a pair of uniformed men lying slumped against a wall by the entrance.

'Duck!' a familiar voice shouted.

A hand grabbed her and pulled her down. She winced as her knees struck the cobblestones under the mud. Hearing cries behind her, she looked back to see a mass of arms and shields filling the narrow gap between the buildings, a cloud of red dust billowing around them.

'*Sonea?*'

The voice was familiar and full of amazement. She looked up, and grinned as she saw Cery crouching beside her.

'She told me the guards were planning an ambush,' the watcher told him.

Cery nodded. 'We knew.' A smile spread slowly across his face, then his eyes flickered past her to the guards, and the smile vanished. 'Come on, everyone. Time to go!'

He took her hand, pulled her to her feet and led her between the youths bombarding the guards. As they did, a flash of light filled the alley with a blinding whiteness.

'What was that?' Sonea gasped, trying to blink away the

image of the narrow street which seemed to hang before her eyes.

'The magician,' Cery hissed.

'Run!' Harrin bellowed nearby. Half blind, Sonea stumbled forward. A body slammed into her back and she fell. Cery grasped her arms, pulled her to her feet, and guided her onward.

They leapt out of the alley and Sonea found herself back on the main street. The youths slowed, lifting hoods and hunching their backs as they spread amongst the crowd. Sonea followed suit, and for several minutes she and Cery walked in silence. A tall figure moved to Cery's side and peered around the edge of his hood to regard her.

'Hai! Look who it is!' Harrin's eyes widened. 'Sonea! What are you doing here?'

She smiled. 'Getting caught in your mischief again, Harrin.'

'She heard the guards were planning an ambush and came looking for us,' Cery explained.

Harrin waved a hand dismissively. 'We knew they'd try something, so we made sure we had a way out.'

Thinking of the guards slumped in the alley entrance, Sonea nodded. 'I should've guessed you knew.'

'So where have you been? It's been . . . years.'

'Two years. We've been living in the North Quarter. Uncle Ranel got a room in a stayhouse.'

'I hear the rent stinks in those stayhouses – and everything costs double just 'cause you're living inside the city walls.'

'It does, but we got by.'

'Doing what?' Cery asked.

'Mending shoes and clothes.'

Harrin nodded. 'So that's why we haven't seen you for so long.'

Sonea smiled. *That, and Jonna wanted to keep me from getting mixed up with your gang.* Her aunt had not approved of Harrin and his friends. Not at all . . .

'Don't sound too exciting,' Cery muttered.

Looking at him, she noted that, though he hadn't grown

much in the last few years, his face was no longer boyish. He wore a new longcoat with threads dangling where it had been cut short, and probably loaded with a collection of picks, knives, trinkets and sweets hidden in pockets and pouches within the lining. She had always wondered what Cery would do when he grew out of picking pockets and locks.

'It was safer than hanging about with you lot,' she told him.

Cery's eyes narrowed. 'That's Jonna talking.'

Once, that would have stung. She smiled. 'Jonna's talking got us out of the slums.'

'So,' Harrin interrupted. 'If you've got a room in a stay-house, why are you here?'

Sonea scowled and her mood darkened. 'The King's putting out the people in stayhouses,' she told him. 'Says he don't want so many people living in one building – that it's not clean. Guards came and kicked us out this morning.'

Harrin frowned and muttered a curse. Glancing at Cery, she saw that the teasing look in his eyes had died. She looked away, grateful, but not comforted, by their understanding.

With one word from the Palace, in one morning, every-thing that she and her aunt and uncle had worked for had been taken away. There had been no time to think about what this meant as they had grabbed their belongings before being dragged out into the street.

'Where are Jonna and Ranel, then?' Harrin asked.

'Sent me ahead to see if we can get a room in our old place.'

Cery gave her a direct look. 'Come see me if you can't.'

She nodded. 'Thanks.'

The crowd slowly spilled out of the street into a large paved area. This was the North Square, where small local markets were held each week. She and her aunt visited it regularly – *had* visited it regularly.

Several hundred people had gathered in the square. While many continued on through the Northern Gates, others lingered inside in the hope of meeting their loved ones before entering the confusion of the slums, and some always refused to move until they were forced to.

Cery and Harrin stopped at the base of the pool in the centre of the square. A statue of King Kalpol rose from the water. The long-dead monarch had been almost forty when he routed the mountain bandits, yet here he was portrayed as a young man, his right hand brandishing a likeness of his famous, jewel-encrusted sword, and his left gripping an equally ornate goblet.

A different statue had once stood in its place, but it had been torn down thirty years before. Though several statues had been erected of King Terrel over the years, all but one had been destroyed, and it was rumoured that even the surviving statue, protected within the Palace walls, had been defaced. Despite all else he had done, the citizens of Imardin would always remember King Terrel as the man who had started the yearly Purges.

Her uncle had told her the story many times. Thirty years before, after influential members of the Houses had complained that the streets were not safe, the King had ordered the guard to drive all beggars, homeless vagrants and suspected criminals out of the city. Angered by this, the strongest of the expelled gathered together and, with weapons provided by the wealthier smugglers and thieves, fought back. Faced with street battles and riots, the King turned to the Magicians' Guild for assistance.

The rebels had no weapon to use against magic. They were captured or driven out into the slums. The King was so pleased by the festivities the Houses had held to celebrate that he declared the city would be purged of vagrants every winter.

When the old King had died five years past, many had hoped that the Purges would stop, but Terrel's son, King Merin, had continued the tradition. Looking around, it was hard to imagine that the frail, sick-looking people about her could ever be a threat. Then she noticed that several youths had gathered around Harrin, all watching their leader expectantly. She felt her stomach clench with sudden apprehension.

'I have to go,' she said.

'No, don't go,' Cery protested. 'We've only just found each other again.'

She shook her head. 'I've been too long. Jonna and Ranel might be in the slums already.'

'Then you're already in trouble.' Cery shrugged. 'You still 'fraid of a scolding, eh?'

She gave him a reproachful look. Undeterred, he smiled back.

'Here.' He pressed something into her hand. Looking down, she examined the little packet of paper.

'This is the stuff you guys were throwing at the guards?'

Cery nodded. 'Papea dust,' he said. 'Makes their eyes sting and gives 'em a rash.'

'No good against magicians, though.'

He grinned. 'I got one once. He didn't see me coming.'

Sonea started to hand back the packet, but Cery waved his hand.

'Keep it,' he said. 'It's no use here. The magicians always make a wall.'

She shook her head. 'So you throw stones instead? Why do you bother?'

'It feels good.' Cery looked back towards the road, his eyes a steely grey. 'If we didn't, it would be like we don't mind the Purge. We can't let them drive us out of the city without some kind of show, can we?'

Shrugging, she looked at the youths. Their eyes were bright with anticipation. She had always felt that throwing anything at the magicians was pointless and foolish.

'But you and Harrin hardly ever come into the city,' she said.

'No, but we ought to be able to if we want.' Cery grinned. 'And this is the only time we get to make trouble without the Thieves sticking their noses in.'

Sonea rolled her eyes. 'So that's it.'

'Hai! Let's go!' Harrin bellowed over the noise of the crowd.

As the youths cheered and began to move away, Cery looked at her expectantly.

'Come on,' he urged. 'It'll be fun.'

Sonea shook her head.

'You don't have to join in. Just watch,' he said. 'After, I'll come with you and see you get a place to stay.'

'But—'

'Here.' He reached out and undid her scarf. Folding it into a triangle, he draped it over her head and tied it at her throat. 'You look more like a girl now. Even if the guards decide to chase us – which they never do – they won't think you're a troublemaker. There,' he patted her cheek, 'much better. Now come on. I'm not letting you disappear again.'

She sighed. 'All right.'

The crowd had grown, and the gang began to push forward through the crush of people. To Sonea's surprise, they received no protest or retaliation in return for their elbowing. Instead, the men and women she passed reached out to press rocks and over-ripe fruit into her hands, and to whisper encouragement. As she followed Cery past the eager faces, she felt a stirring of excitement. Sensible people like her aunt and uncle had already left the North Square. Those who remained wanted to see a show of defiance – and it didn't matter how pointless it was.

The crowd thinned as the gang reached its edge. At one side Sonea could see people still entering the square from a side street. On the other, the distant gates rose above the crowd. In front . . .

Sonea stopped and felt all her confidence drain away. As Cery moved on, she took a few steps back and stopped behind an elderly woman. Less than twenty paces away stood a row of magicians.

Taking a deep breath, she let it out slowly. She knew they would not move from their places. They would ignore the crowd until they were ready to drive it out of the square. There was no reason to be frightened.

Swallowing, she forced herself to look away and seek out the youths. Harrin, Cery and the others were moving further forward, strolling amongst the dwindling stream of latecomers joining the edge of the crowd.

Looking up at the magicians again, she shivered. She had never been this close to them before, or had an opportunity to take a good look at them.

They wore a uniform: wide-sleeved robes bound by a sash at the waist. According to her uncle Ranel, clothes like these had been fashionable many hundreds of years ago but now it was a crime for ordinary people to dress like magicians.

They were all men. From her position she could see nine of them, standing alone or in pairs, forming part of a line that she knew would encompass the square. Some were no older than twenty, while others looked ancient. One of the closest, a fair-haired man of about thirty, was handsome in a sleek, well-groomed way. The rest were surprisingly ordinary-looking.

In the corner of her eye she saw an abrupt movement, and turned in time to see Harrin swing his arm forward. A rock flew though the air toward the magicians. Despite knowing what would happen, she held her breath.

The stone smacked against something hard and invisible and dropped to the ground. Sonea let out her breath as more of the youths began hurling stones. A few of the robed figures looked up to watch the missiles pattering against the air in front of them. Others regarded the youths briefly, then turned back to their conversations.

Sonea stared at the place where the magicians' barrier hung. She could see nothing. Moving forward, she took out one of the lumps in her pockets, drew her arm back and hurled it with all her strength. It disintegrated as it hit the invisible wall, and for a moment, a cloud of dust hung in the air, flat on one side.

She heard a low chuckle nearby and turned to see the old woman grinning at her.

'That's a good 'un,' the woman cackled. 'You show 'em. Go on.'

Sonea slipped a hand into a pocket and felt her fingers close on a larger rock. She took a few steps closer to the magicians and smiled. She had seen annoyance in some of their faces. Obviously they did not like to be defied, but something prevented them from confronting the youths.

Beyond the haze of dust came the sound of voices. The well-groomed magician glanced up, then turned back to his companion, an older man with grey in his hair.

'Pathetic vermin,' he sneered. 'How long until we can get rid of them?'

Something flipped over in Sonea's belly, and she tightened her grip on the rock. She pulled it free and gauged its weight. A heavy one. Turning to face the magicians, she gathered the anger she felt at being thrown out of her home, all her inbred hate of the magicians, and hurled the stone at the speaker. She traced its path through the air, and as it neared the magicians' barrier, she willed it to pass through and reach its mark.

A ripple of blue light flashed outward, then the rock slammed into the magician's temple with a dull thud. He stood motionless, staring at nothing, then his knees buckled and his companion stepped forward to catch him.

Sonea stared, her mouth agape, as the older magician lowered his companion to the ground. The jeers of the youths died away. Stillness spread outward like smoke through the crowd.

Then exclamations rang out as two more magicians sprang forward to crouch beside their fallen companion. Harrin's friends, and others in the crowd, began to cheer. Noise returned to the square as people murmured and shouted out what had happened.

Sonea looked down at her hands. *It worked. I broke the barrier, but that's not possible, unless . . .*

Unless I used magic.

Cold rushed through her as she remembered how she had focused all her anger and hate on the stone, how she had followed its path with her mind and willed it to break through the barrier. Something in her stirred, as if it were eager for her to repeat those actions.

Looking up, she saw that several magicians had gathered around their fallen companion. Some crouched beside him, but most had turned to stare out at the people in the square, their eyes searching. *Looking for me*, she thought suddenly. As if hearing her thought, one turned to stare at her. She froze in terror, but his eyes slid away and roved on through the crowd.

They don't know who it was. She gasped with relief. Glancing around, she saw that the crowd was several paces behind her. The youths were backing away. Heart pounding, she followed suit.

Then the older magician rose. Unlike the others, his eyes snapped to hers without hesitation. He pointed at her and the rest of the magicians turned to stare again. As their hands rose, she felt a surge of terror. Spinning around, she bolted towards the crowd. In the corner of her eye, she saw the rest of the youths fleeing. Her vision wavered as several quick flashes of light lit the faces before her, then screams tore through the air. Heat rushed over her and she fell to her knees, gasping.

'STOP!'

She felt no pain. Looking down, she gasped in relief to find her body whole. She looked up; people were still running away, ignoring the strangely amplified command that still echoed through the square.

A smell of burning drifted to her nose. Sonea turned to see a figure sprawled face-down on the pavement a few steps away. Though flames ate at the clothing hungrily, the figure lay still. Then she saw the blackened mess that had once been an arm, and her stomach twisted with nausea.

'DO NOT HARM HER!'

Staggering to her feet, she reeled away from the corpse. Figures passed her on either side as the youths fled. With an effort, she forced herself into a staggering run.

She caught up with the crowd at the Northern Gate and pushed her way into it. Fighting her way forward, clawing past those in her way, she forced herself deep within the crowd of bodies. Feeling the stones still weighing down her pockets, she clawed them out. Something caught her legs, tripping her over, but she dragged herself to her feet and pushed on.

Hands grabbed her roughly from behind. She struggled and drew a breath to scream, but the hands turned her around and she found herself staring up at the familiar blue eyes of Harrin.